HEAD TIDE

BY

JOSEPH C. LINCOLN

NEW YORK AND LONDON

D. APPLETON AND COMPANY

MCMXXXII

HEAD TIDE

CHAPTER I

THE clock in the belfry below the pointed spire of the old First Meeting House at Wellmouth Four Corners boomed seven times. It boomed solemnly, heavily, and with the deliberation befitting a timepiece of its age and social position. For forty-three years—ever since its presentation to the society by Captain Amaziah Dean, whose brick tomb was a prominent feature of the graveyard before and beside the church building—it had told the time to the citizens of the Four Corners. The fact that, of recent years, it seldom told it correctly was but a trifle in the minds of those citizens. If it erred, it was always on the slow side and this, too, was as it should be. The new clock on the Second Church, down at Wellmouth South Side, was sometimes as much as ten minutes fast. There you were!

The Four Corners, where the South Side road crossed the main road, was deserted. The post office was closed and would remain closed until seven-thirty, when the late mail was due to arrive. The doors of the Wellmouth Bank had been shut since four. The neat, trim little building with the Greek portico and the small, gilt-lettered sign "Joel Dean, Attorney at Law" was locked and untenanted. Only behind the broad panes of Manasseh Eldredge's "Grocery, Dry Goods and General Store" were there signs of animation. Manasseh, always alert for the loose penny, did not close his establishment during the supper hour but kept open until after mail sorting.

The year was one late in the seventies and the day the second of July. The afternoon had been overcast, with a strong wind and a thick haze—the sort of weather which sailors call a "smoky sou'wester"—and beneath the elms and silver leaf

I

poplars arching the main road dusk was deepening. Early **as** it was the windows of the Eldredge store were alight.

As the seventh stroke boomed from the belfry of the First Meeting House another window showed a yellow gleam. About a hundred yards farther up the road, on the same side as Eldredge's and just beyond the iron fence of the graveyard, was a low clapboarded building which, in other respects vastly unlike the miniature Grecian temple occupied by Judge Dean, was also white. The gilt lettering of the sign above its door, however, was faded and weatherbeaten. This sign read, when one came near enough to be able to read it, "B. Higham. Job Printing of All Descriptions. Office of the Wellmouth *Eagle*."

The interior of the little building was a dingy and grimy contrast to its outside. A small public room, divided by a battered counter, with a chair or two for customers before the counter and another chair, a desk and a stove behind it. The desk was heaped high with papers and the walls were thickly plastered with samples of posters, bills announcing auction sales, political "rallies," "Grand Balls" at the town hall, and the like. There was a brass cuspidor conveniently placed on the floor near the customers' chair.

Behind the door leading from the public room was the print shop, twenty-five feet long or thereabouts, smelling of oil and ink and with two old-fashioned presses and another stove. Opening from the shop at the rear and to the right was a third room, so tiny as to be little more than a closet. On the ground glass pane of its door was painted in black letters "Editor's Office." The knob and a liberal section of the door above, about and below it, were smeared with inky finger marks.

Elisha Dodson had just entered this room, and it was he who had lighted the kerosene bracket lamp affixed to the wall. He took off his ancient felt hat and his worn pepper and salt jacket and tossed them both carelessly into a corner.

Then he laid his stout crook-handled cane upon the flat table-top desk by the window, and, sitting down in the armchair before the desk, squared his elbows to the task for the doing of which he had left an unfinished supper and hurried back to that office that evening.

Dodson was a short, thin little man, with a smooth-shaven face and a thick crop of grizzled brown hair which, bristling out in all directions, made his head look not unlike a dry thistle top. He wore spectacles and now, as he prepared to write, he adjusted a green eyeshade above them. He turned back his shirt cuffs and pushed the cane a bit farther out of his way. That cane was no fashionable flourish, but a very real necessity, for Elisha had walked with a limp since he was seventeen years old.

Sheets of copy paper were lying ready for use on the desk before him and he dipped a pen in ink and held it poised above them. This was to be an important editorial, the very first which, during his many years of employment in the *Eagle* office, he had ever written entirely on his own responsibility and which, when completed, would be published just as it was, without supervision or blue-penciling by a superior.

For there was no superior now. Beriah Higham, who founded the Wellmouth *Eagle* in 1846 and had owned, published and directed it until very recently, was dead and buried. And now his assistant, boss printer, and general factotum, Elisha Dodson, must compose and write and, later on, put into type the memorial which, set in double space, bordered by heavy, turned rules, would appear in the next number of the paper. Elisha had not been ordered to write it. Until the will was read and the wishes of the late B. Higham were made known, the future of the *Eagle* was a mystery. Meanwhile some one must carry on and that some one was, obviously, 'Lish Dodson.

He dipped the pen once more. How should he begin? It seemed impossible that the "old man" had gone forever.

3

Old Beriah, with his bald head, his gold-rimmed spectacles, his cracked voice, his black stock and starchy, if frayed, linen— it was very hard to realize that he would never again enter that office, that that dry cough of his would never again be heard by the front door, a signal for "Tip" Cahoon to whisper: "Hide your pipe, 'Lish. Here comes old Ramrod Back."

Dodson wrote a sentence and then drew the pen through it. Rising, he opened the lower half of the window beside him and stood looking out. The window commanded a cheerful view of the First Meeting House cemetery and, in the shadow beneath the ailanthus trees, he could dimly see the newly made grave with the fading floral tributes heaped upon it. Those tributes were many, for the late B. Higham had been a prominent figure throughout all Ostable County. He had made the *Eagle* a paying property. Amid the pullings and haulings of local politics, at the very center of the whirlpool of bitter rivalry between the conservative Four Corners and the bustling South Side, he had managed to make no real enemies, to keep old subscribers and win new ones. To be neutral—always neutral until it was perfectly safe to take sides, that was the Higham policy, and it paid. Benjamin Harrison Cahoon—"Tip," short for "Tippecanoe"—who was errand boy, printer's devil and janitor in the shop—summed it up when he said:

"The old man could walk tight rope with a kittle of hot clam chowder on each shoulder and never spill nary a drop. Ain't that so, 'Lish?"

Elisha Dodson had worked for Mr. Higham almost twenty years. Left an orphan at fourteen he had, in his early youth, "gone fishin'," as did almost every other Wellmouth male of his social status, at that period. When he was seventeen, during a February gale on the Georges, a heavy bit of wreckage had crushed his right knee and put that leg out of active commission forever.

Beriah Higham, then a middle-aged man, seated at that

4

very desk in the little room where Elisha sat now, looked up and saw a slim, rather haggard lad regarding him shyly and somewhat fearfully.

"How d'you do, 'Lish?" he inquired. "Well, how's the leg?"

"So-so, Mr. Higham, thank you."

"Going to be all right again pretty soon, isn't it?"

"No, sir."

"Oh, now come! It may be—you can't tell."

"Yes, I can. . . . Mr. Higham. I—I—you can't give me a job, can you?"

"A job! Why are you bothering about a job yet awhile? You're scarcely out of the doctor's hands."

Elisha smiled, the slow quizzical smile which was characteristic of him.

"Want to stay out of 'em," he observed. "Have to eat once in a while to do that."

Higham smiled; he was in a gracious mood that morning. "I need a printer," he said. "You aren't a printer, are you?"

"No, sir, not yet; but I'm goin' to be."

"Oh, you are, eh? When?"

"Soon's I can after you give me the chance to learn."

Beriah was beginning to be mildly interested.

"Why do you think you want to be a printer?" he asked, curiously.

Elisha shifted from his sound leg to his lame one and back again.

"I always liked printed things," he confessed. "I like to read. I've read most all the books in the Ladies' Circulatin' Library. I—I—" he swallowed and then added: "I'd rather be a printer and—and run a paper than anything else in the world, I guess."

"Hum. . . . Well, I'm sorry, but I'm afraid I can't help you. I can use a journeyman printer, but I can't waste time with a green hand."

5

Young Dodson sighed. "Cap'n Amaziah he said he was afraid you couldn't. Well, I'll have to try somewheres else, I presume likely."

Higham had pricked up his ears.

"Wait," he ordered. "What's that? Did Cap'n Amaziah Dean send you to me?"

"Yes, sir. He said he'd be kind of glad if you could give me a chance. My father was second mate along of him for four voyages."

Captain Dean was a big man in Wellmouth, a well-to-do and influential citizen and a leader in Whig politics in the county. The *Eagle* and its editor owed much to him. Mr. Higham pulled at his chin beard.

"I might take you on as a—well, as a sort of errand boy, I suppose," he mused. "Like to please Cap'n Amaziah when I can. Three dollars a week; how's that sound to you, 'Lish?"

"Fine." Then, wistfully, "Could I have a chance to learn printin'? I'd work at it nights if you'd let me."

"All right—see how you get along." He paused and then asked another question. "You say you read a lot. What do you read?"

" 'Most everything I get a hold of. I've been readin' history lately, about the War of 1812 'twas. Miss Becky Snow, at the lib'ry, she picked out the book for me."

"Hmph! Do you remember what you read?"

"Yes, sir. Cal'late to."

"Well—er—let me see. Who was Isaac Hull?"

Elisha Dodson's shyness vanished; his blue eyes flashed. "Commander of the United States frigate *Constitution*," he announced. Then, rattling on as if repeating a lesson, he added: "Fought a fight with the British ship *Guerrière*." (He pronounced it "Gur-*ree*.") "The *Gurree* opened fire first, but Cap'n Hull he never let the *Constitution* fire back until he had the *Gurree* right in range of his broadside. Then he sung out: 'Now, boys, jam it into 'em!' He had on tight-fittin'

6

britches—pants, I mean—and he stooped over when he sung that out and them pants cracked right open from the top right down to the knee. Yes, sir, split right apart, they did."

The editor laughed. "Who told you that yarn?" he demanded.

"Nobody," stoutly. "It's so, 'twas all in the book. They give Cap'n Hull a big dinner up to Boston afterwards." The slow, quizzical smile again and Elisha added: "Maybe they give him a new pair of pants too—the book didn't say."

Dodson came to work in the print shop the next morning and he had missed few working days since. He learned the printer's trade, and he learned other things, among them the knack of writing fairly correct English. His speech, however, still retained the characteristic expressions and twang which it had acquired in boyhood. Higham, who—perhaps because he had been told that he looked like Daniel Webster—made it a point to dress and speak like that great man, found the twang and the careless use of words irritating.

"Why do you say 'ain't' when you mean 'isn't'?" he snapped irritably. "You write pretty well; why don't you talk the same way?"

Elisha shook his head. "When I write 'ain't' I can see it looks wrong," he explained, "but I can't see what I say. I guess likely that's it."

"Don't say you 'guess likely.' Say you guess. Did you ever hear me say I guessed likely?"

"No, sir, not as I know of."

"You don't know 'of'—you know, don't you?"

"Why, yes, sir, I guess maybe I do, that's a fact."

"If it's a fact you don't have to guess it. . . . Tut, tut, tut! You're a South Sider born and you'll never be anything else till you die. Here," handing him a penciled manuscript, "here are this week's East Harniss locals. See if you can turn them into decent English."

Dodson took the sheets of blue-lined notepaper and departed to edit the notes of Mrs. Sarah Abigail Ginn who was the *Eagle's* East Harniss newsgatherer. Sarah Abigail wrote on both sides of the paper and invariably referred to a defunct person as the "late diseased."

Little by little, year by year, Elisha built himself into the fabric of the printing business and the Wellmouth *Eagle* until he became almost as important a part of them as B. Higham himself. During the last decade of his life the "old man" left the paper almost entirely in his assistant's hands. He—Beriah—wrote the political editorials and supervised the general make-up, but the news columns and their contents were all in Elisha's charge.

When he was but twenty-two, Dodson married. His wife was a Blodgett, one of the Orham Blodgetts, and they rented a small house on the South Side road, half way between the South Side and the Four Corners. A year later he became a father and a widower. Jane Dodson died in childbirth, and Elisha was left with a baby girl, Helen, on his hands. Somehow or other he brought her up and now she was his housekeeper, his guardian and his first interest in life. The second was the Wellmouth *Eagle*. Helen and the *Eagle,* these two occupied his thoughts and kept him busy—little else mattered.

He turned from the window and sat down once more before the desk. "All Wellmouth and all Ostable County has suffered a heavy loss," he wrote. "Heavy" was not precisely the word he wanted, it was not the sort of word which B. Higham himself would have used. Too simple—too everyday. B. Higham had never liked and seldom used everyday words. There must be something—ah yes! "Irreparable," that was better. Two "r's" or one? He refreshed his memory with the dictionary and went on, his pen moving faster as he gained confidence.

The latch of the outer door rattled and lifted. Elisha did not hear it. Neither did he hear the door open nor the steps in the public room and print shop. Only the dignified "Ahem" which heralded the approach of the visitor caused him to look up from his writing and turn his head.

"Why—why, good evenin', Judge!" he exclaimed.

Joel Dean—"Judge" Dean by courtesy—was Wellmouth's leading lawyer. He was counsel for the Wellmouth Bank, as well as one of its directors, and legal adviser to most of the nabobs of the Four Corners, including Captain Gideon Bates, Wellmouth's richest man. In politics he was, of course, staunchly Republican—to be anything else in that neighborhood at that time was to be lonely indeed—and, although Manasseh Eldredge was the active "boss" of the local political ring, behind Manasseh was Judge Dean. No postmaster, no customs collector, no nominee for the State House of Representatives for that district was ever selected without his approval. Captain Bates might be king of the Four Corners, but Dean was prime minister.

Bearded, silk-hatted, gold-spectacled and carrying a gold-headed cane, he stood there in the doorway and regarded shirt-sleeved Elisha Dodson with condescending benignity. Elisha scrambled to his sound foot and stammered a greeting.

"Why—why, good evenin', Judge," he repeated. "I—I—why—er—good evenin'."

Dean nodded. "Good evening, Elisha," he said. "Hard at work, eh? Well, that's right—that's right. The paper must go on even if its late proprietor has—er—passed beyond. Of course—yes. Ahem! May I come in?"

He had come in already and Dodson hastily pushed forward the chair he had been occupying. Judge Dean sank into it with deliberate dignity.

"Don't stand, Elisha," he ordered, graciously. "Be seated—do."

As the chair he had relinquished to his visitor was the only one in the room, Dodson, after a moment's hesitation, compromised by leaning against the desk.

9

"You wanted to see me, did you, Judge?" he asked, rather vaguely.

"Yes. Yes, I did. There is a matter which we—er—felt should, perhaps, be discussed with you before it is—er—brought to public notice. It will, of course, be made public in a short time, but as it is important to the welfare of Wellmouth in general, certain of us who have that welfare at heart feel that you should—er—be made acquainted with it in advance. It may be gratifying to you to know that, with the exception of Captain Bates and myself and Eldredge and—well, one or two more—you are the first to learn of it. Ahem! the very first—yes."

Elisha was bewildered. He could not imagine what was to follow this impressive prologue.

"I see," he faltered. "Yes, yes—I see."

Judge Dean smiled. He stroked his long gray beard. It was a majestic, bushy and carefully tended beard, and he was proud of it. The feminine leaders of Four Corners society often complimented it as the most beautiful beard in the whole town. This was high praise, for to be beardless in the seventies was to be eccentric. Elisha Dodson, as has been mentioned, was smooth shaven.

The Dean hand stroked the beautiful Dean beard.

"I doubt if you do see, Elisha," observed the Judge.

"Yes. . . . I mean no. . . . Well, I guess maybe I don't," confessed Dodson.

"There is no reason why you should. I was—of course you know that—Mr. Higham's friend and lawyer. I had charge of his affairs while he was alive, and under the provisions of his—ahem—last will and testament, which I drew, I am in charge of them now."

Mr. Dodson, feeling that he should say something, said "I want to know!"

"Yes. I know how my friend intended disposing of his property and effects. A part of that property is this business here, the printing business and," impressively, "the Wellmouth *Eagle*. It is about them—the *Eagle* in particular—that I am here to-night to talk with you, Elisha."

He paused. Dodson was thinking rapidly. The late B. Higham was a bachelor; never once had Elisha heard him speak of living kinsfolk. The question of who was to inherit the print shop and the paper had been much discussed in Wellmouth. The gossips at the post office and in Manasseh Eldredge's store had talked of little else since the funeral. Down at the South Side, in the office of the fishing magnates, at the shipchandler's, along the wharves and aboard the schooners unloading fish at those wharves, they were guessing and speculating—or so "Tip" Cahoon reported.

Elisha himself had scarcely mentioned the subject in public, but at home, alone with his daughter, he had mentioned it often. The question of who was to be the new editor and proprietor of the *Eagle* had filled his thoughts for three days and nights. Sometimes he had even dared to dream foolish dreams. Helen, with her usual common sense, had warned him that, in all probability, they were foolish, and he agreed with her. But—well, no one knew the ins and outs of the Higham shop as he knew them; no living person knew the *Eagle* as he knew it. And Beriah, through their long association, had been aware of that knowledge. What was he about to hear? A thrill of expectancy, almost of hope, stirred within him. His knees were trembling.

The Dean beard received another stroking. The throat behind the beard was cleared with another "Ahem."

"Dodson," went on the Judge, with solemn deliberation, "I doubt if more than two people in Wellmouth were aware that Mr. Higham had any relatives living. He never spoke of them; he was—er—shall we say close-mouthed about his private affairs. For instance, he never mentioned to you that he had a sister living in Cleveland, did he?"

"Eh? . . . A sister? No, he never."

"I'm sure he didn't. I shouldn't wonder if there had been trouble between them at some time or other. At any rate he *had* a sister there, a widow, her married name was Cobb; she died five years ago, leaving an only son, Franklin Cobb. Her husband's mother was a Franklin, I believe. Ahem— yes."

Elisha made no comment. The thrill of hope was changing to a quiver of dread.

"Well, Elisha," went on Judge Dean, "I may as well tell you now that this Franklin Cobb is the sole Higham heir. All the property, real and personal, has been left to him."

Dodson caught his breath. "You mean—" he stammered, "you mean—everything? The *Eagle* and—and all?"

"That's exactly what I mean. This Franklin Cobb inherits everything. A little money—not much, for Beriah was far from rich—and a few stocks and securities amounting to, perhaps, two or three thousand dollars. Those and the furniture and personal effects, plus this print shop and the *Eagle,* now, under the will, belong to this young fellow. Yes," with emphasis, "*all.* There were no other bequests of any kind."

The dream castle was a pathetic ruin now. Elisha's eyes, behind the spectacles and beneath the green shade, closed and then opened.

"You don't say!" he gasped. "Well, well! . . . Does he— this Cobb boy—know about it?"

"Why do you call him a boy?"

"You said he was young."

"So he is. About twenty-five or twenty-six, I believe. I don't know whether he knows yet, but he will, of course. I telegraphed him at Cleveland, at the only address I had, which was his mother's home during her last years. It was, I was given to understand, a rented apartment, so the chances are that young Cobb doesn't live there now. I telegraphed him and I have written him, but I have as yet had no answer. Meanwhile," leaning forward, and speaking even more impressively, "there are important matters to be considered and settled. Captain Bates"—he mentioned the name reverently, as all Wellmouth was in the habit of doing—"agrees with me as to their importance and the need of prompt decision. . . . Ahem! . . . In our consultations your name, Dodson, has been often mentioned and I was commissioned to have this talk with you. In strict confidence, of course; you understand that?"

"Why—why yes. I shan't tell anybody."

"You mustn't. As you know, Elisha, the Wellmouth *Eagle* is a—er—power in the town and county." His voice assumed an oratorical roll, such as it was accustomed to assume when he addressed a district convention. "Its editorials," he boomed, "and its news columns have always reflected the views of the wisest political thinkers of this section of the State. In the right hands it can, as it has in the past, do a great deal of good. In the wrong hands it might possibly do considerable harm. You realize that?"

"Why—I guess likely so, Judge."

"I am sure you do. My friend Beriah often expressed to me his confidence in your—er—discretion. . . . Just a minute, please; let me go on. . . . It is not likely that this young fellow, Cobb, will wish to continue his uncle's business—and the *Eagle*—under his own direction. The chances are that he is employed elsewhere and that he will probably wish to sell out at once. Captain Bates and I and—er—some of the rest of us have decided that, for the good of the community, the *Eagle* should continue to be in safe hands—in wise, conservative hands. Therefore we have, among us, pledged a sum of money to buy it. The printing business will, no doubt, have to go with it, so we shall buy that, too. The Wellmouth *Eagle* will, if, or when, we control it, still be issued from this office."

Elisha Dodson nodded dazedly. He still could not understand why this was told to him. Why? Unless as a preparation for notifying him that his services would no longer be needed. Visions of having to look for employment elsewhere crossed his mind. At his age they were disturbing visions.

"And," went on Dean, emphatically, *"and* under the same direction. The very same—yes."

The disturbing visions departed as suddenly as they had come. Elisha's hands moved involuntarily. His cane was knocked from the desk to the floor. He did not notice it.

"I—I don't know's I quite understand you, Judge," he faltered. "You mean—you mean you'll want me to—to work here same as always?"

The Judge's voice lost a little of its platform quality. He was very much in earnest now and, momentarily, he was a trifle less statesmanlike in manner and diction.

"I mean," he declared, crisply, "that we—Captain Bates and I and the rest of us—will want you to run the *Eagle.* That's what I mean."

Dodson pushed the green shade up into his hair. The eyes behind the spectacles were shining.

"You're goin' to let me be editor!" he cried. "You—you *are?*"

"Yes, we are. Wouldn't you like to be?"

"Like to be! . . . My gorry, yes! I'd rather be that than President, don't know as I wouldn't."

Dean smiled. "Well," he observed, dryly, "I doubt if you'll ever be President, Elisha."

Elisha smiled in sympathy. "I doubt it full as much as you do, Judge. . . . I—I must say I'm awfully obliged to you, I am so. And I'll try my best to do a good job."

"We are sure you will. Yes, you are to be the editor. We—some of us—may write an occasional editorial and we shall, of course, have general supervision of what goes into the paper."

"Why, naturally. That's right, that's right. I understand."

"You must understand. The *Eagle* will continue, as it always did under Mr. Higham, to support the right candidates and the proper policies. Who those candidates may be and what the policies are will be matters which the new owners will determine. Otherwise than that you will—er—have a free hand."

He rose. Elisha, who seemed to be in a sort of trance, groped on the table for his cane, then, remembering that it was on the floor, stooped and picked it up.

"I don't know just how to thank you, Judge Dean," he faltered.

"That's all right. As for your wages—why, I suppose that is a matter to be settled later. They won't be smaller than they are now, of course. . . . Eh? What were you going to say?"

"Why—why, nothin' much, Judge. I presume likely you're as good as sure this—this Cobb boy will be willin' to sell out? Don't think likely he'll want to own the *Eagle* himself?"

"Can't imagine why he should. He is in the West somewhere, probably, and at work. This print shop and the paper are of no use to him out there and, if he is sensible, he will be glad to turn them into money. However, nothing is settled yet, and until it is you mustn't mention it to anyone."

"Oh, I shan't, Judge. Except—well, I'd like to tell Helen if I might."

Dean hesitated. "Yes," he agreed, after a momentary pause, "you may tell her. You would anyhow, of course—"

"No, I wouldn't," quickly. "Not unless you said I could."

"She would get it out of you, or I miss my guess. She is a smart girl—everybody says so. Very well, tell her, but don't either of you whisper a word of it outside. Captain Bates himself wished me to impress you with the need of keeping this very quiet. He has great confidence in you, Dodson. Don't disappoint him."

He rose and turned to go. "As soon as the matter is settled you will be notified," he added. "Until then, if any one asks questions you don't know anything. Good night."

"Just a minute, Judge. Shall I keep on gettin' out the paper until it is settled?"

"Certainly."

Dodson, taking the lamp from the wall bracket, lighted his visitor through the print shop and public room to the outer door. Then he limped back to the chair by the desk and sat down to think it over.

The Wellmouth *Eagle* was to go on and he was to be its editor. So much of his dream at least had come true. Helen had never taken much stock in his own faint hope that Beriah Higham might have remembered him in his will. Not very likely, was her opinion. No one had worked harder or more faithfully than Elisha, but, again in her opinion, Mr. Higham was not the sort of man to appreciate that service to such an extent.

"Don't you believe it, Father," she said. "If it turns out that there aren't any Higham relations you'll find that everything has been left to build a monument in the cemetery, or for a memorial window in the church, or to buy a new organ with his name on a silver tablet—something like that. What he has left you doesn't interest me. What I really worry about is the chance that you may lose your place in the *Eagle* office. *That* worries me because I know it would break your heart. I honestly believe you had rather have your name at the top of the editorial page of the *Eagle* than be left a million in anybody's will."

Her father smiled. "Maybe you're right, Nellie," he agreed. " 'Fraid I wouldn't know what to do with a million and there's lots of things I'd like to do with the *Eagle,* if 'twas mine."

And now it was going to be his—or, if not his exactly, he was to be its editor, its real editor, with his name in print.

No less an authority than Judge Joel Dean had told him so, and the voice of Dean was the voice of Captain Gideon Bates, not to mention that of Manasseh Eldredge and others of Wellmouth Four Corners' little circle of ruling powers. They had made their plans and he, Elisha Dodson, was a part of those plans; that was something to flatter a fellow's vanity—if he had any.

Elisha had very little, but he could not help feeling a trifle vain just then. They must have considered him worthy or they would not have laid this trust and responsibility upon him. Captain Bates had great confidence in him—he had sent that message by Dean. By gorry, that was good to hear! Even Helen, who pretended not to share the reverential awe of the majority for the great Captain Gideon—even Helen would find it hard to laugh that off. She would be pleased when he repeated it to her, pleased and happy.

There were lots and lots of ways in which the *Eagle* could be improved. Some of them he had suggested to Mr. Higham, but Beriah was not inclined to accept suggestions from a hired man. Well, there would be no one to bar improvements now. Of course Dean had said something about supervising and directing the policy and politics of the paper, but he had also said that its new editor was to have a free hand. Editor of the Wellmouth *Eagle* and given a free hand to do what he liked with it—gorry, that was wonderful!

He dreamed and exulted and schemed for many minutes. Then, awakening to reality and the passage of time, he resumed work upon the editorial tribute to the late B. Higham. It was, when at last he finished it, a glowing eulogium. He was in the mood to be completely satisfied with the world and its inhabitants past and present and the tribute was a reflection of his feelings. It ended thus:

Beriah Higham has gone from our midst, but the paper he founded and which he made a power for good in Ostable County must and shall go on. Its new editor, whoever he may be, will, we know, continue the fight for truth, justice and freedom. In the future, as in the past, the Wellmouth *Eagle* shall soar onward and upward, "Not a stripe effaced or polluted, not a single star obscured."

The bracket lamp, which Tip Cahoon had forgotten to refill, was burning low and smoking high when he finished. He folded the sheets of copy paper and put them in his pocket. Helen was always accorded the privilege of reading his editorials before they appeared in print. Usually she revised them here and there. "I have made a few changes, Father," she frequently said. "You don't mind, do you?" He did not mind of course. Often some of his choicest flowers of rhetoric were plucked, and he could not understand why, but he seldom protested. Helen had had an education, something he never had. She was what Judge Dean had called her, a smart girl. Doubtless she knew what was right better than he did.

The clock in the belfry of the First Meeting House struck ten as he locked the outer door. The main road was black as Egypt. Above his head the leaves of the elms and silver leaves rustled in the southwest wind. He descended the steps to the sidewalk and, leaning upon his cane, limped briskly toward home.

The Eldredge store was closed now, so was the post office, and almost all the dwelling houses were dark. In the great white house—the *Eagle* invariably referred to it as the "mansion"—of Captain Gideon Bates, however, the lights were still burning. The French windows of the Bates mansion were aglow and behind their drawn shades shadows moved and the tinkle of a piano was audible. Victoria—Captain Gideon's eighteen-year-old daughter—was at home from the Middleboro Academy on her vacation, and Victoria had city ways and city hours for retiring. The young people of the Four

Corners—the select young people—had gay times in that house during Victoria's vacations.

Dodson crossed the road and, leaning upon the white picket fence bordering the Bates front yard, listened for a moment. The piano was playing a lively tune and, as he listened, young voices began singing "There is a Tavern in the Town."

Elisha went on his way humming the familiar words. He was in a musical mood himself just then.

> "'There is a tavern in the town—
> in the town,
> And there my true love sits him down—
> sits him down.
> And drinks his wine both good and free
> And never, never thinks—'"

"I beg your pardon."

Dodson's song broke off in the middle of a line. He turned quickly.

"Huh?" he queried, with a startled grunt. "What? . . . Who's that?"

A figure had stepped from the deep shadow of the clump of syringas at the far side of the granite post marking the Bates driveway.

"I beg your pardon," said the voice again. "Can you tell me how to get to the hotel?"

Elisha peered through his spectacles. It was too dark to see clearly, but the person who asked the question was a man, and, judging by his voice, a young man. He was tall and broad shouldered, wore a straw hat and appeared to be carrying a valise. Dodson leaned forward and peered at him. A stranger, that was certain. Elisha knew every resident of Wellmouth Four Corners and Wellmouth South Side, and this young fellow was none of these.

"Eh?" stammered Mr. Dodson. "Hotel, did you say?"

"Yes. There *is* a hotel, isn't there?"

"Why—why, there's the Vineyard House down to the South Side; that's a kind of hotel, but it's a good ways off."

"How far?"

"About two mile."

"Whew! Nothing nearer than that?"

"Well, there's Mrs. Cahoon's. She takes boarders. I understand she's full up now, though. This is her busy time. City folks down for the summer and over the Fourth. Maybe you could get in there, but I doubt it."

"Is her place nearer than the hotel?"

"'Tisn't too near, maybe a mile and a half."

"Great Scott! This bag weighs a ton. Isn't there *any* place where I can be put up for the night? This isn't a boarding house here, is it?"

He pointed to the Bates mansion. Elisha gasped.

"I should say *not!*" he exclaimed, with horrified emphasis. "That house belongs to Captain Gideon Bates. You've heard of him, I expect."

"Sorry, but I haven't."

"Then you don't belong in Ostable County, I'll bet on that."

"If you do, you win. I landed here about ten minutes ago. I came as far as Bayport in the train, and got off at the station to buy a cigar. When I came out the train was just leaving. I hired a livery rig and driver to bring me here. The driver said he hadn't lived in Bayport long and didn't know where the Wellmouth hotel was, but he guessed it wasn't far off. Looks as if he missed his guess."

"Sho! He ought to have known better. In a hurry to get back to bed, I shouldn't wonder."

"If he was I can sympathize with him. Bed sounds pleasant to me; I was on a sleeper all last night. Sleeper was what they called it, but it was anything but that."

Elisha Dodson had heard of sleeping cars, but he had never seen one. He was impressed.

"I want to know!" he exclaimed. "So you were in a regular sleepin' car, eh? Must have come a long ways."

"I came from Cleveland to start with."

The name "Cleveland" awakened a memory in the Dodson mind. Where had he heard that city mentioned? He had and recently. Why yes, of course; Joel Dean had spoken of Cleveland.

"What did you say your name was?" queried Elisha.

"My name is Cobb."

"Cobb! . . . *Eh?* . . . Why—why, you ain't Franklin Cobb, are you?"

"Yes."

"Well—well! My gorry!"

CHAPTER II

HELEN DODSON, in the sitting room of the little house on the South Side road, heard the click of the latch as the gate opened. She rose from the rocker, put the library book she had been reading on the center table and, going into the little entry—it was not large enough to be called a hall— opened the door leading to the yard. This was the "side door" of course: Elisha Dodson would no more have dreamed of entering his house by the front door than he would of sitting in the best parlor in his everyday clothes.

Helen opened the side door. "Father," she called, "is that you?"

There was no reply. The clump of ancient lilacs blocked the bend in the path and she had left the lamp on the table in the sitting room.

"Father," she said again, peering out into the darkness, "it *is* you, isn't it?"

"It's me," she heard him call. "Comin', Nellie."

"And high time, I should think. Do you realize it is half-past ten? You'll get yourself talked about if you aren't careful."

Then she realized that her father was not alone; he was speaking once more, but this time not to her.

"Steady as you go, Mr. Cobb," she heard him say. "Black-er'n a nigger's pocket in amongst these bushes, that's a fact. Right this way."

She could see him now. He was holding back one of the lilac branches which had grown across the path. A moment later a second figure brushed by the branch and, carrying a traveling bag, approached the doorway. A stranger, that

22

was plain, even though she could not as yet see his face.

"Nellie," said Elisha, limping to the front, "I guess you're surprised to see me bringin' company home with me, but—well, I'll tell you about it in a minute. Mr. Cobb, let me make you acquainted with my daughter. Nellie, this is Mr. Cobb; he's goin' to stay with us to-night."

Helen was surprised, there was no doubt of that, but she said that she was glad to meet Mr. Cobb.

"Come in," she said. "Father, don't forget to shut the door."

She led the way to the sitting room. Seen by the lamplight the stranger was a good-looking young fellow, with dark hair and eyes, an easy manner and an attractive smile.

"You are wondering what on earth I'm doing here at this hour, Miss Dodson," he observed. "Of course you are. Well, I hardly know myself. Your father is responsible. I asked him how to get to the hotel and he said there wasn't any."

"And that's so too," put in Elisha. "I told him there was a boardin' house a mile or so off but that it was shut up and gone to bed long ago. Couldn't very well leave him hangin' onto Cap'n Gideon's gate, so I brought him here. . . . All right, ain't it, Nellie?" anxiously.

There was but one thing to say, of course, and Helen said it. It was perfectly all right, no trouble at all. Nevertheless she was more than a little annoyed. A lifetime of experience had taught her that one could never be sure of what Elisha Dodson might do, except that it would probably be what no one else would do under similar circumstances. She made a hasty mental review of the condition of the larder and the spare bedroom.

"You see, 'twas this way, Nellie." Mr. Dodson's conscience was troubling him, and he hurried to explain. "Mr. Cobb, he's a stranger in town, and he's come all the way from out West—"

"Only from Cleveland," interjected Cobb.

"That sounds pretty far to me. Anyhow, Nellie, the train went off and left him over to Bayport and he hired a livery stable rig to fetch him over here and then—"

"Wait a minute, Father. Don't you think you and Mr. Cobb might as well sit down? It would make us all a little more comfortable."

She sat and so did Elisha, but their visitor hesitated. His eyes had been busy, looking his young hostess over from head to foot, and the inspection seemed to embarrass him a trifle. One might have surmised that this calm, self-possessed, distinctly good-looking young woman was not precisely the sort of person he had expected Elisha Dodson's daughter to be.

"Why now, see here," he blurted. "Let's get this straight. My shoving myself in this way is a confounded imposition, and I know it. Why don't you pitch me out again, Miss Dodson? I would if I were you."

He laughed as he said it and Helen laughed too. "I told you it was all right and it is," she said. "Sit down a minute, please. I suppose you are tired and would like to go to bed, but Father seems to have something he wants to say first. What is it, Father?"

"I—why, I wanted to tell you how he and I came across each other, that's all. You see—"

He went on to give Mr. Cobb's explanation of his belated arrival at the Four Corners and of their meeting by the Bates driveway.

"So there 'twas," he said, in conclusion. "No place to sleep and not a mouthful to eat since noontime. Sounded pretty lonesome to me, so I says: 'You come right along, Mr. Cobb. We've got an extra room and as for eatin'—well, we'll see what the neighbors have brought in.' He didn't want to do it, of course—"

"Strange," interrupted the young man. "I'm odd that way, Miss Dodson. No, I didn't want to do it, of course. All

I wanted to do was to find that boarding house, or whatever it is. If your father had only—"

He paused, for Helen had risen from her chair. "We mustn't waste time," she said, "or your supper will be breakfast. Father, take Mr. Cobb's bag to the spare room. Make sure there is soap in the dish and that the wash pitcher is full. Oh, yes, and that there are clean towels on the rack. Mr. Cobb, if you'll go with him I'll run out to the kitchen and see what sort of a picnic meal I can get together."

"Now see here—please! I'm not hungry."

"I don't believe it. Go now, both of you."

Elisha came hobbling to the kitchen a few minutes later. The teakettle was on the stove, and she was hurriedly setting a place for their guest at the corner of the pine table.

"Goin' to feed him out here?" asked Dodson, doubtfully. "He don't look to me like a fellow who's used to eatin' in the kitchen. Think we're kind of funny folks, won't he?"

She shrugged. "He ought to think himself lucky to be fed anywhere—in Wellmouth at eleven o'clock at night. Father, you—well, I think you must have been born without any faculty of time at all. I told you the other day, when you were three-quarters of an hour late for dinner, that this house ought to put up a sign 'Meals at All Hours' . . . Oh, never mind, don't bother me. I'm planning to make an omelet, if there are eggs enough. Mercy me, where *is* everything?"

Mr. Dodson ran his fingers through his thistle-top hair.

"I know I make you lots of trouble, Nellie," he faltered, contritely. "I don't mean to, honest."

"Why, of course you do and of course you don't mean to. There, there, dear, don't look so distressed, I shall live through it. Whether *he* does or not"—with a jerk of her head in the direction of the sitting room—"will depend on what I put into this omelet. Where is he now?"

"Washin' up. Anyhow that's what he was gettin' ready to do when I left him."

"Let's hope he is doing it yet, and not prowling around the house filling that bag of his with our spoons or anything else that takes his fancy. Who is he, anyway?"

"Why, I told you. His name is Cobb—Franklin Cobb."

"Good gracious, I know that. At least I know he told you his name was Cobb and that he came from Cleveland. And you told me you found him looking in at Cap'n Gideon's gate. What was he doin' there, figuring on *their* spoons?"

"Why, the idea! He ain't that kind."

"How do you know he isn't? I don't believe you know a single thing about him—really."

Elisha had been leaning against the table; now he stood erect. His tone was hurt and indignant.

"I know everything about him," he proclaimed stoutly. "Certain I do. His name is Franklin Cobb and he's Beriah Higham's nephew. His mother was Beriah's sister. She's dead now, and he's come into all Beriah's property—every single thing, the *Eagle* and all."

Helen, the mixing spoon in one hand and the frying pan in the other, swung about to face him.

"Father," she cried, "what are you saying? Did he tell you that?"

"He didn't need to tell me. Joel Dean was into the *Eagle* office this very night—about half-past seven 'twas when he came—and he stayed till 'most nine. He told me all about it. Course he didn't know Cobb was in town, didn't know where he was, hadn't heard a word from the letter he wrote him. But—oh, and say, Nellie, he told me a lot more. Somethin' you'll hardly believe when you hear it. He told me—"

"Sshh!" Helen lifted a warning hand. Footsteps in the dining room warned them of their guest's approach. Helen was too amazed and disturbed by the news she had just heard

26

to greet him, but Elisha was brimming with nervous cordiality.

"Sit right down here, Mr. Cobb," he urged, "here at the end of the table. Hope you don't mind eating in the kitchen. We don't usually do it, but 'twas the handiest place just now, so—"

Helen interrupted. "I imagine," she said, briskly, "that Mr. Cobb isn't so particular about where he eats as that he does eat pretty soon. There is bread and butter to begin with, Mr. Cobb, and I am hoping there may be an omelet, though goodness knows what kind of one. Father, look after him, will you, please?"

The tea was hot and the bread light and homemade. The omelet, when ready, was a success. Franklin Cobb had declared that he was not hungry, but he ate as if he were. As he ate Elisha watched him anxiously. Helen's regard seemed to be a sort of appraising scrutiny. Happening to look up, he caught her eye.

"Of course you are wondering who in the deuce I am and what I'm doing in this neck of the woods," he said, with a smile. "That's it, isn't it?"

She shook her head. "Father says you are Mr. Higham's nephew. I was thinking about that. You see, we didn't know he had any relations."

"And I didn't know I had an uncle, to say nothing of one who would remember me in his will. I don't really believe the whole of it myself yet. Shan't until I see this what's-his-name—the lawyer fellow who telegraphed and wrote to me."

"Judge Joel R. Dean," prompted Elisha, solemnly.

"That's it. All I could think of was 'Sardine.' Hope I don't call him that by mistake."

He chuckled. Mr. Dodson laughed, although he was obviously shocked. Helen's smile was faint and somewhat vague. Her mind was busy trying to grasp this astonishing development. If what her father said was true—that this man was Beriah Higham's sole heir—what might it mean to the Dodson family?

"No," went on their guest, cheerfully, helping himself to a second section of the omelet, "I don't believe it. Why should I? I remember hearing Mother speak of having—or having had—a brother with some ungodly name like Beriah, or Josiah, or Maria, something like that, but she never told me anything about him and I took it for granted he had been dead a long while. Mother died about four years ago and I went to Chicago where I had a job in a bank. It wasn't much of a job and I hated the work, but it paid me a salary, such as it was, so I hung on hoping to find something I liked better. About a month ago the cashier and I had a little difference of opinion—he told me what sort of a bank clerk he thought I was and I told him what sort of a man I knew he was—and so—well, I resigned by 'mutual consent' as the Irishman said."

He seemed to regard the loss of his position as a good joke. Neither of his hearers spoke, and he went on with his story.

He had hung about Chicago for a fortnight, trying to find some other opportunity, but business was bad there and he had no luck. So he returned to Cleveland, where he had friends and where he hoped for better success. Dean's letter, which had been forwarded to Chicago, was reforwarded to him in the Ohio city. Its contents were a complete surprise to him.

"I didn't answer the letter," he said, "because it seemed to me that I should have to come on here anyhow, and I might as well come at once. As a matter of fact I was too excited to waste time in writing. I came and—well, here I am. Now you know as much about the affair as I do. More, I imagine, for you probably know what sort of property, and how much, this uncle of mine owned. I know nothing whatever."

Helen drew a long breath. "It sounds like a fairy story

to me," she mused. "I have often wondered how it must feel to have some one leave you money and things in a will. How *does* it feel, Mr. Cobb?"

"I am too numb from the shock to feel much of anything yet. And I don't dare count on it. More than likely, when the estate—if there is one—is settled and the debts paid I shall find that about all this long-lost uncle of mine left me are his kind regards."

The prospect did not seem to trouble him greatly. Elisha gasped.

"Why, don't you know—" he cried, but his daughter did not let him finish.

"Of course you haven't made any plans yet?" she suggested. "You can't, I suppose, until you know what Mr. Higham has left you."

"Not a plan. What has he left me? Do you know?"

Again Mr. Dodson's mouth opened and again Helen spoke first.

"Father hasn't told you anything about—about anything?" she asked.

Elisha seized the opportunity. "How could I?" he protested. "Didn't I promise the judge I wouldn't tell a soul except you?"

"Oh, did you? When?"

"Why, just to-night. I told you he'd been into the office and—"

"Yes, yes, so you did. Well, if you promised you mustn't tell."

Franklin Cobb looked from one to the other.

"Getting more mysterious every minute," he observed. "Look here, *is* there anything—anything really worth while, I mean?"

"It would seem worth while to Father and me. But you will see Judge Dean to-morrow and then you will know all about it."

29

"You bet I'll see him—and as soon as possible. Miss Dodson, your father didn't say much, but he dropped a hint about some sort of business—printing, I believe it was—and—yes—a newspaper. Wasn't that it, Mr. Dodson?"

Elisha looked guilty. "I—I didn't know I said anything about the *Eagle*," he faltered. "I didn't mean to, but—but I thought you must know about *that*."

"I don't know anything. Oh well, don't break your word to the Sardine. A printing business and a paper, eh? That sounds interesting."

Helen had given her father a reproachful look.

"Father worked for Mr. Higham," she said. "I'm sure he told you that, too. . . . Do you know anything about printing or running a paper, Mr. Cobb?"

"Not a thing."

"Then—then, supposing they have been left to you, what will you do with them?"

"Eh? Sell the whole outfit, probably. That is, if I can find a customer. I wouldn't know what to do with a printing press, but I do know what to do with money—live on it until I find another job, which may take some time. . . . Oh, well, we'll know more to-morrow."

He pushed back his chair and rose to his feet.

"There!" he exclaimed. "As they say in the books I'm a new man again. That was the best omelet I've eaten since Mother used to make them for me, Miss Dodson. You've saved my life and I'm more obliged to you and your father than I can tell you. Just now I'm not going to try. It's high time you kind people were in bed. The word now is—good night."

Elisha would have protested, but Helen, looking over their guest's shoulder, shook her head.

"Father will go with you to your room," she said. "You're sure you have towels and soap and everything? Good night, Mr. Cobb. We have breakfast about half-past seven."

When Elisha returned to the kitchen his eyes were shining. "You heard him, Nellie?" he cried, exultantly. "You heard him say it? He'll sell out quick as ever he can, and Joel and Cap'n Gideon and the rest are all set to buy. And I'm goin' to be editor of the *Eagle*—the judge said so. *I* am!"

Helen put her hands on his shoulders and pushed him into a chair. "Now, Father," she ordered, "stop running in circles, and tell me what the judge said. That is, if you can without breaking your promise."

"Oh, he told me I could tell you. He said you was a smart girl. Yes, he did."

"That was nice of him, although I don't know how he knew."

"Why, everybody knows it."

"Hum! Then they've kept it to themselves. Now tell me."

He told her, his voice cracking shrilly with excitement as he related the marvelous tale of Dean's disclosures and confidences. When, at last, he finished, she bent over and kissed him.

"It sounds perfectly splendid," she declared. "If it really proves to be as good as it sounds I shall feel like hugging them all, Cap'n Gideon and everybody."

"Eh? Hug Gideon Bates? I'd like to see you or anybody try it!"

"Perhaps he would like it, too. I don't believe he has been hugged for a long time—unless it was by Victoria when she wanted a new piano or something. . . . Yes, yes, Father, I am as happy as you are, only—"

"Only what? I don't see any 'only' in it."

"You wouldn't. But we must remember that it hasn't happened yet. Judge Dean's people don't own the *Eagle* and this Cobb man does. He says now that he wants to sell, but he hasn't sold. So until he does we mustn't count our chickens, must we? . . . Now you go straight to bed. I shall go, too, as soon as I finish these dishes. Run along. Yes, and don't lie awake all night—or what's left of the night—writing editorials."

Next morning, after breakfast, their guest announced that he was off to see Dean without losing a minute. Elisha suggested that they walk up to the Corners together.

"Leave your valise right here," he urged. "You can come back and get it any time. Nellie'll be at home all day, and if she wasn't you could get it just the same. Nobody ever locks doors around here, do they, Nellie?"

"Not as a usual thing, Father, but every one with common sense will lock them to-night. Remember, before you go to bed, to take off the front gate and bring it into the house. That is, unless you want to find it hung up in one of Cap'n Gideon's silver leaf trees as you did last year."

Her father whistled. "By gorry," he exclaimed, "to-morrow *is* Fourth of July day; that's so, 'tis. I've been so—so sort of worked up by what's happened since yesterday that I forgot all about it. There'll be doin's around town this night, that's a fact. They tell me there's no less than three mackerel boats and one of the Blake coddin' schooners in port down to the South Side and with that gang of wild Indians loose the night before the Fourth *nothin's* safe. Yes, sir, Mr. Cobb, I spent half the forenoon huntin' for our gate and when I found it in that tree I couldn't get it without a ladder and almost every ladder at the Corners had been stole and burnt up in the bonfire. Well, boys'll be boys, I presume likely."

Helen sniffed. "Yes, and whisky will be whisky," she observed. "Mix up a jug or two of whisky with a fishing crew ashore and you don't need any matches for your bonfire, Mr. Cobb."

When Dodson and his companion reached the Four Corners they saw a crowd of men and boys surrounding the rear entrance of Manasseh Eldredge's store. This entrance was on the Bayport road and almost opposite the junction of the South Side road and the main road. Elisha suggested

that they go across and see what was going on. They did
so and Dodson hailed a stout man, with a perspiring and
troubled countenance, who was rushing about shouting
orders.

"What's up, Manasseh?" he asked.

Mr. Eldredge turned petulantly. "Don't bother me," he
snapped. "Oh, it's you, 'Lish. We're tryin' to get them guns
into my back room and it's a healthy job. Cussed things
weigh more'n a hundred pound apiece. . . . Easy there, Seth!
Easy! Do you want to smash my steps all to thunder?"

He pushed through the crowd, roaring protests. Cobb,
standing on tiptoe, could see over the shoulders of the on-
lookers.

"Why, they're cannon, aren't they?" he exclaimed, in surprise. "Two old cannon. What on earth—"

Elisha was busy questioning others in the crowd. Cobb
pressed closer to the center of action. Each cannon—they
were small ones, rusty, and, by their look, of ancient pattern
—was slung in ropes which a half dozen husky young fellows
had across their shoulders. The weight was considerable and
the bearers moved slowly.

"What are they doing with those things?" he asked of a
boy next him. The youngster looked up and grinned.

"Goin' to lock 'em up in Manasseh's back room till to-
morrow mornin'," he explained excitedly. "Ain't goin' to
let the South Side gang cart 'em down there and fire 'em off
same as they done last Fourth of July. No sir-eee, we'll do the
firin' up here to the Corners this year, you bet you!"

Dodson had finished his questioning by this time, and as
they walked together toward the Dean office, he offered hurried explanations. The two cannon, he said, were Wellmouth institutions, so to speak. They were very old, as old
as the Revolutionary War, having come originally from a
British frigate wrecked on the bars below East Wellmouth
in 1778, or thereabouts. Brought ashore by the wreckers,

33

they were presented to the town and, up to a year ago, had stood on crude mountings at each side of the little grass plot bordering the property of the First Meeting House around the corner on the Bayport road.

"It's only last Fourth that the trouble started," he explained. "You see, Mr. Cobb, there's a whole lot of jealousy nowadays between the South Side and the Four Corners. Up to a few years ago there wasn't any doubt that the Corners was the real head center of Wellmouth township. The town hall was here—it's down yonder beyond the printin' shop—and Cap'n Gideon Bates's big place and the old First Meetin' House and Judge Dean's office and Manasseh's store and the *Eagle* and—well, about everything that was any account. But, beginnin' about the end of war time, the South Side has been growin' and gettin' more and more important. The wharves are down there and the fish boats come in there, and mackerelin' and coddin' have got to be big things in Wellmouth. There are some mighty prosperous firms at the South Side now: the Blakes—Abiathar Blake is a shrewd trader and well off, and his younger brother, Cap'n Carmi, is one of the smartest fishin' skippers that ever hailed from this neighborhood. Then there's the Rogerses and Sylvanus Oaks and Co., and one or two more. And four years ago there was a split in the Congregational society and the South Side part, most of it, pulled out and built a church of their own. That made feelin', of course, and—"

"But about the cannon?" put in Cobb.

"I'm comin' to them. Politics are mixed up in this jealousy business too. For a long spell the crowd that run things in the Republican party—there's precious few Democrats nowadays—was Judge Dean and Manasseh Eldredge—the fellow I was talkin' to a minute ago—and Cornelius Haven, the bank cashier, and Beriah Higham, your uncle, and a few like them, with Cap'n Gideon as a sort of head adviser, as you might say."

Franklin Cobb grinned. The habitual tone of reverence in which his new acquaintance mentioned the Bates name had not escaped his notice.

"This Bates chap must be quite the cheese around here, I should imagine," he said.

"Eh? Oh, he's a big man, Cap'n Gideon is. Worth a million of money, they say; been to the State Legislature, got the finest home in the county and always doin' things to help the town. Yes, yes; Cap'n Gideon is the most looked-up-to citizen we've got."

"I see."

"Now about those cannon: it ain't so much who is to fire 'em on the Fourth; that isn't it, really. It's what's behind the whole thing. The South Siders, so the Corner folks think, are gettin' too big for their boots. If they came and *asked* for the privilege of firin' a salute down at their end of the town, they would probably get it. The truth is they don't intend to ask. They figure they're more important than the Corners nowadays, and they mean to have what they want without askin'. Last year a gang of Southers sneaked up here in the middle of the night, loaded those cannon onto a cart and hauled 'em away. When Manasseh and the Corners crowd went out in the mornin' to get ready for the salute they heard 'em goin' 'Bang, bang' down to the South Side. Then, of course, the committee in charge had to hitch up *their* cart and go after 'em. And how those Southers did laugh when they saw 'em comin'! That's the yarn and that's why Manasseh—he's head of the Fourth committee—don't intend to lose 'em this year. . . . Well, here's Judge Dean's place and here's where you and I part company for a spell, Mr. Cobb. Hope when he tells you what's comin' to you it'll prove better even than you expect. . . . Why—what's that paper stuck up for?"

They were opposite the classic Grecian portals of Joel Dean's office and the "paper" was a business card tacked, wrong side outward, on the closed door. They moved toward it together. It read: "Out. Back at 10 A.M. July 5." and was signed "Joel R. Dean."

Elisha Dodson whistled. He thumped the lawyer's step with his cane. He was staring at the card with disappointment written large upon his face.

"If that ain't a shame then I don't know," he groaned. "He's gone over to spend the Fourth of July day with his niece's folks at Ostable, I bet you. He pretty often does that on holidays. Sho, sho! Now what'll you do, Mr. Cobb?"

His companion shrugged. "Wait for him to come back, I suppose," he replied. "What else is there to do?"

"You could telegraph him, sayin' you was here. Perhaps he'd come right back if you did."

"Well, I shan't. No use spoiling his outing. My fault for not letting him know I was coming. Too bad, though."

"You—you won't go away again?"

"Where could I go? No, I'll spend the glorious Fourth in your—er—metropolis, Mr. Dodson. That is," with a dubious glance up and down the main road where, except for the group at the Eldredge corner, not a soul save themselves was visible, "if you think I can stand the excitement."

The sarcasm was not wasted. Elisha nodded, grimly. "You stick around until twelve o'clock to-night," he said, "and you may find somethin' to keep you awake. There was a Boston drummer down here last night before the Fourth and he didn't sleep much, I shouldn't wonder. . . . Well, I must be gettin' over to work. Want to come along with me, Mr. Cobb?"

Cobb fell into step with him as they crossed the road. "What disturbed the Boston man's rest?" he inquired. "Roosters crow too early?"

"I doubt if he paid much attention to roosters. He was down to the South Side—been to see a girl there, I understand—and a parcel of tough boys off the fish boats met him. They had a jug along—wasn't much left in it by that time—and they asked him to have a drink."

"Generous."

"Um-hm, seems so. Trouble was he didn't appreciate the generosity and said no. So, judgin' he liked water better, they pumped the horse-trough full and set him in it."

"Whew! That sounds more chilling than exciting."

"Little of both, I guess likely. They said they didn't want to spoil his nice clothes, so they undressed him before they put him in the trough. When they left, they took his clothes with 'em. No, no, they didn't steal 'em, they hung 'em on a scarecrow in the minister's back garden."

"Hmph! I hope the drummer found them."

"He did, along about daylight. So did the minister's old maid sister; they both found 'em at the same time. That's the way the story goes, but there's nobody to swear to it. The drummer left town on the first train, and the minister's sister don't seem to care to talk on the subject. . . . Here we are, Mr. Cobb. Come in, will you?"

They were standing before the late B. Higham's place of business. Franklin Cobb looked at the little building, at the sign above the door, and the specimens of printing hung in the windows. Then he followed his companion inside. Elisha did the honors. He proudly displayed the two presses, the type cases, the working paraphernalia.

"Pretty well found shop, of its size, don't you think?" he asked hopefully.

Cobb nodded. "Shouldn't wonder," he agreed, "if you know what it's all about. What do you keep in here?"

He indicated the little editorial sanctum, the door of which was open. Mr. Dodson waxed eloquent.

"Here's where we turn out the Wellmouth *Eagle*," he announced, with pride. "This was where Mr. Higham—your uncle—spent the heft of his time. This was his private room,

37

when he wrote editorials and the like of that. It's seemed odd enough, this past week or so, not to see him sittin' at that desk."

The young man glanced about the little room. He stepped to the window and looked out at the cemetery.

"Bright prospect," he observed.

Elisha was at his elbow. "That's your uncle's grave over yonder," he said, pointing.

"Indeed?" Then, as the thought occurred to him, "I suppose the paper goes on even though he—er—doesn't? Who is carrying the load?"

"Eh? . . . Why—well, I suppose you might say I am. You're right, Mr. Cobb; the *Eagle* has to be out on time. That's one thing about a paper—it can't stop. Folks that pay their two dollars a year expect it to keep goin'—and it has to. I've been doin' my best. Oh, that reminds me," he added; "last night I wrote a—er—sort of memorial piece about Mr. Higham to go on the editorial page. Set in a mournin' frame, 'twill be, you understand. Maybe you'd like to read it, he havin' been your uncle. So I'd like to know if you think it's all right," anxiously.

Franklin Cobb took the sheets of manuscript and regarded them doubtfully.

"Why, as far as that goes, I'm sure it is all right if you did it, Mr. Dodson. You knew my uncle well and I never knew him at all. . . . Oh well, I'll read it, if you wish. Glad to, of course."

"That's fine. Sit right down. Oh, and I'll get you some copies of the *Eagle*. Maybe you'd like to look them over, too."

He went out and tiptoed in a moment later to lay the copies of the *Eagle* on the desk. Cobb read the tribute, at first with a sort of condescending amusement, and then with a curious feeling—almost of respect. This uncle of his must have been a good deal of a personage in the community and his country weekly a very real influence, not only in Well-mouth but in the towns adjacent. Dodson's flowing sentences and spasms of "fine writing" were funny, but behind the stilted phrasing was sincerity, there was no doubt of that. A man could live a worth-while life even in a place like this, apparently; yes, and find it interesting—if he were built that way.

He took up a copy of the *Eagle* and began to read that. The "local jottings" from the towns and villages and hamlets were full of unconscious humor, and he chuckled over them. Obviously, everybody knew everybody else in these places and nothing was too inconsequential to miss being recorded. And the way they were recorded! An East Harniss man did not merely whitewash his fence, he "treated it to a fresh coat of kalsomine." When Mrs. Sarah Tidditt of Bayport spent a Sunday with her married daughter at Wellmouth South Side she "sojourned" there. Mr. Theophilus Snow was "our esteemed fellow townsman" when the Trumet correspondent wrote of his having bought a cow of Philander Bearse, who was "our flourishing undertaker and paper hanger." The young man could not help wondering if these people really were as complimentary to one another in private life as they seemed to be in the public print.

The news from Wellmouth South Side interested him particularly. This, apparently, was, as his new acquaintance, Dodson, had said, a growing and pushing place. The record of schooners unloading fish there, or departing for the mackerel grounds or the Banks for more fish, was a long one. And building was going on. "Blake Brothers are adding a new shed to the upper end of their wharf." Captain Carmi Blake was at home again. His vessel, the *Flyaway,* had made another record trip. "The South Side is proud of Captain Carmi and all the men alongshore are eager to sail with him."

Then and there Franklin Cobb made up his mind to spend

a part of his day of waiting at the South Side. He believed he would find the experience novel and interesting.

The Four Corners items were much more florid and dignified in their wording.

Miss Victoria Bates is at home from the Middleboro Academy on her summer vacation. The Four Corners welcomes Miss Bates as its most charming daughter.

Captain Gideon Bates has purchased a new dogcart. Miss Victoria Bates's appearance in it behind her dashing roan created a sensation on our streets.

Miss Victoria Bates is, so we understand, planning to spend the Fourth and a day or two following with her friend and classmate, Miss Maisie Rogers, who is at home again with her father, Captain Zenas Rogers, at his residence on the main road at the South Side.

Captain Gideon Bates expresses himself as greatly interested in the district choice for State congressman. This township will not, of course, nominate its representative until a year from this fall, but Captain Bates feels that it is not too early for the town to be considering its nominee.

Franklin Cobb decided that Wellmouth Four Corners should have been named "Batesville." Doubtless there were other well-known citizens as Dodson had said, but, if so, they were only "seconds."

When a half-hour later he finished his reading and came out of the editorial office to the print shop, he found Mr. Dodson busy setting type at one of the cases. In the outer office a long-legged, carroty-haired youth was making a pretense of sweeping and dusting. Elisha abandoned his typesetting long enough to introduce this individual.

"Mr. Cobb," he said, "let me make you acquainted with Ben Cahoon. His name's Benjamin Harrison, but we generally call him 'Tip,' short for 'Tippecanoe.'"

"'Tippecanoe and Tyler too,'" recited Cahoon, with a broad grin. "Yes sir, that's me. Pleased to meet you, Mr. Cobb. Any relation to Ezra Cobb's folks over to Bayport?"

"Sorry, but if I am I don't know it."

"Thought maybe you might be. I know them Cobbs first rate. Been to dances with Letitia Cobb a whole lot of times. 'Lettie J.' most folks call her. She's quite a girl, Lettie J. is. Ezra's her old man. You ain't no relation then?"

"Tip is a great fellow for the girls," was Elisha's comment. "You might not think it to look at him, but he is."

"My red hair's what gets 'em, I guess likely," observed Tip with cheerful candor. "That and my dancin'. I can shake a mean leg, if I do say it. Like dancin', do you, Mr. Cobb? I go to about every dance there is around here. Yes sir, I—"

Dodson interrupted. "There, there," he broke in. "You dance that broom a little livelier if you cal'late to get this place cleaned up before ten o'clock. . . . Oh, goin' out, are you, Mr. Cobb?"

Franklin Cobb announced his intention of going for a walk. "I may go as far as the—what do you call it?—the South Side," he added. "I have been reading the *Eagle* and that end of your town has got me interested, Mr. Dodson."

Tip Cahoon snorted.

"Don't waste your time," he counseled scornfully. "Nothin' down to the South Side but fish scales. You hang around up here to the Corners, and you're liable to see somethin'. Say, 'Lish, I had a good look at that new dogcart of Victoria's yesterday. That's a wagon. Cost money, that did; I wisht I was the lucky dog to ride in it."

"You'll be back to the house by noontime, won't you, Mr. Cobb?" was the Dodson query. "Nellie's expectin' you."

Cobb shook his head. "Please tell her not to wait dinner for me. I'll be back some time before the afternoon is over; that is, unless your South Side friends treat me as they did the Boston drummer. See you later."

He walked out of the shop and the building. Cahoon watched him from the front windows.

"He's a city fellow, ain't he, 'Lish?" he asked. "Can always tell 'em, can't you? Swing themselves along as if they owned about everything worth while in all creation. They don't though," rebelliously.

Elisha Dodson sighed. "This one does," he muttered, under his breath. Then, ordering his assistant to stop talking and get to sweeping, he limped back to the editorial office.

CHAPTER III

FRANKLIN COBB was walking briskly along the South Side road. The morning was glorious; in fact so glorious that local prophets would have called it a "weather breeder" and too good to last. The "smoky sou'wester" of the day before had blown itself out, the breeze now came strongly from the northwest and the air was cool and bracing. The horizon, ahead in the direction of the South Side village, with its distant church spire and roofs and tree tops, was as clearly outlined as if cut with scissors and pasted against the deep blue background of the sky. The shadows of the bushes and fence rails bordering the road lay in purple silhouettes upon its dazzlingly white clamshell surface. Exercise was a delight, especially after the long, tedious hours aboard slow moving trains.

Young Mr. Cobb was enjoying himself. And why not? He was young and healthy and heir to—something, although that something might prove to be but little. The old world wasn't such a bad place and Wellmouth—on this morning, at any rate—not the worst place in it. It must be, however, he decided, the "deadest." He had met but one individual, since leaving the Four Corners, an elderly man driving a fat, meditative white horse attached to a blue cart loaded with barrels. The barrels and cart smelled enthusiastically of fish and the driver, with his pale blue eyes and half-open mouth, was himself suggestive of a defunct codfish. In acknowledgment of the pedestrian's "good morning" he languidly nodded but said not a word. Franklin wondered if this were one of the "esteemed citizens" of whose social and business activities he had read in the *Eagle*. The old fellow was certainly not social, nor did he look as if he were ever active.

South Side village, when he turned the corner into its narrow, winding main road, looked as somnolent as the driver and smelled as fishy as the cart and its contents. The stores and shops were set close together; there was an obviously new church which was a white clapboarded replica of the First Meeting House at the Corners, a "Billiard, Pool and Sipio Parlors"—what "sipio" might be he had not the vaguest idea—and a dingy building with the sign "Masonic Lodge" above the entrance to its second story and "E. Rogers, Fishermen's Outfitters" lettered over that of the first.

The only show of life were two or three men and boys on the platform of one of the larger stores, an old woman with a market basket plodding along the right hand sidewalk, and perhaps a half dozen horses and vehicles of various kinds hitched at intervals to posts. Where were all the bustle and hustle the *Eagle's* excited paragraphs had led him to expect?

As he came opposite the "Billiard, Pool and Sipio Parlors" he heard laughter and strident masculine conversation behind its shaded windows. Apparently there was something going on in there, and for an instant he contemplated entering. He did not however—thereby, although unaware of it, saving himself a black mark on the social ledgers of the South Side's select and God-fearing citizens. Caleb Ryerson's billiard room was the "gilded hell" of Wellmouth South Side and carefully respectable people did not visit it.

A sign at the corner of an alley to his left caught his eye. "Blake Brothers, Wholesale Fish Dealers." Mr. Dodson, he remembered, had spoken of the Blake brothers during their conversation that morning; yes, and the *Eagle* had had much to say concerning them. He turned into the alley, bordered on one side by the wall of a wooden building and on the other by a board fence, walked along it for perhaps sixty feet and came out upon the harbor front. There *was* something going on here. He paused to look about him.

The harbor was an artificial one, protected on the sea side

44

by a long stone breakwater, with a beacon at each end. Beyond the breakwater was the open water of the Sound extending to the horizon. Inside the barrier a number of small craft, sloops and catboats lay at anchor and dories were moving back and forth. Before him a good-sized wharf extended out into deep water and two schooners, one topsail rigged and the other a "fore and aft," were made fast alongside it. To the left, a hundred yards distant, was another wharf and to the right, but farther away, a third. At each end of these, vessels were lying and men were busy. The fresh northwest breeze was heavy with the odor of fish.

The wharf at the landward end of which he was standing was the largest and, so it seemed, by far the busiest at that moment. Aboard each of the schooners lying beside it men were working and on the wharf above them were larger groups, all active and all noisy. Orders were shouted, there was much running about, and a great deal of rough and good-natured profanity.

Franklin Cobb sauntered toward the nearest of these groups. They were unloading fish, mackerel, from the schooner's hold, hoisting them in buckets by ropes over a pulley, swinging them up to the wharf and running them in barrows into the broad doorway of the building at its landward end.

The men at the pulleys and trundling the barrows were a boisterous, sunburned, broad-shouldered lot, their bare arms corded with muscle and their big hands cracked and seamed by salt water and the handling of wet nets. They seemed in high good humor, particularly one swarthy individual who looked like an Italian or a Latin of some sort and who, seated upon an overturned bucket, was singing at the top of his lungs. The song was not of the Sunday School variety, but he bellowed it no less lustily on that account.

This fellow was the only one of the crowd to notice the approach of the stranger. His comrades were too busy to heed and, although they occasionally joined in the chorus of the ballad, kept on with their work. When the singer stopped in the middle of a verse, however, they turned toward him.

"What's the matter, Portygee?" asked one. "Forgot the rest of it, have you?"

"Aw, he ain't forgot, Jim," said another, with a loud laugh. "Had to stop to get up steam, that's all. Take another swig at the jug, Manuel. Yes, and pass it 'round. . . . Why, what ails you, 'Gee? What you lookin' at?"

"'Gee" or "Portygee" or "Manuel"—the individual on the bucket appeared to have a variety of names—was staring with bibulous gravity at Franklin Cobb.

"Looka da hat!" he exclaimed. "Oh, by cripe, looka da hat!"

He pointed a very dirty finger. Every one looked where he pointed, which was at the hat worn by Mr. Cobb. It was a straw hat and its brand-newness was spotlessly obvious. Cobb had bought it just before leaving Cleveland and rather fancied it. To have it called to public attention in this unexpected manner was embarrassing. His face showed his feeling, and the crowd surrounding him shouted hilariously.

"It *is* a hat, that's a fact!" declared one.

"It's a new hat," vowed another.

"It's a nice new hat, right out of the store, and I'll bet you a dollar he ain't wet it yet," whooped a third.

Cobb grinned. "Don't you like that hat?" he asked. "What's the matter with it?"

"Sartin we like it. Only—"

But the swarthy man was rising from his seat on the bucket. He rose a trifle uncertainly, but he rose, and, leaning toward the wearer of the straw hat, expressed his opinion.

"*I* don' like it," he growled, thickly. "*I* don' like it. It's a scousy hat. I'm goin' to—to chuck it overboard."

He made a sudden snatch, but Franklin jerked his head out of the way.

"Gimme dat hat," growled Manuel, with another grab in

the general direction of the Cobb headgear. "Gimme it—you! By cripe, you don't I break your neck."

One of the fishermen, a man older than the majority, interfered.

"Heave to, Portygee," he ordered. "You've had too much Fourth of July juice ahead of time. Let the boy alone, Seth. You'll have the old man out here and afoul of you, fust thing you know."

But the larger part of his comrades were not as easily satisfied.

"Back water there, Cal," commanded the man addressed as Seth. "We ain't goin' to hurt the dude none. But this is Fourth of July time, and a new hat has to be wet Fourth of July, don't it, boys?"

"You bet!"

"Sure's you live!"

The agreement was general. "Cal" shook his head but he said no more. With a glance over his shoulder at the open door of the building at the head of the wharf, he backed from the group and turned again to his place by the pulley ropes. No one paid attention to him, however; even the hands aboard the schooners were scrambling ashore to join the crowd surrounding Cobb and the Portuguese.

"See how 'tis, Willie boy," chuckled Seth. "That new hat of yours has got to be wet, that's all there is to it. Soon's it is wet right and proper we'll let you run home to mama. Be nice now and don't make no fuss."

Cobb objected to being addressed as "Willie boy." He was annoyed, but his common sense held his temper in leash. He had no yearning for trouble. Obviously this was a tough crew, the sort of gang who had extended hospitality to the Boston "drummer" in Dodson's narrative.

"What do you mean—wet?" he asked, pleasantly enough. The question was received with a roar of laughter.

"Well, I'll tell you, Willie. It's the habit hereabouts when

47

a feller's got somethin' brand-new, like that tony hat of yours, to take a drink all 'round on it. That's what we call wettin' it. See?"

Franklin saw, but only partially.

"I don't mind standing you fellows a drink," he said, "but where can I buy drinks around here?"

There was another loud laugh. "You don't have to buy none. We've attended to that already. All you got to do is stand by while we take a dose apiece and then take a good healthy one yourself. Where's the jug, Jim? Portygee was afoul of it a minute ago."

A two-gallon jug was produced from beside the water bucket. Seth swung it to his shoulder.

"A good beginnin' makes a job half done," he announced. "Well, here's down the road and back again!"

Before his lips touched the mouth of the jug the latter was pulled from his grasp. It was the Portuguese, Manuel, who seized it. With his other hand he snatched the straw hat from its owner's head.

"We giva da dicer one first, eh, boys?" he crowed. Before any one could remonstrate or interfere, he splashed at least a quarter-pint of cheap whisky into the crown of the new straw hat.

And then Franklin Cobb forgot all about his disinclination for trouble. His fist caught the whooping Manuel full on his prominent nose. The Portuguese fell backward over the bucket and his head struck the wharf with a hollow crack. The jug flew from his hand and fell upon the fish nets. The hat flew in the opposite direction. Franklin stepped forward and retrieved it; the others rushed to the rescue of the jug.

Manuel was up almost as quickly as he went down. His dark face was distorted, and his black eyes flashed fire.

"By gor, I keela you for dat!" he roared and plunged forward. But Seth and Jim and one or two of the others were in his way and he tripped and fell again. Men were running from all parts of the wharf. There was much shouting and excitement.

Seth took charge of the situation.

"Easy, 'Gee," he ordered. "Hang on to him a minute, Jim. Get back there, you fellers. Give 'em room."

The crowd drew back. Franklin found himself on the inner edge of a closely packed circle, with the gesticulating, howling Manuel at its opposite side. He glanced over his shoulder. There was no way out. He had let himself in for a fight and a fight was the last thing he desired. He was not afraid, but he was very much chagrined. This would be a nice introduction of Beriah Higham's nephew to Wellmouth.

But there was to be no fight. As he stood there, awaiting the onslaught by his antagonist, he was pushed unceremoniously to one side. Turning to see who had pushed him he found himself regarding a new arrival, a man he had not seen before. There was no doubt of that, for, having once seen him, he could not have forgotten. Cobb's first impression was that this was almost, if not quite, the biggest man he had ever seen outside of a show. Six feet three at least; lean, broad shouldered, blue eyed, sunburned to a brick red, a small sandy mustache above a square jaw. He was dressed in blue trousers and a blue waistcoat and was without a coat. The stub of a cigar was in the corner of his mouth.

"Well," he asked, quietly, his gaze moving about the circle, "what's goin' on here? Eh?"

No one answered. The outer fringe of the circle was melting away. The inner ring, men who were hemmed in and couldn't escape, shifted uneasily on their feet.

"What's the trouble, Seth?" asked the big man, turning to that individual. Seth looked sheepish.

"Why, nawthin' much, Cap'n," he stammered. "Some of the boys havin' a little fun, that's all. Day afore the Fourth, you know."

49

"I know," crisply. "Manuel, you look a little mite peevish; what ails you?"

The Portuguese was still gesticulating and spluttering profanity.

"He puncha me in da face, dat sucker dere," he snarled, pointing at Cobb. "No man do dat to me. You let go of me, Jim Holway. By gar, you just watch—"

"Shut up, Manuel! Well," turning to Franklin, "is that so? Did you punch him? What for?"

Cobb was calm enough outwardly. "Sorry to make a row," he said. "I didn't intend to. That fellow grabbed my hat and was—well, doing things to it that I didn't like. So I did something to him, that's all."

"Yes," dryly, "looks so, judgin' by his nose. Here, Jim, you probably know about this. You and Seth are liable to be mixed up in most of what goes on—unless it's hard work. What's the yarn? Let's have it."

Jim, still retaining his clutch upon the furious Portuguese, swallowed, stammered and then made answer.

"'Tain't nawthin', Cap'n Carmi. That fellow there," indicating Franklin, "was struttin' 'round here with a new dude hat on and—well, bein' as all hands could see 'twas new, we thought he ought to wet it. When Manuel grabbed the jug and started to pour—er—er—some of what was in the jug into the hat, this fellow got mad and biffed him."

"Jug, eh? Seems to me I said that anybody who brought a jug or a bottle onto this wharf was apt to be sorry. Who brought it?"

No one answered.

"Where is it now?"

The jug was standing, its cork carefully replaced, beside the overturned water bucket. The big man strode across the ring, picked it up, removed the cork and sniffed.

"Humph!" he grunted. "Kill at a mile, that stuff."

He walked to the edge of the wharf and threw the jug as

far as his long arm could send it. There was a stifled groan from the crowd.

"That's that," he observed. "Well, Manuel, what's on your mind?"

There seemed to be much on Manuel's mind. He jerked himself free from Jim's grasp and performed a sort of Comanche war dance.

"What you do dat for?" he screeched. "Dat was mine. I pay two dollars for dat whisky. By gar, you got no right—"

He did not finish the sentence. The big man seized him by the collar and the rear of his scale-spattered overalls, propelled him to the wharf edge and threw him after the jug. There was a tremendous splash, a joyful howl from the crowd and a general rush to the stringpiece.

"If you want it swim for it," said the big man.

The Portuguese was swimming but not toward the spot where the jug had sunk. He pawed his way to shoal water and waded to the beach.

"Go 'round to the office and get what money's comin' to you," his conqueror called after him. "And don't you ever let me catch you around this property or aboard one of our vessels again. Get!"

Manuel "got." He disappeared around the landward end of the long building. The big man turned to the others.

"All hands satisfied now?" he asked, cheerfully. "Nothin' to say? All right, then get to work. These two schooners must be empty by one o'clock. After they are, you can get drunk and be put in the lockup, if it's your notion of a good time; but now—move!"

The unloading began again. Cobb hastened after his rescuer who was strolling toward the building.

"I'm a whole lot obliged to you," he declared, earnestly. "And I'm mighty sorry to have made all this trouble. I walked down from the Four Corners and turned in here just by chance. This fish business is new to me and I was watching the work when—when all this started."

"All right, all right. No trouble—that is, no more than what we expect day before the Fourth. Nobody hurt but that Portugee and water hadn't ought to hurt him inside or out. Too bad about your hat. Spoiled, is it?"

The straw hat dripped with bad whisky and smelled to high heaven, but its owner laughingly replied that he guessed it wasn't hurt much. Just then another man, also tall and broad-shouldered, but older and wearing spectacles, hailed his companion from the doorway of the fish shed.

"Nothin' serious, was it, Carmi?" he asked.

"No, no, Bi. All over now. Everything smooth as a smelt."

He joined the man in the doorway and they entered the building together. Franklin Cobb looked after them. One of the barrow pushers was passing and he detained him.

"Who are those two?" he inquired. "That big chap and the other."

"Eh? Them? Oh, they're Blake Brothers. Own this wharf and them two schooners and a lot more. The one with the specs is Abiathar Blake. T'other, him that chucked the Portygeezer overboard, is Cap'n Carmi. Be consider'ble of a feller when he gets his growth, won't he?"

He went on, chuckling. Franklin walked through the alley to the main road.

It was almost six o'clock when he entered the gateway of the little Dodson home. The gate itself, he noticed, had been lifted from its hinges and was nowhere in sight. Elisha met him at the side door.

"Well, well!" he exclaimed, "you've made quite a day of it. Nellie and I had begun to think maybe you'd gone over to Ostable to hunt up Judge Dean, after all. I told her I wouldn't blame you if you had. If it was me I'd gone there if I had to walk. Though," he added, "if anybody left *me* anything in a will I probably wouldn't be able to walk."

At the supper table their guest told of his tramp to the South Side and a portion of his later experiences there. He had wandered about, lunched at a boarding house recommended by one of the shopkeepers, and spent the first part of the afternoon at the South Side, and the hours between four and six at the Corners.

"I have looked those two sections of your town over pretty thoroughly, Miss Dodson," he said.

Elisha nodded. "It's a pretty fine town, too; I guess you'll agree to that," was his comment. "Of course the Four Corners is the finest part of it, but there's consider'ble goin' on down to the South Side these times, I'll own up."

Cobb smiled. "*I* found something going on there," he observed.

Helen turned to look at him. "Now what does that mean?" she asked, quickly. "You haven't told us everything, Mr. Cobb, I guess."

"Well, no, I haven't. I had a lively experience there this morning. Not as lively as it might have been—but lively enough while it lasted."

He told of his visit to the Blake wharf and his adventure with Manuel and the rest.

"So I had to buy a new hat," he said, in conclusion. "Mr. Elkanah Rogers—I think that was his name—sold it to me. He had a fresh stock just come in. Said he did a pretty good trade in hats after the Fourth. I should say he might, if what happened to mine was a sample."

His hearers were interested and excited, Mr. Dodson particularly.

"Well, by gorry!" he exclaimed. "Say, I know that Portugee. He's no account and always was. So Cap'n Carmi hove him overboard. Well, well! That's just like Carmi Blake. That's one reason why he is so popular."

"I doubt if he is popular with Manuel just now. He saved me from a rough and tumble though, and I'm grateful to him.

What a whale of a man he is! You know him well, I suppose?"

Helen nodded. "Yes, we know him," she said briefly.

Her father stared. "Why, how you talk, Nellie!" he exclaimed. "Know him? Know Carmi Blake? Why, of course we do. Everybody does, far's that goes; he's gettin' to be a pretty big man in Wellmouth."

"*Getting* to be?" Franklin Cobb whistled.

"Oh, I don't mean big up and down and across. He's that all right. I mean big in town affairs, politics and the like of that. He skippers that mackerel schooner you saw down to his wharf. As for our knowin' him—Nellie and I—why, he drops in to see us here at the house two or three times a week when he's in port. Nobody knows Cap'n Carmi better than Nellie and I do. That's so, ain't it, Nellie?"

Miss Dodson changed the subject.

"Have you had enough supper, Mr. Cobb?" she asked. "All right, then you and Father go into the sitting room while I do the dishes. You're sure you've locked up everything, Father? This is the night before the Fourth, you know."

Cobb went to his room early. He was tired after his long walk and fell asleep almost immediately. He dreamed a good deal—fried clams and doughnuts for supper are a combination conducive to dreaming—and he woke from one particularly distressing nightmare to hear the First Meeting House bell ringing frantically and the distant popping of firecrackers. Wellmouth Four Corners had evidently begun to celebrate.

He rose and went to the chair by the window. The northwest wind had died away and a heavy fog, almost a drizzle, had drifted up from the Sound. The night outside was black and wet. Along the South Side road all was quiet.

That is, it was quiet at first. Then, along that road from the direction of the Corners came a peculiar murmur. The tread of many feet, the occasional jolt of a heavy wheel, the low grumble of voices. The sounds drew nearer. Franklin, leaning from his open window, could see nothing, but he could hear. People—a good many people—were coming down the road. Some one gave an order in a hoarse whisper.

"Easy with that truck, Hosea, can't you! If you can't be quieter than that, the whole South Side will be up waitin' for us."

The listener at the window lit a match and looked at his watch. A quarter to three. The doughnuts and clam fritters were not tempting him to sleep again, and, besides, he was curious. He remembered Dodson's story about the two old cannon, and what had happened to them the year before. He jumped from the chair and, lighting the lamp on the table, began putting on his clothes. Then he blew out the light and tiptoed carefully downstairs to the door.

CHAPTER IV

THE road was deserted when he reached it, but he hastened on in the direction of the South Side village. Soon he could hear the jolt of the wheels and an occasional low voice ahead and, a few minutes later, caught up with the stragglers at the rear of the crowd. They were strapping young fellows for the most part, and, to his surprise, not a boy among them. He learned afterwards that every boy had been ordered not to follow under threat of a licking. They plodded steadily on, speaking seldom and only in whispers; apparently this was a serious business.

He ventured to ask a question of the man nearest him. The answer was a peremptory demand to be told who the devil he was and where he came from. He hastily explained that he was a stranger in town, staying with the Dodsons.

"I'm not poking my nose in your affairs, understand," he added. "I was awake and at the window when you went by, so I came along to watch the fun—if there was any."

His companion grunted. "If you're staying with 'Lish Dodson I guess likely it's all right," he said; "'Lish is a good square Four Corners man. Fun? Well, you're liable to see some afore we get through, I shouldn't wonder. The gang down yonder may be expectin' us, though we're hopin' they ain't. They most likely figure we don't know they've got the guns; cal'late we won't find it out till daylight. That's where we'll fool 'em," vindictively.

"The guns? The old cannon, you mean? Why, they are locked up in Eldredge's back shop, aren't they?"

The man beside him swore in disgust.

"We thought they was locked up there," he growled, "but

56

there's been some funny business somewhere. Somebody blew the gaff and we'll find out who 'twas afore we finish. A few of us looked in Manasseh's back room about half an hour ago to make sure everything was all right and we found the door open and the guns gone. We know well enough where they're gone and now we're goin' after 'em. We'll get 'em too, or know the reason why."

It was not until the next day that Franklin learned the whole story. Some time between eleven and twelve that night a group of South Siders, with a cart and a pair of horses, had visited the Corners, had unlocked the Eldredge door—where and how they got a key to fit is still a mystery—loaded the cannon on the cart and departed as secretly as they came. In other words they had practically repeated their triumph of the previous Fourth. This time, however, the Four Corners had discovered the theft before the night was over, had hastily gathered a posse and set forth to retrieve what they considered their property.

Little by little Cobb moved forward in the crowd until he came abreast the slow moving team and the four wheels and under body of a lumber wagon which they drew. The leaders of the expedition walked beside the horses. One of them was, so he discovered to his surprise, the fussy Mr. Eldredge himself. Those nearest him were middle-aged men whom the young huskies forming the bulk of the expedition addressed with respect. Obviously this must be something more than a Fourth of July lark. The visitor from Cleveland began to understand. As Elisha Dodson had said, the cannon did not matter so much in themselves; it was what their transfer represented that had aroused the solid citizens of the Four Corners. It was one more piece of impertinence on the part of the upstart South Side, and the South Side must be kept in its place. Franklin Cobb began to feel a curious thrill of interest, almost of partisan bias. For the time, at least, he was a Four Cornerite.

Just before reaching the first clump of houses at the edge of South Side village the expedition halted. These houses were dark and quiet, but above the roofs ahead was a ruddy glow and from that direction sounded the occasional explosion of a firearm. The leaders drew together for consultation. Then Manasseh turned to the crowd pressing about him. He was perspiring and out of breath, but very earnest.

"We're goin' to turn the team off on this side road here," he pointed. "No use goin' straight up the main road. They'd see and hear us and we'd have to fight before the time came for it. They've got them guns hid somewheres, of course, and it's 'most likely where they hid 'em last time, in Solomon Hawkes's pines over back of the meetin' house. May be somebody set to watch 'em there too, you can't tell. We'll drive the truck around this back road till we get abreast of the pines and wait there till we find out somethin' definite. Anybody got any better notion? If they have we'd like to hear it."

Apparently no one had. There was much whispered conversation but no helpful suggestions. The truck moved on and the crowd moved with it. The back road was little more than a bypath through the fields, rough and rutted. Several times they stopped to readjust the bagging and odds and ends of cloths with which the wheels were muffled. At last they reached the outer fringe of a pine grove.

"Now," whispered Eldredge, "we can't do no more till we find out somethin'. Is there anybody in this gang that ain't known from one end of the South Side to the other? If there is I'd like to talk to him."

No one came forward. Then Franklin felt a hand laid upon his shoulder. The man who had given him the information concerning the theft of the cannon was pushing him to the front.

"Say, Manasseh," he whispered, "here's a fellow I guess nobody knows. He's from out of town, or so he says, and he's stayin' at 'Lish Dodson's. Maybe he could spy out the lay of the land for us. How about it, boy?"

Cobb suddenly became the center of interest. Eldredge and the other leaders clustered about him. Manasseh bent to peer into his face.

"Who are you?" he asked, unceremoniously.

"My name is Cobb. I'm in town for a few days; staying with the Dodsons, as this chap says."

"Anybody know you down here to the South Side?"

"No; that is, they don't know who I am or where I'm staying."

"Huh! Well, are you in on this game with us? Know what it's all about, don't you?"

"Yes." And, impulsively, "Why, yes, I'm in it. Glad to help if I can."

The leaders drew apart to whisper. Then Eldredge again came close to his side.

"You can help if anybody can, I guess," he said. "Now, I'll tell you what to do. You go on along this road till you come to the first one crossin' it. Then turn left and keep on till you come out on the main road about abreast the new meetin' house. There's a little square there, as you might say, and that's where the bonfire is and where the crowd will be, if there is one. 'Tain't likely to be much but boys, for this drizzle will have drove most of the grown-ups inside; at least, we hope 'twill. Boys generally know what's goin' on and, if you listen, you may hear somethin' about where those cannon are hid. Find out all you can, without lettin' anybody know you're tryin' to find out anything, and then come back and tell us what you've heard. For thunder sakes don't keep us waitin' long. It'll be daylight in an hour or so and all hands'll be turnin' out. . . . Oh, I know!" turning to the younger element who were muttering behind him. "Some of you fellers are lookin' for a free fight. Well, I ain't—not

59

unless it's needful. Now you, what's-your-name—Mr. Cobb, you run along. And *hurry!*"

The crowd opened to let him through and, almost before he knew it, Franklin Cobb found himself alone and stumbling on through the wet grass and low bushes bordering the lane at the edge of the pines. He could not help thinking that perhaps he was a fool for letting himself into this business. He had done it entirely on impulse. The secrecy of the whole affair, the intense, solemn earnestness of the crowd from the Four Corners, the thrill of adventure, all these had lured him and trapped him. But it was fun, there was no doubt of that. Well, he was in it now and must go through with it.

When he reached the corner of the main road he saw the little open grass plot which Eldredge had called a square. It was directly opposite him on the other side of the road. A bonfire was burning in the center of it and perhaps a dozen boys, their coat collars turned up, were standing about it, trying their dismal best to believe they were having a glorious adventure. Not a grown person was in sight, as far as he could make out. The shops along the road were all dark and shuttered, but an occasional house beyond the little square showed a lighted window. One larger and more pretentious dwelling on the corner where he stood showed several. The drizzle was now a steady rain.

He crossed the road and, by a circuitous route, strolled toward the bonfire. The youngsters, their ages ranged from ten to fifteen, scarcely looked up at his approach. The rain was obviously dampening their enthusiasm. As a matter of fact, it was dampening his, and he was more certain than ever that he was a fool on a fool's errand.

"Hello!" he hailed, stepping into the circle by the blaze. "Having a good time? Got a fine fire, haven't you?"

The smaller boys edged away. One of the older ones sniffed. "Ain't much good," he grumbled, with a shiver. "Darn

60

rain's spoilin' everything. Aw, come on, fellows! I'm goin' home. No use gettin' soaked through."

He walked off, his shotgun under his arm and his hands jammed in his trousers' pockets. Several of the others followed him.

"Aw, Ike," pleaded a comrade, who still lingered, "ain't you goin' to wait till they fire off the cannon?"

"Won't fire 'em off afore half-past five or six. Might's well keep dry till then. You can stay by your old bonfire if you want to, I'm goin' home."

There was a moment's hesitation and then, to Cobb's surprised chagrin, every boy in sight started to leave. He hastily detained one of them.

"Where will they fire the cannon?" he asked. "I don't want to miss that."

"Eh? Why, right here, of course. They fired 'em here last year and wa'n't the Four Corners folks mad? Aw, gee!"

"Where are the cannon now? I don't see them anywhere."

"'Course you don't. They've hid 'em, that's why. Hold on, Tom, can't you! I'm a-comin'."

He jerked free and ran. Another minute and Franklin Cobb was alone by the bonfire. Alone and with the conviction that his scouting expedition was so far a complete fizzle.

He wandered toward the church building and stood beneath the projecting roof above its wide doorway to keep out of the rain and think. The thinking did him no good and he had about decided to go back to Manasseh Eldredge and report failure when he heard the noise of wheels and the "clump" of horses' hoofs approaching along the road. A covered carriage passed and drew up before the big house diagonally opposite, the house with the lighted windows. There was much youthful chatter and feminine laughter. He walked over to the clump of shrubs at the far end of the grass plot and stood there. He had no definite reason for doing so, other than the faint hope that he might hear something concerning those confounded cannon.

Two young men got out of the carriage, opened its door and assisted two young women to alight. By the lamplight shining from the door at the top of the house steps he could see that the quartette were dressed as if they had come from a party or dance. The young women's flounces and furbelows were conspicuously noticeable. They ran up the steps out of the rain and the young men followed them.

"No, no, George," protested one of the girls, "of course you can't come in. It's almost morning. We've had a perfectly gorgeous time, good night."

"Good night, Maisie," called one of their escorts. "Good night, Vic. See you both to-morrow—or to-day, I suppose it is. Good night. Sweet dreams."

"Say, Maisie," put in the other young fellow, "don't let Vic lie awake thinking about those guns. Perhaps we hadn't ought to have told her. She may be sneaking out and spiking them or something."

The other girl, the one who had not before spoken, tossed her head.

"I only wish I could," she declared, with a little stamp of her foot. "I only wish I had known about them while we were at the party. I should have put a word in somebody's ear, you may be sure of that, Ed Howes."

Her companion laughed. "Too bad, Vic, too bad!" jeered Ed. "Tough on the poor old Four Corners, that's a fact. Well, you'll have to own up that the South Side is the only live place. Good night."

The door closed. The carriage moved off. Cobb strolled to the sidewalk and looked after it. Then, with a shrug, he turned and, crossing the main road, started along the lane which led to the juncture of the other lane bordering the pine grove where Manasseh and the rest were waiting. He did not look forward to meeting them.

The house on the corner stood in a good sized yard which extended along the lane he was traveling. A white fence, scroll-sawed and fretted in the style of the period, bordered this yard. The wall of the house was but a short distance from the fence. Suddenly one of the windows on this side of the house sprang into light and, an instant later, it was opened.

Franklin paused involuntarily and turned to look. He could see into the room, a bedchamber evidently, for he saw the corner of a black walnut, marble-topped bureau, a marble-topped commode with a lamp on it, and the back of a walnut chair. He saw these, but only as a fleeting picture. Two young women were in the room, obviously the two he had just seen at the front door. They were talking and what they said caused him to halt in his tracks.

"I don't care, Maisie," said one. "I'm just as provoked about it as I can be. You South Side people are altogether too smart. If it wasn't raining I honestly believe I would climb right out of this window and run all the way to the Corners to tell Manasseh Eldredge and father and the rest. They wouldn't let those old cannons stay here long, indeed they wouldn't! Oh, yes, yes! I know it's all a joke, but I don't like jokes when they are on the wrong side. And that Ed Howes is too fresh to live; he makes me mad all the way through. There, there, dear, I'll get over it. Now run along to bed or your family will never invite me again. Good night."

There were whispers and a feminine giggle, then the sound of a closing door. Franklin Cobb, a trifle ashamed of himself for listening, moved on again. He had taken but a few steps when he turned to look back. The window was still open and, against the lamplight, he could see the silhouette of one of the girls. She was leaning upon the window sill, looking out. She was, he was sure, the one who had expressed a wish that she might tell Eldredge about the cannon. He had half a mind—

63

The "half a mind" became a whole one. He stepped over the low fence and moved toward the window. She saw him and drew back with a startled exclamation. He took off his hat.

"Don't be frightened," he said, in an eager whisper. "It's all right. I want to speak to you a minute, that's all. Please listen."

He could see her face now. She was a pretty girl, a very pretty girl.

"Who are you? What do you want?" she faltered.

"You don't know me, but my name is Cobb and I am staying at Mr. Dodson's up at the Corners. I heard you say something about the cannon. Do you know where they are now? Oh, don't call any one! Don't! If you do it will spoil everything. You see, we've come to get them."

She had started toward the door, but now she hesitated. She came back to the window.

"Come to get them?" she repeated. "Who has? What do you mean?"

"I'll tell you. I heard you say—I was passing and the window was open and—and I couldn't help hearing some things you said to that other girl. You're from the Four Corners, aren't you? You'd like to have Eldredge and the rest of us get those cannon back again, wouldn't you? Well, if you know where they are maybe we *can* get them. We've come down here to do it. Honest, we have. *Do* you know?"

She was leaning on the sill again, peering out at him through the screen. She *was* a pretty girl; the prettiest he had ever seen, or so he thought at that moment.

"Tell me all about it—quick!" she whispered.

He told, in a half-dozen hurried sentences, of the discovery of the theft of the cannon, the expedition and its purposes, of his so far unsuccessful scouting excursion. She clasped her hands.

"Oh, lovely!" she exclaimed, with a little squeal of delight.

"Splendid! Yes, I know where the cannon are. They have them hidden in the empty hearse house at the back of the old cemetery—not the one they use now, the old one. Mr. Eldredge knows where it is. Oh, *do* you think you can get them? You'll have to *hurry!* They are going to fire them by six o'clock."

"We'll get them. And say, thanks a lot. Good night."

He was over the fence and running up the lane. A glance over his shoulder showed her still leaning on the sill.

Manasseh and two or three more had, in their impatience, come part way to meet him. He breathlessly panted the news. Eldredge relaxed his grasp on his shoulder and turned to his followers.

"Come on, boys," he ordered.

"Hold on, Manasseh," said one. "They may have set somebody to watch them guns, you know. What'll you do if they have?"

"Leave a couple of somebodies to watch him—yes, and keep him quiet. Get goin', all hands. We haven't got any spare time."

It was half-past five when Franklin Cobb tiptoed up the Dodson stairs to his room. He hurriedly removed his wet clothes and lay down on the bed. The morning was dark and the rain was pouring. He was tired out, but somehow he could not get to sleep. The retrieving of the cannon had been exciting and lots of fun. He thought it all over from beginning to end. No, Wellmouth wasn't such a dead place, at any rate on the day and night before the Fourth of July. There was his adventure on the Blake wharf and then this. And that girl at the window—he could see her now. Her hair—her eyes —her expression as she listened to his story! Who was she, anyway?

He was still wondering when, at last, he did drop off to sleep.

A "boom" which shook the windows woke him a half-hour later. He sat up in bed, realized what was going on, and grinned triumphantly.

"Boom!" thundered the other old cannon before the First Meeting House at Wellmouth Four Corners.

CHAPTER V

FRANKLIN COBB was a trifle heavy-eyed when he came down to breakfast. The Dodsons had, of course, been awakened by the cannon firing and Elisha was inclined to gloat over the obvious fact that, if the South Siders had planned to repeat their trick of the previous Fourth, their plans had been frustrated.

"Smart notion, that one, of Manasseh's lockin' those guns up in his back store," he chuckled. "He's a wise old owl, Manasseh is. . . . *Now* what are you smilin' to yourself about, Nellie?"

Helen looked up from her coffee pouring.

"Did you say 'owl' or 'eel,' Father?" she asked, innocently.

"Eh? Why, I said 'owl,' of course. Never heard that an eel was 'specially wise, as I know of."

"He's especially slippery. . . . There's your coffee, Mr. Cobb. You look to me as if you needed it. Didn't you sleep well?"

He told of his morning's adventure. Elisha's excited exclamations punctuated the telling. It was not until Franklin described his interview with the girl at the window that Helen interrupted.

"Victoria Bates," she put in. "That's who it was. She is spending the Fourth with Maisie Rogers; I heard she was going to."

" 'Twas in the *Eagle*," chimed in her father. "I remember now. Alma Perry had it in the 'Gleanings' last week. She finds out everything, Alma does."

Cobb remembered the local. Stupid of him not to think of it before. The girl was Victoria Bates, of course; she who owned the new dogcart and whose father ap-

67

peared to own the Four Corners—or the larger part of it.

"Maisie and her go to the same boardin' school together," Elisha went on. "They're great chums, those two. Stick together in about everything—except when it comes to stickin' up for the parts of the town they live in. Cap'n Zenas Rogers, Maisie's father, is one of the big men down there. He and Cap'n Bates used to be hand and glove in runnin' district politics, but lately the story is that they don't get on so well together."

Helen nodded. "The South Side is beginning to take a hand in its own politics," she observed. "Well, Mr. Cobb, how are you going to spend the Fourth?"

Cobb had been doing a little thinking and he answered promptly.

"The first thing I shall do," he announced, "is look up that boarding house your father mentioned when he and I first met. It looks as if I might have to stay in Wellmouth for several days at least, and I must find a place to stay in."

Elisha and Helen looked at each other.

"Father and I have been talking about that," she said, "and we both think you had better stay here with us. It probably won't be long and you're not the least bit of trouble. We have a spare room and it is as easy to cook for three as two. Stay here for the present. We want you to, don't we, Father?"

"Certain sure. Come now, you stay, Mr. Cobb."

Franklin protested that he shouldn't do any such thing. They had been more kind than he could express, but he must not think of imposing upon their hospitality any longer. The Dodsons were insistent, however, and the argument ended by his consenting to stay until after his interview with Dean.

As a matter of fact, in spite of his protests, he was only too pleased to remain in his present quarters. He was beginning to like his hosts. Elisha was an interesting old bird and Helen was a bright and attractive girl, good-natured and good company and with a lot of common sense. Pretty too, in a whole-some sort of way. He gave her looks but a passing thought however; the picture of Victoria Bates at that window was still in his mind, and he could not have forgotten it if he had wished—which he most distinctly did not.

After breakfast he and Dodson walked up to the Four Corners. Elisha limped briskly along beside him, pointing out places of interest and crowing delightedly over the disappoint-ment of the South Side gang. On the grass plot at the Bay-port road side of the First Meeting House the two old can-non were proudly enthroned on their mountings and a small crowd of exultant citizens, both sexes and all ages, was gath-ered about them. It was no longer raining, although the sky was gray and overcast.

In the crowd Franklin recognized several of his early morn-ing associates, Manasseh Eldredge among them. Mr. Eldredge was obviously the hero of the day and, just as obviously, he did not shrink from the spotlight. He was garbed in a checked suit which was a celebration in itself and his Ascot tie sported a horseshoe pin. He espied Dodson as the latter limped toward him and recognized his companion.

"Why, hello, there!" he exclaimed, bustling over to meet them. "Well, 'Lish, we kind of got ahead of 'em—what? Oh, that you, young fellow! Heard the salute, I presume likely? Cal'late they heard it down to the South Side; we meant they should. Ho, ho! Say, 'Lish, this young chap gave the Corners a helpin' hand last night. Told you about it, didn't he?"

"You bet he did!" Elisha waxed gleefully enthusiastic over his guest's share in the rescue of the cannon. Manasseh listened rather absently and interrupted before the finish.

"Oh, yes, yes," he broke in, with a condescending wave of the hand, "he helped us considerable, but we'd have pulled it off anyhow. When I set out to do a thing it most generally gets done. 'Twas Victoria that turned the trick for us, really.

She's a smart one; wouldn't be her old man's daughter if she wasn't. How long you down for, Mr. —er—"

"Cobb," prompted Elisha.

"Yes, Cobb, that's right. Now who did I hear talkin' about somebody named Cobb lately? Cap'n Gideon, was it? Or Joe Dean? Oh, well, don't make any difference; wouldn't be you they was talkin' about, of course. Cal'latin' to stay in Wellmouth a spell, Mr. Cobb?"

"Not long, probably."

"Better come to the ball at the town hall to-night, if you haven't got anything 'special to do. Bridgewater Silver Cornet Band is comin' down, and 'Lish'll tell you that means music. Lucky to get that band, we were. There was two or three other towns after 'em, but I straightened it out. I've got a little pull up to Bridgewater; done a few favors around election time for some of the boys, you understand," with a wink.

"Better not miss that ball, Cobb," he added. "If you like dancin' and want to know some of the right girls, hunt me up and I'll see you're fixed. If I ain't there when you first come don't worry. I've got a date with Judge Dean, but it ain't liable to keep me long."

He was moving off but Elisha's exclamation detained him.

"Judge Dean! Why, I thought the judge was over to Ostable with his niece's folks."

"Eh? So he is. Planned to stay till to-morrow mornin', but I had a telegram from him sayin' he'd be back this afternoon and wanted to see me after supper to-night. I don't know what for; heard somethin' new in the politics way, I shouldn't wonder."

He strolled away biting the end from a fat cigar. Franklin Cobb shook his head.

"I'll bet that fellow takes off his hat to himself every time he looks in a mirror," he observed. "Eh? What's the matter?"

Elisha was excited.

"Why, Mr. Cobb!" he cried. "Didn't you hear what he said? That about Judge Dean? Accordin' to him the judge will be here this afternoon. If that's so you won't have to wait till to-morrow to see him."

CHAPTER VI

THE Joel Dean residence was a white house on the main road
about an eighth of a mile beyond the Higham printing office.
It was what New Englanders of that section used to call a
"square top"; that is, a two story house sitting broadside to
the street, with a colonial doorway in the middle, and a huge
chimney in the center of the roof. It was painted white, and
the window blinds were, of course, green. The walk leading
to the front door was of brick, bordered by trimmed hedges.
The walk was very straight, swept very clean, and the hedges
were trimmed with exact evenness. There was—or so it
seemed to Franklin Cobb as he approached its front door—an
air of self-satisfied respectability about the establishment. To
his fancy it seemed to advertise its owner as a person of strict
party regularity and unswerving orthodoxy, one who had
made those qualities pay.

He pulled the glass knob beside the door. Within, apparently at the end of a long hall, a spring bell jolted and clanked,
the clankings dying away to a quivering jingle. After an interval—a decorous, dignified interval—footsteps sounded at
the other side of the door and it was opened. A feminine
head, bespectacled and white-capped, looked out.

"Well, young man?" inquired the owner of the head.

Cobb had learned from the Dodsons that Joel Dean was
a widower and that his housekeeper's name was Higgins. He
lifted his hat.

"Is the judge in?" he asked.

Mrs. Higgins opened the door a very little way. She gave
him an appraising inspection.

"What do you want to see the judge for?" she asked, crisply.

"If you're sellin' law books or anything it won't be any use. He's been away and he's just got back and he's busy."

"I'm not selling anything. I want to see him because—well, because I know he wants to see me."

"Oh, does he? What for? Does he know you're comin'?"

"No, but I have a letter from him. My name is Cobb. If you tell him that I think he'll understand."

Mrs. Higgins said "Umph." Then, after a moment, she added, "Well, I'll tell him. You stay here."

She went away, closing the door carefully behind her. Franklin grinned, looked up and down the road, and waited. When she returned her manner was more gracious.

"Come in," she ordered. "Judge Dean says he'll see you. I declare I don't know how to act when a stranger rings this bell nowadays. There's so many everlastin' peddlers and book agents around, and the judge gets *so* provoked when I let 'em in that— Here's the man, Judge. He's in there, Mr.—er— What's-your-name. Go right in."

She opened a door opening from the hall. Cobb entered. The room was a sort of combination sitting room and library. There were two cases of books along one wall, gilt-framed steel engravings and "crayon-enlarged" portraits hung about, a black walnut sofa upholstered in black haircloth, several walnut and haircloth chairs, a tall "gas burner" stove in a corner and a walnut table-desk by a window. The windows, there were two of them, were topped with lambrequins and hung with lace curtains.

At the table-desk, in an armchair, sat Judge Joel Dean. He looked just as Franklin Cobb, his imagination helped by Elisha Dodson's sketchy description, had expected him to look.

The judge stroked his beard and looked at his caller. The caller bowed and said, "How do you, sir?"

Dean cleared his throat. "How do you?" he repeated, with dignity. "Well, Mr.—er—Hobbs, what can I do for you? Mrs. Higgins, my housekeeper, tells me that you have a letter from me. I don't remember writing it, but I write a good many letters and I may have forgotten."

"My name isn't Hobbs, Judge Dean. I am Franklin Cobb, from Cleveland—Beriah Higham's nephew, you know."

The lawyer's demeanor underwent a great change. It might be an exaggeration to say that he sprang to his feet—it had been many a day since he sprang to anything—but he certainly rose from his chair with almost undignified alacrity.

"Why, dear me!" he exclaimed. "Why, dear me! Yes, yes, of course. I *beg* your pardon, Mr. Cobb. That—er—woman of mine is a trifle hard of hearing— Yes, yes! Well, well! I am very glad indeed to see you, Mr. Cobb. Sit down, sit down."

He came from behind the desk and shook his visitor's hand. He pressed him into a chair.

"This is an unexpected pleasure, Mr. Cobb," he declared. "I have been a good deal disturbed by getting no answer to my letter and telegram. My friend Higham's nephew! Well, well! Your uncle's sudden—er—passing away was a heavy blow to me—and to all Wellmouth, Mr. Cobb. When did you arrive?"

Franklin told of his arrival and of the Dodsons and their hospitality. He said nothing of his participation in the cannon episode.

"Yes, yes." The Dean head bowed with patronizing graciousness. "I know the Dodsons well. They are very—er —respectable people. . . . Of course," with a keen glance from behind the gold-rimmed spectacles, "they know who you are and why you came?"

"I told them. But," quickly, "I am sure that made no difference. Judging from what I have seen of them, I am sure they would have been just as kind to any one else under the circumstances."

"Oh, no doubt, no doubt. Did—er—Elisha mention my calling on him at the *Eagle* office night before last?"

"He said you did call, but that was all."

"I see, I see. Yes, yes. . . . Well, now, Mr. Cobb, what are your plans? How much time have you to spend with us here in Wellmouth?"

The young man was tempted to reply that he had more time than money to spend anywhere, but he did not yield to the temptation. He explained that he had no definite plans, having hurried to Wellmouth as soon as he received the lawyer's letter. He added that the news of his legacy had come as a great surprise to him; he had not known, or had forgotten, that he had an uncle.

Dean nodded. "Beriah gave me to understand that his sister —your mother, Mr. Cobb—and he had some—er—slight disagreement at one time. A good while ago, I believe he said it was. Something about the division of your grandfather's property, I gathered, but he gave me no particulars. It could not have been very serious, I should say; certainly he held no grudge, for he has made you his heir, his only heir."

"Yes, so you wrote. It seems scarcely possible."

"It is a fact. All that your uncle owned—everything—is yours under the will."

Franklin drew a long breath. Judge Dean regarded him keenly.

"Don't expect too much," he cautioned, after a moment. "Beriah Higham was not rich, I tried to make that plain in my letter."

"Oh, I know. Honestly, Judge Dean, I haven't really dared expect anything. *Is* there anything? Anything beside the printing business and the paper? The Dodsons told me about them and Mr. Dodson showed me the shop and the presses yesterday."

"Oh!" thoughtfully. "He did?"

"Yes. You were away, and I didn't have anything particular to do, so I went up to the shop with him."

"I see." The judge stroked his beard. "Well," he said, "the printing business is not a—er—large affair. You realized that, of course. It wouldn't be in a town like this. And the paper —the *Eagle*—well, you know what a country weekly is, Mr. Cobb. Not a Boston *Advertiser,* exactly."

"I suppose not."

"No. . . . You are—er"—another glance through the spectacles—"you are not a newspaper man, Mr. Cobb?"

"Don't know the least thing about it."

"So I imagined. Then I suppose you will wish to dispose of that outfit, the business, including the *Eagle,* as soon as possible?"

"Sell them, you mean?"

"Why—er—yes. Turn them into something tangible—that is, money."

"Could that be done? Do you know of any one who would be likely to buy them, Mr. Dean?"

Joel Dean waved his hand. He smiled pleasantly. "That remains to be seen. We never can tell till we try, Mr. Cobb. I may have an idea—ahem—but that we will consider later, of course. Plenty of time for that."

"I don't know," doubtfully. "I shall need whatever money I can get; need it now, so far as that goes. I am out a job, as it happens, and so, if I decide not to stay in Wellmouth, the sooner the whole estate is turned into cash the better, I should say."

Judge Dean leaned back in his chair. The eyes behind the spectacles narrowed.

"If you decide," he repeated, slowly. "Have you been thinking of staying here—permanently?"

Franklin Cobb hesitated. "I don't know why I said that, exactly," he confessed. "I haven't decided anything. I have been working in a Chicago bank, but that is over and done with, and I never liked it, anyhow. I must work somewhere though, and the sooner the better."

Dean was smiling again. "You are a city man, aren't you, Mr. Cobb?" he asked.

"Yes. That is, I have never lived in a town as small as this, if that is what you mean."

"Exactly. Well, Wellmouth is a good town. It is my town and I am—ahem—proud of it. But I am old enough to be your father. If I were young again—"

He paused. Cobb finished the sentence for him. "You would go somewhere else?" he suggested.

"Oh, I'm not sure of that. I have—er—I think I may say that I have—er—got on fairly well as a country lawyer. But," impressively, "I was born here, I am accustomed to country ways. Wellmouth is—er—Wellmouth. It isn't Chicago, for instance. There are opportunities for a young man in a large city—great opportunities."

"I wish I knew one of them just now. . . . But you're probably right. Then you advise me to sell my uncle's business as soon as possible and for what it will bring? Is that it?"

The Dean smile broadened. "That is a decision you must make, Mr. Cobb."

"I know, but I am asking your advice."

"Well, then, speaking not only as a lawyer but as your friend —I was your uncle's friend and I should like to be yours—"

"Thank you. As a friend then, your advice is—sell out?"

"Why—er—everything considered, frankly—yes."

"I see. Much obliged."

Franklin looked at the floor. Joel Dean stroked his beard and looked at him. Suddenly the young man raised his eyes.

"Judge Dean," he said, bluntly, "I believe you do know some one who might buy that print shop and the *Eagle*. Do you, sir?"

The judge seemed a trifle disconcerted. He met his visitor's look for a moment, then fumbled with the papers on his desk. He turned one of them over.

"It seems to me," he observed, "that you are taking a good deal for granted. That is what we lawyers would call a leading question, Mr. Cobb. What makes you think I know anything of the kind? I didn't say that I did."

"No; but you said you had an idea and the way you said it set me to wondering if you hadn't some particular person in mind. Have you?"

Dean turned the sheet of paper back to its original position. He still seemed somewhat put out.

"You are a sharp young man," was his comment. "I—er—mustn't answer your question directly; I am—er—not empowered to do so. . . . I will say this: I *do* know of a certain group of substantial responsible people here in Wellmouth, who, rather than see a long-established business like Mr. Higham's go out of existence altogether, might—I say *might* —possibly consider taking it over at a low figure. Just as a matter of sentiment, of course. They might—or they might not. That is all I can say now."

Franklin nodded. "Well, that's something, anyway."

"Something, but not very definite. However, all that can wait—a little while, at any rate. Now I suppose you would like to know more about your inheritance, the rest of it, I mean—what that amounts to."

"There is something else then?"

"Oh, yes, not a great deal, I told you that. The will is in my safe at the law office, we'll see that later, but I have a list here of the stock and securities and you and I might go over it together. Here it is. Pull up your chair."

The list was not a long one, but to Franklin Cobb the items were welcome surprises. When the inspection was finished, he found himself struggling to realize that he was the possessor of a trifle over three thousand dollars in stocks and bonds. Considering that his hitherto available resources had dwindled to less than six hundred dollars in the savings bank this was a windfall indeed. And there were, so Dean informed him, a few books and some furniture in the rooms his late uncle had occupied. They might be sold at auction, although the return would not be likely to exceed another hundred and fifty, if as much.

They rose from the desk as the clock struck six, having fixed upon ten the next morning as the hour for another conference, this one to be at the lawyer's office. Dean accompanied him to the door and shook hands with him at parting.

"I should be very happy to have you make my house your home while you are with us here in Wellmouth, Mr. Cobb," he said. "I am alone now, since my wife's—er—passing. Mrs. Higgins and I will do our best to make you comfortable. I know every one in the town and, if you care to meet the—er— best people, I should be glad to introduce you."

Cobb thanked him. "I have promised to stay with the Dodsons to-night," he explained. "After that—well, I haven't any definite plans. You're very kind, Judge Dean."

"Not at all, not at all. You are my friend Higham's nephew, I don't forget that. To-morrow at ten at my office. Good night, Mr. Cobb."

Franklin, as he walked down the South Side road, thought over the interview. As to accepting the Dean offer of hospitality his decision was already made. The idea of spending more time than was necessary in that gloomily majestic abode, with the prim Mrs. Higgins and her patronizingly dignified employer, was not in the least appealing to a person of his years.

As to Judge Joel R. Dean himself, his impressions were mixed. The lawyer had been gracious and cordial, almost effusively so, but he had not been altogether open and frank with the nephew of his "dear friend" Higham. In fact he had admitted as much, under pressure. He had advised the sale of the print shop and the Wellmouth *Eagle* and, then, a minute later, had hinted at knowledge of a "group" who might possibly buy if the price were low enough. Further than this he would not go, saying that he was "not empowered" to do so.

That must mean that the "group"—whoever they might be —had discussed the subject and that Judge Dean had either taken part in those discussions or knew all about them. The "not empowered" phrase sounded as if he might have been present in the capacity of legal advisor. Was it possible that he, himself, was one of the group?

Two things seemed certain: The Higham business was a saleable property; and certain people considered it worth buying. These certainties were, as he had said to the lawyer, something, but the terms of the sale were something else. It behooved Franklin Cobb—who had recently heard himself characterized as a "sharp young man"—to be careful, to watch his step. There was something behind this, something that Judge Dean was keeping from him.

Supper was waiting when he entered the Dodson dining room. Elisha was hovering about and Cobb expected to be bombarded with questions concerning his session with Judge Dean, but the little man asked not a single one. Helen, when he came in, was dressed in what their guest imagined to be her best gown. It was simple, but in good taste and very becoming, so he thought. She laughingly explained.

"Excuse the best bib and tucker, Mr. Cobb," she said. "I am going to the dance this evening, that's all. Now, Father, we're ready."

Mr. Dodson bent his head and galloped through a blessing. He looked appealingly at Cobb and then at his daughter when he had finished. She caught the look and smiled.

"No, Father," she continued. "You know what I told you. It isn't our business. Give Mr. Cobb some of the fish."

Franklin, too, had noticed the exchange of looks.

"I suppose you'd like to hear what the judge had to say to me," he suggested. "Well, it didn't amount to much. I am to have a few shares of stock and a bond or two; that is about all the ready assets."

Elisha could hold in no longer. "But about the *Eagle?*" he blurted. "Didn't you and the judge talk about the *Eagle* at *all?*"

"Oh, yes, but only in a general way. He thinks I ought to sell, if I can find a customer."

"Customer! Why, didn't he—?"

"Hush, Father! Remember."

"I know, Nellie, but I supposed of course he'd— Oh, all right, all right."

"He and I are to have another get-together to-morrow morning at his office," put in Cobb. "Probably we shall talk more about the printing business and the paper then. . . . Miss Dodson," he added, turning toward her, "just what sort of a man is this Dean?"

Elisha answered the question. "He's one of the biggest men in Ostable County," he declared. "Lawyer for the bank and for Cap'n Gideon and for 'most everybody that is anybody around here. And when it comes to runnin' town politics, he—"

"Oh, yes, you told me that. He's a big gun and knows he is; that's plain enough. That isn't just what I meant. Is he square? Can you trust him?"

It was Helen he was addressing.

"Cap'n Bates trusts him, I'm sure," she said.

"No doubt, but I'm not Bates, you see. Suppose, for instance, there was a deal to be made with—oh, with Bates, for instance, on one side and a—somebody he didn't know very well and wasn't likely to profit much by on the other; would he play even and according to Hoyle, or would he be likely to have an ace or two in his sleeve?"

Helen hesitated. "Well," she said slowly, "he has handled politicians for a long while." She looked up suddenly. "In a case like the one you mention, Mr. Cobb, I think I should keep an eye on that sleeve."

Elisha was horrified. "Why, Nellie!" he said. "What a way that is to talk!"

Franklin nodded. "I guessed as much," he said. "Thanks a lot."

He went to his room soon afterward. There were several copies of the *Eagle* on the table, and he looked them through with a new interest. The paper looked prosperous. It carried a pretty fair amount of advertising, and advertising, so he remembered having heard somewhere, was the really profitable end of the newspaper game. He wondered what the circulation might be. He must ask Elisha.

In spite of his lack of sleep the night before he was not sleepy now. He had a mind to go out somewhere, if there were anywhere to go. Then he remembered Mr. Eldredge's suggestion concerning the "Grand Fourth of July Ball" at the town hall. He shaved, changed to a blue serge suit and went downstairs.

Elisha was alone in the sitting room. Helen, he explained, had departed for the dance at the town hall. Was Mr. Cobb cal'latin' to go out? Well, 'twas a nice night for a walk.

The town hall was ablaze with lights when Franklin reached it. There was a crowd on the platform, mostly young fellows who, judging by their sunburned faces and hands, which contrasted acutely with the white of their collars and cuffs, were members of the fishing crews Dodson had mentioned. They were boisterous and loud of speech, but good-natured and peaceable enough. An elderly man, with a solemn and important manner and a metal star prominently displayed upon the breast of his coat, was strutting up and down among them. Cobb guessed him to be an officer of the law. He evidently took himself seriously, but the rest of the crowd treated him as a joke.

Franklin paid a dollar to another elderly man at the little window inside by the door, received a ticket in exchange, and mounted the broad flight of stairs to the ball room. The hall was crowded. The Bridgewater Silver Cornet Band, on the platform at the farther end, was earning its wages, and a quadrille was in progress.

He pushed through the lookers-on by the door and stood, looking over the assemblage. Mostly young people, the men in their best clothes, and perspiringly conscious of them, the women and girls in summer gowns, trained and tucked and hooped. A brisk little man, standing on the edge of the platform—he was the "prompter"—screamed orders for the dance.

"First four forward and back."

"Lade-es change."

"Grand right and left."

"Tur-rn your partners."

The skirts ballooned, chignons bobbed up and down, there was much shrill laughter and masculine whooping. They were having a good time, there was no doubt of that. In the set nearest the center of the floor Franklin saw Mr. Eldredge. Manasseh was grand in a "Clay-diagonal" cutaway coat, white waistcoat and striped trousers. When he "balanced corners" he performed a solitaire jig and made a hit with it, too.

"All promenade" shrieked the little man on the platform. The quadrille was over.

As the floor cleared and the couples moved to the seats along the walls Franklin heard his name. He turned. Helen Dodson was standing at his elbow and with her was the young giant who had intervened between the Portuguese and himself the morning of the day before.

"Why, it is Mr. Cobb," exclaimed Helen. "I didn't know

you were coming here. Carmi, this is Franklin Cobb; he is at our house, you know. . . . Oh, but you and he have met, haven't you? Of course you have."

Captain Carmi Blake smiled and held out his hand. "How are you, Mr. Cobb?" he said. "Done any more fightin' since yesterday?"

"No. I didn't do much then. You saw to that."

"You gave Manuel somethin' to remember you by," with a chuckle. "I met him this forenoon and his nose looked like a whole Fourth of July."

"Was he any more peaceable?" asked Franklin.

"Seemed to be. And sober, for a wonder. Wanted to know if he came down to the wharf to-morrow mornin' if I'd give him his job back. I told him I'd guarantee to give him somethin' if he tried it."

The prompter was shouting from the front of the platform. Blake turned to listen.

"Umph!" he grunted in disgust, "a polka. Too bad, Nellie. Here's where I have to stay ashore. I can manage to navigate through a square dance, but I'm no good in these new round ones, even with as smart a pilot as you are. But you're booked for the passage anyhow, aren't you?"

Helen consulted her dance card. "Oh, dear, yes!" she groaned. "I promised this polka to Ben Cahoon. He's a perfectly terrible dancer, but I had to give him *one* number. He works with Father on the *Eagle,* you know, Mr. Cobb."

Franklin suddenly remembered. "You don't mean 'Tip,' do you?" he asked.

"Yes, that's what every one calls him."

The music began. Evidently "round" dances were not popular in Wellmouth, for only a few couples were spinning in the polka. There was no sign of Tip. Helen's foot was patting the floor in time to the catchy tune. Cobb was tempted.

84

"It doesn't look as if he were coming," he suggested. "Shall you and I try it, Miss Dodson?"

She glanced up at her escort.

"Why, yes indeed," said Captain Blake, heartily. "If Tip heaves in sight I'll smooth his fur. Go ahead, Nellie."

Franklin was a good dancer, but he was surprised to find that his partner was equally good. She was as light as a feather in his arms and her timing was perfect. He had not expected to enjoy that polka greatly, there had been a trifle of condescension in his invitation, but when the music ceased he found himself clapping enthusiastically.

"That was bully," he exclaimed. "You dance wonderfully, Miss Dodson."

"Thank you. I like it very much," she said, simply.

There was an encore and, when it was finished, he led her back to where Blake was waiting. A gorgeously arrayed youth, with a fiery red tie which matched his hair, was there also and received them with mingled apologies and reproaches.

"Judas priest!" exclaimed the red-haired one. "I never thought you'd give me the go-by this way, Nellie. I was a little mite late, got on new shoes and I have to haul out every little spell to take 'em off and give my feet room. I hurried much as ever I could, but when I got here Cap'n Carmi said you was hoofin' it with another feller. How be you, Mr. Cobb? What do you think of this for a ball? Some high-toned time, ain't it? Yes sir-ee! How about this next dance, Nellie? Lancers. The girls'll tell you if there's any dance I'm 'specially good at it's lancers."

Carmi Blake pushed him unceremoniously aside. "You run along and listen while they tell you, Tip," he ordered. "Come, Nellie."

She lingered a moment. "Thank you very much, Mr. Cobb," she said. "I enjoyed the polka."

She and Blake moved out on the floor. Tip Cahoon

grinned. "Cap'n Carmi's all right," he commented, "but he don't hanker to have anybody else swingin' Nellie Dodson around. While you and she was polkain' just now he had a face on him sour as a cranberry pie. Haw, haw, he never thought I noticed it, but I did. Well, you'll have to excuse me, Mr. Cobb; I got a date. . . . Aw, Christmas, them plaguey shoes!"

He hobbled away. A few minutes later Franklin saw him prancing through the lancers like a jumping jack, his partner a plump girl whose pudgy face was lifted to his adoringly. Evidently Mr. Cahoon was a favorite with the ladies—some of them.

Cobb lingered for a while, strolled aimlessly among the on-lookers, and then, finding himself bored, decided to go home. He would have liked another dance with Helen, but he had caught a glimpse of her card and it was full. There were far more "C.B.'s" than any other—Carmi Blake's initials, of course.

As he moved toward the doorway at the head of the stairs there was a sudden stir before him. Manasseh Eldredge came hurrying.

"Stand back there, some of you folks, can't you?" he de-manded, testily. "Give 'em room. . . . Ah, good evenin', Cap'n Gideon. Well, well, this is fine! Glad you could run in for a minute. Everybody's havin' a good time, I guess. Let me find you some seats over yonder."

He spread his arms and opened a path for the newcomers. A portly, gray-haired, gray-bearded man; a plump matron, dignified, but smiling; a girl of eighteen or so, whose face was vaguely familiar; two young men—and then another girl whose face was familiar indeed. The girl at the window—the girl who had given him the information about the cannon.

He was in the front row, just beyond the spread of the important Mr. Eldredge's arms; and he and this girl came face to face. She recognized him at once. Without an instant's hesitation she crossed to where he stood.

"Why, what fun!" she cried, her hands extended and her eyes sparkling. "I've been wondering all day when I should see you again. Last night—this morning, I mean—at the window. Don't you *remember?*"

CHAPTER VII

FRANKLIN'S expression must have assured her that he had not forgotten. They shook hands. She was bubbling with delight.

"Wasn't it *splendid!*" she cried. "I didn't sleep a wink after you left. And when I heard them firing those cannon up here at the Corners I just *screamed,* I couldn't help it. Did you find them right away? Was there any one watching them? Oh, I want to hear all about it, about everything! You see—"

"Victoria!" It was the plump lady who was calling.

"Yes, yes, Mother, I'm coming. . . . Oh, dear, I suppose I *must* go! . . . And I don't even know your name, do I? I think you told me but I was so excited I didn't pay any attention."

"My name is Franklin Cobb. And you are Victoria Bates, of course."

"Yes. . . . I'm *coming,* Mother, I tell you! . . . You are going to stay here—here in the hall, I mean—for a while, aren't you, Mr. Cobb? You're not going yet?"

Five minutes before he had had every intention of leaving at once; but now—

"I'll stay," he promised.

"You must. Stay right here, just where you are. I'll come back in a few minutes. Yes, yes, Mother; *do* have a little patience."

She turned and hurried back to the group who, still under the guardianship of the important Mr. Eldredge, were waiting by the door. Headed by the gray-haired man and the plump matron, they moved across the floor to seats below the platform. One of the young men in the party offered her his arm, but over his shoulder she flashed a smile in Franklin's direction. He drew a long breath. The impression formed during the brief and romantic meeting in the rain at the Rogers' window was confirmed. She was very lovely.

Obedient to her instructions he remained exactly where he **was**. The prompter's shrill voice bade his hearers, "Choose partners for the Virginia Reel." The lines formed up and down the hall. The young fellow who had been her escort when she entered the hall was her partner in the reel, and Franklin noticed that although there was another "head couple" already in position, the place of honor was promptly relinquished to them. The Silver Cornet Band broke loose with the jiggy strains of "The Irish Washerwoman" and the bowing and advancing and retreating and whirling began.

It lasted a long time, but it was over at last, and he saw her return to the seat beside her family. She and the gray-haired man were deep in a whispered conversation. They glanced in his direction. Then they rose and moved toward him.

"Mr. Cobb," she cried. "Oh, there you are! I was so afraid you might have gone. I want you to meet my father. Papa, this is Franklin Cobb, the one I told you about."

Franklin and Captain Gideon Bates shook hands. The manner of Wellmouth's great man, was, so Cobb felt, not unreservedly cordial. His daughter doubtless had told him of the unconventional meeting at the South Side. Possibly he did not altogether approve of a member of his family making acquaintances in that way.

"Hum," observed Captain Gideon. "Yes, yes. How do you do, Mr. Cobb? Well, you and Vic had a—hum—what you might call an adventure this morning, I understand."

"Why—why, yes, sir. She helped us—I mean the Four Corners people—out of a bad scrape. I'm sure we should never have got the cannon if it hadn't been for her."

"Yes, Eldredge told me. I heard it from him long before I did from you, Vic. . . . Well, Mr. Cobb, you are a stranger here in Wellmouth. Visiting at Elisha Dodson's, I understand."

"Not exactly visiting, sir. I am staying there for a day or two, because they were kind enough to take me in, that's all. I came to Wellmouth from Cleveland on a business errand. Judge Dean telegraphed and wrote me of my uncle's death and—"

Bates interrupted. "Eh?" he exclaimed, sharply. "What's that? Your uncle?"

"Yes, sir. Mr. Higham was my uncle."

Captain Gideon seemed very much surprised.

"Are you Beriah Higham's nephew?" he cried. "You are? Well, well! Hum! Queer that Joel didn't tell me you were in town."

"He didn't know until late this afternoon, sir. He was away—in Ostable I believe. I tried to see him yesterday but he didn't get back until a little while ago. I spent an hour with him just before dinner—supper, I mean."

The Bates hand picked at the Bates beard. That beard did not, like Judge Dean's, descend upon his waistcoat in an unchecked cataract; it was short and closely trimmed beneath a shaven upper lip. Captain Gideon pulled at it thoughtfully. There was a decided change in his manner.

"Well, well!" he said again. Then, heartily, "We're very glad to know Beriah's nephew, of course. When Vic here told me about a strange young fellow coming to her window at three o'clock in the morning, I—"

Victoria broke in. "It wasn't three, Papa," she corrected, with a mischievous laugh; "it was ten minutes past four."

"Hum! I wouldn't say that made it any better. This girl of mine, Mr. Cobb, likes to keep the old man guessing. . . . But my wife will want to meet you. Bring him along, Vic."

He led the way back to the seat below the platform. Victoria and Franklin followed more slowly. She was very excited.

"Are you really Mr. Higham's nephew?" she whispered.

"Yes."

"Then I feel as if I had known you a long while. Father and Mr. Dean have talked a lot about you. You own the *Eagle* now, don't you?"

"I guess I do. Judge Dean says so, anyway."

"It's the *weirdest* paper. It tells everybody's business. They send it to me up at school, and the girls just *shriek* when I read them some of the things in it. Everybody in Wellmouth considers it very important, though. Don't you think this a funny little town?"

"Why, I don't know. I haven't seen much of it."

"You must have seen enough to realize that. Look at the crowd here to-night. Aren't they just *too* funny?"

"Well, I—"

"Oh, we're not all like Ben Cahoon; that is, I *hope* we're not. Our family just had to come to this ball, but we're not going to stay, of course. Father makes us come. He adores Wellmouth—you see, he has lived here all his life—and the people just worship him. He feels it is his duty to look in at public meetings and dances, and— Oh, dear! we must move faster, I'm afraid. Mother is watching us, and she is scowling already."

Franklin was introduced to the Bates party. Mrs. Bates was majestically cordial. She was garbed in black silk and her plump fingers sparkled with rings. The diamond drops in her ears flashed as she told the young man that she was *very* pleased to meet poor dear Mr. Higham's relative. He met Miss Maisie Rogers, a jolly, vivacious girl, and shook hands with George Bradley and Ed Howes, the young men of the party.

"Now, Gideon," urged Mrs. Bates, "you won't stay much

longer, will you? We have shown ourselves here and that is all they expect us to do. The young people are anxious to get home, I'm sure. We are entertaining a few of Victoria's friends, out of town friends most of them, at the house this evening, Mr. Cobb, and we mustn't neglect them, of course. . . . What *is* it, Vic? Don't nudge me like that; you make me feel positively uncomfortable."

Victoria was not in the least disconcerted by this reproof.

"You deserve to be uncomfortable, Mama," she declared. "Why don't you ask Mr. Cobb to come around to the house with us? Of course he is expecting you to. You are, aren't you, Mr. Cobb?"

Mrs. Bates was not the only uncomfortable individual at that particular moment. Maisie Rogers giggled, Howes and Bradley grinned, and Franklin Cobb felt decidedly foolish. Captain Gideon seemed greatly amused.

"She's a ticket, this girl of ours," he said, patting his daughter's shoulder. "Better come along, Cobb. Glad to have him, aren't we, Mother?"

His wife's lips tightened, but she replied that, of course, they would be delighted.

"But Mr. Cobb may have other plans, Victoria," she added, reprovingly. "Perhaps he had rather stay here."

"I don't believe it. You will come, won't you, Mr. Cobb?"

Franklin hesitated. He was tempted, but he had a shrewd idea that acceptance might be a mistake just then. He certainly meant to know Victoria Bates better, but her mother's antagonism would not be a help toward acquiring that knowledge.

"I'm afraid I can't to-night," he replied. "Some other time, though, if I may."

"Any time—any time," this from Captain Gideon. "You're going to be in Wellmouth for a while, of course?"

"Yes, sir. I don't know how long. I have an appointment

with Judge Dean at his office at ten to-morrow morning. After that I suppose I shall know more."

Bates picked at his beard. "You and Joel have had one session already, seems to me you said," he observed.

"Yes, sir. I was with him for several hours this afternoon."

"Hum. . . . Oh, well, I shall see him myself before long. Shouldn't wonder if he was waiting for me at home now. I want to know you better, young man. I knew your uncle first-rate and we had a good many interests in common. A fine fellow, Beriah. Well, good night. . . . All ready, Mother? Come on then."

Mrs. Bates rustled to her feet. Franklin stepped aside to let them pass. Victoria caught his arm.

"You are coming to see me, you know," she whispered. "We have so much to talk about. I wish you could have seen Maisie's face when I told her you and I were responsible for the Four Corners getting those cannon back again. She's a dear girl but she is the stubbornnest little South Sider that ever lived. Good night. I shall see you at the house very soon. Oh, you will be there! Don't worry, I'll attend to *that*."

With a wave of the hand she was off. The ubiquitous Eldredge was clearing the exit for them. Franklin watched until the crowd by the door had come back to its place. Then he walked slowly toward that door. Captain Blake and Helen Dodson spoke to him as he passed a set which was forming for another quadrille. He replied, but absently. A few minutes later and he was walking toward the Dodson cottage.

Elisha was sitting by the center table in the sitting room, poring over the editorial page in a recent number of his beloved *Eagle*.

"Hello!" was his greeting. "Have a good walk, did you?"

"What? . . . Oh, yes."

"Goin' to turn in right off? Well, I don't blame you.

93

You didn't have much sleep last night—no, nor the one before."

"That's right. . . . Oh—er—I say?"

"Eh? Yes?"

"Is that Bates girl engaged to that Bradley fellow?"

"Engaged? No, no. He's hangin' 'round after her considerable, but so are a lot of others, far's that goes. She isn't engaged to anybody; too fond of a good time for anything serious as that, I guess likely. What made you ask?"

"Oh, nothing. Good night."

CHAPTER VIII

Precisely at ten the next morning he entered the Dean office. The judge met him at the portal and ushered him into a private room at the rear.

"Sit down, Mr. Cobb," he urged. "You're right on time. That's good, that's good. Promptness is a fine habit in young men—yes. Now—ahem—let me see. You would like to look at your uncle's will, of course. Here it is."

They looked over the will together. It was brief and contained nothing of which Franklin was not already aware.

"I will attend to the probate and whatever is necessary," Dean assured him. "As to the sale of the furniture and personal effects, I will arrange for that too, if you like. The really important matter is the disposal of the business. You have—er—made up your mind to turn that into money, I take it?"

"Why—you seemed to think I had better."

"Well," with a smile, "you said yesterday that the idea of living here in Wellmouth didn't sound attractive to you. Then the only alternative is to sell out, isn't it?"

But Franklin had done a good deal of thinking since yesterday.

"Judge Dean," he asked, after a moment, "what do you suppose my uncle made, on the average, in a year from his print shop and the paper?"

"Eh? Why, I don't know. He made something, of course. Not a large amount."

"Mr. Dodson says, from all he has heard, Mr. Higham was a poor man when he came here to live. When he died he owned the building and the printing outfit and the *Eagle*.

They are free from debt, you say that yourself. Now, if that is so—and of course it is—he must have made a living from them—yes, and more. He must have."

The lawyer adjusted his spectacles. He stroked his beard.

"Why—er—yes, that is so, I suppose," he admitted. "But you must remember that your uncle was a bachelor and lived very—er—simply. A single man who is not extravagant can live in a town like this without spending much money."

"Yes. . . . So it seems to me. What do you suppose his income was? Outside of any investments, I mean."

"Oh, perhaps two thousand dollars a year. That is just a guess, of course."

"Two thousand!" in surprise. "Really? Why, that isn't so bad. It's a lot more than I was earning in the bank."

The lawyer moved in his chair.

"That is a—er—liberal estimate," he added, quickly. "It may have been less—very likely was."

"What is the *Eagle's* circulation? Do you know, sir?"

"Eh? Circulation? . . . Why—er—no, not exactly."

There was just enough hesitancy in the reply to cause the young man to look up. He caught the Dean eye. It may have been because of his own vague suspicions, but it seemed to him that there was a puzzled questioning in the other's regard, a trifle of uneasiness, just as there had been the previous afternoon when he—Cobb—had forced from him the admission that he knew of possible purchasers of the Higham business. If so, however, it vanished instantly.

"That could be—er—ascertained, of course," said the judge, with a tolerant nod. "That is, if it interests you."

"The *Eagle* is the only paper published in the county, isn't it?"

"Oh, no, no!" There was no hesitancy now. "There are others. The Ostable *Beacon* and the *News* are well-established papers. The *Eagle* is—er—well, pretty local, pretty much

Wellmouth, of course; I told you yesterday that it isn't a Boston *Advertiser*. You remember that?"

"I remember. . . . But—well, I can't help thinking that my uncle must have made a profit from it or he wouldn't have kept it going."

The justly famous gray beard received another stroking. The Dean manner became impressive.

"Your uncle, Mr. Cobb," he said, "was a man of wide acquaintance here in town and, besides, he was an experienced newspaper man. As you say, he probably did make a profit, a small profit, from his weekly paper. Because of his friendships and—er—long residence here he was able to do that when an outsider, particularly an inexperienced outsider, would have lost money. I think that is a fair estimate of the facts in the case."

"Perhaps it is. . . . I only—"

"Just a moment. Now, Mr. Cobb, I don't want you to think that I have any personal bias in this matter at all. You understand that, I hope?"

Franklin understood; that is, he could easily understand Dean's wishing him to think that. It was possible to make an equivocal reply, so he did so.

"Certainly, sir, I understand," he said.

"I want you to. In our talk yesterday afternoon I advised you to sell your uncle's business. You are not a practical printer and you know nothing about running a newspaper. Therefore, provided there was an opportunity for you to sell out, it seemed to me that selling was the most practical and least risky thing you could do. You see my point?"

"Yes, sir."

"Of course I don't know what, if anything, may be behind your questioning me concerning Mr. Higham's income and the *Eagle's* earnings, but—"

He paused, smiling. Franklin said nothing. The smile

97

broadened. "Well," asked Judge Dean, "*is* there anything behind them, Mr. Cobb?"

It was a blunt question and called for a straight answer. Franklin's hesitation was but momentary.

"Perhaps there is," he admitted. "Why, yes, sir, I guess there is, in a way. At least—well, I have been thinking things over and it seems to me that I ought to look at this matter from both sides before I make a decision. I am not earning anything now and I don't want to be a loafer for any length of time, even if I could afford it."

"Certainly, certainly. The right spirit, of course. Well?"

"Here is an established business. It was my uncle's and, apparently, he made a living out of it. It is mine now. I have never lived in a small town, but I suppose I could if I had to."

"*If* you had to."

"Oh, I know you think I wouldn't like it. Maybe I wouldn't, but, if necessary, I could try it and see. I don't know a blessed thing about printing or about running a paper, but I suppose I could learn. Mr. Dodson might teach me a lot, I should think. He was with my uncle for years. He is a printer and, as for the rest of it, he is what you might call temporary editor of the *Eagle* now, isn't he?"

Judge Joel R. Dean's heavy eyebrows drew together. Obviously he believed he had found the answer to his puzzle. His tone, when he spoke, was no longer graciously bland.

"I see," he said, sharply. "So 'Lish Dodson has been talking, has he? Hmph! I might have expected it."

"Talking? Why, what do you mean, Judge Dean? When I was with him at the print shop day before yesterday he showed me the editorial he was writing. I gathered that he was in charge, for the time, at any rate. As for talking, I don't quite—"

He stopped in the middle of the sentence. A door had opened and there were heavy footsteps in the adjoining room, that nearest the street. Joel Dean rose hastily from his chair. He was still frowning, and his expression, as he looked from his caller to the door of that other room, was even more disturbed.

"Hmph!" he grunted. "Pshaw! . . . Excuse me for a minute, Mr. Cobb."

He walked briskly to the outer office, closing the door behind him. Franklin heard the growl of masculine voices. Then the door opened. A portly figure entered.

"Nonsense! Why not?" said Captain Gideon Bates. "Oh, hello, young fellow! How are you this morning?"

Franklin, scrambling to his feet, murmured the conventional reply. He and the emperor of Wellmouth shook hands. Bates spoke over his shoulder.

"Come in, Manasseh," he ordered. "What are you waiting for, Joel? I haven't any time to waste, if you have."

Dean reappeared, ushering in Mr. Eldredge. Apparently they had been interrupted in the middle of a whispered conversation. Captain Gideon took charge of the gathering.

"Sit down again, Cobb. Pull up chairs, the rest of you. Let's get this thing under way."

He had already commandeered the chair the lawyer had just vacated. Dean and Eldredge took others. Captain Gideon settled his glasses firmly on his big nose.

"Well, Joel," he said, "how far have you and this young fellow got along with the proposition?"

Judge Dean stroked his beard. He looked from the questioner to Franklin. Manasseh Eldredge, who was holding the stump of a partially smoked cigar between his fingers, shifted in his chair. The chair creaked and Captain Gideon turned.

"Whew!" he sniffed, disgustedly. "I thought there was something! Throw that thing out of the window, will you, Manasseh. I'll give you a *good* cigar when we get outside."

Mr. Eldredge meekly raised the window and cast forth the cigar stump. Bates grunted in relief.

"Smells like a rope-walk on fire," he observed. "Well, come, Joel; how far have you two got?"

Dean shook his head. "Why, Gideon," he admitted. "I—er—well, I am afraid we haven't got very far."

"Why not? Thought you told me you had as good as settled it yesterday. He wants to sell, doesn't he? And we're willing to buy, if the price is right. He understands that, of course?"

Again the lawyer glanced at the Cobb face and the expression of surprise upon it. He looked, or so it seemed to Franklin, as if he would like to bite some one—his undiplomatic cross-examiner from choice.

"Why no, Gideon," he said, "he doesn't understand that—yet."

"Why not? You and he have had a good half-hour together. Manasseh and I waited to give you time enough. Do you mean to say you haven't told him we are going to buy his uncle's business?"

Franklin, himself, answered the question.

"Judge Dean hinted that he knew of a 'group'—that is what he called it—who might possibly buy, if I decided to sell," he said. "That is as much as he would say yesterday. We hadn't got even as far as that this morning."

"Then what in the world have you two been talking about?"

Dean shrugged, resignedly. "Mr. Cobb tells me he has been thinking. I gather that he has changed his mind since last night. He doesn't seem to be sure now that he wants to sell."

"What? Doesn't want to sell—to us, you mean? Who else has been getting after him? Look here, Joel; if that Ostable *Beacon* crowd have been cutting in here, I want to know it. I warned you that I heard they had been trying to get hold of the Wapatomac *News* and that they might try to buy the *Eagle*. We can't have that. We need more than one paper in this county."

This emphatic declaration had a varied effect upon his hearers. Manasseh Eldredge looked decidedly uncomfortable. Franklin Cobb's eyes opened. He stared at the speaker, then at Dean. The latter looked more than ever as if he wished to bite. The young man grinned broadly, he could not help it. He was learning rapidly.

"Well?" demanded Bates. "That's all true, isn't it? True, isn't it, Manasseh? You were the one who told me you heard the *Beacon* was after the *News*."

Eldredge, thus appealed to, made his first contribution to the conversation.

"I guess likely maybe that's true enough, Cap'n Gideon," he muttered, "only—"

"Only what? What are you looking at Dean for? Come, Joel, say something."

The lawyer's impatience and chagrin got the better of his usual tactful suavity. He sighed, as one who surrenders to the inevitable.

"I think you've said all that is necessary, Gideon," he blurted. "You are handling this affair now."

"Handling it? What do you mean? I thought you had it settled already—all but the price."

Franklin spoke. "Nothing has been settled, Captain Bates. Judge Dean and I have only discussed the possibility of selling my uncle's business. I am interested, of course. Just what is your proposition?"

The magnate leaned back in his chair. He jingled his heavy gold watch chain.

"So far as price goes," he began, "why, that's a matter to be gone into. The judge has done a little figuring, I know, and he's come to some general idea of what the outfit is worth. If you would sell the *Eagle* without the print shop we would be just as well satisfied; but as you probably want to get rid of the whole affair, why we'll have to take the tail with the rest of the cat. That's about it, isn't it, Joel?"

Dean had recovered a little of his suavity. While his patron was delivering this information he had been fidgeting.

"Why—ahem—yes," he affirmed. "Mr. Cobb—er—if you and I had had a few minutes longer in conference I should have told you—er—practically what Captain Bates has already told. Your—er—hint that you might not wish to sell at all rather—ahem—well, it rather threw us off the track. If you are ready to sell—*if* you are—"

"Just a minute, Judge Dean, please. I am not sure yet what I want to do. Tell me first just who it is that wants to buy. Captain Bates—and who else? You said there was a group."

"Well—er—in a way there is—in a way, yes."

Gideon Bates again took charge.

"What's all this backing and filling?" he demanded. "I'll answer that, young man. We three—the judge and Eldredge and I—are the 'group' he talked about."

"Oh, Judge Dean is an interested party, himself?"

"Certainly. . . . There, there, Joel, I'll tell him. . . . Yes, he is, a good deal interested. It is the Wellmouth *Eagle* we want to hold on to. It isn't much of a paper, but everybody in this town and this part of the county reads it and it has some political influence in this neighborhood. As long as Beriah Higham owned and ran it it was sure to stand for the right things and the right people. With an outsider at the head of it—especially that *Beacon* crew—well, you can't tell what or who it might stand for. So, as we three think a good deal of the welfare of the town we live in, we put our heads together and agreed to put something from our pocket-books behind it. There's a reasonable limit to how much we take from those pocketbooks, but otherwise than that— well, there you are."

Franklin nodded. "I see," he said. "That's clear enough. Thank you, sir."

"All right. Then let's get down to brass tacks. I'm in a

hurry just now. Promised Vic I'd take her over to Bayport this afternoon. Somebody over there has got a dog or something she wants to buy, I believe. Joel, what about the figures? You've got them on paper somewhere, haven't you? Get 'em out and let's finish up."

Dean opened a drawer of his desk.

"The values I have here," he said, "are only roughly estimated, of course. The building itself isn't worth much—five hundred dollars at the outside. The presses and—er—other fittings were second-hand when Beriah bought them years ago. He got rid of the—ahem—other antiques he had at the time and bought these. Not more than another five hundred in a sale, that is sure. As for the *Eagle,* the subscription list and the advertising contracts—the—er—good will, and so forth, are hard to appraise. Hum, suppose we say—"

"Oh, bosh!" Captain Gideon broke in. "You and Manasseh and I have been over all that. See here, young fellow: we've decided to offer you five thousand, cash, for the whole ship and cargo. It's a pretty liberal offer too, more than Eldredge and the judge thought we ought to give. But you are Beriah Higham's nephew and Beriah and I were good friends, so I want you to be satisfied. . . . Five thousand, cash down. What do you say?"

Franklin Cobb said nothing immediately. And yet his mind was already made up on one point. When he came to that office his resolution was wavering, even then he was not perfectly sure that he should sell at once. The idea of remaining in Wellmouth, for a time at least, was not as repugnant as it had been. A town that a girl like Victoria Bates lived in could not be altogether a dreary place. And her father had always lived there and had, somehow or other, managed to grow rich—very rich. Then, too, the revelation of Joel Dean's double-dealing—the confirmation of his suspicions—had aroused other and stronger doubts. Whatever he might do in the end, he would do nothing definite yet.

He would wait and investigate and ask questions. The need of money was not so urgent now; he had several thousand in those stocks and bonds which his uncle had left. He could afford to wait.

"Well, boy, what do you say?" repeated Bates.

Franklin raised his head and looked his questioner in the eye.

"I am not going to sell just yet, Captain Bates," he said. "Perhaps later—I don't know—but not right away. I am much obliged to you gentlemen and I haven't any doubt you have made me a fair offer, but I'm going to hang on for a while."

He rose from his chair. The trio stared at him. Judge Dean was frowning and pulling his beard. Manasseh Eldredge's red face was about purple, his fat chin was quivering.

"Well, I'll—be—damned!" he burst forth in an incredulous splutter. "If this ain't—"

He left the rest to inference. Gideon Bates's fingers toyed with his watch chain. He leaned forward.

"What's this?" he demanded. "Hang on? To what? Do you mean you're thinking of running the Higham business *yourself?*"

Young Mr. Cobb grinned cheerfully.

"I may take a shy at it," he said.

CHAPTER IX

WHEN Elisha Dodson came home for dinner that noon his first questions were concerning their guest.

"Has he told you yet, Nellie?" he whispered eagerly. "Have they bought him out? How much did they give?"

His daughter smiled. "You can answer all that just as well as I can, Father," she said. "Mr. Cobb hasn't been here and he won't be here—for a while at any rate."

"Gorry, that's too bad! How do you know?"

"Because he sent word by the Simmons boy that he wouldn't be here for dinner."

"Tut, tut, tut! Pshaw! . . . Where do you suppose he's gone?"

"I haven't the least idea. Perhaps Cap'n Bates asked him to his house. There, there, Father, don't look so distressed. We'll know all about it by and by. Possess your soul in patience."

Elisha possessed his soul as best he could and, when, at one o'clock, he limped in at the front door of the Higham shop, Tip Cahoon had news for him. Tip was excited and mysterious.

"He's in there," he whispered. "He's in there now."

"Eh? What are you tryin' to say? Who's in where?"

"That young Cobb feller. He's in yonder in the *Eagle* room, lookin' over subscription lists and things. Wanted me should get the old man's account books so's he could look at 'em, but I told him they was in the safe and you had the key. Say, 'Lish, why didn't he eat dinner to your house? Sent me out, he did, to fetch him some grub. Only place I could think of to fetch it from was down to the depot, and I told him, says I, 'All they have there in the eatin' line is stale bakecart doughnuts and apple turnovers.' Didn't make no difference, go get 'em, was his orders. Say, 'Lish, there's a story goin' 'round that he's Beriah's nephew. Is that so?"

"Eh? . . . Yes, I guess so."

"Does that make him boss?"

"I suppose so. For a while anyhow."

"Well, if he ain't boss he better not be sendin' me to do errands for him. I never got home from that dancin' shindig till most six o'clock this mornin' and my feet's trod out flat as them turnovers I bought him. Say, 'Lish, what—"

"There, there! Go home to your dinner and don't forget to be back when your hour's up."

Tip departed and Dodson hobbled to the little editorial office at the rear of the building. There, at the Higham desk, he found Franklin Cobb, the subscription lists before him and a heap of back numbers of the Wellmouth *Eagle* on the floor beside his chair.

"Well, well, Mr. Cobb!" cried the little man. "What's this I hear about your eatin' depot turnovers for your dinner? Gorry, if I'd been here I'd have told you not to tackle those things. Last time I bit into one of 'em—waitin' for a train I was—I told Henry Baker, he's depot master, that I bet that turnover was older than he was. And he helped win the Mexican War."

"So? Well, he never would have won in a fight with one of the doughnuts he sells. Mr. Dodson, Cahoon tells me the account books are in the safe. Will you please get them for me?"

Elisha took a bunch of keys from his pocket and, to the accompaniment of rattling and clinking, opened the door of the small safe in the corner. He returned to the desk bearing several worn, leather-covered books which he deposited on the desk. He had been holding in his curiosity by main strength, but now it got away from him.

"I—I presume likely you had a pretty busy session this forenoon?" he blurted. "Up to the judge's place, I mean."

Franklin's reply was provokingly noncommittal.

"Oh, yes, pretty busy."

"Did you—did they—"

Cobb looked up. "'They?'" he repeated. "Whom do you mean by 'they'? Did you expect there would be others there beside the judge?"

Elisha reddened and stammered. His confusion was so obvious that the young man laughed aloud.

"Don't let it trouble you, Mr. Dodson," he said, good-naturedly. "You dropped a hint, the first time we met, about Judge Dean's having been in to see you, so of course I guessed you knew a good deal more about the old boy's schemes—his and the others—than you could tell me. It's all right. I know them myself now, so don't worry."

Elisha's embarrassment was still keen.

"I gave Joel my solemn word that I wouldn't tell a soul but Nellie," he stammered. "Might know I'd let the cat out of the bag one way or another. Just like me."

"You haven't let the cat out, Captain Bates did that this morning. I'll tell you and your daughter the whole story by and by. Just now, though, I want to get better acquainted with this outfit here. Are these all the account books? Who keeps them?"

"Why, Beriah always did that himself. He was pretty close-mouthed and private about money and the like of that, your uncle was. Never liked to have anybody else foolin' with those accounts."

"I see. . . . You have your work to do, of course, so go and do it. I'll call you when I want to ask more questions."

There was a ledger, a journal, a cash book and another, a smaller one, for the petty cash. Franklin, turning their pages, shook his head. Bookkeeping was the one detail of business in which he had had some slight experience and even this cursory examination showed him that the books of "B. Higham" had been kept in a decidedly offhand manner.

An hour or so later he called Elisha again.

"Are these *all* the records there are?" he asked, incredulously.

"Why yes, so far's I know. Of course there's the subscriptions to the *Eagle*. Tip gave you those before I came, he said. When a subscriber pays up we always put it down—whichever one of us happens to take the money—on a piece of paper and then, when we got the chance, we write 'Paid till such and such a time' opposite the fellow's name. Like that there. See?"

"There seem to be a good many who haven't paid for some time."

"Yes, yes, I know, but they'll pay when they get around to it. They're good honest folks, most of 'em, and it don't do to dun 'em too much. Wellmouth folks don't like to be dunned for money. Think it's a kind of reflection on 'em, seems as if they did."

"How about the contracts for the advertising?"

"Oh, most of the ads from out of town, the patent medicine ones and such, are sent in by an agency up to Boston. You'll find the agency's name in the books. The Wellmouth advertisin' and that from the county neighborhood—well, Beriah took care of that, too. Most of it is in the books under the different one's names—that is, I suppose it is. Your uncle was pretty private, Mr. Cobb, same as I told you. He kept a good many things just in his head, I shouldn't wonder."

Cobb was forced to the same conclusion. There were moments during his examination of the Higham accounts when the offer of five thousand dollars in cash seemed alluring and unbelievably extravagant. And yet, those people—Bates and his associates—must know what they were about. He could not imagine Joel Dean offering an extravagant figure for anything; no, nor even all that it was worth. And he had not forgotten that the lawyer, in an unguarded moment, had estimated his uncle's net profit at two thousand dollars a year.

Later he strolled out into the shop, watched Dodson and Tip Cahoon set type, asked questions concerning the printing jobs at hand, occasionally made penciled memoranda. People came into the outer office and, when this happened, he wandered out to look and listen. Cahoon, who usually attended to the wants of the visitors, made jottings on the backs of envelopes or whatever scraps of paper were nearest his hand and dropped the slips into a basket on the desk behind the rail.

"Don't any of those things get lost, Cahoon?" asked Franklin.

"Hey? Oh, no, no, not none to speak of. Me and 'Lish come out here just afore shuttin' up time and fetch that basket in and put it on the old man's desk in his back room; that's what we used to do when Beriah was alive. 'Lish takes care of 'em himself now. . . . Ah hum! this is a long day. Seems as if I hadn't had no sleep for a week. Nothin' like girlin' 'round to keep a man broke of his rest."

One of the callers was a dried-up little woman, whose dress and bonnet were of a pre-Civil War fashion, whose manner was decidedly prim and who spoke with a precise gentility which Cobb found amusing.

"These are the 'Gleanings' for next week, Mr. Dodson," she said, handing Elisha a neat package of sheets of pink note paper tied with a cord. "There are more of them than usual. Victoria and the Rogers girl are at home now, and they have planned many gayeties. The Ball, of course, I have described fully, with a list of the—ahem—best people present. The text of the sermon for next Sunday is *not* given, because the Reverend Mr. Copley told me that he had not quite decided upon it yet. You will find a short note about last Sunday's discourse and the names of the reward of merit scholars in Sabbath School. I *think* I have covered everything. I have done my best, poor as that best may be. My dear mother used to tell me that angels could do no more."

She finished with a prim little cough.

"Did you say anything about the cannon business?" asked Dodson. She bridled.

"Indeed I did not!" she declared, with an indignant sniff. "*That* sort of thing I do *not* care to soil my pen with. They tell me there was a great deal of liquor drinking on the Fourth of July and that the Selectmen are going to see what can be done to stop it. I didn't mention that either. I *try* to be a lady, Mr. Dodson."

"Why yes, yes, of course. I only—"

"If the *Eagle* feels obliged to give space to the doings of a pack of rowdies I can't stop it I suppose, but I shall certainly not aid nor abet it. I have heard my dear mother say *so* often that a true lady may be obliged to see and hear but she is *not* obliged to speak. I have ignored the cannon, Mr. Dodson."

Having withered the acting editor of the *Eagle* with this blast, her manner became much more gracious. In her left hand she had been holding a small roll of the pink note paper. This roll she now passed across the rail.

"Here is a small contribution for the 'Corner,'" she said, with a simper. "If you find it acceptable you are quite welcome to use it. A little thought that's all. Good afternoon, Mr. Dodson."

She walked mincingly from the building. Franklin Cobb was grinning.

"Who is that miniature edition of Queen Victoria?" he asked.

"Eh? Oh, that's Alma Perry, the one who does the 'Social Gleanin's' for the *Eagle*. She's a kind of straight up and down old maid, but nobody can beat her when it comes to pickin' up news around the Four Corners. She won't have anything to do with the South Side though; that isn't high-toned enough for her."

"What is the 'little thought' she gave you?"

Elisha opened the roll of pink paper.

"I presume likely it's one of her poems. I don't hardly know how we'd keep the 'Poets' Corner' filled up if it wasn't for her. Like to see this one, would you, Mr. Cobb? She's pretty smart at makin' up verses. She can make words rhyme that you wouldn't believe ever could."

The "thought" was neatly written in violet ink and was entitled "To my Beloved Home." Franklin read the first of the six stanzas.

> *Oh, home my home in Wellmouth here,*
> *How sweet thou art, to me how dear.*
> *Let others sigh for crowded cities,*
> *For such as they I have only pity.*
> *Dear Wellmouth Four Corners, thou art my home,*
> *From thy loved scenes I ne'er will roam.*
> *Thy wooded hills, although not mountains,*
> *Are more precious to me than Afric's sunny fountains.*

"Are you going to print this?" he asked.

"Eh?" Elisha seemed surprised. "Print it?" he repeated. "Why yes, certain. We 'most always print whatever's sent in for the Poets' Corner. Always print Alma's poems. Her kind of poetry is hard to get."

"I should think it might be. Do you pay for these contributions?"

"No, no. We don't pay for much of anything, so far as that goes."

"Not for the 'Gleanings'?"

"Why, Mr. Cobb, Alma Perry don't write those things for money. She loves to rummage around and pick up news. It's her main interest in life. When folks tell her that was a fine piece she wrote about the church fair or the Odd Fellows' supper she's as proud as a bantam rooster. Pretends she isn't, but she is just the same."

Franklin learned that most of the *Eagle's* newsgatherers, in Wellmouth or elsewhere, received no pay for their labors. A few did, but for the majority the glory of seeing their contributions in print was recompense sufficient.

"How about your political articles?" he asked.

"Oh, Beriah attended to those. He wrote all the editorials boomin' this candidate or that. Of course Cap'n Bates and Judge Dean and Manasseh, and two or three more leadin' Republicans like them, decided who the candidates are goin' to be. After they picked their men, Mr. Higham would start hurrahin' for 'em in the *Eagle*. He knew how to do it, too. Runnin' for office without the Wellmouth *Eagle* behind you is a poor payin' business in this district. Two or three fellows that used to think themselves pretty smart have found that out before now, Mr. Cobb."

Franklin's lip curled. He was learning—oh, yes, he was learning. The reasons why the trio in Dean's office were willing to pay five thousand dollars to keep the Higham property from falling into other hands were becoming plainer every minute.

He and Elisha walked home together. During supper he talked very little and, when the meal was over, went to his room. After dishwashing, however, when the Dodsons entered the sitting room, they found him there waiting for them.

"If you and your father haven't anything important to do this evening, Miss Dodson," he said, "I should very much like to tell you a few things and have you tell me some others. I won't say that my mind is made up on a certain point, but it will be soon, and I should like your help. Can you spare me an hour or so?"

"Of course," was Helen's answer. "I was not going out tonight and I'm sure Father wasn't, either. What is it, Mr. Cobb?"

"I'll tell you. This is the way the situation stands at present."

He began by describing his interview with Dean in the latter's home. Then he went on to tell of the meeting of that forenoon in the lawyer's office. The mention of the price offered for the Higham business caused a mild sensation. Helen, obviously, was surprised and Elisha awed.

"Five thousand dollars!" he gasped. "Whew! Gorry, that's a lot of money!"

Helen nodded. "It is a lot," she agreed. "But if Judge Dean offered it I'm sure it isn't more than it is worth."

Franklin turned to look at her. "Your conclusion is the same as mine," he said, with a smile. "When that old rooster makes a bid I'll bet his generosity isn't running away with his cagyness much. I called him a sardine once or twice; and what was it you called Eldredge? Oh, yes, an eel. Well, now I should say that our friend the judge was a cross between the two. Oily *and* slippery, that's my estimate."

Elisha was, as usual, shocked. His lifelong residence in Wellmouth and his close association with Beriah Higham had inculcated in his being a deep-seated reverence for the tin gods of the Four Corners.

"Oh, now, Mr. Cobb," he protested. "You hadn't ought—"

"Hush, Father, please. Mr. Cobb has a great deal more to tell us, I am sure."

"No, there isn't a great deal more. These people want to buy the *Eagle*. The printing business they care little about; Bates said so. But they do want the *Eagle*. Why do they want it?"

Helen was regarding him steadily.

"I think you know," she said.

"Perhaps I do. Bates said that they didn't intend to have the control of the *Eagle* in any outsider's hands. Which means, I imagine, that they propose to keep it in their own, where it has always been. My uncle owned and managed the paper, but they managed him. Is that right?"

Elisha was again moved to protest. His was a loyal soul and Beriah Higham had been his employer.

"Oh, now, Mr. Cobb!" he cried. "I wouldn't go so far as to say that."

"How far would *you* go, Miss Dodson?"

Helen hesitated. Then she laughed.

"Just about as far," she confessed. "Of course I don't know anything about Mr. Higham's private affairs, but Gideon Bates and Joel Dean manage most things—and most people—in Wellmouth Four Corners."

"Of course. And they mean to keep on managing. I rather like Captain Bates. There is a good deal of bowwow about him, but I like a dog better than I do an eel. They had it all fixed to buy me out. It was settled before I came here. Their scheme was a good one—from their end of it—but they omitted one little thing."

He paused. Elisha could not wait for him to continue.

"What was it they left out?" he demanded, eagerly.

"Me. They forgot that I might not care to sell."

"Eh?" Mr. Dodson jumped in his chair. His jaw fell. He looked at the speaker and then at his daughter.

"What's that?" he cried, aghast. "You mean you ain't goin' to sell them the *Eagle?* Why—*why*—"

"Wait a minute. I don't say that. I told you I hadn't made up my mind. . . . Now, Mr. Dodson, it is your turn. Considering that I know what I know, is there any reason why you can't tell me what Dean said to you when he came to you that night when I blew in unexpectedly?"

Elisha swallowed. He did not know how to reply. Helen, too, was silent. She seemed to be considering the question.

Cobb smiled. "Suppose I guess," he suggested. "You needn't answer unless what I say isn't true. My guess is that Dean told you of the will, about me, and then went on to tell you of the plan to buy this Wellmouth business from me, taking it for granted that I would be only too happy to sell.

Then he spoke about the *Eagle* and about you. I am guessing he told you, Mr. Dodson, that, after the paper was theirs, you would be its editor. That's pretty near the truth, isn't it?"

Elisha was staring at him as if he were a clairvoyant possessed of magical mind-reading powers. Helen bit her lip.

"It *is* the truth, isn't it?" persisted Cobb.

Helen surrendered.

"Of course it is," she said. "Considering what has happened since, you couldn't help guessing that, Mr. Cobb."

Franklin nodded. "I couldn't conceive of their finding another editor right away," he declared. "From what I have seen up at the shop and from what Cahoon told me this afternoon, your father has been the real editor of the *Eagle* for a good while. Come now, Mr. Dodson; isn't that a fact?"

Elisha was troubled. "Beriah wrote all the politics himself," he faltered. "And the editorials. Of course he did leave about everything else to me, but that didn't make me the regular editor. 'Twas Mr. Higham's name that was printed top of the editorial page."

"Certainly." Then, with a flash of inspiration, "And Dean told you that, when he and Bates and the rest owned the *Eagle,* your name should be printed there? I'll bet he did!"

Dodson sighed. "Well—yes, he did," he admitted.

"You would have liked that?"

Helen answered. "Father told the judge that he would rather be editor of the Wellmouth *Eagle* than President of the United States."

Again Elisha sighed. "I meant it, too," he vowed. "Gorry, yes!"

Franklin Cobb's fingers tapped the table. Then he nodded once more. That nod, although the Dodsons were not aware of it, was the signal that his decision was made.

"All right," he said, briskly. "All right. Editor you are going to be, Mr. Dodson. You can put your name at the head of the editorial page to-morrow, if you want to."

Father and daughter gazed at him in bewilderment. He did not keep them waiting.

"I said my mind was not made up, didn't I?" he went on. "Well, it is made up now. I won't say that I shall never sell the paper and the printing business; I may have to sell them some time or other. But I shan't sell now—to Dean and his 'group,' or anybody else. I've got to go to work somewhere, and here is a job already provided. I'm no printer, and God knows I'm not a newspaper man, but your father is both, Miss Dodson. Unless I'm the complete fool I can learn and he can teach me. So far as salary and terms and all that are concerned he can settle those himself. Whatever, in reason, suits him—and you, of course—will suit me. I'm going to stick right here in Wellmouth and have a shot at earning a living. I may not earn one, but I'll have the fun of trying. Now, please listen. I've only begun."

It was nearly one o'clock when the conference broke up. Franklin went to his room. Elisha and Helen lingered.

The former spoke first.

"Well, Nellie," he observed, "there goes my notion that I was goin' to be head boss of the *Eagle*. I'll be hired man just as I always was."

She put her arm about his shoulder.

"You will be a good deal more of a head boss, as you call it, than you were under Mr. Higham—yes, and more than you would have been with Joel Dean and Gideon Bates to crack the whip over you. Mr. Cobb, just as he says, knows nothing about printing or papers and you know it all. And you will be ever so much better paid."

Elisha shook his head. "He never ought to have raised my wages like that," he declared, conscience-stricken. "You and I hadn't ought to have let him. . . . Well, he'll be a nice man to work for, seems to me. I like him first-rate, don't you, Nellie?"

"Oh, yes, I like him."

"What are you smilin' to yourself about?"

"Why, Father, I was just thinking. He says he will have fun trying to make a go of the business. If he runs contrary to what Cap'n Bates and Judge Dean and their crowd want done and printed he *will* have fun—plenty of it."

"Eh? Why, Nellie, you don't suppose likely he'd think of buckin' against folks like them, do you? He's only a young fellow, after all."

Helen Dodson shook her head. "I have an idea," she observed, "that he may be like that white horse Manasseh Eldredge bought last year at the auction in Middleboro. That horse was not much more than a colt, but he just would *not* be driven."

CHAPTER X

THE following morning, when Cobb came down to the dining room, he found that Helen and her father had already breakfasted and that the latter had departed for the printing office.

"I am glad you didn't wait," he said. "I am late, I know."

"Not very. Father asked me to tell you that there were some things connected with this week's paper which he wanted to attend to and, as he had been up and about for a good while, he thought he might as well go on ahead and see to them. As a matter of fact," she added, "I heard him moving about his room at half-past four. I doubt if he slept a wink all night."

"Why?" asked Franklin, innocently.

She smiled. "You gave us an exciting evening, Mr. Cobb," she said. "I didn't sleep very soundly myself."

"That's funny. I slept like a top—if you know what that means."

"I know what it is supposed to mean. So you really slept? I should think you had more reason to lie awake than any of us."

"Not now. Now that my mind is made up there is no use worrying, as I see it. I know what I'm going to do—or try to do—and what comes next is the doing. That's all, isn't it?"

She nodded. "Yes . . . that's all," she agreed dryly.

That Elisha had broken the news to his assistant was evident as soon as Cobb crossed the threshold of the print shop. Mr. Benjamin Harrison Cahoon was sweeping with an energy Franklin had never seen him display before and his manner

118

toward his new employer was almost respectful—for the first few minutes.

"Good mornin', good mornin', Mr. Cobb," was his greeting. "You'll find your desk and chair all dusted up in yonder, waitin' for you. Got some fresh ink in the bottle and a couple of new pencils all sharpened. All you've got to do is set right down and lay into work. Nice day, ain't it?"

Elisha was in the little back room. He rose from the desk chair when the young man entered.

"Good mornin', Mr. Cobb," he stammered, rather nervously. "Hope you don't mind my settin' down in your place till you came. You see, I had a little mite of touchin' up to the *Eagle* to do and—er—so I took the liberty. Made myself kind of free, I know."

Franklin waved the apology aside.

"Keep on sitting just where you are," he said. "Your work is much more important than mine this morning. Now how about this week's paper? Is it ready for the press?"

Elisha nodded. "Part of it's already printed," he answered. "The patent inside and the Poet's Corner and the like of that, they're done. And the rest is all set up and waitin'. I was just hangin' back on the editorial page. You see, I—well, I didn't just know what way you'd want that headed. It always said 'B. Higham, Owner and Editor.' Now that Beriah's dead and—and, recollectin' what you said last night, I—well, I didn't know."

"So far as the 'editor' part is concerned you do know. 'Elisha Dodson, Editor,' that's what we want there, of course."

"You—you ain't changed your mind then? You really mean it?"

"I certainly do. Set it up at once."

"Well, if you say so. 'Twill look pretty queer, I'm afraid. Some folks'll laugh, that's sure. Now about your name. That's got to go in—and in big type, too."

"No bigger than yours. To be absolutely honest we should

make it smaller. You're the big gun around here, Elisha.
Say, if you don't mind I'm going to call you by your Christian
name; we're likely to know each other pretty well from now
on. And you better call me Franklin—or Frank, when we
are alone, anyhow. It will save time."

"Why now, Mr. Cobb, that wouldn't sound—"

"It will sound shorter. Besides, the 'Mister' business would
always make me feel as if I were on stilts. If I am they are
mighty shaky ones and I don't care to be reminded of them.
Run along and change that heading."

"But don't you think there ought to be some—well, sort of
announcement about your takin' things over? Of course
we've got the memorial to Mr. Higham—that'll have to be
run first, I presume likely—but seems as if you ought to say
somethin' about yourself."

Franklin shook his head. "Not this week. Let it go as it
is, except for the new heading. Next week—well, I'll try and
write a word or two."

Elisha limped out to the type cases. In a few minutes he
returned with a proof.

"Think that'll do, Mr.—er—Franklin?" he asked, rather
nervously. "I know it looks funny, but 'twas your orders."

Cobb glanced at the new heading.

" 'Franklin Cobb, Publisher and Owner. Elisha N. Dodson,
Editor,' " he read aloud. "First rate. Run it that way."

"You don't mind my puttin' the N in? I don't very often
let folks know I have a middle name, but this was such a—
well, important occasion, as you might say, that I kind of
spread myself."

"Why on earth should I mind?"

"Maybe you would if you knew what it stood for. It stands
for 'Napoleon.' Yes, and that ain't the worst of it. There's
a B that belongs after that. I've never been sure whether my
father and mother couldn't see a joke or thought I was one.
My whole name is Elisha Napoleon Bonaparte Dodson.

Gorry! Ain't that—? Well, I'll go outside so you can laugh in comfort."

All that day, with a brief interval for luncheon, the publisher of the Wellmouth *Eagle* sat before the desk in the little room while without in the print shop, the presses, operated by Dodson and Cahoon, clanged and thumped turning out the next week's issue of the paper. When, at six o'clock, he walked with Elisha down to the cottage on the South Side road, he was weary. He had been going through the tangle of accounts pertaining to his new business, and, more than ever, he was coming to a realization of how much of those accounts and records Beriah Higham must have, as Dodson said, "kept in his own head." Straightening them out and arriving at even an approximate estimate of the amount of subscriptions and printing bills owed his uncle at the time of his death was going to be a tremendous job.

On the other hand, and fortunately, there seemed to be almost no unpaid bills—bills owed by the late B. Higham, that is. Elisha, when questioned, declared the old man " 'most generally paid cash for everything." "Kind of a prejudice he had against buyin' on tick, seemed so," said Elisha. Franklin was thankful for that prejudice.

That evening he and the Dodsons reached an agreement concerning his permanent place of residence. Helen said that she had been thinking it all over since the night before, and she saw no reason why he should not remain with them at the cottage.

"We have more rooms than Father and I ever use," she declared.

"Scarcely ever have comp'ny," put in Elisha.

"Yes. And, if you think you can get along and be comfortable, Mr. Cobb, you can have the bedroom where you are now and the room next to it, that on the front of the house. We could fix that up as a sort of sitting room for you."

"Sure thing, Mr. Cobb—that is to say Franklin. He orders

me to call him that, Nellie. Wouldn't hear to anything else. He's boss now, so I've got to mind him, ain't I?"

Cobb was very much pleased with the idea. "I had much rather live here than anywhere else in Wellmouth," he declared. "As for my meals—"

"You can eat here, too, if you think you will be satisfied with my cooking. I like to cook and I have plenty of time. . . . Now wait a minute," she put in, before he could protest or reply. "This isn't just kindness on our part—it is business. Father and I have often considered renting those rooms, or even taking a boarder or two. We can use the money, can't we, Father?"

Then followed a lengthy argument as to the amount of room rent and board, but it ended by Franklin's gratefully accepting the offer, although at a rate which he considered ridiculously low. He wrote that very night to the hotel in Chicago where his trunks and personal belongings were stored, asking them to be sent on at once.

There remained, of course, the matter of settling the estate and that involved calling again upon Judge Dean. He anticipated a rather unpleasant session, the first of a series of unpleasant sessions, but, to his surprise, the lawyer was affable almost to the point of cordiality. Patronizing, of course, and inclined to regard his young client's plunge into a business of which he knew nothing as a rash venture—but ready to help in any way. The formalities concerning the will were trivial and those he—Dean—would attend to at once.

The pair visited the rooms occupied by the late B. Higham. Several articles of furniture, including a good-sized bookcase and its contents, Franklin decided to keep. These, and the personal effects, wearing apparel, trunks, letters and papers, were to be carted down to the Dodson cottage. The papers and letters could be looked over at leisure and retained or destroyed as seemed best. The garments could be given away. Possibly Elisha or Tip could make use of some of them. The remainder of the fittings in the room it was arranged to sell to the second-hand dealer in Denboro.

Cobb and Dean parted by the door of the latter's law office.

"I'm ever so much obliged to you, Judge," said Franklin, heartily. "I realize that I have upset your plans a good deal— yours and Captain Bates's—and perhaps I'm making a fool of myself by not accepting your offer, but—well, the more I see of this game the more it seems to me worth playing. I am sure to make a lot of mistakes and I may go broke in the end, but, as I said to some one—I think to you and the captain— I believe I shall have fun for a while, anyhow. . . . Hope there will be no hard feeling on the part of you or your associates."

The judge's smile was almost benignant.

"Not in the least, my dear boy," he declared. "Not in the least. Our offer was made purely in the interests of Wellmouth. Captain Bates is not the sort of man to hold a grudge. The purchase of the *Eagle* is a matter of small moment to him; he has too many really important—er—business affairs to be concerned with—excuse me—trifles. As for myself, I wish you every success. And, if, later on, in any way, I can help you by—er—advice or—ahem—counsel as to policy, and so forth, I shall be only too glad. Don't hesitate to call upon me, please. I have lived here all my life and my experience is at your service. Good day, Mr. Cobb, and good luck."

He proffered his hand and Franklin took it.

"Drop in at the office whenever you can," he urged. "Dodson and I will always be glad to see you."

"Thank you, thank you. I shall accept your invitation. I used to call frequently while your uncle was alive, and it will seem like old times."

Cobb described the interview to the Dodsons that evening. Elisha was impressed by the judge's broad-minded attitude.

"He's a pretty big man, Joel Dean, say what you mind to," he vowed. Helen smiled.

"I imagine he has had his orders," was her surmise.

"From Bates, you mean?" suggested Franklin. "I shouldn't wonder. The old captain was square enough, and blunt enough, during the session when I issued my declaration of independence. I got the impression that he rather likes a fighter."

"He has always been one himself. And I'll admit that he isn't likely to hold petty grudges. But if you think—you or Father—that he will sit still and let you run the Wellmouth *Eagle* in any way contrary to his wishes, *I* think you're mistaken. He won't interfere—perhaps he may even give you a helping hand—so long as you run it in orthodox, Four Corners, Beriah Higham fashion. If you don't—if you put any monkey wrenches in the regular machinery that has kept this town going since before the war—*then* you'll hear from him, or I miss my guess."

"I can't see why 'tis you don't like Cap'n Gideon, Nellie," grumbled Elisha.

"I do like him. I like him a million times better than I do Judge Dean. It isn't his fault that he thinks he is the Almighty; if a whole county got down on its knees to me as it does to him I should probably get to believe I was."

The third member of the Dean "group" was—when Franklin next met him—not quite so patronizingly gracious as the judge had been, or as Captain Gideon was reported to be. Manasseh Eldredge was, in fact, rather grouchy.

"Well, young fellow," was his greeting. "I suppose likely you're feelin' your oats these days. You and 'Lish got your names on top of the page in the *Eagle* already, I notice."

Cobb smiled. "Somebody's name had to be there," he replied, cheerfully.

"Yeah. And somebody'll have to pay the bills when they come due. I judge that don't bother you though. You must have money to burn."

"I haven't started the fire yet. Why do you say that?"

"Huh! Anybody that turns down a five-thousand cash offer the way you did must either be rich or—"

"Yes? Or what?"

"Oh, nothin'. None of my business, as I know of."

Manasseh was "sore," of course, and Franklin realized that to make him sorer would be poor policy; the Eldredge store, he had noticed, was a regular advertiser in the *Eagle* as well as an occasional customer of the print shop. So he merely laughed and walked away.

He spent the next week in hard work at the office, returning home—he was already beginning to consider his rooms at the Dodsons' as home—tired and headachy from the labor of straightening the accounts and getting further acquainted with the numberless details of the business. That business was small, but it was fussy. He decided that, as soon as he possibly could, he must hire some one, a girl or a young fellow—whichever came cheapest—to help with the bookkeeping. He, himself, would find plenty to do outside, picking up news and soliciting advertising and orders for job printing. If he were to net two thousand a year—yes, or half of that—from this venture of his he must hustle. Franklin was already beginning to question that two thousand a year.

He wrote his first editorial for the next issue of the *Eagle*. It was brief—he worked hard to keep it so—but he tried to make it sensible, free from cocksureness and to the point. In it he stated that in taking over Wellmouth's weekly paper, particularly in stepping into the shoes of the able, experienced and respected Mr. Beriah Higham, the new proprietor and editor had undertaken a very real task.

The present owner of the *Eagle* [he wrote], is a stranger in Wellmouth. He intends, however, to become a citizen here and, he ventures to hope, in time a useful citizen. The Wellmouth *Eagle*, under its new ownership, has no axes to grind, no hobbies to ride, and no pet policies to exploit. It means to be a paper which every subscriber may read with confidence in its truth telling and find interesting, up to date, and informative. Its new owner and its new editor intend especially to make it a newspaper, not for any one section of our community, but for all sections alike —a fair field and no favor. It asks your coöperation in this attempt.

He spent more than two hours of writing, scratching out and rewriting in the production of this manifesto. When, at last, it was finished, he wiped his perspiring forehead and called Dodson from the print shop. Elisha hobbled in, his hair every-which-way and the green eyeshade hanging over his left ear.

"Read this, will you, Elisha?" Cobb asked. "See how it compares with what my uncle used to write? Don't spare my feelings. Kindly omit flowers. Give me your honest opinion. If it's rotten, say so."

Elisha adjusted his spectacles and read. Then he readjusted them and read again.

"First-rate," he declared, heartily. "Mighty good job, 'specially for a green hand. I was kind of afraid you might make it a little too long, but you ain't, not a mite."

Franklin shrugged. "If you knew how I have sweat blood to keep it short," he observed. "So you wouldn't change it at all?"

The little man hesitated. "Why—no-o," he said, slowly. "If you mean just what you've said I wouldn't change it."

"What do *you* mean by that?"

"Why—er—you say here that you and me want to make the *Eagle* a paper for all sections of the community. That sounds a little as if you meant it would play up the South Side just as strong as it does the Corners."

"All right. What's the matter with that?"

Elisha shook his head. "I don't believe Beriah would have put it just that way. You see—I don't know as I ought to say this to you about your uncle, Franklin—Beriah was always pretty careful. He printed all the South Side news and advertisin' he could get, but, if you'll notice, it was always the Four Corners that had the front page."

Cobb leaned back in his chair. He had labored hard on that editorial and, possibly for that reason, the Dodson hint irritated him.

"If the South Side earns front page space it is going to get it," he snapped. "Judging from the little I have seen so far it is the livest section of this town. If that is your only criticism, I say set it as written."

Elisha took the manuscript and turned toward the door, Cobb called him back.

"Look here, Elisha," he said, "don't get the idea that I don't appreciate your advice. I do—and no doubt my uncle's policy was a safe one. But—oh, confound it, all this being afraid to whisper for fear of disturbing the self-satisfaction of Bates and Dean and their 'group' is making me sick. There's no need to drag you into it though. Cut out that mention of the editor, why don't you, and say 'the new owner intends.' I'll take the responsibility."

Mr. Dodson made no comment, but when Franklin was shown a proof of that editorial, mention of the editor had not been elided.

Tip Cahoon read the proof, and he had something to say.

"Whew!" he whistled. "Say, 'Lish, did you read this? Ain't goin' to let him put it in that way, be you? He as much as says the South Side is goin' to get as much space as the Corners. How do you cal'late Cap'n Gideon and Joe Dean and the rest of us that live in the right part of town are goin' to like that? Why, old Beriah would no more have—"

Elisha turned on him. "Beriah's dead," he said, crisply. "If anybody don't know it yet then I shouldn't wonder if the Wellmouth Weekly *Eagle* proved it to 'em. Yes, sir, the old man's dead enough, but I wouldn't wonder if his paper was just comin' to life."

At home and alone with Helen that evening, he said a little more. He showed her a copy of the proof.

"He told us he was goin' to have a little fun out of his new job," he said, with a shake of the head. "And I recollect you said if he run contrary to the tide up here to the Four Corners he would have it. Looks as if the fun was beginnin' early, don't it?"

She nodded. "Good for him!" she exclaimed, her eyes sparkling. "This will be talked about."

"Huh! That's no exaggeration."

"And the South Side will like it. Carmi Blake has always said that what this town needed was a paper that would give his people down there a square deal. . . . Come now, Father, you are glorying in his spunk yourself. You like it—you know you do."

Elisha rubbed his chin. "I like hot mince pie," he retorted, dryly. "I can have fun eatin' that, but an hour or so afterwards I don't feel nigh so funny. I'm gettin' on in years, and I've got you and my wages to think about."

"Father, don't you worry about me. I can earn my own living at any time, if I have to."

"I know, but I'd hate to have you earnin' mine. And you'll notice that I'm supposed to be standin' behind that 'fair field and no favor' stuff just as much as he is."

"But you needn't have been. He told you to cut out the 'editor' part; you just said so."

Her father snorted. "When I was a kid fo'mast hand on a fish schooner," he grumbled, indignantly, "I took it for granted I was supposed to do my share of the work, fair weather or foul. I never sneaked below and turned in soon's it came on to blow."

The new editor's announcement, when it appeared in the *Eagle,* did not appear to create the sensation that the Dodsons and Tip Cahoon prophesied. There was some comment, of course, and on his visits to the South Side, which he made almost daily in search of news, Franklin Cobb was the recipient of congratulations and, in some instances, promises of support. Captain Abiathar Blake, the senior member of Blake Brothers and Captain Carmi's partner, was more cordial than he had been at their previous meetings. A large, sturdy man, although not as huge as his younger brother, he tilted back at shirt-sleeved ease in the chair behind his desk, and, puffing steadily at a black cigar, expressed his approbation.

"I liked that 'fair field and no favor' piece of yours, Mr. Cobb," he declared. "We South Siders, the heft of us, are beginnin' to realize that, long as we pay consider'ble more than half of the taxes in this town, it's time we had our share of the say-so about runnin' it. Back in the old square-riggin' days, when all the big-bugs like Amaziah Dean and Cap'n Seth Bangs and Gideon Bates and a dozen more lived at the Four Corners, and goin' fishin' was looked on as a sort of no-account job—back in those days the South Side wasn't cal'lated to be much account. When the Corners piped to quarters all hands down here jumped. It's different now. Square-riggin' is dead so far as Wellmouth is concerned, and the Four Corners is dyin', even if it don't know it. You mark my words, young fellow: In another ten years this end of the town will be the big end."

Franklin nodded. "I should guess that that was very possible, Captain Blake," he agreed.

"It's more than possible, boy—it's sure. Some of us South Siders are wakin' up to it now and we don't intend to have the whip cracked over us much longer. We're sick of havin' every three out of four selectmen hail from the Corners and every time it's Wellmouth's turn to pick out a representative for the Boston State House havin' a Corners man picked for that, too. You don't know much about Ostable County politics yet awhile, I presume likely."

"Very little, sir."

"Then I'll drop a flea in your starboard ear. Next year it's goin' to be this town's turn to pick a man for the House of Representatives up to Boston. Probably you've heard a little about the way it's done. There's two towns in our district—Orham and Wellmouth. It's got to be the habit—just politeness, that's all—to let each town in turn pick out one of its own citizens for the job. The term is one year, but usually, if the fellow elected has done pretty well, he's given another year—what they all call 'courtesy' nomination."

"Mr. Dodson told me something like that. He said the nomination was equivalent to election."

"'Tis if it's Republican nomination. You could haul a seine through Ostable County since the war and not fetch aboard enough Democrats to make a mess for breakfast. Well, as I just said, next year is Wellmouth's turn to nominate and this is the word in due season that I promised you. Don't you be in a hurry to have the *Eagle* come out for any one candidate too far ahead of the caucus. Oh, you'll have hints enough dropped your way up yonder—I know that. Joe Dean and Manasseh Eldredge and Cap'n Gideon and a few more of the Republican Town Committee have got their heads together even now. But don't let 'em wheedle you into pledgin' the *Eagle's* support until you *know* who's goin' to be nominated. The South Side isn't sayin' anything yet, but—Hum! Well, maybe *I'm* sayin' too much; it was that 'fair field and no favor' thing of yours that got me started. Look here, Mr. Cobb, nobody owns you, do they?"

"No one that I know of."

"Nobody up to the Four Corners has got you pledged up to anything? You ain't under any obligations, or like that?"

"No."

"Good enough! Then you keep right on playin' square for the whole town, that's all I can say now. You nor the *Eagle* won't lose by it in the end. . . . Oh, Carmi!"

Captain Carmi Blake had strolled in from the wharf. His bulk filled the doorway.

"Carmi," said Abiathar Blake, "I've been talkin' to Mr. Cobb here. I told him we South Siders liked that piece he had in his paper and that, as long as he stood by it, we'd stand by him. That's right, isn't it?"

Carmi nodded. "Yup," he replied, laconically.

"Well, how about our puttin' that advertisement of ours back in the *Eagle?* The firm always used to run a card in the paper, but we and Higham had a—hm—sort of disagreement, and we took it out. Might's well run it again regular, hadn't we, Carmi?"

"Don't see why not. . . . Oh, Nellie Dodson tells me you've arranged to stay at her and her father's house right along, Mr. Cobb. Like it there, do you?"

"Yes, very much."

There was an emphasis in his tone which Captain Carmi seemed to notice. For just an instant his eyes narrowed as he regarded the visitor.

"Should think likely you would," was his only comment.

Franklin had not spoken to Victoria Bates since the evening of the "Grand Ball." He had seen her a number of times, driving in her new dogcart. When she saw him she always waved a greeting, but she had never stopped to talk. He was not greatly surprised. In spite of Judge Dean's assertion that her father was too big a man to hold a grudge, Franklin could easily imagine that the new owner of the *Eagle* was not in high favor in the Bates household. Doubtless Victoria, like Dean, had had her orders.

But as he was walking back from the South Side, after his call at the Blake Brothers office, he met her again. She was alone on the high seat of the dogcart and, as she saw him striding along beside the road, she turned the horse's head toward that side and stopped.

"Good morning, stranger," was her greeting. "How do you do?"

Franklin took the gloved hand she bent down to offer.

"I am disgracefully healthy," he replied. "How is the new rig working out?"

"Splendidly. Like it, do you?"

"How could I help it? It is the swellest turnout I've seen since I landed in Wellmouth."

"It ought to be. Papa got the bill for it the other day, and he has been grumbling about extravagance ever since. It's fun being extravagant, don't you think?"

"I don't know. I haven't tried very often."

She laughed. "Oh, I wouldn't say that. Anybody who tosses a five-thousand-dollar offer into the wastebasket the way Papa says you did can't be so dreadfully in need of money."

"That was careless of me, I suppose. Your father thinks so, I am sure."

"He says you are either a smart boy or a—er—well, something else. He doesn't seem to be quite certain which."

"I am uncertain myself."

She did not answer immediately and he, taking her silence as a hint, lifted his hat and was moving on, but she stopped him.

"Wait!" she exclaimed. "Goodness gracious, you're not running away so soon, are you? I have been dying to see you. I think I should have come into the printing place soon if I hadn't met you like this. Why haven't you called at the house? You told me you would."

Franklin did not remember telling her any such thing. Her last whispered remark to him had been that she should see that he was invited there.

"Well? Why haven't you?" she insisted. "Don't you care to? Have you seen too much of me and my family already?"

He smiled. "Don't you think it possible that your family

may have seen too much of me?" he suggested. "Considering what has happened, I mean."

She laughed. "I understand. You are one of those very correct people who must have a formal invitation. That is all right. Good by, Mr. Cobb. We're going to meet again soon—very soon."

She waved her hand, jerked at the reins and the dogcart moved down the road, the dust rising behind it. He walked on toward the Four Corners. In the excitement of his new business venture Victoria Bates had been, if not forgotten, at least relegated to a second place in his thoughts. Now he was thinking of her again: he thought of her all the rest of that day and evening.

The following afternoon, as he sat at his desk in the little rear office, Tip Cahoon came to the doorway, agitation and awe written large upon his freckled countenance.

"Say, Mr. Cobb," he whispered, behind his hand, "who do you cal'late is out here askin' to see you? Gideon Bates, that's who. Yes, sir, Cap'n Gideon himself. Land sakes! you mustn't set there. Didn't I tell you he was *waitin'* for you?"

Before Franklin could answer, Mr. Cahoon was pushed unceremoniously out of the doorway. Captain Bates, portly, dignified and commanding as always, brushed by him.

"Hello, young man," he hailed, pleasantly. "Well, here you are, eh?"

Franklin rose to his feet. "Why—why, yes, sir," he stammered, rather inanely, "here I am. Glad to see you, Captain Bates. Won't you sit down? Tip, bring in another chair."

Cahoon hurried out and returned with the customer's chair from the front room. The visitor lowered himself into it. He looked about the tiny sanctum.

"Hum!" he observed. "Seems odd to see any one except Beriah at that desk. I've seen him there more times than you are months old, I guess. Well," with a glance at the disordered desk top, "you look busy. Are you?"

"Why, yes, I am. Plenty to do, especially when I haven't learned how to do it yet. . . . You needn't wait, Tip."

Tip departed. In the print shop he whispered in Elisha Dodson's ear that he bet there was goin' to be Tophet raised in that other room right off that minute.

"I been expectin' it," he vowed, hoarsely. "Gideon's come to ask the whys and wherefores about that 'fair field and no favor' piece. Darned foolishness *that* was and you heard me say so. Shouldn't wonder if you'd be huntin' a new job afore long, 'Lish. Well, they can't lay it onto *me; I* wasn't asked what I thought of it."

As a matter of fact some such idea as to the purpose of the great man's visit was in Cobb's mind. It did not remain there long, however. Captain Bates did not mention the editorial announcement. He chatted about the *Eagle,* its past and present, but he made no criticisms nor did he offer any advice. He asked how Dodson was bearing up under the weight of the editorial crown and chuckled as he asked it.

"Good, honest, well-meaning chap, Elisha Dodson," he observed. "A hard worker, too. Whatever he's got in this world he has earned himself. His people were common as they make 'em and his father, Amusa Dodson, was what Vic's college crowd calls a 'character.' Has Elisha told you yet that his middle names are 'Napoleon Bonaparte'? He has, eh? Generally he doesn't like to be reminded of it. That was Amusa's doing, naming him that. Amusa had got hold of a life of Napoleon—somebody lent it to him—and, as the baby came along about that time, he hung the name on the poor child. Ho, ho! If there ever was any one less like Napoleon than 'Lish Dodson I never heard of him."

He had a good many stories to tell of Beriah Higham who, he declared, was an able man and a shrewd one. He remained for a full half-hour and it was not until he rose to go that the listener heard a word which gave him the slightest clew as to the purpose behind the call.

"Oh, by the way," said Captain Gideon Bates, as he picked up his hat; "my wife and Vic have been wondering why you hadn't dropped in to see us. We asked you to, that night at the town hall, you remember. Olivia—Mrs. Bates, I mean— would like to have you take dinner with us to-morrow night, if that's convenient to you. Can come, can't you? Good! We usually eat about half-past six. See you then. Good day."

He departed, nodding graciously to Dodson as he passed through the print shop. Franklin, left alone, smiled. He had been wrong in his surmise that Victoria had had her orders and was acting under them. Obviously, it was she—as Helen Dodson had intimated—who gave orders in the Bates household. Mrs. Bates's offer of hospitality was but the echo of her daughter's voice. This, of course, was the "formal invitation" for which Victoria had accused him of waiting.

So, shortly after six the following evening, arrayed in his blue serge—he had looked longingly at his dinner coat, but decided it would be out of place if the raiment displayed at the Grand Ball was a criterion—he left the Dodson cottage for the Blake "mansion." He had, of course, told the Dodsons of his invitation and they were properly impressed, Elisha particularly so.

"Well, well!" he exclaimed. "So you're goin' to eat with the big-bugs, eh? Now, Nellie, you can't say that Cap'n Gideon ain't broad-minded. A narrow gauge man would be disappointed and hold it against a fellow that stood up against him the way Franklin did. Instead of that he comes to see him and asks him to supper at his house. Goin' the limit of broadmindedness, I call that."

Helen shook her head reprovingly. "Not supper, Father," she corrected. "They don't have supper at the Bates house."

"Eh? Now what sort of nonsense is that? Why, I've

heard Victoria, when she was a little girl and used to be with her father when he'd come into the shop to see Mr. Higham—more'n once I've heard say they must hurry or they'd be late for supper."

"Yes, Father, but that was before she went away to school."

"What on earth has her goin' to the Academy got to do with it?"

"Oh, a great deal—with lots of things."

"Tut, tut, tut! I don't know what you mean."

"Neither does Franklin, I'm sure. He looks on as if he thought I had gone crazy. We mustn't keep him any longer or *he* will be late—for dinner."

CHAPTER XI

SUPPER might be dinner in the Bates home, but it was by no means the stiff and stately affair Cobb had expected and dreaded. True, the dinner itself was far more elaborate than the majority of evening meals in that town at that period— there was a neat and adequate "second girl" to serve it and there were several courses—but there was little or no formality. Captain Bates was a genial host and his wife, although dignified and inclined to patronize, as became her royal station, was kind and pleasant.

If she had been much less so Franklin would scarcely have noticed. Victoria sat opposite him and she claimed most of his attention. Prettier than ever, in a very becoming gown, her hair glistening in the light from the prismed hanging lamp above the table, her eyes sparkling as she laughed and chatted, she made a picture from which he found it hard to keep his eyes. Not that she seemed in the least anxious to have him do so, rather the contrary, but he occasionally awoke to the realization that his answers to Captain Gideon's questions were absently given and that he was not, perhaps, heeding as closely as he should Mrs. Bates's extended comments upon the lack of really worth while social events in Wellmouth or the shortcomings of the Shakespeare Reading Society under its new president.

After dinner they went into the parlor—Mrs. Bates referred to it as the "drawing-room"—where Victoria, at her father's request, played several selections upon the obviously new grand piano, smiling over her shoulder at their visitor as she did so. When, however, after the third of these, the captain urged her to continue she rebelled.

"Of course not, Papa," she said. "That's quite enough. Nobody wants to hear me pound any longer—no one but you, that is, and you don't count. Poor Mr. Cobb is bored to death already."

Franklin, embarrassed by this unexpected accusation, hastened to deny it. He was not bored in the least, far from it.

"Of course you are. Anybody would be; I am, myself. No, Papa, I simply won't. The only reason I did it at all was to please you. You mustn't mind him, Mr. Cobb," she added, with a mischievous toss of the head. "I am his only child and he thinks anything I do is wonderful. He's quite sane otherwise."

Her father laughed heartily. "She's enough to drive anybody crazy, isn't she, Cobb?" he demanded. "I spoil her, always have, and she takes advantage of it. Well, I can't help it; too late to change now. And her mother's just as bad, aren't you, Mother? Come now, be honest."

Mrs. Bates smiled indulgently. "*We* think," she said, "that she plays *very* well. From a child she was always inclined to be musical. Her teacher used to say—poor Mr. Saunders, it was; *he* is dead now—that *he* considered her to show traces of real genius."

Victoria jumped from the piano stool. "And he died soon after he said it," was her comment. "Now what is the next exciting number on the program? Would you like to look at the family photograph albums, Mr. Cobb? We have no less than three."

Her mother took the suggestion seriously.

"Oh, I don't believe, Victoria, that Mr. Cobb would be interested in *that*," she protested. "All our relations are perfect strangers to him."

"I know, but don't you think he should make their acquaintance? He really ought to see that photograph of great-aunt Keziah and second cousin Lemuel, taken together. You never saw anything in the least like it, Mr. Cobb, I'll bet a cookie."

The "second girl" entered the room just then to announce that Mr. and Mrs. Haven had called and were in the sitting room. Mrs. Bates looked at her husband and he at her. The lady rose, with a rustle of silk.

"I suppose we might ask them in here, Gideon," she suggested, doubtfully.

Victoria's veto was prompt and emphatic.

"Indeed you won't do any such thing," she declared. "They'll stay forever—they always do—and Mr. Cobb and I are not going to have our evening spoiled by that tiresome frump and her husband. He'll talk about what has happened at the bank, and she'll talk about what a dreadful time she has been having with their new hired girl. Oh, I know them. Papa, you and Mother go out and make martyrs of yourselves, and we'll stay where we are. Run along, like good children."

Her parents departed and she closed the door after them. Then she threw herself into an easy chair with a sigh of relief.

"That is the first time I ever was glad to have those Haven people call," she announced. "Of all the tiresome creatures! He is cashier of Papa's bank, you know, so we just have to be decent to them."

"I didn't know your father owned a bank."

"Oh, it isn't his—all of it. It's the Wellmouth National and Savings, but Papa is president and the biggest depositor, so Cornelius Haven and the directors always do what he tells them to. But don't let's waste time with banks. Tell me all about yourself. I know your name and that funny old Mr. Higham was your uncle and that you used to live in—Cleveland, wasn't it? And of course I know about your refusing Papa's and Judge Dean's offer for the *Eagle*. *That* was a surprise for them. The judge was awfully mad."

"I was afraid your father might be mad, too."

"He wasn't. He called you an impudent young squirt, but that was just his way of talking. And I heard him tell Judge Dean that, so far as he could see, you might as well run the *Eagle* as any one else, so long as you ran it the right way."

"Oh . . . and what is the right way?"

"Why, the way he and the judge want it run, I suppose; the way Mr. Higham ran it. . . . But don't let's talk about the *Eagle* either. Tell me all about yourself. I don't know you at all, really; and yet it seems as if I had known you for ever so long. As if we were old friends. I never felt just that way about anybody before. Isn't it queer?"

It was flattering certainly. And the look which accompanied it gave him a peculiar thrill. He forgot his flash of resentment at having been called a "young squirt" and the stubbornness which any reference to Dean and the "group" aroused in him. He forgot everything except that this attractive and extraordinarily pretty girl already considered him her friend and was obviously greatly interested in him. He had known as many girls as the average young fellow of his age, but he was quite sure he had never known one like Victoria Bates.

He told of his life in Cleveland, of his years at college, of his mother's death and of his disastrous experience as a would-be banker.

"And that's about all," he concluded. "I hurried on here to find out about my legacy and—well, here I am."

She nodded. "And now you're going to stay," she said, with satisfaction.

"I'm going to stay—yes. If I can make a living from a business I know nothing about."

"Oh, you will! Of course you will. But why did you do it? Why did you refuse Papa's offer? He said it was a generous one."

"It was, I suppose. I just—well, I don't know. I—I liked

Wellmouth, the little I had seen of it, and I liked the people I had met. Some of them, particularly."

"Oh," with delightful innocence. "Which ones were they?"

"Well, the Dodsons and—yes, your father—I think I am going to like him."

"I see. Just those few."

"Not exactly. There was some one else. Of course I had met her only twice and the first time only for a minute, but—"

He paused. She maintained her expression of naïve innocence for a moment and then burst out laughing.

"That first meeting was rather—oh, what do I want to say? —unconventional, that's the word. Never mind, it was great fun; just like something in a book. Are you romantic, Mr. Cobb? I am—oh, terribly. I'm just silly over romantic stories and things like that. But there isn't much romance in Wellmouth—not usually. Now tell me all about what you did that night. How you happened to see me at the window and—oh, everything."

They were sitting together upon the walnut and haircloth sofa, one of the family photograph albums within reach but unopened, when the rattle of the knob heralded the return of Captain and Mrs. Bates to the parlor. Victoria broke off her story of a boarding school escapade, snatched the album and opened it at random.

"And this," she said, primly, "is Papa's cousin Joshua—he is dead now. He— Oh!" looking up with an air of surprise, "you are back again already? Have those Haven people gone so soon? It doesn't seem possible—as early as this."

Captain Gideon chuckled, but Mrs. Bates, with a significant glance at the clock, observed that it was not so dreadfully early, after eleven. Franklin, who had risen when they entered, took the hint.

"I must be going too," he said. "I didn't realize it was so

late. I've had a wonderful dinner and a wonderful evening. I am ever so much obliged."

Victoria pouted. "Eleven o'clock isn't late," she declared, petulantly. "At least it wouldn't be anywhere but in dead old Wellmouth. Don't go, Mr. Cobb. Why," with a demure twinkle, "we haven't half finished the photographs."

"No need to hurry, young fellow," urged the captain. "That's so, isn't it, Mother?"

Mrs. Bates's smile was gracious, but possibly a trifled forced.

"Certainly, Gideon. Mr. Cobb is welcome as long as he cares to stay; he knows that, I'm sure. But if he feels he *must* go—why, we can't be selfish."

Franklin, of course, not being entirely an imbecile, insisted that he must. Victoria accompanied him to the front door.

"You'll come again—soon?" she whispered, looking up at him.

"Indeed I will," he whispered in return. "I've had a—a perfectly wonderful evening."

"So have I. We are going to be awfully good friends, you and I, aren't we?"

"I certainly hope so."

"I know we are. . . . Well . . . good night—Franklin."

He looked down into her upturned face. It was alluring—it was—

Then, at the other end of the hall by the parlor door, he heard the dry rustle of a silk gown.

"Good night, Victoria," he whispered and walked hurriedly down the steps.

To his surprise the sitting room windows of the Dodson cottage were alight as he approached along the South Side road. As he neared the gate it opened and a man came out. No need, dark as it was, to guess this person's identity. There was but one pair of shoulders like those in Wellmouth.

"Who's that?" demanded Captain Carmi Blake. "Oh, hello, Cobb! Long spell of fair weather we're havin'."

142

When Franklin entered the cottage Helen called to him from the sitting room.

"Did you have a good time?" she asked.

"Yes. First-rate. You're up late, aren't you?"

"Rather. No later than you, though."

"That's a fact. Good night."

So Carmi Blake had been calling on her. Elisha had hinted that he called pretty often. Well, Blake was all right; rather a rough diamond maybe, but square and honest and a good fellow. Helen Dodson, though, was a very nice girl, an especially nice girl. If there was anything serious between them it seemed almost a pity, because——

He could not, at the moment, think of any satisfactory "because." Somehow, vaguely, he did not like the idea, that was all. He did not dwell upon it long, however. His mind was filled with thoughts of another girl, a marvelous girl, who had declared that he and she were going to be great friends. He must be careful and not let this friendship develop into something more intimate and tender on his part. She was rich, and he had only a few thousands. Her parents, of course, had all sorts of ambitious plans for her; and they were the most influential people in the county, every one said so. His business—this new venture of his into which he had plunged on impulse and for the fun of it—its success depended upon his making no enemies in high places. Yes indeed, he must be careful.

He would be; he would see her often, but not too often. She would be going back to the Academy in the fall anyhow. . . . And probably all this was ridiculous—of course it was. She had dozens of friends, fellows like young Howes here in Wellmouth and goodness knows how many more elsewhere. He need not flatter himself that he counted with her for more than those others. But, all the same, she had said——

By George! she *was* a wonderful girl.

CHAPTER XII

THE summer passed very quickly, quicker for Franklin Cobb than any he had before known. He was beginning to feel at home in Wellmouth, not only at the Four Corners, but at the South Side and in West Wellmouth and North Wellmouth also. He was becoming acquainted with the townspeople, sufficiently so to call many of them, the men especially, by their Christian names and to be hailed as "Franklin" or "Frank" wherever he went. Along the wharves and aboard the fishing vessels he was accepted as a neighbor and good fellow, and even his former antagonist Manuel, when in port and sober, greeted him with "Hello dere, Frankie! How she go, eh?"

Local news items were very much easier to get because of this familiarity and although, true to his promise of a fair field and no favor, the South Side was now accorded its share of front page space, so far there had been no open remonstrances from the Four Corners "group." Manasseh Eldredge occasionally sneered at "playin' up them Blakes and Rogerses as if they were somethin' more than 'seconds' in this town," but even Manasseh was usually good-naturedly genial. The job printing side of the business was fairly prosperous and, owing to Cobb's entire lack of condescension when dealing with the South Siders, the Blake Brothers and several other firms down there were giving him their office printing.

The *Eagle* continued to fly at about its customary height; not very high, but no lower than when under Beriah Higham's piloting. Franklin, on the whole, had reason to be moderately satisfied. True, these first months of his first year's net earnings were not averaging quite their proportionate share of the two thousand annual profit, but they were gaining a bit. He was beginning to like the game and to understand its workings better and better.

He was ambitious, however, and already he could see that the Higham outfit was old-fashioned and far from economical in its waste of time and labor. Elisha Dodson agreed with him.

"Yes," said Elisha, "these presses, especially that one over yonder, are pretty well wore out. They were second-hand when Beriah bought 'em and they've been used hard since. One good-sized, up-to-date job press would save us a whole lot and two would save consider'ble more than twice as much. But presses cost a lot; by gorry, yes!"

Franklin made some inquiries and learned that he was right. Presses of the right kind were very expensive. He could not think of such extravagance for the present, nor for a long time to come. Collections were amazingly slow, particularly in the case of subscriptions and payments for local advertising. Obviously Dodson had not exaggerated when he said that Ostable County folks paid when they felt like it.

He did, however, engage some one to help with the books, a girl named Elsie Barker, who had spent a few months in a Brockton business school and was fairly competent. She was anxious to gain practical experience and, therefore, was contented to work for very low wages.

This gave him more time to spend in news collecting and picking up local advertising and printing jobs. The regular contributors from the adjoining towns in the county sent in their weekly installments of "Jottings" and "Gleanings" and there was always Alma Perry to be depended upon for a "thought" for the Poet's Corner.

Without Alma that Corner would have been practically vacant, or dependent upon clippings. The little woman's prim gentility and mincing elegance amused Franklin, and he made it a point when she called to see her if possible. His flattering interest met with an immediate response. Her first utterance, following her polite "Good morning, Mr. Dodson," or condescending "How do you do, Benjamin?" was an inquiry as to whether or not Mr. Cobb was in. Tip considered this a huge joke.

"What's got into you, Alma?" he demanded, on one occasion. "You always used to hand over your stuff to me or 'Lish, whichever one of us happened to be nighest. Now nobody'll do you but the boss. Common folks ain't good enough for you any more, it looks like."

Miss Perry's straight little back straightened still more.

"I'll thank you not to call my writings 'stuff,' Benjamin Cahoon," she said, crisply. "Good day."

Dodson happened to be within hearing and he limped hastily from the back room.

"What's the trouble?" he asked. "Anything wrong?"

Cahoon was grinning broadly. "Alma's goin' off mad," he explained. "Her beau ain't around, and she won't talk to anybody else."

Miss Perry turned to wither him.

"My dear mother always taught me," she observed, haughtily, "that time was precious. That is why I shall not waste mine in answering such remarks from *such* a source."

"Be still, Tip," ordered Elisha, impatiently. "If you only talked as funny as you look you'd make us all laugh. Don't mind him, Alma. Mr. Cobb is down at the South Side and he won't be back till late afternoon. Can't I do anything for you?"

Miss Perry hesitated. Then her black-mitted left hand produced from behind her back the inevitable roll of pink note paper.

"I have written—that is, composed," she said, "a little offering which I thought possibly Mr. Cobb might care to use in the *Eagle*. I should have preferred that he read it while I

146

was here. He usually reads my poems aloud and he reads *so* well—with such feeling."

Cahoon choked and hastily turned his back.

"Too bad he's out, Alma," said Elisha, "but I do wish you'd leave your poem. You see we need it for next week's paper and time's gettin' short."

The lady, but with evident reluctance, surrendered the pink roll.

"Please tell Mr. Cobb I left it," she requested, "and that I shall appreciate his opinion—his personal opinion—of it very much indeed. Good day, Mr. Dodson."

She nodded graciously to Elisha, ignored Tip's good-by completely and minced out of the building.

Cahoon doubled up with a whoop of laughter.

"Haw, haw!" he shouted. "You know what's the matter with her, 'Lish? She's gettin' soft on Franklin. Ho, ho! Say, 'Lish, *there's* somethin' to put in the *Eagle*. 'It is rumored about town that Miss Alma Perry, our famous poetry factory, is seen very frequent nowadays droppin' in at a certain office up to the Corners. Careful, Alma; we're watchin' you.' Eh? How'd that do? Put that in this week, why don't you, 'Lish?"

Elisha handed him the "offering." "Put that in first," he ordered. "Set it up right off. Stop talkin' and go to work."

After a short session at the case Tip came into the editorial office, his grin broader then ever.

"What did I tell you, 'Lish?" he crowed. "Read that and then say I don't know what I'm talkin' about."

Dodson took the proof and read as follows:

To My Happy Yore

Backward, turn backward, as said by another,
(That is, by Adelaide Proctor, in "Rock me to sleep, Mother.")
Turn backward, Time, and give to me

Sweet days of yore by the deep blue sea,
Where soft and low the breakers mingle
All up and down along our South Wellmouth shingle,
Where as a child so oft I sat,
Free from care and strain and all like that,
And dreamed of the future's gladsome store—
Oh, give—oh, give to me my yore!

"Well, what's that got to do with Franklin Cobb, I'd like to know? All she's wishin' for is to be young again. She ain't the only one that's wished that."

"Huh! *He's* young and that's why she'd like to be. Now you mark my words; I've had consider'ble experience with women—"

"Sshh! You're girl crazy, that's what ails you."

"Aw, rats! But say, talkin' about bein' crazy! Did you notice what she says in that piece about breakers runnin' up and down the shingles over to South Wellmouth? *That's* crazy enough. I've seen some high tides in my day but I never see one high enough to reach the shingles on *no* building, even a scallop shanty. I'm tellin' you, 'Lish, that Alma's head's softenin' up and Franklin's responsible. She never wrote such foolishness when Beriah was here, did she?"

"Go to work. Yes, and before you go home you might look up 'shingle' in the dictionary."

Tip slouched off, grumbling that he didn't need to look 'em up, he'd nailed enough of 'em on in his time.

If Mr. Cahoon was right in his surmise and Miss Perry's middle-aged susceptibilities had been touched by the young proprietor of the *Eagle*, at least she was not the only Ostable County female similarly affected. Franklin Cobb was becoming popular with Wellmouth's young people. He was invited to picnics, clambakes, dances and church socials. Occasionally he was asked to dine by some of the older residents, by Abiathar Blake at the South Side and by Judge

Joel Dean at the Four Corners. The Blake dinner was a rather enjoyable affair. Captain Carmi was present and Cobb heard many sea yarns and learned a little of the perils and risks of the fishing business. The meal at Judge Dean's was heavy and the table conversation was even more so. Rather to the guest's surprise, however, the judge did not once offer advice as to the *Eagle's* contents or policy.

True to her promise, or prophecy, Franklin and Victoria Bates were meeting frequently now. He discovered that there were many social sets in Wellmouth, but Victoria's was the *crème de la crème* and she was its leader. The Bates mansion was a gay center during the vacation period. There were many guests, girls whom Victoria had met at the Academy and young college fellows. They played croquet, held archery matches, went boating and occasionally tried the new game of lawn tennis, which was just beginning to be popular.

Most of the dances and parties Cobb attended, but invitations to the daylight excursions and picnics he invariably declined. Victoria took him to task.

"I don't think I shall ever ask you again," she declared, with a pout. "I thought you and I were going to be *such* friends and yet I hardly ever see you."

Considering that she had seen him the evening before and the evening before that this was something of an exaggeration. He told her so. She tossed her head.

"Oh, yes," she admitted, "you come to a dance once in a while. You like to dance, so I suppose that is why you come. But, even if you don't care for picnics and such things I should think you might say yes occasionally, if only to be polite."

"I do care for them. And I hate to say 'no.' That's the truth, Vic, I hate it."

"Then why do you always say it?"

"I must. If I am going to make a living from this job I've

tackled I can't afford to neglect it for a minute. I've learned that already."

"Oh, bother! Sometimes I wish you had let Papa have his way and sold him the old *Eagle*. . . . Oh, no, I don't!" with a sudden flash of repentance. "No, I don't wish that at all."

"Why, Vic?"

"Oh, because— Are you sorry you stayed in Wellmouth, Frank?"

She looked up at him when she asked it, just as she had looked when they parted after his first evening at the Bates home. And now, as then, he found that look hard to withstand.

"You bet I'm not!" he answered, fervently.

"I'm glad you're not. . . . And you'll come to the picnic to-morrow?"

"Oh, Vic, don't ask me. How can I?"

"Won't you—to please me?"

"Vic, I just can't. I've got an appointment down at the South Side that may mean twenty-five dollars' worth of advertising."

"Please!"

"Now, Vic—"

She turned away. "Oh, very well," she said, carelessly. "Of course if you like the society at the South Side better than you do ours here—why, that's all."

"Vic! . . . Oh, well! I'll come—this once."

He attended the picnic and, during almost the entire day experienced the doubtful pleasure of seeing her in the company of one of the Rogers guests, a young fellow from Boston. The fact that Maisie Rogers did not seem to enjoy the spectacle any more than he did was little consolation.

But an hour before the party started for home she dropped her Boston acquaintance and, coming over to him, took his arm.

"You've scarcely spoken to me since morning, Frank Cobb,"

she said, reproachfully. "Aren't you ashamed of yourself? Come, let's walk somewhere. There are lots of things I want to talk about."

During their stroll she was her bewitching, tantalizing self, apparently quite unconscious of any previous neglect, alternately tempting him by whispered confidences and holding him at a distance by sudden intervals of sedate and demure coolness. As they were walking back to join the rest of the party she surprised him by showing a new and apparently real interest in his business. How was he getting on? Did he really believe he would succeed? He mustn't think she did not care, for she did—truly she did. Only he must not let that old printing place of his take all his time and keep him away from his friends; that was not fair.

He found himself telling her his plans and hopes. He mentioned the need of new presses.

"Why don't you buy them?" she asked, naïvely.

"Can't afford it. They would cost two thousand dollars—or almost that."

"My, that's a lot—just for printing presses! Do you really need them?"

"I think I do. . . . Yes, I need them and I need a number of other things, but I shall have to get along as I am, for a while anyway. What I need is a rich partner."

He was joking, but she seemed to take the remark seriously.

"Why, so you do, don't you?" she agreed. "Yes, of course you do. I wonder— Oh, let me think. . . . No, don't ask me what I mean. Probably I don't really mean anything."

He had no idea of what she could mean, and he did not try to guess. Doubtless, as she said, she did not really mean anything beyond a wish to help him. Well, that was something; it was a great deal. He forgot the young man from Boston entirely and went home that evening confident that he never before had enjoyed himself as he had at that picnic.

Even next morning, when he made his trip to the South

Side and found that the extra day of deliberation had convinced Mr. Elkanah Rogers that he did not need to advertise in the *Eagle*—even then he did not wholly regret his expensive holiday. He remembered her good-by at the Bates gate.

"You're glad you came with me—with us, aren't you, Frank? *I* am—awfully glad."

He was glad too. Business wasn't everything.

By the way of penance, however, he decided not to accept more invitations for a time, but to give his evenings as well as days to work. He and Elisha held long sessions in the Dodson sitting room over questions of policy, changes of make-up in the paper, all sorts of things. Helen was always present at these conferences and her common-sense advice was a valuable check upon Elisha's somewhat impractical visions of improvement and prosperity. Elisha was in favor of buying this or that because "we need 'em."

"But you can't afford it. Wait until you can," was her counsel.

One evening, when they were discussing prospects for next year she made an unexpected disclosure. They had been talking of advertising, and her father had mentioned politics.

"A year from this fall is Wellmouth's turn to nominate somebody to send to the State House of Representatives up to Boston," he said. "Things'll be lively around here then and the *Eagle* ought to pick up some political advertisin'. That'll help us along."

Franklin nodded. "Who is likely to get the nomination?" he asked. "Heard any rumors, Elisha?"

"Oh, yes, I've heard names mentioned. Cornelius Haven would like it—or his wife would like to have her husband in the State House—but I don't think he's got much show. Cap'n Gideon ain't anxious to have him away from the bank for any length of time. And Manasseh Eldredge has always wanted it, but he isn't exactly the man—or so I've heard tell Cap'n Bates thinks."

"Why not? Eldredge strikes me as a pretty smooth politician."

Helen smiled. "Possibly Cap'n Bates prefers to have him where he can watch him," she observed.

Elisha chuckled. "Maybe so," he admitted, "but I understand Manasseh says he's done about all the hard work for the party committee in this town, and it's time he had a little somethin' to show for it."

"What sort of work has he done?" Franklin inquired. It was Helen who answered.

"The sort that the captain and Joel Dean and Haven are ashamed to do themselves, I imagine," was her suggestion.

"How about the Sardine himself as a nominee?" asked Cobb.

"No, no. Joel Dean is after somethin' bigger than that. The story is that he wants to be appointed a reg'lar judge some day and that Gideon has promised him he shall be soon's the cap'n feels he can spare him down here."

Franklin laughed. "Why bother with caucusses and conventions and elections?" he suggested. "Let King Gideon the First pick his man and send him to Boston. That should save trouble and expense and amount to the same thing in the end."

"Yes," put in Helen, "and *he* is contented so long as he runs them. . . . You notice, Frank, that every possible candidate Father can think of is a Four Corners man."

"Well!" Elisha sniffed. "Who else is there left for the job?"

Franklin was suddenly reminded of his recent conversation with Abiathar Blake.

"It was hinted to me not long ago," he said, "that the South Side might have a word to say about next year's nominee. Hinted rather strongly, I thought."

Mr. Dodson shook his head.

"Guess likely they may say things, but the doin' will be done up at the Four Corners."

And then Helen sprang her surprise.

"I am not so sure," she said, impulsively. "I think—yes, I know that influential people of the South Side are determined to have one of their own sent to the State House next year. They have decided on the man, and they intend to nominate and elect him."

Both her hearers turned to look at her. Franklin whistled.

"By George!" he ejaculated. *"That's* news, Elisha. Do you really mean it, Helen?"

"Yes. . . . Now wait, Father. . . . I do mean it and I know who the nominee will be. At least I know who all at that end of the town mean to fight for tooth and nail. You mustn't mention it in the *Eagle,* though," she added, hastily. "Unless you promise not to do that, I shan't tell you another word."

"Now, Nellie—"

"Hush, Elisha! Of course we'll promise, Helen. By George, this begins to sound like happy days to come! Who is the man? How did you know about him? What is his name?"

Helen hesitated. Her color heightened just a trifle. "I know because he told me, himself, the last time he was here—in this house."

Elisha, obviously, was very much puzzled. Cobb, however, guessed instantly.

"Here in this house?" he repeated. "Then I know, of course. Captain Carmi Blake! . . . Well, I'll be hanged!"

Elisha Dodson leaned back in his chair.

"Carmi Blake!" he murmured. "Carmi. . . . Sho! . . . By gorry!"

Helen nodded. "It is a dead secret," she insisted, "and it must be for a while, but it is true. Carmi—Cap'n Blake, I mean—is about ready to give up active going to sea. He is away at the Banks now and he may make a few more voyages,

154

but not many. He intends to remain in the business, of course, and, up to a very short while ago, he had no idea of going into politics. His brother and a dozen of the leading men at the South Side have coaxed and pleaded with him and, at last, he has decided to run. They think he will make a strong candidate and a good representative for the district. I think he will. I know he is absolutely honest."

Dodson's sole comment was another "By gorry!" Franklin was becoming excited. A lively political campaign would be "nuts" for the *Eagle*.

"But how on earth does Blake expect to get the nomination?" he asked. "He'll have to fight Bates and Dean and the rest that have been ruling the roost."

"He hopes he won't have to. Abiathar and Mr. Rogers and the rest tell him that he will have the whole South Side and East and North Wellmouth behind him and that when Cap'n Gideon and Dean and Manasseh find that to be true they may give in rather than risk such a fight as that would be. . . . Father, don't look as if you were struck dumb. What do you think about it?"

Her father drew a long breath. "By gorry, I—I don't hardly know what to think. Carmi's mighty popular. Every fellow that ever went fishin' will be for him and that means a lot of Republican votes. And what few Democrats there is would vote for him if only to spite Dean and Manasseh. He'd be strong all through the district. If he came to the polls on the reg'lar ticket he'd have one of the biggest majorities ever. But how will he get there? The Republican Town Committee makes up the slate, the town caucus ratifies it and the district convention ratifies what the caucus does."

"And the Bates crowd is the Committee and the caucus— or it amounts to that, I suppose?" was Franklin's surmise.

"And two-thirds of the convention," added Helen. "Yes, Carmi knows that, of course. If Cap'n Bates puts his foot down and says he shan't be nominated he won't be, of course.

But that doesn't necessarily mean that his name might not be voted upon on election day."

Elisha whistled. "An independent nominee!" he exclaimed. "Whew! *That* would set the fur to flyin'. There hasn't been anybody run independent since Ezra Silver came out for County Sheriff six years ago. And *he* didn't get votes enough to fill a quart measure. Folks down here are pretty hard shell reg'lars; you can generally depend on 'em to vote straight. . . . But Carmi Blake! I do honestly believe he'd give 'em a run for their money, even with Cap'n Gideon and Joe Dean workin' against him. . . . Although," he added, with emphasis, "I *don't* believe even he could be elected that way, with any good reg'lar's name on the ticket. Wellmouth is only one town and Orham's another, after all."

Cobb rubbed his chin.

"Wonder where the *Eagle* would stand, if it came to anything like that?" he said. "By George, Elisha, we'd be skating on thin ice, wouldn't we! With the South Side on one side and the Four Corners on the other there would be plenty of toes to be trodden on. How would Uncle Beriah have handled such a mix-up?"

Helen answered, "He would have waited as long as possible and then have endorsed the regular nominee, whoever he might be. There would be an editorial praising Carmi to the skies as a man and a citizen and regretting that the call of duty made it necessary to urge every one to vote against him at the present time. 'The party that saved the Union, the grand old flag, the land of the free and the home of the brave, hip, hip, hurrah'—and a lot more of the same. Then Mr. Higham's skirts would be clear, the Four Corners crowd would be satisfied, and if there were any political plums in the way of advertising to be picked the *Eagle* would get its share. That is how your uncle would have handled it, Frank."

She paused. Then she added: "And Judge Dean would have read and amended the editorial before it went to press.

There! I know that sounds spiteful, but it is the truth. Isn't it, Father?"

Elisha looked uncomfortable, but he nodded.

"Why, about like that—yes," he admitted. "Beriah was a shrewd man, Franklin. And, of course, he did have to think of his business. I don't know's you can blame him."

Franklin was amused. "And I suppose I ought to think of mine?" he suggested.

"Why," after a moment's hesitation, "yes, I presume likely you'd ought to."

"What do you think, Helen?"

She, too, hesitated. Then she said, "Yes, of course you should. You must consider your future and your own interests. No one has the right to expect you will do anything else."

This was not precisely the reply he had anticipated from her. It surprised and, for no really good reason, irritated him a bit.

"Well, I'll tell you both this," he announced, crisply. "Whatever I do will be done because I decide to do it. And neither Bates nor Dean nor anybody else will decide for me; no, nor read and revise the *Eagle's* editorials either."

He rose to his feet as he said it. And now came another surprise. Little Elisha Dodson rose also. His lined face was redder than usual, and the eyes behind his spectacles were flashing.

"That's the talk!" he exclaimed, his fist descending with a thump upon the table. "That's what I've been waitin' to hear all the years I've worked on the *Eagle,* and I've never heard it till now. Gorry! That sounds good!"

Franklin was amazed. He turned to look at his assistant; then at Helen. She, too, was flushed and her eyes were sparkling. Franklin guessed the reason, or thought he did.

"Don't misunderstand me," he said, quickly. "This doesn't mean that the *Eagle* is going to support Carmi Blake. It doesn't mean that it won't support him, either. It may or it may not; that remains to be seen. I—"

But Elisha cut in. "I—I don't care if it supports Judas Iscariot," he sputtered. "That ain't the thing. It's your sayin' that it'll do what it darned well thinks right that's got me goin'. I felt the same way when you put in that 'fair field and no favor' piece. That did me good, too. By gorry, yes!"

Cobb was more astonished than ever.

"But you were the one who advised me not to print it," he remonstrated. "You said it was bad policy."

"I know. And I was ashamed while I was sayin' it. But I—well, I'm gettin' old. I've got Nellie here to look out for. I have to think of my job—I *have* to. But if I was you, young, and with nobody but myself on my hands, I'd say, 'To the devil with policy.' I would! And I'm mighty glad to hear you say it. And I'm stickin' right with you, job or no job. There!"

He wiped his forehead with his shirt sleeve and sat down again. Helen came over to put a hand on his shoulder.

"Good, Father," she said, softly. "But I have told you before, and so often, not to worry about me."

Franklin was much moved. He realized something of what Elisha's pledge of loyalty might mean to the hard-working, self-sacrificing little man.

"I have been talking big, I'm afraid," he observed, with a shrug. "What I said must have sounded pretty cocky. It was—too cocky, I guess. These moguls rile me, and I am not very practical—never have been. I wouldn't have you lose your place and your living for worlds, Elisha. I shan't—at least I shall try not to make an absolute fool of myself. As for backing Blake—well, that you and I must think about very carefully. As I feel now I should like to do it. He—well, he seems like a good fellow and, for Helen's sake, if nothing more, I should enjoy helping him."

He would have gone on, but Helen interrupted. "Why for my sake?" she asked, quickly.

"Eh? Why—why, because he is—he seems to be such a friend of yours. . . . I mean—"

Again she broke in.

"I have other friends," she said; "at least I hope so. And they will never lose my friendship by standing for what they believe to be fair and right and honest. . . . Good gracious, we have all of us taken to stump speaking—it must be the effect of politics, I guess. Come, Father, it is long past bedtime."

Elisha went to the kitchen to lock up for the night and she and Cobb were alone together for a moment. Then she said, earnestly, "Franklin, you mustn't let our talk to-night, or anything that may happen later, influence you—you really mustn't. Father is a good deal of a dreamer, bless him, and I—well, I am a rebel by nature, I suppose. You have your success and your future to think of, and you must think of them. You can't afford to make enemies who could ruin you here in Wellmouth. Of course Carmi Blake is a friend of ours, we like him, but that should not count beside more important things."

"Well, I like him, too. I'm not always sure that he likes me, but that isn't his fault probably."

"Why, what do you mean?"

"Oh, I don't know. Perhaps it is funny, but it has seemed to me recently that he is rather short and—well, cool. I don't know why he should be. I'd like to be friends with him, if only because he is—is such a very good friend of yours, Helen."

He had not meant to emphasize the "very," but he did, just a trifle. She glanced at him and then turned away.

"He is an old friend," she said. "I've known him ever since we were at school together. And Father and his father were friends long before that. As to his not liking you, that is nonsense. He does; he has told me so. . . . But you have friends too. How do you think Victoria Bates would like your taking sides against her father?"

It was his turn to flush. Before he could frame an adequate reply Elisha appeared, announcing that he was ready to turn in if the rest were. There was no more said that evening nor, so far as Captain Blake or his candidacy were concerned, for many evenings thereafter. Nor was, between Helen Dodson and himself, Victoria Bates's name again mentioned.

CHAPTER XIII

On the twelfth of September Victoria went back to the Academy at Middleboro. Franklin called, the evening of the eleventh, to say good-by. He had been calling rather frequently of late and his calls seemed to be, by the Bates household, taken as a matter of course. He was not the only caller by any means; George Bradley, the young fellow who had been Victoria's escort at the Grand Ball in the town hall, was still holding on, although he did appear, on the few occasions when he and Cobb met, somewhat disgruntled and peevish. He was present on this particular evening and after he had gone Franklin mentioned his odd behavior to Victoria.

She laughed. "Oh, he is just silly, that's all," she said. "He'll get over it. He's only a boy, you know."

"Boy! He must be almost as old as I am. He is old enough to know good manners from bad. Why should he be grouchy toward me? I haven't done anything to him."

They were in the drawing-room at the time. Victoria, at her father's request, had been playing the piano and Franklin was standing beside her. Mrs. Bates had been called from the room by the maid and Captain Gideon, in the big chair by the far window, was reading the Boston paper. He had heard neither question nor answer.

Victoria, turning on the piano stool, looked up into Franklin's face.

"Of course you haven't," she declared. Then after a glance in her father's direction, she added, in a lower tone, "I shouldn't worry about George, if I were you, Frank. I think he is a good deal crosser with me than he is with you, only he doesn't dare show it as plainly, that's all."

"But why should he be cross with you?"

She smiled. "You are awfully innocent sometimes," was her murmured comment. "Oh, yes, yes, Papa! I will play again in a minute. Do give me a chance to breathe."

They had no further opportunity for confidences until, an hour later, he rose to go. Victoria's good night to young Bradley had been said in the drawing-room, but she accompanied Franklin to the door. On the occasion of his first visit to that house they had parted in the hall. Now she stepped with him out upon the brick walk, between the rows of fragrant box bushes. It was a clear, cool, early autumn night, scarcely a breath of wind and the sky was spattered with stars. Wellmouth Four Corners, most of it, was already in bed and the stillness was absolute. They talked in whispers.

"I am going to-morrow," she said. "Back to the old school again. Goodness, how I hate it!"

"Hate it! Why, I thought you had wonderful times there. You have said so, over and over again."

"Oh, I know. I used to like it and be glad to go back. Now it is different; I don't want to go one bit."

There was a little catch in her voice as she made this confession. Franklin knew she was looking up at him and it took all his strength of will to prevent looking down at her. He realized, only too well, that this sort of thing was dangerous. He had steeled himself against this danger many, many times. He must not be a fool. He had resolved.

She came closer to him. "Franklin," she whispered.

"Yes, Vic."

"Are you sorry I am going away?"

"Yes."

"I mean really and truly sorry? Awfully sorry?"

"Yes."

She was silent for an instant. Then softly, "You haven't said so. You haven't said once that you were going to miss me. . . . Frank—?"

162

"Yes, Vic."

"I am going to miss *you* dreadfully. I never dreamed that saying good-by could be so—so awful. . . . Frank, why won't you even look at me? You won't see me again for months."

He looked at her then and it was, so far as his high-minded resolutions were concerned, a fatal mistake. He looked down into her eyes—a trifle wet they were—at her face lifted toward his, at her hair, a soft velvety shadow against the darker shadows of the box bushes. He looked—and all his common sense and his resolves went to rack and ruin. He took her in his arms and kissed her. . . .

And then—or shortly after then—they heard Mrs. Bates calling from the hall.

"Vic! . . . Victoria! Where in the world are you?" The couple in the shadow of the box hedges sprang apart. Franklin was in a decidedly nervous, not to say frightened, state of mind, but Victoria seemed cool enough.

"Coming, Mother," she called. "It is such a lovely night that I walked down to the gate with Mr. Cobb. I'll be right in."

Mrs. Bates appeared to be satisfied; at least she called no more. Her daughter turned swiftly.

"You'll write to me—every day, won't you?" she whispered.

"Yes."

"And send me your photograph? I *must* have your photograph for my room."

"Yes, Vic."

He had no photograph on hand, but that made no difference. He would have promised to send a portrait by Rembrandt if she had asked for it just then.

"Oh, you *are* a dear! And I'll send you mine. And you won't forget me? And you *will* write? And I shall be home for Thanksgiving—and for the Christmas holidays. And—Oh, dear! Mother's coming; I hear her. . . . Good night, Frank. . . . Quick! Good night."

The good night was quick, but intoxicating. Before he realized that it was over she was running up the steps. The door closed behind her. He remained where he was for a moment. Then, slowly, he walked toward the Dodson cottage. Thank goodness, neither Elisha nor Helen was awake when he reached there.

Keeping his attention fixed upon business was difficult for the next few weeks. She wrote regularly and at length, and he as regularly replied. He visited the photographer in Orham and, in the course of another week his likeness, in—for him —an extravagantly expensive frame, was on its way to the Academy. The letter acknowledging its receipt was enthusiastic. She was *so* proud of it. Did he realize how handsome he was? There! she shouldn't have said that because it might make him vain, but it was true, nevertheless. The photograph was on the dresser in her room, and all the girls were just crazy about it. She was having new ones taken of herself and he should have one just as soon as they were ready. "But of course you won't be as proud of mine as I am of yours, I mustn't expect *that*. I wonder where you will keep it. Somewhere where you will see it very, *very* often, I *hope*."

As a matter of fact he kept it, when it came, in his bureau drawer. Helen took care of his room and, for reasons which were rather vague, and yet in a way definite enough, he preferred neither she nor her father should know that he had the photograph in his possession. Some day, when the situation was a bit more clear, if it ever was, he would show it to them, but not yet awhile. Were he and Vic actually engaged? He did not know. In that short but fervid parting between the box hedges not a word had been said concerning betrothal.

Nor was it mentioned in their letters. Hers began "Dearest, dearest Frank" and were signed "Your own lonesome, loving Vic," but she never hinted at the existence of an engagement nor intimated that she was giving any thought to their future together. Neither did he. In his present financial condition, and with business prospects as shaky as they now were, marriage with the daughter of the Emperor of Wellmouth—or marriage at all—seemed too remote a possibility even for dreams. And yet he and Vic were engaged. . . . Or weren't they?

In one of his letters he mentioned being worried over the need of money for new presses and improvements at the print shop. It was his first reference to the subject since their conversation at the picnic. In her reply she declared that she had not forgotten.

"I have an idea," she wrote. "I am only a girl and I don't know one single thing about rubbishy old printing presses and all that, but I do know how to get what I want. Yes, and I usually get it, too. You wait and see; perhaps you will have a pleasant surprise."

He frowned when he read this paragraph and regretted having referred to his monetary troubles. If her great idea meant anything, if there was anything behind it other than a desire to comfort and cheer him, she must be contemplating asking help from her indulgent father. Perhaps she intended coaxing Captain Gideon into renewing his offer for the *Eagle,* possibly raising his five-thousand-dollar bid for the paper. Well, that was off, clean off. He might have been a stubborn, impractical idiot in refusing that offer when it was made, but he had refused it; with his hat on one side, figuratively speaking, he had told Bates and Dean and Eldredge to go to the devil. Yes, and had boasted to the Dodsons of his independence, then and often since. He would not back down and eat humble pie now; he would go through with it even if the finish was in the poor debtors' court. Joel Dean should not have the satisfaction of preparing a bill of sale for the Wellmouth *Eagle*—at least not until that proud bird had made its last dying flutter.

He set his square chin as he made this resolution, but, nevertheless, his courage was sorely tried in those October days. Developments entirely unforeseen came one after the other. His Uncle Beriah's legacy, aside from personal effects and furniture and a few hundred dollars in cash, consisted of stocks and bonds and, of course, the printing business and the land and building on and in which it was conducted. When the need of new presses became urgent he endeavored to sell some of the so-called securities. Then he discovered that the majority of them were not securities at all. Several hundred shares in an Ostable cranberry growing company, par fifty dollars a share, proved to be worth, at a forced sale, less than five. Moreover, he was advised that to sell at that figure would be extremely bad judgment, for the company was in process of reorganization and might make good, later on, under its new management. The bonds, there were two of them, he did sell at their face value, five hundred dollars cash, and used the greater part of the money in absolutely necessary repairs to the print shop building. The floor had sagged in places, and when the carpenters crawled beneath the sills to investigate they found those sills so rotten with age that the entire lower framework must be replaced. This necessitated employing masons to strengthen the brick piers and foundations. The thousand-dollar proceeds from the bond sales dwindled to less than ninety when the job was done.

Then, just as he was drawing an easier breath, the oldest and weakest of the two presses gave out altogether. To put it in working condition would have meant almost the cost of a new press. He called Dodson and Tip Cahoon into consultation over the patient, and the opinion of the two specialists was that the case was hopeless.

"I'm afraid it ain't much use, Frank," confessed Elisha. "She's worn out here and she's gone there. Fix up those places—and that would cost a lot of money—and what you'd have left would be—well—"

"A mess of nawthin'," Cahoon finished for him. "Most of what ain't wore out is busted, and what ain't busted has got the shakin' palsy. She's worth so much a pound for old iron and that's all she is worth. I've got a cousin to Bayport in the junk trade. I'll send for him to come after her if you want me should."

Cobb turned to Dodson. "Is that right, Elisha?" he asked.

The little man sighed. "I hate to say it, Franklin," he replied, "but—but I guess Tip's talkin' sense, for once in his life."

Franklin whistled mournfully. "By George, this is a punch in the eye for us just now," he admitted. "What are we going to do?"

Tip was prompt with his counsel.

"Buy a new one, Mr. Cobb. There's presses on the market nowadays that would make this derelict look like Noah's ark alongside of Carmi Blake's new mackerel schooner. You and 'Lish don't need to bother. Just send me up to Boston and I'll pick out a press for you. . . . I'd just as soon go to Boston as not," he added, complacently. "There's a girl lives in Somerville that's been writin' me to come see her when I was up that way. Waited on table down to the Vineyard House last summer, she did. Had sort of yaller hair and was 'most generally laughin'. You see me with her up to the post office one time, 'Lish, didn't you? . . . Eh? Didn't you?"

Elisha's answer was absently given.

"I've seen you—yes, and heard you, with a good many, Tip," he observed. "Was she the fat one?"

"We-ll, some folks might call her a little mite fleshy, but I don't mind; I like 'em that way. I knew you'd remember her. She ain't the kind a feller forgets."

Elisha sighed. "No one man could forget all of her at once," was his comment. "There, there; be still, Tip! Mr. Cobb is waitin' to say somethin'."

Franklin said the only thing to be said, under the circumstances; buying a new press was out of the question, and he made that clear.

"We've got a good deal of job work on hand, I know," he added. "Ordinarily I should be glad of that, but now—it's a problem. The *Eagle* must have preference, of course. *That* must be out on its regular days. Can we get along for a while with one press, Elisha?"

Tip broke in, vehemently.

"Eh? With *one?*. Cripes t'mighty, we've had to break our backs to get along with two. Me and 'Lish have been all foamed up to a lather every night at knockin' off time for a month; ain't we, 'Lish? No sir-ee, we couldn't get along with one. Possible is one thing and impossible is another."

"I was speaking to Dodson. *Could* we get on with one for a while, Elisha?"

Elisha nodded decisively. "We could and we've got to," he declared. "Tip and I will have to work extra hours, that's all."

Cahoon's remonstrance was almost a shriek.

"Extry hours! Why, what are you talkin' about, 'Lish Dodson? I'm all sewed up with dancin' dates and town hall times for a fortni't—yes, I be. And, besides, that other press is pretty nigh as much of a cripple as this one here."

Elisha grinned. "You can get consider'ble work out of a cripple, if you try hard," he observed. "At least I've got a whole lot out of myself durin' the last thirty-odd year. Tip and I'll tackle it, Frank."

Of course Cahoon vowed he would do nothing of the sort but, when reminded that he would receive extra pay for the extra work, he reluctantly agreed to try it for a while and see how his health "hung out."

"I ain't very strong, though," he declared, "had the cholery instantum when I was a baby. I'll try it for a spell to help you, Mr. Cobb, but I can see right now that I'll be needin' a vacation afore long. . . . How far is Somerville from Boston, 'Lish? Close by, ain't it?"

The extra pay for overtime was another drain upon the exchequer, for, although Elisha declared he would not take another cent, Cobb insisted on paying him as he did Cahoon. To offset this, however, Miss Barker, the bookkeeper, was offered a position in Bridgewater and decided to accept it. Franklin hired no one in her place. He, too, would work evenings and handle the bookkeeping himself.

But now Helen Dodson had a suggestion to make.

"Why not let me come up to the shop after supper two or three nights a week?" she said. "It is lonesome here, with Father away, and I should enjoy having something to keep me busy. I don't know much about keeping books, but I could learn, I guess. If you can put up with a greenhorn I should be glad to try, Frank."

Franklin hesitated. She guessed the reason for his hesitation for she added, quickly: "Of course I wouldn't expect to be paid. I'd like to do it, just for fun."

Franklin shook his head. "Do you suppose I would let you work for nothing?" he demanded, indignantly. "Hardly!"

But she insisted. It would be a favor to her. She was tired of sitting at home alone, evening after evening. Then her father put in a word.

"Why don't you let her, Frank?" he urged. "She wants to do it, I know. Cal'late she *is* lonesome, with you and me gone. Cap'n Carmi, he's off on another Banks cruise," he added, as an afterthought.

Helen was as near to losing patience as Franklin had ever seen her.

"I believe Manuel, that Portuguese that Frank had his trouble with, has gone to the Banks, too," she observed, with sarcasm. "Why didn't you tell him that, Father?"

"Eh? Why—why, what's that Portygee got to do with it, for mercy sakes?"

"What has Carmi Blake got to do with my trying to keep books? But you will let me try, won't you, Franklin?"

This was but the beginning of a long argument, but she had her way in the end and it was agreed that, for a while at least, she was to join her father and Cobb and Cahoon two or three evenings a week at the print shop. Franklin still insisted that she should be paid for her services, but she was firm in her refusal.

"If I were paid it would be work," she declared, "and I should feel that I must keep regular office hours. Now I can come or stay, just as I please."

She did know very little about office work, but she was quick to learn and she possessed qualities which Elsie Barker lacked, namely initiative and discretion. She took a very real interest in the *Eagle* and her advice, given only when it was asked, was of value. Cobb found himself relying more and more upon her judgment in the printing or omission of news items sent in by out-of-town correspondents.

CHAPTER XIV

Victoria came home for the Thanksgiving week-end and Franklin was invited to the Bates's home for Thanksgiving dinner, which, as it was Thanksgiving, was served at noon. It was a dinner to remember, and the nonchalance with which plump Mrs. Bates absorbed heavy plum pudding and mince pie would have caused shudders if any one had dreamed of dieting in those days. There were other guests, Judge Dean among them, so the young people had little opportunity for intimate conversation.

Franklin, not having been invited to remain to supper—not that he felt the need of eating again that day—left about four o'clock in the afternoon. Victoria whispered to him that he must call the following evening.

"It's a shame that you can't come to-night," she said, "but Papa and Mother have a lot of stupid old townspeople coming in for whist, and I am supposed to help entertain them. But I shall expect you to-morrow evening."

He demurred. "Truly, Vic," he said, "I ought not to leave the office. I am working there every evening now. So is Elisha—yes, and Tip."

She pouted. "Oh, well," she said, "of course if you had rather spend your time in that precious printing place than with me—"

"But I hadn't and you know it. . . . Well, I'll come."

Her father's back was turned, so she threw him a kiss. Friday night, at supper, he excused himself to the Dodsons, saying he could not be at the office that evening, having another engagement which must be kept.

Elisha was disappointed. "Well, now, that's kind of too

bad," he said. "I was figurin' to go over that editorial piece with you, that one I wrote about the need of an addition to the post office. If it's goin' into next week's paper it ought to be set up to-night. Couldn't stop in just a few minutes before you kept your appointment with this other fellow, could you, Frank?"

Helen was quietly smiling. "I am sure the other fellow wouldn't like to be kept waiting, Father," she put in. "I'll go over the editorial with you; that is, if Franklin isn't afraid to trust my judgment."

Franklin hastened to say that he was quite satisfied to trust it. He knew that he was blushing, and it angered him to know it. Helen had hesitated, ever so little, before she repeated the word "fellow." Confound the girl! she was altogether too clever. He departed immediately.

That evening was a very pleasant one, so pleasant that Helen Dodson's cleverness was forgotten a few minutes after his arrival at the Bates mansion. Captain Gideon and his wife went out to prayer meeting at the First Meeting House vestry and Victoria and he had the drawing-room to themselves until their return. Victoria was as alluringly provocative as ever, one moment sitting confidentially close to him on the sofa, the next drawing away and changing the subject to school happenings or something in which he was but mildly interested. She teased him by telling him of letters she had had from George Bradley and then, when she had brought him to the point where he was losing his temper, she snuggled next to him once more, looked up into his face with those wonderful eyes of hers and whispered:

"You don't really mind, do you, Frank? I couldn't help his writing to me, could I? You know I don't care two cents for him or any one else except—well, except some one who isn't *very* far away this minute. All the girls get heaps of letters from fellows. It is part of the fun. But, of course, if you really want me to, I will tell George he must never write me again. . . . Oh," with a little gurgle of glee, "what *would* he say if he knew how the other girls laugh over those foolish letters of his."

Franklin's arm, which had fallen from the back of the sofa to a position infinitely more comfortable and agreeable, was withdrawn in a hurry.

"Look here, Vic!" he exclaimed, sharply. "Do you mean to say you show letters like that to—to other people?"

"Why, of course! We always read each other's letters. . . . Why, what is the matter? Good gracious, you don't think I show *your* letters to any one else, do you? You don't think that of me, Frank Cobb! You can't!"

He did not know exactly what to think. She slid to the other end of the sofa.

"If you can't trust me," she declared; "if you are going to be silly and jealous, I—I— Oh, how *can* you! Well, I could be jealous too, I suppose, if I were made that way, which, thank goodness, I'm not. I understand that Nellie Dodson is spending her evenings at the printing office now. No wonder you weren't anxious to come here to-night. I thought it was very queer when you hemmed and hawed about coming. Now I understand."

This was a staggerer. He was entirely innocent, of course, but that fact did not prevent his looking extremely guilty.

"Why—why, this is ridiculous," he sputtered. "You know perfectly well that—that—"

"Oh, she is rather pretty, in a country sort of way, I realize that. But I *did* think, after that night when you and I— Oh, I thought *you* were different."

He spent the next five minutes explaining how different he was and that Helen was at the office merely to help with the bookkeeping.

Reconciliation, when it came, was as sweet as the quarrel had been bitter. And, when the older members of the Bates family returned from prayer meeting the couple on the sofa were looking over the photograph album, holding it upside down. The parting in the dark hall was sweet also, and Franklin promised faithfully to call again on Sunday evening.

"I hardly dare ask you for to-morrow night," whispered Vic. "Mother and Papa expect me to go to the church entertainment at the hall, and if I pretend I have a headache or anything they won't go themselves. But Sunday evening—I shan't think of anything but Sunday evening till it comes. *Good* night."

And yet, when Franklin Cobb sat alone in his room an hour later, he found himself still wondering whether he and Victoria were engaged or not. Their conversation, now that he had leisure to think it over, had not dealt with the future at all.

Sunday morning the Bates man of all work brought a note to the Dodson cottage. Helen took it from the messenger and handed it in at the door of his room. Characteristically she made no comment when delivering it, nor did she refer to it afterward. Obviously she had not mentioned it to her father, for Elisha did not ask a single question. Franklin was grateful for those omissions; there were some subjects a man did not care to be questioned about.

The note, opened in the privacy of his bedroom, contained disappointing tidings. Victoria could not see him that evening, after all. Her parents had accepted an invitation to supper with relatives in Harniss, and they had accepted for her also. She just had to go and, goodness, how she hated it. Would he forgive her? Her last paragraph contained a hint which set him to speculating.

"I think," she wrote, "that that surprise I told you you were likely to have pretty soon is almost a sure thing now. I can't be with you to-day, more's the pity, but I shall be thinking of you every minute—yes, and working for you, too. You don't know what that means, my ownest boy, do you? Never mind, you will know very soon, and then I think you will be grateful to your little Vic."

All that lonely day he guessed and speculated, and the next morning he entered the *Eagle* office with a certain vague, but excited expectancy. And at ten that forenoon, as he sat at his desk in the little back room, the door opened and, looking up, he saw the impressive figure of Captain Gideon Bates on the threshold. He sprang to his feet but the captain entered without waiting for an invitation.

"Hello, Cobb," was the great man's greeting. "All alone, eh? That's good. I wanted to talk with you a minute or two. Mind if I shut the door?"

He shut it himself without waiting for a reply. As in their former interview in that room, Bates took the editorial chair and Franklin perched on a far corner of the desk. The visitor cleared his throat.

"Cobb," he began, "my daughter has been talking to me about you and, from some things she said, I thought perhaps it would be a good idea if you and I had a talk—a private talk."

Franklin said, "Yes, sir," but he scarcely knew that he said it. This introductory speech was disconcerting and alarming. Victoria and her father had been talking about him. What had she said? Had she told—?

The color rushed to his face, but he squared his shoulders. He had done nothing to be ashamed of.

"Captain Bates," he began, "I don't know what Victoria has said to you about me, but—"

Bates interrupted. "There, there!" he broke in, "I know you don't. She said you didn't. She gave me to understand that you have had heavy expenses you hadn't counted on, and that you needed more money in your business and didn't know where it was coming from. That right, is it?"

Franklin drew a breath of relief. So she had not told him —about the other matters. He nodded.

"Why—yes, sir; it is."

"Um-hm, so she said. She tells me one of your printing presses has gone on the rocks and that you need another. That right, too?"

"Yes, sir. I need a new press badly; need two, so far as that goes. But I shall have to go on needing for the present."

"Can't afford to buy 'em, eh?"

"Most decidedly not."

"Humph! Your Uncle Beriah left you some stocks and bonds, seems to me Joe Dean said. Have you thought of turning them into cash?"

Cobb, wondering what was to come, told briefly of his experience with the cranberry company stock and of his selling the bonds. Then he went on to relate the disastrous story of the repairs to the building. Bates did not wait for him to finish.

"I know, I know," he broke in. "Always that way when you start fixing up an old building like this one. I used to tell Beriah he'd have to make this shanty of his over or 'twould fall down on him. He always said he guessed it would last as long as he did. Well, it did, but not much longer, eh? . . . Humph! Yes, yes, I can see where your money's gone. Now let me ask you a question or two more. Is there anything worse than a shortage of cash behind this, young fellow?"

Franklin looked at him. "What do you mean by worse?" he demanded rather sharply. "There's nothing that isn't honest."

"All right, all right. Needn't get mad. I've got my reasons for pumping you this way; you'll hear 'em pretty soon, probably. I mean is there anything wrong with the business as a whole? You're making a go of it, aren't you? I've inquired around a little, and from what I hear you are doing about as well as Higham did; better, some say."

"I have been doing as well as I had any right to expect. I have been learning a good deal, and I am sure I can make a living here. But, in order to keep on and do better than that I ought to have the tools to work with. If I had realized that this building was not much more than a mess of rotten lumber covered with paint and my two presses junk, or just about, I—well, I don't know. Possibly your five thousand dollars might have been in my pocket and I somewhere else. Possibly—or possibly not, I'm not sure."

"I see. Well, maybe it isn't too late even yet. Provided I can get Dean and Eldredge to stand in with me now, would you consider selling at that figure? Very likely they wouldn't stand in, of course—people do change their minds; but if you would—are you willing to sell out?"

"No."

"Eh? . . . Humph! You sound pretty positive. Five thousand is a fair bid, and that isn't horse swapping talk either."

"I know. But I'm not going to sell. I like this game, particularly the newspaper end of it, better than I ever liked any hard work before in my life. I'm going to stick to it; I've made up my mind to that. I won't be licked until I am."

"I see," with a quiet chuckle. "Make or break, eh?"

"Make or break; that's it exactly. Just now it looks more like break, but—I'm not down and out yet."

Captain Gideon leaned back in his chair. Franklin expected almost any sort of remark from him—except that which he made.

"Good boy!" he grunted, with emphasis. "That's the way to talk. Never say die till you're dead and then somebody else can say it for you. I like that."

Cobb was astonished. He suspected irony but apparently his caller was very much in earnest.

"Well!" he exclaimed. "You surprise me, Captain Bates. I thought you would probably say I was a fool."

"Perhaps you are; it may turn out that way. But you're no quitter. I can sympathize with a fool—been one myself a good many times in my day—but I have no use for a fellow who curls up and quits as long as he's able to fight. Never giving up got more than one vessel of mine into port when I was going to sea for a living. . . . There, there!" impatiently. "I've got things to do and so have you, I guess likely. Your business here is all right enough. Oh, I know; I've taken pains to find out. You are in a close hitch just now because you need a little extra capital. Would three or four thousand dollars tide you over, think?"

"What? . . . Indeed it would. Two thousand would do on a pinch."

"Might as well get enough while you're getting it. Look here, young man, have you ever thought of borrowing money?"

Franklin had thought of it, but he had dismissed the idea almost as soon as it came. He shook his head.

"I shan't think of it," he said, with decision.

"Why not? Borrowing money is a part of business. I have borrowed a barrel of it, myself."

"Yes, sir, but you were in a position to pay it back. Borrowed money has to be paid some day or other."

"Sure as shooting it has. But that day needn't be to-morrow or next month—no, nor next year, provided the interest is paid on the days it comes due. If you know the right way, and the right place, a note of hand can run a long, long while. My advice to you is—borrow."

Another shake of the head. "No. Thank you, Captain Bates, but I can't do it. It is very good of you to offer and of Victoria to suggest your doing it—of course that is what she did—but—"

"Here, here, here!" testily. "What are you talking about? I'm not offering to lend you money. I'm not in the money lending business. My bank is, though; that's how it makes its profits. You give the Wellmouth National your note payable on demand for, say, three or four thousand dollars and I'll see that the loan goes through. Yes, and you needn't be afraid that the demand will be made till you are ready to have it. I'll attend to that, too. Then you can get your new press and whatever else you need. What do you say?"

Franklin did not know what to say. Here was a way out of his present troubles, but it might be the way leading to others, and worse ones, later on. He hesitated. Bates took a big cigar from his pocket and lighted it.

"Of course you are wondering why I'm offering to do this for you," he observed. "Well, I'll tell you. I'm doing it partly because Vic's been telling me about the tight corner you are in—yes, probably I shouldn't have thought of it if it hadn't been for her. She seems to like you pretty well, and she's a smart girl and doesn't take a fancy to every Tom, Dick and Harry. But even to please her I wouldn't lend the bank's money without security and good security, too. There's something behind it, just as you are guessing this minute. I've been watching the way you run the *Eagle*. You are making a live paper of it, and we need that kind of paper in this county. My idea—Joe Dean's and mine—was to buy it from you and let 'Lish Dodson run it the way we wanted him to, but you put your foot on that notion. All right, I don't find fault with you for that. I've got a will of my own and I have considerable respect for anybody who will stand up in his own boots and say no when he feels like it. You can own the *Eagle* and run it, so far as I'm concerned, but I don't want any outsiders to own it—that I *won't* have. I don't want to see you go to smash and any Ostable or Wapatomac crowd stepping in and buying it. I mean that the Wellmouth *Eagle* shall be edited and printed by Wellmouth men *in* Wellmouth. That's what I mean and what I intend to have. So that is what is behind my offering to help you get the money you need."

He rose, knocked the ashes from his cigar into the waste basket, and turned to the door.

"There!" he grunted. "I've talked a lot more than I meant

to when I came in, but I don't think I've said anything I'm sorry for. There will be three or four thousand dollars waiting for you at the Wellmouth National whenever you are ready to go and get it. Think it over, but think carefully. . . . Morning."

He strolled out, puffing at his cigar. Cobb heard his casual greetings to Dodson and Cahoon and their deferential acknowledgments. Then the outer door slammed. Franklin sat down in the chair to do a little of the recommended thinking. This, or something like it, was Victoria's promised surprise of course. She had promised to help him out of his business troubles and this was her—or her father's—way of doing it.

Tip was openly curious concerning the reason for the Bates call and Elisha obviously, although he asked no questions, was in the same state of mind. Franklin did not satisfy their curiosity. The captain had just dropped in, he said, to chat about things in general and the *Eagle* in particular; they had to be satisfied with that explanation.

Tip, however, had his own answer to the problem, and he whispered it to Elisha across the type case.

"You know what I think, 'Lish?" he whispered, shading his mouth with his hand. "I think the old man had some consider'ble to say about Frank's hangin' around Vic the way he's been doin' lately. Oh, all hands knows about it; some of 'em go so far as to cal'late he's figurin' to keep comp'ny with her."

Elisha was scornful. "He's a long way from bein' the only young fellow who's been hangin' around her," was his observation. "She's never been contented, since she was fifteen, unless there was a half-dozen boys trailin' alongside to carry her parasol and hop when she whistled. Tip, you ought to sign some anti-girl pledge. Just the sight of a female in the offin' makes you drunk. Franklin Cobb keepin' company with the daughter of the man he wouldn't sell out to! Rubbish!"

Nevertheless, the Cahoon suggestion, wild as he pretended to think it, troubled him a bit. He mentioned the subject to Helen the next time they were alone together.

"I can't see that it is any of our business, Father," she said, indifferently. "Even if it is true—what of it?"

"Why—why, I don't know's there anything of it, in a way, Helen," he admitted. "Only—only—well, if he was to marry her he'd be—he'd be—"

"He would be the son-in-law of Captain Gideon Bates. And practically every one in Wellmouth will tell you what sort of a position that would be."

He turned to look at her. "You don't act as interested as I thought you'd be, Nellie," he observed, in mild surprise. "I thought you liked Franklin same as I do."

"Of course I like him. Why shouldn't I? But what has that to do with this silly gossip Tip Cahoon has been whispering to you?"

"Why, nothin'. Only—well, Franklin has always talked and acted so sort of—of independent and all, that for him to— Ah, hum, he's young of course and Victoria *is* a real pretty-lookin' girl."

"So she is. . . . Good night, Father."

Franklin's thinking lasted through another day. On the morning following that he dropped in at the Wellmouth National Bank and found Mr. Cornelius Haven smiling a welcome from behind the cashier's rail.

"Good morning, good morning, Mr. Cobb," gushed Cornelius. "I have been expecting you. Captain Bates told me you might call almost any time. Come in to the directors' room. It won't take us long to handle our little matter, I imagine."

It did not. Fifteen minutes later Franklin Cobb emerged from the bank's portals leaving behind him the sum of four thousand dollars to his credit and his signature on an untimed note for that amount. And that evening he wrote Victoria what he had done, expressing the hope that his action might not prove to be a mistake. Inwardly he had his misgivings, but he tried to dismiss them from his thoughts. It was done, anyhow; now he could equip the establishment which had belonged to the late B. Higham as that gentleman should have equipped it but never did.

He still kept the matter of the loan a secret—to every one except the bank people and Victoria, that is. Helen had never mentioned the call of Captain Bates at the editorial office although he was sure her father must have told her about it. She came regularly twice, and sometimes three times a week to spend the evening at her bookkeeping and was still firm in refusing pay for her services.

"I enjoy doing it," she declared. "Sitting alone there at home is poky and lonesome. This is interesting. When it isn't I'll let you know, I promise you."

They usually walked home together, the three of them. One evening in early December the Masonic lodge to which Elisha belonged was holding an especial meeting, with speakers from out of town, and Cobb insisted that he take that evening away from work and attend. He did so, after much persuasion, and Franklin and Helen walked home without his escort.

As they entered the cottage, the door of which had been left unlocked, of course, Franklin, lingering to close that door, heard Helen utter an exclamation.

"Why, Carmi!" she exclaimed, in surprise. "Where on earth did you come from?"

The deep voice of Captain Blake answered.

"From the Grand Banks," it said. "Come flyin', too."

"You must have. You weren't expected in until next week, were you?"

"No, but a man who is skipperin' his last cruise wants to make it a record one, if he can. I'm goin' to be a shore bird from now on."

"You mean you are going to stay at home for good?"

"Yes, I am. Unless they send me to the State House or somethin' like that. . . . Well, Nellie, is that all you've got to say? Ain't you glad to see me?'

"Why, of course I am. What a silly question!"

"Is it? I didn't know. You haven't as much as asked me to sit down yet."

"But you have been sitting down. How long have you been here?"

"For an hour or so. And where have *you* been?"

"Why, up at the *Eagle* office. I am helping with the book-keeping there, two or three evenings a week. You knew that; of course you did."

"Heard about it from Bi after I made port this very evenin'. Hadn't heard it before. What are you doin' that for? Thought Frank Cobb had a bookkeeper already."

"He did have, but she left and so— But he will tell you about it. He is here now. . . . Franklin, what are you waiting for? Come in; it's no one but Carmi."

Franklin, who had waited, uncertain whether to enter or not, obeyed the summons.

"Why, hello, Captain Blake!" he cried, extending his hand. "Welcome home again. Glad to see you."

Blake did not appear to see the hand, at least he did not take it. Nor did he smile.

"How are you, Cobb?" he said gruffly. Then turning to Helen, he added: "Well, I suppose I better be runnin' along. Gettin' late."

"Running along! Why, you've just got here—or I have. Of course you're not going yet. Sit down and behave yourself. Running along; the idea!"

Cobb decided to take the hint, no matter whether one was intended or not.

"I am going to my room," he put in, hastily. "Got some

letters to write. Good night, Helen. Good night, Captain Carmi."

Helen said good night, although she looked rather troubled. Carmi Blake's good night was curt enough. Franklin climbed the stairs, lighted a lamp and sat down to write his letter to Victoria. In the sitting room below he could hear the murmur of voices.

Blake's odd behavior disturbed and irritated him. He had been grouchy the last time they met. What was the matter with the fellow? Apparently now he resented Helen's working at the *Eagle* office; but why? Could he imagine that— He couldn't be such an idiot.

Well, he was a queer duck anyway. Honest, and capable in his way, but rough and with a temper of his own, there was no doubt of that. Not good enough for Helen Dodson, he had felt that from the beginning.

None of his business, however. He dipped his pen in ink and began the letter.

"Dearest Vic:"

CHAPTER XV

CARMI BLAKE had been at home but a few days before political rumor became active in Wellmouth. As a matter of fact there had been whispered reports for some time, but there was nothing authoritative behind them. Now, however, it was said openly that Carmi was "out" for the nomination as district representative at the State House. Franklin heard this at the post office, at the barber shop and in Manasseh Eldredge's store. Just for amusement—for he felt certain that he, himself, knew more of the facts than most—he asked Manasseh for information.

"Anything in it, Eldredge?" he asked. "If it is true the *Eagle* ought to be giving it some attention, don't you think?"

Manasseh gave him a quick glance and then, teetering on his toes, looked out of the front window.

"If it's just talk," he observed, "then gettin' it into print won't help the *Eagle* a whole lot. Do it more harm than good, way I look at it. Better wait a spell, hadn't you, Frank?"

"Suppose we quote you as saying that there is nothing in it? You are supposed to know about all the politics in the county. 'Mr. Manasseh Eldredge, when asked concerning a certain rumor dealing with a prominent South Side citizen's candidacy for the State Legislature, laughed and declared it nonsense.' How would that do? It would prove that the *Eagle* had its ears open and knew where to go for information. We'll print it about that way, Manasseh."

Mr. Eldredge's plump figure ceased bobbing up and down. The superior smile faded from his lips.

"Here, hold on, Frank," he protested, anxiously. "Don't

fetch my name into it. *I* ain't sayin' nothin'; nothin at all, you understand? And if you'll take my advice, the *Eagle* won't either—not yet."

"But a lot of people are saying a good deal."

"Let 'em. The ones whose say-so counts are keepin' pretty quiet, you'll notice. When the time comes they'll say somethin' and what they say generally goes. You just wait till the word comes to you and then you and your paper can back up that word. Frankie, you trust your Uncle Manasseh; he generally knows what's what. You just wait and— Why, here! smoke a good ten-cent cigar on me while you're waitin'."

Cobb gathered from this that the powers were quite aware of the Blake candidacy and were not a little disturbed. That afternoon he walked to the South Side and dropped in at the office of Blake Brothers. A stiff, raw wind from the sea was rattling shutters and whistling about the eaves of the building, and, in spite of the hot fire in the office stove, the two clerks at the high desk were working with their coat collars turned up. One of them told him that Captain Abiathar was out.

"How about Cap'n Carmi?"

The clerk jerked his thumb over his shoulder. "In yonder —inside," he said.

The rear office was even chillier than the other, but Carmi Blake was in his shirt sleeves, the stump of a cigar between his teeth. He was writing busily.

"Good afternoon, Captain," hailed Franklin.

Blake looked up. "Oh, hello!" he grunted, gruffly. "Well? How's news bitin' these days?"

"Not too briskly. Perhaps I don't use the right bait or have been fishing in the wrong places. I came down here hoping you might help me out. You could, I imagine, if you wanted to."

"That so? How?"

"Oh, by just giving me leave to announce your candidacy for the State Legislature. Better still by giving the *Eagle* your signed statement. Perhaps," with a grin, "that is what you are writing now. I hope it is."

Blake tossed aside his pen and crossed his legs. His brows drew together.

"How do you know I'm a candidate?" he asked.

"Every one knows it. Or, at least, the whole town is saying it is true. It is, isn't it, Captain?"

Blake's big hand waved the question aside. "Where did you hear it first?"

"Oh, I don't know. I heard it a good while ago."

"There ain't many who knew it a good while ago. I only made up my mind lately."

"Well—er—I heard it somewhere and from those who seemed to know what they were talking about. At any rate, it is an accepted fact nowadays and—"

"Wait a minute. Did Nellie Dodson tell you?"

Cobb, caught unawares by this blunt demand, hesitated momentarily.

"Why—" he stammered, "why should she tell me? What makes you think that?"

"Because she knew before anybody else—except Bi and two or three others. So she told you, eh?"

"I didn't say she did."

"You didn't say she didn't, either."

Franklin's temper was beginning to simmer. The tone and manner of his companion were distinctly irritating.

"I haven't said anything and I don't intend to, Captain Carmi," he said, with decision. "You are taking a good deal for granted, it seems to me. I heard it and where I heard it doesn't matter. What I am here for now is to ask if you are willing that the *Eagle* should print something about it. Are you?"

"I don't know's I am. Suppose I'm not, what then?"

"Then? Well, then I guess we shall have to print it anyhow. The *Eagle* is a newspaper, and it prints the news. Your candidacy is getting to be old news by this time and we can't ignore it any longer. I had rather print your own statement but if you won't give it to any one I shall have to print one of my own."

He turned toward the door. Blake leaned across the desk.

"Hold on!" he ordered. "I didn't say I wouldn't give out a statement, as I know of. Maybe I will—when I'm ready. Ought to give out somethin' to some of the county papers, I presume likely; anyway Abiathar seems to think I ought to. . . . Look here, Cobb; suppose I did give the *Eagle* a statement—what would you do with it?"

"Print it, of course."

"Just as I write it?"

"Certainly."

"Humph! . . . How do you know Gideon Bates and Dean and the rest of 'em would like you doin' that? Have they told you you could?"

Franklin looked at him. Then he stepped forward and laid a hand on the desk.

"Now what do you mean by that?" he asked, sharply. "What have the likes or dislikes of Bates's crowd got to do with the *Eagle*? Do you suppose I take orders from them?"

"Don't you? Your uncle used to."

"Perhaps, but I don't. Nor from any one else. If you haven't understood that before you must understand it now."

Captain Carmi was silent for a full minute. He was regarding the young man before him with an odd expression. Cobb said nothing further; he was very angry. At length Blake shook his head as if giving up a puzzle.

"Be darned if I can make you out, Cobb," he declared.

"You don't have to, you know."

"No, I don't, that's a fact; but I'd like to. You set me to guessin'."

"There we're even, for you've got me guessing too. For some reason or other you don't like me. Oh, you don't; I've known it for a long time. Now why? Let's have it out. This is as good a time as any. Come."

Carmi Blake leaned back in his chair to thrust his hands into his trousers' pockets.

"I like the way you're talkin' now," he said, grudgingly. "Nellie tells me you talk the same way to her and her father. She thinks you mean what you say."

"And I'm to take it that you don't think so?"

"I don't know what to think. Come now, Cobb, you're askin' for plain speakin'; here's a little of it. You and Nellie are pretty friendly these days—mighty close friends you are, I judge. You've coaxed her into workin' up at your place nights."

"Rot! I didn't coax her. She insisted on doing it to help me and her father with the bookkeeping. . . . At any rate, I don't see what that has to do with—"

"Wait! Let me finish. You've got her there with you, and I've heard from a dozen or more who have seen you that you and she walk home together every other evenin' just as you had the other night when you found me waitin' at her house. . . . Well? You're thinkin' that ain't any of my business, I supppose?"

"Yes, I was. And now I say it."

"I hear you; and I'll say it is. It wouldn't be, maybe, if I was dead sure you were playin' a straight game. If I'm licked in a straight, fair game—why, then I— But I'll be darned if I'm sure just what your game is, Cobb. No, by godfreys, I ain't!"

He had withdrawn one huge fist from his pocket and now he struck the desk with it. Franklin was in a curious state of mind. This was so entirely unexpected, so undreamed of, so—so ridiculous. He was furiously angry and yet he did not know what to say; or, rather, of the hundred things he wanted to say, which to say first.

"Why—why, you—" he began, and paused. Then, choking back his fierce resentment and choosing his words with care, he added, "Blake, suppose you tell me just what you mean by that? Don't hint—speak what you think. And hurry; I'm not too patient just now."

Blake shrugged his great shoulders. "Told you I was goin' to be plain, didn't I?" he queried. "I say I can't make out what your game is. You are thick as thieves with Nellie, but, if what I hear's true, you're even thicker with Vic Bates. When she's home you're with her every minute; you're wearin' out the steps up at her house, eatin' there, stayin' there till the middle of the night. When Victoria's around you're all Bates; when she's away you're all Dodson. Now—"

Franklin's face had been flushed; now it was white. "Blake," he broke in sharply, "shut up! If you don't mean what you say you're a fool. If you do mean it you're a liar. Either way I warn you to shut up."

Carmi Blake started. He rose from the desk chair.

"Young fellow," he said, slowly, "I ain't in the habit of takin' that kind of talk from anybody."

"You'll take it from me."

Blake had come around from behind the desk and was standing before him, looking down at him, his brows drawn together, and his clenched hands at his side.

"And if I don't take it?" he said, slowly. "If I don't choose to take it, then—well, then you'll make me, I suppose?"

"I'll certainly try."

"Humph! . . . How far do you figure you'll get in a fight with me, boy?"

"As far as I can," grimly.

Blake still stood there. Franklin, looking up into his rugged, sunburned face, had a feeling that the man was sorely tempted. The fingers of his right hand were opening and closing. Well, he should have a run for his money, a short run probably, but lively while it lasted. His own glance did not waver. And suddenly, to his amazement, the menacing scowl faded from Carmi Blake's brow, and his lips twitched in a reluctant grin.

"I guess likely that's so," he grunted. "Yes, you'd try anyhow. Darn you, Cobb, you've got spunk, I'll say that for you. You say I don't like you. Most of the time I don't, but there's others—just now, for instance—when I can't help it. . . . Oh," crisply, "don't get the idea that I want to kiss and make up or anything like that. I doubt if there is anything in this world I'd enjoy better than givin' you a lickin'. I've done it in my mind a dozen times since I got back from this last cruise."

"Well, here I am."

"Oh, lay off! What would a fight between you and me settle except which of us two could manhandle the other? There's nothin' to that."

He turned and, walking back to his chair, sat down heavily. With his elbow on the desk he rested his chin on his hand and gazed gloomily at his visitor.

"You ordered me to tell you what I was thinkin', Cobb," he went on. "I did and, instead of answerin', you want to fight. Why? Ashamed to answer, are you?"

"No," hotly. "You know I'm not."

"Said 'Let's have it out,' didn't you? Well, why not? Are you keepin' company with Vic Bates?"

"Why—what do you mean?"

"Goin' to marry her, are you?"

"I—I don't know. That is my affair—and hers."

"How about Nellie? Do you know whether you want to marry her or not?"

"Look here, Blake! This is—"

"Shh! Don't tell me *she* isn't any of my business, because she is. She is, d'you hear? *I* know—" He paused, his jaw set and his face suddenly haggard. Then looking down and shuffling the papers on his desk, he added gruffly, "I'm talkin' too much. . . . Humph! Say, Cobb, you keep this to yourself. Understand?"

"Oh, *don't* be a fool! You know I will."

"Hum. . . . Well, yes, I guess you will. And I *am* a fool, been talkin' like one. . . . But here's just how you stand as I see you, Frank Cobb. You're hangin' to Vic Bates's skirts, and the whole town knows it, and half of it is talkin' about it. But you're livin' at Nellie Dodson's house and now you've got her up to your damned print shop and the town knows it and sees you goin' around with her, and some are talkin' about *that*. Now—"

But Cobb did not let him finish.

"Do you mean to say," he demanded, aghast, "that—that the people in this town are so—so foul-minded that they—that they—"

"I mean to say that they're talkin' about you and both girls—both of 'em. And they ain't any more foul-minded than any other lot of folks who talk for the sake of havin' somethin' to say. They're talkin' about it and wonderin' and guessin' and I don't blame 'em. If you're playin' square with one girl you must be hog selfish to let the other one get talked about. And if you ain't playin' straight with either then you can't be trusted. And it's the same way with the Four Corners gang and us South Siders. You can't play with both ends. I never had any use for a fellow that was all butter to one side and all soft soap to the other. Either the butter or the soap is bluff, it's bound to be. So when you come struttin' to me blowin' about the *Eagle's* independence I don't take much stock in it. The *Eagle* can go to the devil so far as I'm concerned. Until I have a whole lot better proof that you are a square dealer than I have so far, you can keep my name out of your paper. . . . There! I guess likely we understand each other."

He threw himself back in the chair and picked up the pen he had dropped when the interview began. Franklin Cobb did not speak immediately; he did not trust himself to do so. And, at that critical moment the office door opened and Abiathar Blake entered.

"Godfreys, Carmi," he exclaimed, "it's chilly weather for this time of year! Gives you an idea that winter's close aboard. . . . Oh, hello, Frank! How's the great American Eagle these days? Flyin' high, eh?"

Neither his brother nor Cobb answered. He looked from one to the other.

"Why, what's the matter with you two?" he demanded. "Humph! *you* fellows don't look chilly, I'll say that for you. What in the world—?"

Captain Carmi shrugged. "Cobb and I have been havin' a little talk," he growled. "It's all over now, though."

"Not quite." It was Franklin who said it and, although he did not raise his voice, there was a frigid emphasis in his tone which caused the elder partner to turn and stare at him. "It isn't quite over," he said. "Captain Carmi, you are partly wrong when you say we understand each other. I'm beginning to understand you, but you're a long way from understanding me. What you have said about—well, about certain people, is what I said it was a while ago—a lie. I have played square, as you call it, and I hadn't the slightest idea that— that behaving like a friend *to* a friend would be misinterpreted by a pack of filthy gossips. No, and I'm dead sure that the friend hadn't, either. . . . Hold on! I'm almost through. When it comes to the *Eagle* I want to say this: I'm not anxious to print your name in my paper—not after this, God knows! but so long and so often as you are news your name will be printed."

Carmi Blake sprang to his feet.

"I told you—" he threatened.

"I'm telling *you* now. It will be printed, just as will Captain Bates's or any one's else if I choose to put them there. And if I don't choose they shall be left out. What you, or Bates, or the whole town may say will make not the least difference. So that's that and now *you* may go to the devil."

He took his hat from the desk and walked from the office. He heard Abiathar Blake swear in amazed wonder as he crossed the threshold.

During the two-mile walk to the Four Corners he was too angry to do any connected thinking. His mind was reviewing, again and again, the interview with Carmi Blake and with each recollection of the things the man had said, he became angrier still. The impertinent boor! The insulting, bullying idiot! To suppose—to dare to think that— And apparently half of Wellmouth township was thinking the same things—yes, and whispering them to each other. What a low, mean hole it was he had chosen to live in. A decent fellow couldn't be friends with a decent girl without— Oh, *what* a set of sewer rats! And Carmi Blake who, up to that time he had considered a good chap—had rather liked him, as a matter of fact—why, Blake was the meanest rat of them all. It was a pity they had not actually come to blows. There could have been but one end to the battle—he was sane enough to realize that—but at least he would have had the memory of landing one or two solid punches on that sneering, sarcastic, lying mouth. And what a satisfaction that memory would have been. . . . And so on, over and over.

He was still red-hot when he entered the print shop and when hailed by Elisha and Tip he merely grunted acknowledgment. He remained in the office but a little while. No use, he could not think of business; all he could think of was Carmi Blake. He gave up trying and, offering the time-worn excuse of a headache, said he was going home to his room to lie down for an hour or so. Elisha was very solicitous and sympathetic, but Tip, after his employer's departure, was inclined to be cynical.

"Headache nawthin'! He's mad about somethin'," was Tip's diagnosis. "Bet you Vic Bates and him have had some sort of a row. Come now, 'Lish, what'll you bet?"

Mr. Dodson was scornful.

"Vic Bates is up to the Academy, and he's down here. Folks don't usually row when they're seventy-odd miles apart. Honest, Tip, you ought to see a doctor. There was a girl went past the window half an hour ago and you ain't been the same since."

Tip was unabashed. "You can have a first-class row with just letters back and forth," he announced. "Judas priest, don't I know it! Why, one time there was a girl up to Providence; worked in a laundry up there she did. She was down here visitin' a cousin of hers to Orham and I met her to a dance twice at the Odd Fellers' Hall over there. She got—well, you might say kind of interested in me—"

"Never saw anything like you before, probably."

"Aw, rats! She was dead stuck on me, that's what she was. And she used to write me every day and I wrote her—well, whenever I got around to it. And them letters strung along and strung along till somebody must have wrote her that I was—was, well, kind of sociable with another girl—one from Fairhaven 'twas, as I remember. And *then!* Say, 'Lish, you ought to have read what she wrote me. You'd think I— Hey? What are you goin' away for? I ain't half finished."

"I know. That's why I'm goin'."

Helen was in the kitchen when Franklin entered the cottage. She heard him enter and called, but he did not answer. He went up to his room and, throwing himself into a chair by the window, sat there until supper time, nursing his ill temper. During supper he ate little and spoke only when spoken to. Both the Dodsons noticed his manner and, later, when she and her father were alone, Helen referred to it.

"What has gone wrong with him, Father?" she asked. "Do

you know? He said very little to you and practically nothing to me. I can't think of anything I have done to offend him. Do you suppose it is something about my bookkeeping? Dear me! I hope not."

Of course, Elisha, the always loyal, declared he was sure it was just the headache. But there was little conviction in his tone. He, too, was puzzled and disturbed. And when his employer called to them that he should not go to the office that evening, he was more troubled than before.

It was late before Franklin fell asleep that night but he did at last and, when he woke in the morning, he was in a far better frame of mind. The interview with Blake, now that he looked back at it, was not so very serious a matter, after all. The man was jealous, that was all. He had guessed as much before, but now there was no need of guessing. Captain Carmi was head over heels in love with Helen Dodson and, therefore, was looking for rivals in every possible, or impossible, place. And, after all, in some ways he had behaved pretty decently. Suppose they had actually fought there in the Blake private office. The story would have traveled from one end of Wellmouth to the other and, if there was any truth in the story that a portion of the town was "talking" about Helen Dodson and himself, her name might have been dragged into the limelight in a new and particularly disgraceful way. Yes, it was distinctly decent of Carmi Blake to ignore the challenge and go back to his desk chair.

All this, now that he was cool enough to think calmly, set him to considering the affair from the Carmi Blake viewpoint. Of course Blake had no rational cause for jealousy, but, equally of course, a chap as deeply in love as he must be, was not rational. He had heard the gossip—some people would gossip; Wellmouth, probably, was no different in that respect from any other community—and it had made him angry. It was too bad that as fine a girl as Helen should be talked about, even if there was no atom of truth behind the talk. Perhaps he, Franklin Cobb, was a bit to blame; perhaps he had been a trifle careless of appearances. After all, he *was* living in her house—hers and her father's. She *was* working with him at the *Eagle* office and he *had*, quite innocently, fallen into the habit of walking home with her afterward.

Yes, he was obliged to admit that Carmi Blake was not entirely without justification. He had had these things reported to him—along with all the rest of it that about Victoria. Confound them! they had better keep *her* name out of it!

Well, one point could be settled and should be. Blake was a candidate. Practically every one knew that before and now he had admitted as much. Statement or no statement, the next issue of the paper should print the news of his candidacy and each succeeding issue until after the district nomination should report the progress of his campaign, just as it reported those of whatever other candidates there might be. *Just* as it reported them; fair field and no favor stuff again—that was it. But how Carmi Blake would squirm and how furious he would be to see the *Eagle* treating him just as fairly as it treated others. Good enough! Serve him right! Franklin's forgiveness was by no means complete even yet.

But Helen— When he went down to breakfast, his mind was made up in one particular. Helen must not continue to work on the books at his place of business. He must either find some one to take her place or do the bookkeeping himself, one or the other. She should not be gossiped about if he could help it. That was only fairness—not to Carmi Blake but to her.

He had a substitute in mind already. A young fellow named Enoch Bearse had called at the print shop several times recently to inquire if there was any chance of employment there. Enoch was only a boy, eighteen years old, and had recently graduated from the Bayport high school. He wanted to do clerical work, almost any kind, and, as he expressed it, was eager to begin at the bottom and "work up." Elsie Barker, when she resigned as bookkeeper had suggested young Bearse as a possible successor. The only point in his disfavor was that he was a distant relative of Tip Cahoon's, but that, of course, was his misfortune rather than his fault.

Without consulting Elisha—who would be sure to tell Helen —Franklin sent for the boy and engaged him, on trial, at the depressing salary of four dollars a week. He was to make his début at the office on the following Monday morning. As it was Friday when the arrangement was made, Cobb was faced with the unpleasant necessity of notifying the Dodsons at once.

He did it after supper that evening. He had a carefully prepared story ready to tell, and there was no hint of Carmi Blake in it. Helen heard the news of the hiring of her successor without any outward show of resentment. Franklin, of course, explained carefully that he had taken the step because of what seemed to him two good reasons. The first that he simply would not continue to employ Helen's time and energy any longer without recompense. The second that the business needed some one on the books and bills all the time.

"I did it without telling either of you," he went on, "because I knew you would insist on carrying on just as we have been doing. That, to my mind, was not fair nor right. I couldn't take more of your evenings, Helen, without paying for them and you said at the beginning that you wouldn't accept pay. So I took the bull by the horns and settled it this way. And it *is* settled. . . . I hope you both understand that I hate like blazes to give up our work together. We've had lots of fun up there these past few weeks, haven't we?"

Elisha agreed that indeed they had and added, ruefully, that, so far as he was concerned, he didn't see why they couldn't keep on having them.

"Nellie, she likes the job. You do, don't you, Nellie?"

Helen nodded. "I liked it very much," she replied, "but Franklin knows what he wants, and it is his business, Father. I hope the new bookkeeper will do better work. I'm sure he will."

Franklin turned toward her in earnest protest.

"Oh, see here, Helen!" he cried. "You mustn't take it in that way. It isn't at all what I want. You've been a brick to help us out the way you have. The Lord knows I'm more obliged to you than I can tell; but it couldn't go on forever, now could it? I'm thinking of you, you know."

Helen smiled. "How did you happen to think of me—in just this way?" she asked, quietly. "Was it all your own thought?"

Franklin was startled, but he lied, promptly and gentlemanly. "Why, certainly it was," he declared. "What do you mean, Helen?"

"Nothing, of course. That was ridiculous, wasn't it? . . . Oh, I almost forgot! There is a letter for you on the sitting room table. I meant to hand it to you when you came home, but it slipped my mind."

The letter on the sitting room table was in a very familiar handwriting, and the postmark on the envelope was unusually clear. Franklin looked at the postmark and then turned to look back toward the dining room. Helen had seen that postmark, of course. Was it possible that she thought Victoria had— Oh, no, of course not; she could not think that.

The new bookkeeper took up his duties on Monday morning. He was very, very green, but he was eager to learn and showed symptoms of ability. Franklin's conscience was easier, but the evenings at the print shop were not half as pleasant as they had been. He should have been well satisfied at finding a way out of his difficulty so soon, but he was not altogether so.

One of his first bits of work at the editorial desk was the preparing of an item concerning the Blake candidacy for the

State Legislature. He began with "It is rumored that—" tore up the sheet and began again with, "The political pot in our community is beginning to boil already. It now seems about certain that one representative citizen of the South Side will permit his name to be presented at the Republican district convention as a candidate for the nomination of representative to the State Legislature. Captain Carmi Blake—"

Here he paused. This did not suit him, either. Too banal, too trite, too much like a "local jotting" sent in by one of the out-of-town correspondents. He would like to print something more direct and outspoken, something which should prove to Blake that the *Eagle* was not in the least afraid to publish the truth concerning anybody or anything. He laid aside the pen and went out to the post office. Possibly something he might hear from the crowd there would give him an idea for a better start.

While there he asked for and was handed the morning mail. One of the envelopes addressed to the *Eagle,* bore, in its upper right hand corner, the printed words: "Blake Brothers. Wholesale Fish Dealers. Wellmouth, Mass." Wondering what this might mean, he tore it open. There was no personal letter, merely a brief, formal written notice.

I have decided to be a candidate for the Republican nomination as representative from this district to the Massachusetts Legislature. It is a long time before the convention, but my friends have asked me to make this early announcement so that there may be no question about my candidacy. This notice has been sent to all the county papers.

CARMI BLAKE

Franklin Cobb laughed aloud when he finished reading. So the stubborn skipper had had to knuckle under, after all. He had sworn that his name should not appear in the *Eagle,* and now he had sent it in, himself. He must have reached the conclusion that Cobb meant what he said about printing it anyhow. Something of a triumph, this was. First blood for the Cobb side.

And then it occurred to him to wonder whether Helen's no longer working at the print shop had caused this change of heart. Carmi had called several times and Helen must, of course, have told him that she was through as bookkeeper. Did Blake think that he—Cobb—had knuckled under? This surmise was not so pleasant.

He called Dodson into the little back room, when he returned to it, and showed him the Blake announcement. Elisha put on his spectacles, read, and whistled.

"Whew!" he exclaimed. "Gorry! Well, *now* the cat's clear out of the bag. Goin' to print this, are we, Frank?"

"You bet!" with decision. "Print it on the front page. Yes, and if you get any news about Blake and his candidacy—anything, no matter how trifling—we'll print that, too. You and Tip keep your ears open and I'll keep mine. We'll show friend Carmi that the *Eagle* is a newspaper."

Elisha was regarding him over the top of his spectacles. He seemed much pleased, or so Franklin thought.

"Goin' to support him, are we, Frank?" he asked, after a moment.

"Support him? Why should we?"

"Eh? . . . Well, I didn't know. He's a mighty square, able fellow, Carmi is. Your tellin' me we was goin' to print every bit of news about him made me— But there, I presume likely you're right; better policy to wait a spell."

"You and Helen would like to have the *Eagle* support him, I suppose?"

"Eh? . . . Why, he'd make a pretty good representative, I shouldn't wonder. I've known him ever since he was a boy; and Nellie—"

"Yes, yes," impatiently, "I'm quite aware that Helen knows him. . . . Go ahead and get that notice into print."

Elisha limped toward the door, then turned and hesitated.

"I hope you don't think I blame you any for not comin' out for him, Frank," he faltered. "I understand. There'll be other candidates, of course, and the *Eagle* can't afford to take chances. We haven't heard from Cap'n Gideon nor Joe Dean yet."

Franklin was decidedly out of sorts already and this ingenuous hint was too much. He had picked up his pen, but now he threw it savagely across the room.

"Oh, for heaven's sake!" he snapped. "How many times must I tell you fellows that the *Eagle* is mine and not Bates's or Dean's—no, nor Blake's? If I want to support Carmi Blake, I shall support him. If I decide to support the village idiot, I'll support *him*. Or, if I choose, I'll support nobody. I've made that sort of statement from one end of Wellmouth to the other, and not a soul seems to believe it. You and Tip might print a few posters to that effect and we'll hang 'em in the post office; maybe that'll help. You make me tired."

Elisha shook his head. "Sorry, Frank," he said. "I know you're independent as a hog on ice. I like you for it—yes, and so does Nellie. It must be fine to know, same as you do, that you're your own boss, and don't owe nobody a single cent. . . . Gorry, yes!"

He limped out, shaking his head. Franklin Cobb rose from his desk and, walking to the window, stood gazing out over the First Meeting House graveyard. Elisha's parting remark had cooled his temper like a bucket of ice water. It had reminded him that he owed Captain Gideon Bates—or the Wellmouth Bank, which appeared to be the same thing—four thousand dollars.

Not that he had been unaware of it before. It was not news. But what else was it Dodson had said? "There will be other candidates, of course, and the *Eagle* can't afford to take chances."

By George, it couldn't! that was a fact. He did not like the idea.

CHAPTER XVI

THE formal announcement of Blake's candidacy caused no great sensation. As Cobb had told Blake himself, it was old news by this time. The *Eagle* mentioned the subject several times and in several different ways in its news columns and continued to do so. There were rumors that there would be other candidates in the field, but there were, as yet, no other names mentioned with certainty. The town's Republican caucus would not be held for many months. Wellmouth was already talking politics, but not—as it would be later—to the exclusion of anything else.

Victoria came home for the Christmas holidays. There were parties and dances and dinners, to all of which Franklin was invited and most of which he attended. He saw Captain Bates frequently, and at two of the dinners Judge Dean was a guest. Neither of them mentioned the Blake name in their conversations with the *Eagle's* proprietor nor did they refer to the succession of news items in which the paper featured Captain Carmi's candidacy. Franklin could not help wondering if the threat of secession at the other end of the town really troubled them as little as it appeared to do.

Victoria continued to be just Victoria. Each function which he attended found her, or so it seemed to him, wearing a new frock, very becoming and also, he imagined, very expensive. Her father's present to her at Christmas was a pendant which must have cost quite as much as the *Eagle's* net profit amounted to in six months. His own gift, a plain gold brooch, looked very cheap and trivial compared with it; yet he had spent more for it than he should have afforded, he knew. How in the world could he ever hope to support a wife who had been accustomed to such luxury?

He mentioned his misgivings to her on Christmas afternoon, one of the very few occasions when they were alone together in the Bates's parlor.

"I ought to give you a ring, Vic," he said, ruefully. "I shall some of these days, of course, but, if you don't mind, I had rather wait until I can buy one such as I want you to have. That I can't afford yet."

She did not appear to understand.

"Oh, but I like the brooch ever so much. Truly I do. And I've got lots of rings."

"Yes, but I mean a—well, a particular sort of ring, you know."

She looked at him quickly—and rather oddly, he thought.

"Oh!" she said, demurely, "does that mean that we are engaged?"

"Why—why, we are, aren't we?"

She laughed. "Oh, I suppose it amounts to that. You haven't told any one we were, have you?"

"No," indignantly. "Of course I haven't."

"I'm glad. You mustn't—for ever and ever so long. An engaged girl doesn't have half as good a time. She must do this, and she can't do that. Besides, it is lots more fun to keep people wondering and suspecting and guessing. Oh, now, *don't* look so solemn and woebegone and unhappy. You are happy, aren't you, Frank? I think you ought to be."

He declared that he was very happy indeed.

"So am I. And I must go back to that old Academy in a week. Now don't let's spoil everything by talking about solemn engagements and marriages and money. They make me feel as old as Mrs. Methuselah. Let's be happy just as we are; shall we?"

They were—very happy indeed. And, as he reflected after his return to his room in the Dodson cottage, perhaps, all things considered, it was just as well—for the present, at any rate.

He saw her almost every evening during that next week, and, on one occasion when they happened to be speaking of the *Eagle* and his business, she dropped a hint concerning the political situation which gave him an insight into the minds of the Four Corners "group."

"I hardly see Papa at all nowadays, except at meal times," she said. "Judge Dean and Manasseh Eldredge—isn't Manasseh the *weirdest* name you ever heard?—are running in to see him almost every hour in the day, or he is holding 'conferences' with them and Mr. Haven somewhere. He won't tell me what it is all about, but I'm sure it is politics. They seem to get the greatest fun out of their stupid old politics, just as if it was some sort of a game. Do *you* know why they are so much interested just now, Frank?"

Franklin could guess. "I imagine it may be Captain Blake's candidacy that is troubling them," was his suggestion.

She tossed her head. "I don't believe anything Carmi Blake could do would trouble my father much," she observed, contemptuously. "Those Blakes are just South Siders and pretty common ones at that. It is the Four Corners that counts here in Wellmouth."

"But this time the South Side seems to have a mind of its own. It wants something."

Another toss of the head. "Who cares what it wants? It will have to take what the Four Corners gives it. It always has, and it always will."

She left on the morning of January second and Franklin settled himself to the dull routine of news gathering, printing, and paying and sending out bills. The new bookkeeper seemed to be learning his duties and was hard-working and faithful, so it was no longer necessary that Cobb and Elisha should spend their evenings at the office. Nevertheless, now that Victoria's society was no longer available, Franklin occasionally did spend an evening there. It was a quiet spot in which to write letters. At the Dodson house he ran the risk of meeting Carmi Blake and, although the pair always exchanged nods and brief greetings when they did meet, there was awkward embarrassment on both sides, especially when Helen was present.

On one of these evenings, late in the month, as Franklin sat at the desk in the little back room, writing his daily letter to Victoria, some one knocked on the front door of the shop. He rose and, walking through the dark press room and outer office, opened the door. A dignified voice bade him a gracious good evening. He leaned forward to peer at the speaker.

"Who—" he began. And then, "Why, yes, of course, Good evening, Judge. Won't you come in?"

Judge Joel Dean cleared his throat.

"Why, thank you," he said. "Are you alone? Good. Very good. I hoped you might be. Yes, with your permission, I will come in. . . . Oh, I can find my way. I used to know it very well in your uncle's day."

In the little room at the rear—there were two chairs now— the judge seated himself. He put his tall hat on the desk, stroked his beard, crossed his knees and regarded the young man benignantly. Franklin, tipped back in the desk chair, returned the look, trying his best to appear casual and not in the least curious. He was curious, however. Joel Dean had once promised to drop in at the *Eagle* office frequently, but that was months ago and this was the first call. What had brought him there now, at nine o'clock at night?

"A fine winter evening, Judge," said Cobb. Dean nodded, thereby giving the impression that he was doing the weather a favor by approving of it.

"Very, very—yes. A cozy little office you have here, Franklin."

"Cozy—and little, that's a fact."

"Yes—yes. It seems strange not to see my dear old friend,

Beriah. Well, this is a world of change; we are here to-day and gone to-morrow."

Franklin agreed with this not too original statement, but made no comment. His visitor stroked his beard and fidgeted with his spectacles. Then he leaned forward.

"Franklin," he said.

"Yes, sir."

"Franklin, I—er—I called here this evening—I came—ahem—well, I came to talk with you concerning the political situation in our township. It is—well, shall I say somewhat unusual."

"Oh, indeed?"

"Yes. Yes, it *is* unusual. Heretofore, as you doubtless know, a certain few of us—men who have the interests of Wellmouth at heart—have been intrusted with the—er—selection of our public office holders and representatives. We —this little group of public-spirited citizens— Yes? . . . You were about to say?"

Franklin had not spoken, nor had he any intention of doing so. He had smiled, involuntarily, when the judge used the word "group," that was all.

"Nothing. Go on, please."

"Yes—er, yes. Well, as I say, for a number of years, our little group at the Corners has used its best judgment and effort, with considerable sacrifice on its part, in selecting the town's candidate for public office."

"You mean the Republican candidates?"

"Certainly," with dignity. "This is, by a large majority, a Republican district. The Republican nomination is equivalent to election. Most of our nominees for—ahem—important offices have been Four Corners men, simply because the Corners is—as of course you have come to realize during your residence among us—the most important and—er—solid section of our community. The town as a whole understands this and had been quite content to have the Four Corners

represent it in—er—the Legislature, on the bench, and—er—
elsewhere. This has been the rule among us for some time
—since the beginning of the late war in fact. But—*but*—"
he paused, and then added impressively, "there must be, at
times, exceptions to all rules."

Franklin, who had begun to feel that he was again a small
boy listening to a stump speech, stirred impatiently.

"And this year," he said, with a nod, "the South Side is
making the exception. I know that, Judge. It promises to
be a lively exception, too. They mean business down there."

Dean was obviously a trifle taken aback by this abrupt
coming to the point. Having been, however, so unceremoniously pushed off the platform, he made the best of it and the
tone of his next remark was more human.

"They say they do," he agreed, with a patronizing smile.
"Yes, they say so. But, if the Four Corners— Oh, well, that
is not worth discussing at this hour in the evening. They are
anxious to have a South Side man represent us in the State
Legislature for the next term—or two terms—and Captain
Blake is their candidate for the nomination. Your paper published his statement, and it has published various news items
concerning his candidacy."

"Just as it will publish statements and news of any other
candidates, provided there are any."

"Certainly, certainly. That is perfectly right. I am glad
you are publishing the Blake news, Franklin. Captain Bates
is glad; he wished me to tell you so. We hope you will keep
on publishing it. And," lifting a hand and speaking very
earnestly, "we are hoping you may be willing to do more than
that."

Franklin did not understand at all.

"More?" he repeated.

"Yes. We are hoping that the *Eagle* will support Captain
Blake for the nomination—editorially, I mean."

This was a stunning surprise. Cobb could scarcely believe he had heard correctly.

"You want the *Eagle* to support Carmi Blake?" he gasped. "*You* do—you and Captain Bates and the rest? You *want* a South Sider in the State House? Why, you just said—"

"One moment. I said there were exceptions to all rules. We have decided that this is the year for an exception. The South Side is, after all, a considerable part of our town and a busy part. There is no reason why, occasionally, it should not—ahem—receive political recognition, provided, of course, that the—er—rest of us are satisfied with the caliber of the person it selects."

"And Blake satisfies you? . . . Well, well!"

"You are surprised? Why?"

"Oh, well—somehow I should have expected a—but it doesn't matter. This is very interesting, Judge Dean."

The judge stroked his beard thoughtfully. When he spoke it was with a slight return of the oratorical roll.

"Captain Blake," he declaimed, "is, in his way, a very able man. Self-educated, of course, and—er—perhaps a trifle less polished than the type Wellmouth has been in the habit of selecting for its nominee; but shrewd and—er—competent and —er—well, in general admirably fitted for public office. You know him quite well, I understand?"

"Yes, I know him."

"What do you think of him?"

"Do you mean as a man, or a politician?"

"Why—er—both, I suppose."

Franklin smiled. "As a man," he said, "I think he is all right. Blunt and with opinions of his own, but absolutely honest. I'm not as sure, though, that he will make a good politician. I very much doubt if he can be led except where he wants to go, and I'm dead certain that he is no diplomat."

Even the solemn Dean was obliged to smile at this estimate.

"Let us hope he won't need to be led," he observed. "I see you do know him. Well, Franklin, I'll tell you this in confidence—all of this talk of ours must be strictly confidential, of course—I'll tell you that the Republican Town Committee, of which I am one, have been in conference with Captain Carmi and he seems to agree with us on all points of public policy. All, at least, that were discussed at the conference," he added, apparently as an afterthought.

"Does he? That is interesting, too. Then he is to be the Committee's choice at the caucus?"

"Well—yes. But that need not be stressed in your paper just yet."

Franklin had by no means recovered from his surprise, but he believed that he was beginning to understand. The powers were convinced that an open fight in the party would be bad policy, and even dangerous, with an opposition such as the South Side could arouse throughout the district. Therefore they had decided to swallow the Blake pill. Whew! it must have been hard to swallow.

"Well, Judge Dean," he asked, "just what is it you want me—or the *Eagle*—to do?"

His caller leaned forward; he was not orating now. His language was no longer stilted, and he spoke briskly and to the point.

"Why, begin to play up the Blake candidacy in your paper. Give him all the favorable news items you can and mention his name on the editorial page. Not too often at first, but more and more often during the winter. Then, later on, when the caucus is held, you will be in a position to pitch in and support him until convention time and, after that, until election day. Oh, I know it is early now, months early, but Wellmouth and the district are in for a lively campaign this year. If there should be any opposition we want it stepped on before it starts. You see what I mean?"

"You think there will be opposition?"

"There is bound to be some. Orham—or the committee there—may not entirely agree with us as to the advisability of Blake's nomination. Of course it is Wellmouth's turn to nominate, but—well, some of the South Side people have been talking a good deal and there is an impression that Blake is their candidate and not the choice of the Wellmouth Committee. We want that impression wiped out. He *is* to be our candidate and, before long it must be understood that he is. We want the *Eagle* to prepare the way."

Franklin nodded. Judge Dean had, possibly, been a trifle more frank than he meant to be and in Cobb's mind the situation was now as clear as day. The group had been forced, no matter how much against its will, to the realization that Carmi Blake must, for safety's sake, be given the nomination; but it had no intention of losing its position as political dictator in Wellmouth. The flag of rebellion having been hoisted, the wise procedure was to proclaim that the established government had hoisted it and that, therefore, there was no rebellion at all.

"Will you do this for us, Franklin?" asked Joel Dean. "I told you, I think, that Captain Bates asked me to say he very much hoped you would."

Franklin hesitated, but not for long. There was no love lost between Carmi Blake and himself, but, as a matter of common decency, that should not influence him. And, in spite of himself, he could not help respecting and, in a way, liking the fellow's outspoken, dogged honesty. Besides, Carmi had definitely refused to accept the *Eagle's* support—moreover, had at first ordered him to keep his name out of the paper entirely. Supporting his candidacy, under such circumstances, would be fun. Sneer at the *Eagle's* independence, would he!

"All right, Judge," he said, shortly. "I don't see why not. . . . Yes, I'll do it."

Judge Dean's countenance, as much as could be seen of it

above the majestic beard, beamed. He rose and extended his hand.

"Thank you, Franklin," he said. "You are a—er—public-spirited and patriotic young man. The *Eagle* will lose nothing by this, I assure you."

Franklin rose, too. "Oh, just a minute, Judge," he said. Then, quizzically: "How does Captain Bates like the idea of the nomination of a South Sider? Delighted, is he?"

Dean shot a glance at him through the gold-rimmed spectacles.

"Captain Bates never permits personal preference to stand in the way of the community's welfare," he proclaimed grandly. "The good of Wellmouth and the party are, in his mind, above everything else."

"I see. It is really settled then. You and Blake are in complete agreement. By George, this is the most surprising news I have heard for a long time."

"Surprising? . . . Why?"

"Oh, I don't know. . . . Yes, I do, too. To be frank, Judge Dean, I didn't think the Four Corners and the South Side were likely to come to an agreement so easily; they have been pretty sore down there for some time. I rather expected a fight."

The Dean smile was bland. "The surest way to cure a sore is to soothe rather than irritate it," he observed, with a dignified wink. "Captain Bates will be pleased with your attitude, Franklin. He is greatly interested in you and your future, young man. He is a friend worth having. I think he has proved that to you in a substantial way, hasn't he? Ha, ha! Yes. . . . Well, good evening, good evening."

Franklin accompanied him to the outer door and then returned to the desk chair to think. The reference to Captain Gideon's "substantial" proof of friendship could mean but one thing—the four-thousand-dollar note at the bank. Of course Dean would know about that, he was one of the bank directors, but nevertheless it was irritating to have him refer to it in that patronizing way. There were no strings tied to that loan, no outside obligations of any kind—he had Bates's word for that.

And then came the comforting reflection that this decision of the group to endorse and support Blake would make it very much easier for the *Eagle* in the coming campaign. There would be no fight now. No friendships broken, no—quoting Elisha Dodson—"chances" to be taken. The Wellmouth *Eagle* had always been a staunch Republican paper supporting the regular candidates of that party. It could support Carmi Blake for the State Legislature now without running any risks and with a clear conscience. And the best of it was that Blake himself could find no reasonable fault with that procedure. He might, and probably would, resent it, but he could not accuse Franklin Cobb of taking orders from the Four Corners. After all the defiant threatenings and bluster of Blake and his South Side backers, when the group offered its endorsement that offer had been promptly and meekly accepted. And Carmi had called him—Cobb—a bluffer! Good Lord, what a joke!

He wrote his first editorial reference to the Blake candidacy the next morning. It was not long, nor overemphatic. He merely referred to the coming campaign, to Wellmouth's opportunity that year to nominate an able citizen to represent the district in the State Legislature, and expressed the hope that the right man would receive the nomination. Then he went on to add that there was already one Republican candidate openly in the field, one whose reputation for ability and integrity was highest.

"All Wellmouth—yes, all Ostable County—knows and admires him," he wrote in conclusion. "There will doubtless be other names offered for our consideration—the caucus is still a long way off—but a high standard has been set and should the nomination fall to Captain Carmi Blake each Republican voter in Ostable County will cast his ballot next fall with confidence and trust."

Elisha, hobbling in with his eyeshade over his left ear and a packet of proof slips in his inky hand, read the editorial with astonishment. He was obviously pleased but a little doubtful.

"Why—why, Frank," he stammered. "This sounds as if you are goin' to support Carmi, after all. Thought you said the *Eagle* would support who it darned pleased."

"Well, so it will. That doesn't pledge us to anything, does it?"

"Don't know's it does, only—"

"Only what?"

"Only Cap'n Gideon and Joe Dean and the rest may get the notion that—that—"

"That we're darned pleased to support Blake. Suppose they do—what then?"

"Why—well, you and I might as well face facts, I cal'late—they may not like it, that's all."

Cobb laughed aloud. "You'll be surprised to see how well they like it, Elisha," he declared. "I've got a story to tell you sometime—not yet though. Don't worry. Everything is all right."

Dodson was by no means so assured that everything was all right and Tip, when he read the proof of that editorial, was absolutely certain that it was all wrong.

"I'm goin' to look for another job," he vowed. "This paper's on skids and headed down hill from now on. Judas! I wisht I was rich. If some of them girls I've had mashed on me in my time had had money, I'd have married by now and wouldn't have to work. Well, maybe 'tain't too late yet."

But when the editorial appeared there was no remonstrance from the Four Corners magnate nor his henchmen. Elisha and Cahoon were not the only ones who were surprised by their placid attitude. Other references of a similar complimentary nature were printed in later issues and these, too, seemed to provoke no resentment. Then it began to be whispered about that the Republican Committee were inclined to favor, rather than oppose, Carmi Blake's nomination. And, when the spring weather burst the buds on the lilac bushes in Wellmouth's yards, and daffodils splashed with yellow the beds by the doorsteps, the Blake campaign was in full bloom and, generally speaking, in full favor with the Republican voters. Of course there was some grumbling among certain irreconcilables at the Four Corners, but even they were coming around. Manasseh Eldredge expressed himself as willing to admit that there were a lot worse fellows at the Boston State House than Captain Carmi ever was or ever would be. "He ain't a Gideon Bates nor a Joel Dean, I give in," proclaimed Manasseh, "but, leavin' out them—and maybe one or two others I could mention—he's as good as any candidate we're liable to scare up. Vote for him? Why, sure I will. He'll get the nomination; looks that way now, anyhow."

The *Eagle's* support was no longer hinted at nor guarded. It was open and avowed. Other names which had been whispered about as those of possible rivals for the nomination were withdrawn or their owners stated publicly that they had never contemplated making the race. The story was that in Orham, the other town in the district, conditions were similar to those in Wellmouth. Blake seemed assured of undisputed support there also. The "lively campaign" which every one had prophesied appeared to have become a walk-away. The town Republican caucus would be but a formality, the district convention another, and the election merely a matter of counting the majority.

CHAPTER XVII

JUDGE DEAN called frequently at the *Eagle* office nowadays and Captain Bates semioccasionally. To Franklin's surprise neither of them had offered to supervise the political editorials nor to criticize those written. The other members of the Four Corners "group"—Manasseh Eldredge and Cornelius Haven in particular—were friendly. Elisha Dodson ceased to be apprehensive and even Tip, although he still professed to be "sick and disgusted" with the idea of a South Sider representing him in the State Legislature, spoke no more of hunting another situation. All was serene, like the proverbial calm before a storm, but in this case there seemed no indication whatever of even a light wind.

Bates, when he called one day early in June, had a suggestion to make. Coming from him it was, of course, offered more as a command than a suggestion.

"Frank," he said, puffing at his usual black cigar, "have you ever thought of getting into politics yourself?"

"I?" with a laugh. "Well, hardly, Captain Bates."

"Why not? It isn't a bad thing for a young fellow like you, and owner and editor of the leading paper in the county."

"Elisha is the editor, sir. I'm only the owner."

"Yes," dryly, "so I hear you say. But I doubt if 'Lish Dodson would get very far in politics, and I shouldn't wonder if you might—in time. . . . See here, Frank, you will be on hand at the caucus, of course?"

"Why, yes, sir, I surely shall unless I'm sick or something like that."

"Humph! Don't expect to be sick, do you?"

"No, sir," with a laugh, "but—well, the caucus is a good way off."

"Not so far—couple of months, that's all. I want you to be on hand and if you should make a speech there, it wouldn't do you any harm. You've been whooping for Blake in the *Eagle;* whoop for him in the caucus. Let's see what sort of a talker you are; we know you can write well enough."

Cobb found the idea amusing.

"I never made a speech in my life," he said, grinning. "Besides, the way things look now, speeches won't be necessary. The Committee's slate will go through without any opposition, or so every one seems to think. The convention delegates appointed will all be instructed for Blake, won't they, sir?"

"Guess likely they will. Looks so now, but that's all right. We're going to make you one of those delegates and, in case the Orham crowd aren't instructed at their caucus, we want you to help instruct them."

Franklin whistled. "You're going to make *me* a delegate to the district convention?" he repeated. "Why, nobody knows me—outside of Wellmouth, I mean."

"Oh, yes, they do. Orham folks read the *Eagle,* and I have heard a number of them say good things about it lately."

"Well, that's nice of them. But I can't quite see why you should feel that the Orham delegation are likely to come uninstructed. From what I hear Orham is all for Blake."

"Yes, yes, I know it is." He knocked the ashes from his cigar into the wastebasket. "We're wasting a lot of time over nothing," he went on. "You're going to be made a delegate to that convention, boy, and the better impression you can make on the crowd there the better for you. Oh, stop arguing," impatiently. "Do you suppose I'm telling you this for my sake? I'm not, I'm giving you a tip for your own good. There are chances for a smart young fellow like you in politics in this district and there will be more as time goes along.

Some of these days we may be sending *you* to the State House; queerer things than that have happened. . . . One of 'em is happening right now. Lord A'mighty!" with a snort, "I never thought I'd live to see the day when *I* should help send a South Sider there."

He rose to go, but Cobb was curious.

"Excuse me, Captain Bates," he said, impulsively, "I—I suppose you're right; it might be a good thing for me, with my business, to become better known through the district. But—"

"But what? What else is on your mind?"

"Why—I can't help wondering how you—for I'm sure you are responsible—ever happened to think of giving me this chance?"

The mogul regarded him good-naturedly; he even chuckled.

"Oh, it just happened to strike me," he replied. "For one thing it is time we had some new blood in the party around here. Joe Dean and I are getting older, we won't live forever, and it is a good idea to train somebody to handle things the right way after we're gone. Then, besides, I have a notion it will please Vic. You and she seem to be pretty chummy and I like to help her friends when I can. She's a smart girl, Victoria is, even if I am her father," with another chuckle.

At the door he made one more remark, one which Franklin did not understand at all.

"We're going to miss her this summer," he said. "Her mother and I will be lonesome enough. . . . No, no, I can't stop any longer. Got to go to another one of Joe Dean's 'conferences.' He is holding 'em now every few minutes. I tell him he's got the conference disease. Good-by."

What on earth did he mean by "missing" his daughter? In her letters she had said nothing about going away.

She said it in her next letter, however. She had some news to break to him, perfectly dreadful news she was sure it would be for him and—he just must believe this—it was dreadful for her, too, in a way. But it was such a wonderful opportunity; she had never really traveled in all her life and these people she was going with were the loveliest, kindest, nicest people. He could not blame her; she was sure he wouldn't when he thought it over. And he would forgive her, wouldn't he? If he did not she would never, never, *never* forgive herself.

And so on for another page. Then—perhaps considering that, by this time, he ought to be prepared for almost any shock—she told her plans.

A very dear friend of hers at the Academy—"the dearest girl you ever can think of, Frank; you simply *must* meet her some day"—was going, with her parents, to visit relatives in Michigan. "They have a summer home on the lake up there —a sort of glorified camp it is, with boats and fishing and lots of young people and everything—and Belle—that is her name, you know—has invited me to spend two whole months there. At first, of course, I said I couldn't possibly leave home. I was thinking of some one—I *hope* you can guess who— when I said that, but she coaxed and coaxed and then I said I would see. And so, at last, I wrote to Papa and Mother about it and, when *they* said they were willing I should do it, I said 'yes' to Belle. I didn't write you, dearest boy, because I *hated* to; I knew *just* how you would feel; but now that it is really settled and I am going, I knew I *had* to tell you. Oh, I shall see you before I go, of course. Belle and I don't start until nearly the last of the month after commencement, you know—and I shall come to Wellmouth for three or four days before I leave for Michigan. You *do* forgive me, don't you? Please write that in your very next letter. If you knew how terribly I feel—" etc., etc.

Franklin's feelings when he read the last word of this twelve-page epistle were an odd mixture. He should have been wretched at the prospect of a summer without Victoria. In a measure he was, he would miss her very much; but there

were some compensations. This was sure to be a busy summer—now that he had enlisted in the political ranks it would
be busier than ever—and, at least he would be free from social
distractions and could give all his time to work. And underneath all was a certain feeling of resentment. Why had she
waited until the very last moment, until everything was settled and her plans all made, before she wrote him a line
concerning her project? She had consulted her father and
mother; she had asked their advice. Surely, if all her protests of undying affection meant anything at all, his wishes
and his feelings ought to count as much as any one's with
her. He did not like her keeping such a secret from him. He
could not help wondering how many other secrets she might
be keeping.

He dismissed the thought, however—or tried to—and wrote
at once that he considered her quite right in taking advantage of such an opportunity. He and she would talk it all
over when she came home. Then, as a help to temporary
forgetfulness, he began a long editorial urging all Wellmouth's
Republican voters to get together, overlook all sectional differences, and work from now until after election for the
nominees of the party.

He told the Dodsons of Captain Bates's call and the great
man's announcement that he—Franklin Cobb—was to be a
delegate to the district convention. He told it as a grand
joke.

"So your boarder is going into politics," he said, with a
broad grin. "He'll be a howling success at it, won't he?"

"Course you will," vowed Elisha. "That's the best news
I've heard for a long spell. Fine for the *Eagle,* too. You'll
be right on the inside from now on, won't you, Frank? Say,
this'll tickle the South Side folks; they're strong for us down
there these days. The South Side advertisin' has picked up
fifty per cent since you came out for Carmi."

"Why don't you think you will make a success of politics,

Frank?" asked Helen. He looked at her; she seemed perfectly sincere.

"Why?" he repeated. "Well, for one reason because I am such a tactful rooster. The first day after I landed in Wellmouth I had a fight with Manuel, that Portuguese chap; and inside of that same week I had a row with the Sardine and his 'group.' That was a good start. And then, a month or two ago, I had one with—"

He stopped short. He had been very careful never to mention his lively disagreement with Carmi Blake. He was certain that Blake had not mentioned it, either. And now the latter's name was on the very tip of his tongue. He almost bit that tongue in his anxiety to cut the sentence short.

"With who?" asked Elisha. "I didn't know you had any more fights, Frank. Who was this one with?"

"Oh, nobody," hastily. "What I am trying to say is that a fellow with as little diplomacy in his make-up as I seem to have isn't likely to make friends in a slippery game like politics. I ought to take lessons from Manasseh."

Helen smiled. "His slipperiness hasn't got him very far yet," was her comment. "He has been trying to wiggle himself into some sort of office for a long time, but he is just where he started. I don't believe he could be elected pound-keeper—or even nominated."

Her father chuckled. "Lots of folks would feel that he'd have to be locked in the pound himself afore they could depend on knowin' just where he stood for five minutes at a time."

"Huh!" grunted Franklin. "I had gathered that Manasseh Eldredge was a very popular man in the community. Every time I go into his store there is a circle of admirers around him, watching and listening."

"Mainly watchin', I guess likely. . . . Oh, I don't suppose I ought to talk like this. Manasseh's a smart fellow, in his way. Only—only—well, the last time I talked with him—

yesterday it was—he sort of made me mad. I was sayin' somethin' about Cap'n Carmi, what a big majority he'd have at the polls and all that, and I'm blessed if he would do anything but sniff. 'Got to get himself nominated first,' he said. I stared at him. 'Why, he's as good as nominated already,' I told him. 'I've heard you say so, yourself, much as a dozen times. And everybody else says it, too. What in the world are you blowin' hot and cold like this for? *Ain't* he goin' to be nominated?' He laughed and thumped me on the back, same as he always does, and I wish he wouldn't. 'Certain sure he is,' he says. But what a way that was to talk! By gorry, yes! he did make me kind of mad."

It took a good deal to make Elisha Dodson "mad" and this outburst from him was decidedly unexpected. Helen's next question harked back to the beginning of the conversation.

"I can't see that what you call your lack of tact has hurt you much so far, Frank," she said. "So far as your trouble with Judge Dean and Captain Gideon goes they seem to be your stoutest backers just now. Why, it was Captain Bates who picked you for a delegate and came to tell you so. And Judge Dean must have agreed with him, I should say. And as for Carmi—well, he told me recently that he thought you were just the sort of man Wellmouth needed to own and run its newspaper. I never heard him say that about your uncle."

Franklin turned quickly, but Elisha asked his question for him.

"What makes you say 'As for Carmi,' Nellie?" he queried. "We was talkin' about folks Frank had had rows with, wasn't we?"

She nodded. "Yes, I believe we were," she replied, and went into the kitchen.

Franklin followed her there a few minutes later. The hint she had dropped, or he imagined she had dropped, made him uneasy. If Carmi Blake had told her the story of their quarrel—he could scarcely believe the big fishing skipper had done such a thing, it did not seem like him—but *if* he had, he, Cobb, was at least entitled to the opportunity of stating his side of the case.

He was standing beside her, wondering whether or not to broach the dangerous subject, when she saved him the trouble.

"Frank," she asked, putting down the dish towel and facing him squarely, "what is the trouble between you and Carmi?"

"Trouble? . . . Why, what trouble do you mean?"

"Don't you know? I think you do. You don't, either of you, mention the other, in my presence anyhow, unless some one like Father or me drags it out of you by main strength. . . . Oh," cutting in ahead of his remonstrance with an impatient gesture, "I don't mean about his running for office or his political chances. You are always ready to talk about those things. But you never refer to him personally, never speak of him as a friend. Now do you?"

He dodged the issue.

"Does he ever speak of me in that way?"

"Well—no, he doesn't. His praise of your management of the *Eagle* was only an answer to my straight question. And when you two·meet—oh, I have watched you often enough— you both are as short and formal, almost, as if you were strangers. Something must have happened to make you that way. Now please tell me the truth. There was something, wasn't there?"

He hesitated, and that hesitation was a blunder for she accepted it as an affirmative.

"I knew it," she declared. "Now what was it? I want to know."

She should never know if he could help it, but he realized that she must be partially satisfied somehow or other.

"Oh, well," he said, with a shrug, "he and I had some words down at his office one day. He accused me of being a—a hired man for Bates and Dean and ordered me never to mention his name in my paper—which, so he said, was their paper. I told him that it was my paper and that I should mention his name, or any one else's, in it as often as I saw fit. We ended, I believe, by telling each other to go to the devil. I haven't gone there yet, and he doesn't like it, I suppose."

"And that was all?"

"Oh, there was more—of the same sort. We were both pretty hot under the collar."

She appeared to be thinking it over. Then she smiled ruefully.

"You men are ridiculous creatures, if you only knew it. And when two of you are as much alike as Carmi and you are, that makes everything ridiculously worse, of course."

"Alike! Blake and I alike? How, for heaven's sake?"

"In almost every way. You are both proud, and stubborn as mules, and both so afraid that people won't believe in the independence you are always talking about. In all common sense you ought to be bosom friends, but you are not because two people so very much alike seldom are. Each thinks, I suppose, that there can't possibly be another person quite as all right as he is."

His momentary resentment vanished and he laughed aloud. If she was satisfied with this explanation of the quarrel he certainly was—and very much relieved. He hoped that Blake, when she questioned him, would tell the same story. The chances were he would; he could scarcely tell the entire truth.

"Franklin," she said, "tell me truly now. Don't you like Carmi Blake—underneath all this foolishness, I mean."

He nodded. "Yes, I do," he admitted. "I like him well enough. . . . At least I don't dislike him as he does me."

"He doesn't dislike you—not really; I'm sure he doesn't. Frank, you said to me once, when we were talking about this very thing, that you would like to like him because he was a friend of mine. He is—and so are you—and I like my friends to like each other."

The result of this conversation was that the next time Franklin and Carmi Blake met—it was at the South Side a day or two later—instead of returning the latter's nod with another as curt, Cobb stepped in front of him and held out his hand.

"Cap'n Carmi," he said, with a smile, "you and I had a few short and snappy words in your office a while ago and we haven't had many words together since. It seems rather foolish to me. I'm willing to forgive and forget, or something like that. What do you say?"

Blake looked down at him.

"Nellie been talkin' to you?" he asked, gruffly.

"Yes. Has she been talking to you?"

"Um-hm. . . . See here, you didn't tell her what we was really fightin' about? You didn't fetch her name into your yarn anywhere?"

"Hardly . . . and, if you will remember, it wasn't I who brought it in that day at your office. You did that."

"I know it. . . . Seemed to me then that I had good reasons."

"And of course you know now that you didn't have."

"Why, it looks—well, you've acted square enough since, far as I can make out."

"Good. Are you satisfied with what the *Eagle* is doing to push your campaign?"

"Couldn't very well help bein'. Tell me this, though: Did Dean, or any of his committee, ask you—after they and I had had our conference, I mean—did they ask you to have the *Eagle* come out for me?"

"Why—well, yes, they did."

"Would you have supported me if they hadn't asked?"

"I don't know. I think I should. I might have waited to see who the other candidates were before I made any decision, but when I had made it I should have stuck to it, committee or no committee."

"You mean that?"

"Certainly I mean it. Look here, Blake—"

"There, there, I believe you. Nellie says she told you that you was as stubborn a mule as I am, and I presume likely she's right. Both of us too stubborn for our own good, maybe."

He frowned, seemed to be about to add something further and then to change his mind. "Well," he said, after a moment, "if you feel like droppin' in for news same as you used to, you can, I guess."

"Thanks, I will. Congratulations on winning your fight, Captain."

"What fight? Oh, for the nomination, you mean? So it's won, is it?"

"I should say so. With no other candidates in the field and both caucuses, here and at Orham, sure to send delegations instructed for you to the convention, it can't help being won, can it?"

Blake grunted. For a certain winner he seemed rather gloomy, Franklin thought.

Victoria came home as she had promised, the last week in June and, considering that it was to be their last week together until September, he saw distressingly little of her. She and her mother were busy with dressmakers and milliners, there was a great deal of packing to be done, friends of the family were calling every evening to say good-by, and Franklin found himself, figuratively speaking, pushed into a corner whenever he visited the Bates mansion. Even their own good-bys were hurried and not very satisfactory. He went to the railway station to see her off and, after watching the last car, with its handkerchief fluttering from the window, out of sight, he walked down to the *Eagle* office feeling, in spite of himself, rather neglected and with that same consciousness of resentment which he had felt when her letter came with the—to him—belated tidings of her going away.

But now, as then, there was plenty of work to help him forget any sense of injury, and her letters, when they began to arrive, helped still more. It did seem to him that she was not writing quite as frequently as she might have done or as he wrote her, but she explained that there were *so* many things going on, her hosts were giving her such a perfectly *wonderful* time, that she had scarcely a minute to herself.

July came and went and then August. The Republican caucuses in the two towns were to be held on the second of September. The candidates for minor offices on the ticket were selected, and Carmi Blake was reported to be absolutely assured of instructed delegates, not only in Wellmouth but in Orham, and, therefore, unanimous nomination at the convention which was to be held in Wellmouth on September fifteenth. Franklin Cobb's name as delegate was among those on the Committee's slate; Judge Dean smilingly showed it to him. The political weather forecast for Wellmouth and the district was "'Calm and Continued Fair." There were no clouds in the sky.

One afternoon, however, a few days before the date of the caucus, Franklin, on his way from the Dodson cottage to the print shop, saw Manasseh Eldredge standing by the steps of the Dean law office deep in conversation with the judge. They both looked troubled, or so it seemed to him. Manasseh was scowling, and his face was flushed and Dean, too, appeared disturbed and angry.

They did not notice his approach and, as he came within earshot, he heard Eldredge say: "It ain't any use, Judge, I tell you. He says he won't promise."

"But he has already promised. You told him that, didn't you?"

"Course I did, but he says the promise he made had nothin' to do with this thing as it looks to him now. He don't say he won't do it, but he does say he means to look into it first. He's heard somethin', somebody's been talkin' to him. Fact of the matter is, Joel, he's been spoiled. Everything has been goin' too smooth for him, and it's swelled his head."

The lawyer nodded. "You and I have seen swelled heads shrink before now, Manasseh," he observed, grimly. "And we have helped to shrink them. Look here, he will keep his other promise—not to mention a word about it? He swore not to whisper it to a soul until after election."

"Oh, yes, he won't tell. But that ain't goin' to help us much if— Oh, hello, Frank! You must wear them new kind of shoes they call 'sneakers'; I didn't hear you comin'."

Franklin did not linger. The fragment of conversation he had overheard vaguely interested him, but he forgot it almost immediately. And yet, if he had known, he might have established his reputation as a prophet by changing the political weather signals to "Squally and Threatening, with Storms to Follow."

CHAPTER XVIII

THE day of the caucus dawned dark and threatening, and by noon there was a drizzle of rain. When at half-past one Franklin mounted the steps of the town hall and entered the building, he was surprised to find so few of his Republican fellow townsmen present. Considering that the South Side was, for the first time in history, to take the initial step toward sending one of its residents to the State House, he had expected a crowd. His hasty look about resulted in an estimate that there were not more than forty men in the hall. Manasseh Eldredge was conspicuous, hat atilt, left thumb in his vest pocket, right hand, with a cigar stump between his fingers, gesticulating as he chatted with Noah Holway from East Wellmouth. Manasseh appeared serenely cheerful; evidently here, in the heart of the political puddle, he was a big frog and quite aware of it.

Judge Dean was nowhere in sight, nor was Captain Bates. Quite as surprising was the absence of South Side leaders. Abiathar Blake was not there, nor Captain Zenas Rogers, Maisie's father. And Captain Carmi, the hero of the hour, was nowhere in sight. Mr. Elkanah Rogers, the South Side shopkeeper, was on hand, however, and Franklin sought him out and asked questions.

"Ain't liable to be much of a turnout to-day," explained Rogers. "Oh, of course, if they knew there would be any kind of a fight on they'd come, but with everything all cut and dried the way 'tis, and it rainin' and all, they won't take the trouble. Carmi's goin' in, the slate with his delegates' names on it is made up. Just what you'd call a formality, I suppose likely 'tis, as you might say."

Franklin asked another question.

"Oh, yes, yes," replied Elkanah, "there'll be more comin' all the time now; we're early, you know, Frank. Bi Blake'll be here, of course, and Cap'n Zenas and Seth Briar and all the heads of Carmi's crowd. . . . Eh? Carmi himself? Well, I don't know. He's kind of funny, Carmi is. The Blake Brothers are unloadin' a schooner down to their wharf and, from what I hear, Carmi didn't want too many of the men nor both him and his brother away from there unless 'twas real necessary. 'Bi knows more about politics in a minute than I do in a year,' Cal Hammond told me Carmi told him. 'Bi'll look out for everything.' Now what do you think of that? The very man that all the fuss has been about! If 'twas me I'd have been camped on the steps afore the doors was open, but not Cap'n Carmi; he don't get excited easy. . . . Ha! See, Frank? What did I tell you? There comes Bi and Cap'n Zenas now."

Other arrivals followed. Elkanah, who was excited even if Carmi Blake was not, pointed them out.

"Here's Cornelius Haven," he said. "He's secretary of the Republican town committee. Joe Dean'll show up any minute now, and then we'll be ready to get goin'. Dean'll be permanent chairman and so we've got to wait till he comes."

"How do you know he'll be permanent chairman? The caucus elects its chairman, doesn't it?"

"Sartin sure, but it'll elect Dean. He's been chairman and Cornelius has been secretary ever since there was any Republicans. . . . Here he comes! You'd think he was king of Ostable County to look at him, wouldn't you?"

The remark had some truth in it. Judge Dean's progress toward the front of the hall was almost regal. Manasseh Eldredge hastened to shake hands with him. "Good afternoon" and "How d'you do, Judge?" greeted him, not only from Four Cornerites but from many South Siders as well. Force of habit is strong and the Honorable Joel R. Dean was still a force and a personage even where rebellion had reared its head.

"Humph!" grunted Franklin. "But he is only an imitation, after all. Where is the real emperor? Doesn't Captain Bates attend caucuses?"

It was evident from the tone of Mr. Rogers' reply, that, although the South Side had at last dared openly oppose the Four Corners, the majority of its citizens still stood in awe of their township's only millionaire.

"Oh, Cap'n Gideon don't have to tend up caucuses, nor anything else, unless he feels like it. He knows what's goin' to be done, you bet you, but he quite often don't bother to be around when the meetin' opens. He'll drop in by and by; leastways he always has."

The clock in the tower of the Four Corners First Meeting House boomed twice. Through the open windows of the hall—they had been opened to permit a modicum of pure air to dilute the clouds of tobacco smoke—the boom was audible.

"Two o'clock," whispered Elkanah Rogers. "Better set down, Frank; they're goin' to begin."

The settees filled. The buzz of talk subsided. Mr. Cornelius Haven, as secretary of the town committee, moved to the platform and, standing beside the table at its front center, rapped with the official gavel and bade the meeting come to order. His was not a powerful voice and, when he raised it to demand silence, it squeaked like a defective slate pencil.

Under the law of the Commonwealth of Massachusetts, he announced, this caucus of the Republican voters of the township of Wellmouth had been called. The first business before the meeting was the election of a permanent chairman and secretary. He had scarcely ceased speaking—or squeaking— when Manasseh Eldredge rose to propose the nomination of the Honorable Joel R. Dean as chairman. There was applause, more or less hearty, and several cries of "Second the motion." There being no other nomination Mr. Haven called for a vote, the Honorable Joel was unanimously elected and, majestically ascending to the platform, took the chair vacated by Cornelius, who slid into the chair at his elbow.

Then Dean, after a preliminary beard-stroking, suggested that, if it were the pleasure of the meeting, Mr. Cornelius Haven be chosen secretary. "If there are no objections—"

There were none, so Haven, who had already straightened the papers before him on the table and picked up the official pen, was duly installed.

Mr. Rogers whispered in the Cobb ear.

"See," he whispered. "I told you. It's always this way."

Judge Dean proceeded to make a speech. He paid tribute to the grand old flag, to the free and glorious country of which they had the honor to be citizens, to the wise and patriotic party to which they belonged, to their responsibility as free and independent voters to choose for their nominees men of unquestioned integrity and staunch loyalty. This, he declared, Wellmouth voters had always done and he was proudly confident that they would do it now and in the future. He finished with a peroration in which the names of Washington and Lincoln and the President and the Almighty were favorably mentioned. Then he paused for applause, which was gratifyingly loud and prolonged.

"Whew!" whispered Elkanah, with a sigh of admiration. "He's a slick speaker, Joe Dean is. Godfreys, I wish I could talk like that!"

The judge continued by saying that the caucus here gathered was particularly important because, according to established custom, it was Wellmouth's privilege and duty this year to send to the district convention delegates whose honor it would be to cast their ballots in that convention for one of Wellmouth's own citizens who, later on at the polls, would be the party's candidate for representative of the district in the State House of Representatives at Boston.

Great and continued applause. Judge Dean raised a hand
for silence.

"A moment, gentlemen, if you please," he begged. "The
present incumbent, our present representative from this district, is, as we all know, an Orham citizen of high repute
and established ability in the service of the party and the
people. He is retiring from public life to a well-earned rest
in the bosom of his family amid the happy surroundings of
his native town. All here present are acquainted with the
public-spirited work done by this man and for it, I am sure,
every man, woman and child in our community is deeply
grateful."

A voice from the floor—Franklin guessed it to be Manasseh
Eldredge's—called for three cheers for the Honorable Sylvanus
Shotwell. The cheers were duly given and a "tiger" added
for good measure. The chairman stroked his beard and
beamed, Mr. Haven nodded approval, and the assemblage
seemed to be enjoying itself. As the tumult subsided Mr.
Rogers, who had apparently taken upon himself the duty of
mentor to his young neighbor, whispered in the latter's ear:
"Sylvanus is Isaac Shotwell's brother. Ike Shotwell is quite
a fellow over to Orham. He's worth lots of money and him
and Cap'n Bates and Joe Dean and the rest are great chums.
All Gideon or Joel has to do is whistle and both Shotwells
come a-runnin'. Ike's a big-bug too and I bet you, down
underneath, he don't like the notion of sendin' a South Side
fishin' skipper to the State House any better than Dean does.
Well, I'm glad I've lived to see the day, that's all."

"And now," went on Judge Dean, "it devolves upon us to
proceed with the business before the meeting. As you know,
delegates must be named by this caucus to attend the State
convention in Boston, others to express, in the district convention to be held here on the fifteenth, our preference in the
choice of member of the upper house—the State Senate—and
for representative in the governor's council; and, last, but not

least," with a fatherly smile, "to vote in the said district convention, for the nominee who is to be our party's candidate at the polls for the high honor of acting as our representative in the assembly hall beneath the gilded dome on Beacon Hill."

More applause, whether for the chairman or the gilded dome Cobb was somewhat uncertain. Dean turned toward the expectant Haven.

"As is its duty," he announced, "your Republican town committee has prepared tentative lists of the various delegates. With your permission I shall ask the secretary to first read the names presented, for your approval, of course, to attend the Boston convention."

Mr. Haven, who had been holding slips of paper in his hand for a long ten minutes, rose and read. The names of the delegates to be sent to Boston were approved without discussion. Plainly the meeting was not particularly interested in them. So far, at least, the caucus was, as Elkanah Rogers had termed it, a "cut and dried" affair.

But, when the secretary began again to read, it was quite different. Every one was bending forward to listen.

"For delegates from this township to the district convention to be held here in Wellmouth on the fifteenth of the current month," squeaked Cornelius, "your committee presents the following names."

He proceeded to read the names. There were seven of them. Franklin Cobb's was one. He was more or less intimately acquainted with the owners of the others. Three of the seven—Eldredge, Dean and himself—were Four Corners men. Two—Abiathar Blake and Zenas Rogers—were from the South Side. The remaining two, Noah Holway and Darius Ward, hailed, respectively, from East Wellmouth and North Wellmouth.

"As you see," explained Judge Dean, blandly smiling, but with his glance roaming over the faces before and below him, "the committee has endeavored to make this a representative delegation, impartially—er—representing all sections of our community. If there are no objections, or other nominations, the list, as read, will now be voted upon. . . . *Are* there any objections?"

He paused. There was a buzz of whispering in several sections of the hall. Two or three men—South Siders—had risen and were clustered about Abiathar Blake and Captain Zenas Rogers. They seemed to be in earnest consultation.

The chairman rapped for order. "Is it the pleasure of the meeting that we proceed to vote upon the list as read?" he inquired.

Elmer Taylor, clerk in the Eldredge store, and one of Cobb's first acquaintances in Wellmouth—they having met the night of the cannon adventure—had risen.

"Mr. Chairman," he said, "I move that the list of delegates be approved unanimous. It's a good bunch of names, and I guess we all feel we couldn't do any better."

There were several cries of "Second the motion."

"It is moved—" began Dean, but he was interrupted. Captain Zenas Rogers was on his feet and demanding attention.

"Mr. Chairman," he began, "speaking as a citizen and a Republican voter, I want to say that I think the committee's list is a good one." (Cheers and cries of "That's right," "So it is," etc.) "Under ordinary circumstances I should be glad to vote for it just as it stands. But," emphatically, "it doesn't seem to me that the circumstances are ordinary, just now. It is the feeling among us South Side people that it is high time our section of the town sent a representative to the State House. We've made up our minds to do that very thing, everybody knows we have, and everybody knows, too, who we intend sending there."

But he got no further at the moment. There was a burst of hand clapping and stamping, punctuated with shouts. Some one whooped, "You bet they do!"

Judge Dean pounded with the gavel.

"Order! Order, gentlemen, if you please," he commanded. "Captain Rogers has the floor. Have you finished, Captain Rogers?"

The South Side magnate shook his head. "Not yet," he said. "What I want to say is just this: In that list of yours, Mr. Secretary, you've got one man from East Wellmouth, one from North Wellmouth, three from the Corners and two from the South Side. I am one of the two South Siders, and although I'm not anxious for the job—I'm getting older and electioneering and politics don't appeal to me the way they used to—nevertheless I'll take it if the caucus votes me in. But that's all to one side. What I say—and what I know a lot of my South Side neighbors and fellow citizens must be thinking—is that, with a South Side man as our candidate, it is the South Side, and not the Corners, who ought to have the most names on that list. Three South Siders, two from the Corners and one each from North and East Wellmouth. That's my only objection and the only change I suggest. Otherwise than that I'm satisfied."

He sat down, but the tumult and disorder grew and spread. Half a dozen lively altercations broke out in different parts of the gathering. No less than four men were trying to obtain recognition from the chair. Haven and Judge Dean were in whispered consultation. The latter rose, after an instant, and pounded with the gavel.

"A moment—one moment," he shouted. "Please be quiet. Mr. Haven has a word to say to you. Will you grant him the courtesy of silence?"

The courtesy was granted, but not too graciously. Mr. Haven's squeaky voice squeaked more than ever as he began to speak.

"Fellow citizens," he began, "we have all, of course, been much interested in what Captain Rogers has just said. And I guess we all realize that there's considerable sense in it, too. But as one of the town committee I just want to make it clear that, in picking out our delegates, we had his very point in mind. As he says, there are two from the South Side and one each from North and East Wellmouth. *But* when he says there are three from the Corners it seems to me that he is mistaken. Judge Dean and Mr. Eldredge are Four Corners men—yes. But the third name is that of a comparatively newcomer to our town and, although he does live a little nearer the Corners than he does any other section, it seemed to us that, as owner and managing editor of our local paper, he really represents all sections and that we might call him a—well, a sort of delegate at large. That was the committee's idea when it put him on the list and it seemed to us—and I must say it seems to me now—perfectly fair for everybody. . . . You see what I mean, Captain Rogers?"

He sat down, out of breath. The caucus hummed like a disturbed beehive. Every one was whispering to his neighbor. Rogers and Blake and several others were in council. Franklin, thus suddenly projected into the center of the limelight, felt conspicuous indeed. After a moment's hesitation he rose. Dean, who had been watching him intently, nodded in apparent approval and rapped with the gavel.

"Mr. Cobb," he said. "Quiet, please. . . . Yes, Mr. Cobb?"

Franklin hesitated. He looked about him; all faces were turned in his direction.

"Mr. Chairman and gentlemen," he said, "I—well, let me say at the beginning that this isn't a speech, merely a word of explanation. When it was intimated to me, a few days ago, that the committee had added my name to its tentative list of delegates to the district convention, I was surprised and rather doubtful whether or not to accept. I appreciated the honor, but I realized that I was, as Mr. Haven has termed me, a newcomer to Wellmouth and that, therefore, it might be better if some one more widely known and who had lived longer among you were selected. I do believe that my interest in Wellmouth is as keen and honestly unselfish as

any one's can possibly be, and, had I been chosen, I would
have done my level best to vote for what seemed to me the
best interests of the party and the town—and by that I mean
the whole town, not any section or sections of it. (Applause.)
Nevertheless, I can see Captain Rogers' point. I am not,
as far as residence is concerned, strictly speaking a South Side
man, and if it is your pleasure that I withdraw my name in
favor of one who is, I shall do it without the least regret or
ill feeling. . . . And," with a broad smile, "the *Eagle* will
keep on working for the nomination and election of Carmi
Blake just as hard and just as sincerely as it is doing now.
That I promise you."

He had had no intention of mentioning the Blake name
when he began. He had added the last statement purely on
impulse and the fact that he did so before that name had
been put forward as the nominee of the caucus evidenced his
utter lack of experience in practical politics. Nevertheless, it
was that impulsive utterance which ended what might have
been a long and perhaps bitter dispute. He took his seat
amid a chaos of enthusiastic yells and cheers. Elkanah
Rogers was hugging him like a bear. Men leaned over the
back of the settee to pound his shoulders.

But the applause, loud as it was, was not universal. Here
and there, men sat silent, some of them frowning. On the
platform Judge Dean, who had listened to the first part of
his short statement with benignant approval, was now stroking his beard and looking somewhat disturbed. Cornelius
Haven bit the end of the official penholder.

Captain Zenas Rogers was on his feet once more. He
and Abiathar Blake had finished another hurried conference.

"Mr. Chairman," said Rogers, "I want to say that I was
wrong. I guess likely the list of delegates *is* a good one and
all right just as it stands. Particularly," with considerable
emphasis, "so long as Mr. Cobb's name is on it. I am satis-

fied, and I'm sure the South Side will be. I withdraw my objection and ask you to call for a vote."

The vote followed almost immediately. It was unanimous —that is, there were no negatives.

Elkanah was jubilant. "There!" he crowed, with satisfaction. "That's settled. You're in politics now, Frankie, my boy. Did you know it?"

Franklin shrugged. "I know it," he admitted. "But I don't know what to do now that I am in."

"Don't let that worry you. You'll have plenty of folks to tell you. . . . And *now* comes the real article. . . . See?"

Seth Briar, the South Side dealer in marine outfittings, had risen to speak.

"Mr. Chairman," he began, "I move you that each delegate chosen be given the privilege of appointing a substitute in case any of them should be sick or unable to attend the conventions."

This motion was approved without opposition. Mr. Briar again rose.

"And I also move you," he said, raising his voice, "that the delegates to the district convention on the fifteenth—or their substitutes, as the case may be—be instructed by this caucus to cast their votes for Carmi G. Blake of this town, as the party nominee for representative to the State Legislature."

This was what the caucus—or a large part of it—had been awaiting. The cheering and stamping shook the windows. Judge Dean made no attempt to still the tumult nor did he interfere when Elkanah, waving both hands above his head, called for three cheers for Carmi Blake, and the cheers were given. The motion was seconded by Captain Zenas.

"You have heard the motion? Are you ready for the question?"

"Question! Question!"

"Then— Yes, Mr. Holway?"

Noah Holway, the delegate chosen to represent East Wellmouth at the coming convention, had risen slowly from his seat in the center of the hall. He was a lean, elderly man, with a smooth upper lip and a grizzled chin beard, wearing spectacles which, as he spoke, slid gradually down his long nose and, therefore, required readjusting every minute or two.

"Mr. Chairman," he said, in a nasal drawl, "I've just been voted in as a delegate and so maybe I hadn't ought to say anything now. But if I don't say it now, it looks as if I might not have a chance to say it—and so," with a nod which caused the spectacles to slip to the very tip of his nose, "I *am* sayin' it. I don't know as I like this notion of bein' sent to the convention 'instructed' for anybody. . . . Now, now, hold on!" raising his voice and turning to look about him; "I realize you South Side fellows don't like that, but it's the way I feel, just the same. Let me tell you what I mean."

He rehoisted his spectacles to the masthead and continued.

"As I understand it, if I'm sent to that convention 'instructed' for any one man—no matter who he is—I've got to vote for him, whether or no. Now the convention's two weeks off. A whole lot can happen in two weeks, in politics same as anything else, and people's minds can change in that time; I've seen it happen. I've no objection at all to bein' sent to the convention 'recommended' to vote for Cap'n Blake, but I have consider'ble objection to bein' 'instructed' for him. . . . Yes, or, as I said before, for anybody else. That's how I feel."

He stopped speaking, but he did not sit down. His hearers had been listening in complete silence; evidently, to the majority at least, what they heard was a great surprise. As he ended the meeting burst into uproar. Dean's rapping for order was ignored. Franklin Cobb, turning hastily to his neighbor, asked a question.

"What is all this?" he demanded. "I thought—I supposed—"

Elkanah was as bewildered as he.

"I—I— Why, dummed if I know!" he sputtered. " 'Twas

all settled long ago. All hands knew 'twas. The old rapscallion! What's got into him, anyhow?"

"Mr. Chairman! . . . Mr. Chairman!" Abiathar Blake was on his feet; so was Briar.

"Silence! Order! Order, gentlemen!" Judge Dean was quite imperturbed; presiding over turbulent gatherings was no new experience for him.

"Order, if you please! Mr. Holway still has the floor. You have not finished, have you, Mr. Holway?"

"Why, no, Judge, I ain't. I told you how I feel, that's all, but I'm willin' to bet there's a good many folks in this town feel the same way as I do. I *know,*" with another nod which sent the spectacles coasting to the verge of peril, "that a whole lot of East Wellmouth feels that way. And they would tell me—fact is, they *have* told me—that before I cast my vote for anybody—yes, sir, *any*body—I ought to be sure how that person stands on certain matters of importance to this township. *I* don't know how one particular one of 'em stands. I did think I knew, but lately I've heard things that haven't made me so sure. I've known Carmi Blake since he was a boy, and I've been strong for him right along. I was all set to work for him and vote for him. I am yet if he satisfies me on one thing. It's a mighty important thing, too; it has been talked about for three or four years, and now at last it's comin' to the point where somethin' will be done. The State engineers, as I understand it, have at last agreed that the State use some of its money to deepen and improve Wellmouth harbor. The good Lord knows that such improvement is needed and us Wellmouth folks know what a benefit 'twould be to every one of us to have it done. The engineers—again as I understand it—have two kinds of propositions for such improvement. One of 'em is to just do a part of the job; just deepen and fix up the present harbor. The other is to do the whole thing at once, dredge out and fix up, not only the harbor where it is, but go on and do the same thing to the east'ard end of it and to Blue River for a half mile or so from where it empties into that east'ard end. Those are the two propositions and one or t'other will be decided on afore the comin' year's over."

The caucus was again growing unruly. It had listened, with some patience, to the first portion of this harangue, but now it was all astir. There were shouts of "Sit down," and one of "Aw, dry up! we know all that."

Holway heard this shout. He wheeled and pointed a long forefinger in the direction from which it had come.

"You know it?" he cried. "Yes, you do know it, and you know, too, or you ought to know, that whichever one of those two plans is put through will depend a whole lot on the recommendation and influence of our member of the State House of Representatives from this district. You ought to know that, I say."

"Oh, shut up! Of course we know it!"

"Yes? All right so far. But," the long forefinger quivering, "does any one of you know just how Carmi Blake stands on that subject? Do you know whether he's for the two-for-a-cent halfway plan or for the whole one, the sensible one? . . . Now—now, wait a minute! I did think *I* knew. From some things I've heard said that *he* said I figured he was for goin' the whole hog. But a few days ago I heard he was kind of doubtful; wouldn't promise one way or another. That ain't enough for me; it ain't enough for a lot of us East Wellmouth folks who live up there to the east'ard and would like to see wharves and schooners and vessels up our way, same as they are down here. . . . There, I guess I've made myself plain. Until I *know* that our nominee for representative is sure to work for the right plan for our harbors I don't want to be instructed to vote for him. If or when I know it—know it for sure and sartin—I'll vote for him without any instructin'. I've said my say, so I'll obey the polite orders I've been hearin' and shut up."

He sat down, snatching at his spectacles barely in time to save them from destruction. He had indeed "said his say" but even as green a hand in local politics as Franklin Cobb could foresee a little of the effect of that say. The caucus might be cut and dried but a haystack is cut and dried also and when a lighted match is tossed into it certain results follow. Almost every one was talking or shouting. Some were calling for "Question!" and demanding a vote. A half-dozen were on their feet claiming recognition from the chair. The meeting which had begun so peaceably was now developing into a riot. The gavel thumped and thumped.

"Order! Order! Quiet!" Then, as the turmoil subsided ever so little, "Yes, Mr. Bascom. . . . *Quiet!*"

Sylvanus Bascom, a man with whom Cobb was scarcely acquainted, but whom he knew by reputation as a well-to-do resident of North Wellmouth, began to speak. It was more than a minute before he could be heard. During that minute the gavel pounded as regularly as the ticking of a clock.

"Mr. Chairman," shouted Bascom. "Mr. Chairman! . . . Oh, for heaven's sake, is this a dog fight or a respectable meeting of respectable folks? . . . Mr. Chairman, I only want to say that I think what Mr. Holway has just said has a lot of sense in it. If *I* was a delegate to that convention I'd want to know how a candidate stood in regard to important matters before I let myself be instructed to vote for him. The harbor improvement *is* important. And Noah there isn't the only one who has heard reports about Cap'n Blake being sort of undecided which plan he's going to recommend and work for. He isn't here himself or I'd ask him. As it is I'd like to ask his brother. With your permission and that of the caucus, Mr. Chairman, I'd like to ask Abiathar Blake if he knows that Carmi is in favor of the Blue River plan? Will he pledge himself to work for it and not let 'em put us off with just the improving of the present harbor?"

He paused. Every head turned toward that section of the

hall where Abiathar Blake was seated. And Abiathar rose, slowly and—so it seemed to Cobb—with some reluctance.

"Well, now, Sylvanus," he said, after a momentary hesitation, "far as I'm concerned I'm for the Blue River plan and I presume likely Carmi is. He was, I know, a while ago and if he's changed his mind he hasn't told me so. No," more emphatically, "and I doubt very much if he's told anybody else so. You say—you and Holway—that there's talk goin' around about him and the harbor improvement business. Where does the talk come from? Who started it? Yes, and *why* was it started—now, at this late day? I'd like to have somebody answer me *that*."

There were cries of "That's it" and "Tell us that, Sylvanus," but there were others—"Don't dodge, Bi" and "Why don't you answer the question?" Amid the disturbance Franklin heard Elkanah shouting in his ear; Elkanah was very much agitated.

"I—I don't know what to make of this," sputtered Mr. Rogers. "There's somethin' up we don't know about. And—and—look, Frank! have you noticed how many of them East and North Wellmouth fellows are here this afternoon? Oh, my soul and body! Why didn't Carmi come here himself? And *why* did he keep all that gang of his at work instead of sendin' 'em here to vote?"

Sylvanus Bascom was waiting for silence. When it was, to a degree, accorded him, he said, with a shrug: "You're a little off the subject, seems to me, Abiathar. I asked you if you knew that your brother was willing to pledge himself to the Republican voters of Wellmouth township to use his influence, after he is elected, for the Blue River improvement plan? That's what I asked. You haven't answered me yet, and," with a grim smile, "you ought to know, if any one does, it seems to me."

There was silence now, scarcely a murmur; every one seemed to be waiting for Blake's reply. And Abiathar, apparently, was not too eager to reply. He opened his mouth, then closed it as Zenas Rogers pulled at his coat. He bent to catch the Rogers whisper, nodded, and straightened once more.

"It strikes me that *I* ain't the one who's off the subject," he protested. "This caucus is supposed to be a—"

He was interrupted. There was a stir by the door. A murmur, a shout, more shouts rising to a series of yells. Carmi Blake had entered and was standing at the rear of the hall. In a moment he was surrounded by an excited crowd of his fellow South Siders, all talking at once.

The Honorable Joel saw and recognized his opportunity. The gavel rose and fell again and again.

"Fellow Republicans!" he shouted. "Kindly listen to me one moment. . . . Thank you. . . . As I think Captain Abiathar Blake was about to remind us, this meeting was called to transact certain—er—business, and the hour is growing late. Captain Carmi, for your benefit and for that of other late arrivals, if any, let me briefly explain that this caucus has selected and approved delegates for the district convention and there is a motion before the house that the said delegates be instructed to cast their votes in the convention for you as the party candidate from the district for the State Legislature. (Cheers.) Certain questions have been asked concerning your —ahem—probable action on a certain matter. It occurs to me that your answering those questions yourself would do away with further discussion. With your permission—er—Mr. Bascom, I suggest that Captain Carmi Blake be given the floor."

Bascom nodded. "I'll be glad to give it to him," he declared, "if he'll tell us what we want to know—what, as I see it, we have a right to know."

Judge Dean bowed graciously. "Thank you, Mr. Bascom. Gentlemen, Captain Carmi Blake."

The assemblage, the greater part of it, rose and yelled. Carmi Blake came slowly down the center aisle. His huge shoulders rose high above those on either side of him and Cobb was reminded of an elephant in a circus parade. He reached the open space before the platform and turned.

"All right, Mr. Chairman," he said, with deliberation, "I shall be glad to answer any questions—any that I can, I mean. What are they?"

Dean was about to speak, but Zenas Rogers was shouting his name.

"Hold on, Joel!" cried Rogers, heatedly. "Before there is any more of this I want to remind some of this crowd that this isn't a church debating society. There's a motion before the house. Let's vote on it."

And the tumult began again. Cries of "Vote! Vote!" and others of "No! No!" The chairman raised his hand.

"Captain Rogers," he said, "it is true that there is a motion before the house, but that motion, being duly seconded, is open for debate. Captain Carmi Blake has the floor."

Captain Carmi's big voice broke in. "All right, Zenas," he said. "Heave aboard with your questions, Mr. Chairman."

"I believe Mr. Holway was the first to—ahem—propound the question. I will ask him to repeat it. Mr. Holway?"

Noah Holway rose. Having carefully adjusted the troublesome spectacles he turned them in the direction of Carmi Blake.

"Cap'n Blake," he drawled, "my question is just this. If you are elected to the State Legislature will you promise to use every bit of influence you've got to have the Blue River harbor scheme put through? To have it—and not any halfway flumadiddle of just deepenin' the harbor where 'tis—put into the reg'lar River and Harbor bill this year? That's my question and it's Sylvanus Bascom's and a whole lot of other folks's. Will you give us your solemn promise, right here in this caucus, that you'll do just that?"

The murmuring and whispering ceased. For the first time in many minutes the hall was still. Carmi Blake looked at his questioner, up at the blandly smiling Judge Dean, at his brother and Captain Zenas fuming and fidgeting in their seats, at the rows of faces all turned toward him. He smiled slightly, a rather grim smile, so Franklin thought.

"So that's it, eh?" he observed. "Humph! Yes, yes, I see. . . . Why no, Holway, I won't."

There was an audible and universal gasp of astonishment. Blake went on.

"I won't, I say," he repeated. "Now that don't necessarily mean that I'm against the Blue River plan. Fact is, a while ago I was pretty much in favor of it. It looked to me like the most sensible proposition in the long run and I was for it. But lately I've begun—" He paused, then, with a shrug, he added, "That's neither here nor there, not yet anyhow. I'm still willin' to say that I may decide in favor of it, but I'm goin' to look into it—into both plans—before I decide anything. I'm goin' to look into 'em and"—with a snap of his jaws—"into all that may or may not go with 'em, before I decide anything. This much I will say though," his voice was rising just a little, "if I go to the State House as representative from this district, I'll go there with my hands untied, free to work and vote for what seems in my judgment the best interests of the people who sent me there. If they can't trust me that much, then they hadn't ought to trust me with the job. That's all there is to that."

He started to walk up the aisle, but Holway caught his sleeve.

"Just one second, Cap'n," insisted Noah. "That's all right and fine so far as it goes, but to my notion, and that of some of the rest of us, it ain't quite enough. Let's get this straight. You won't pledge yourself to work for the Blue River plan? You won't promise it?"

Carmi turned, his heavy brows drawn together. "I'll promise to do what I think is best—and honest and square— for the whole district," he said, with sharp emphasis. "And that's the only pledge or promise I'll give to anybody—now or later."

The five minutes which followed were lively ones. All the chairman's efforts to restore order and proceed with business were unavailing. Even to Franklin's inexperienced eyes it was plain that the assemblage was dividing into three factors, one staunchly and unswervingly demanding that the delegates be instructed for Carmi Blake, the man they had come there to support; another opposed to instructing at all; and the third, and largest, undecided what to do.

"Gentlemen! Gentlemen!" Dean was imploring; his voice was husky, but still adequate. "*Will* you come to order? There is a motion before the house. Are you ready for the vote?"

They paid no attention to him. And, in the midst of the excitement, another new arrival came pushing his way through the crowded center aisle. As he moved forward the disorder hushed, the accusations and denials ceased or changed to respectful greetings. By the time Gideon Bates reached the space before and below the platform the Republican caucus of Wellmouth township was once more a comparatively orderly gathering instead of what Bascom had sarcastically termed it, "a dog fight."

Elkanah Rogers, who had charged away to the spot where the argument was hottest, now came plunging back again.

"Godfreys!" he panted, squeezing into his seat beside Franklin Cobb. "Godfreys mighty, I'm glad he's come! *Now* we'll have a little common sense. Holway and the rest of them dum fools will listen to him; they won't dare not to."

Dean and Cornelius Haven were plainly relieved; their faces showed it. They bent forward to shake their sovereign's hand. The judge was whispering, obviously explaining the situation. After a moment of questions and answers Bates waved his hand. "Yes, yes," Franklin heard him say impatiently, "I know all that; heard the most of it. Let me talk to 'em."

He mounted the steps to the platform. His doing so was a signal for great and prolonged applause. Manasseh Eldredge, his voice sounding as if his throat had been sandpapered, proposed three cheers for Captain Gideon Bates. And—so Franklin noticed—even the South Siders, most of them, joined in the cheering.

The Honorable Joel was beaming once more.

"Fellow Republicans of Wellmouth," he announced, "we have now with us a man whom, not only this township, but all Ostable County delights to honor. His life has been spent among us, he has brilliantly represented our district in the State House and he is, as we all know, a leader in our party's councils. I am sure you will all wish to hear a word from Captain Gideon Bates."

It was evident that they did; certainly most of them did and proved it by their greeting. Only in the section where the Blakes and Rogers and Briar and their immediate followers were seated was there silence. Wellmouth's great man nodded appreciation of the plaudits and faced his fellow citizens with a smile upon his face and his thumbs in his waistcoat pockets.

"Friends and neighbors," he began, "I understand that some of our opponents on the other side—the outside—of the political fence have been prophesying that a Republican caucus in this town is just a matter of routine like—well, like a well-run orthodox funeral. They seem to think—or, at least, they want people to believe they think—that everybody present has had his orders and that nobody will say yes if those orders were to say no. According to them all that is expected of a voter who attends is to sit quiet and listen to the ceremony.

"Well," his smile broadening, "whenever I hear that I feel like reminding those fellows that they have made a mistake in the date. There *is* a political funeral held in this district every year, but it is held in November—on election day. And it *isn't* the Republican candidates who are buried."

If his purpose was to bring the meeting back to good humor he was undoubtedly succeeding. The roar of laughter and the handclapping which followed this sally were sufficient proof of that.

"And," he went on, still smiling, "if some of those opponents of ours had been standing as I have stood for the past quarter of an hour, just outside the door in the lobby yonder, and had heard, as I heard, what has been going on in here, I rather guess they might have figured that—there—well, to explain what I mean I'll tell you a story my father told me years ago. Over at Denboro in the old days there was a fellow named Obed Sampson who went to sea before the mast. One voyage he was washed overboard in the night. They heard him yell and threw over a life preserver, but the vessel was running before a stiff gale of wind and by the time she could be hove to and they got over a boat she had gone ahead so far they couldn't find hide nor hair of him. When they got to Liverpool, where they were bound, the skipper wrote to Sampson's sister in Denboro telling her the sad news. Of course there wasn't any Atlantic cable, same as we have now, and no steamers—everything was sail, and naturally it took that letter a long time to get there.

"When the letter came, Susanna, that was the sister's name, felt that some sort of memorial service ought to be held. She and Obed had fought like cats and dogs—he was a good deal of a no-account, I guess—but she felt that way anyhow. So they had the memorial service in the church. Right in the middle of it Obed himself walked in at the door. Seems that he had got hold of that life preserver, hung on to it till morning and then was picked up by a vessel bound for Savannah. She was a slow tub, and they had a spell of head winds and calms, so they didn't make Savannah for weeks. Anybody else but Obed would have written home, but he didn't. He waited till he got a chance to ship north on a schooner and he got down to Denboro just a few days after the letter from Liverpool got there. When he walked into his own memorial services there was a sensation, naturally. After a minute or two the minister, probably feeling that he ought to say something, announced that under the happy circumstances, the services were called off, or something like that. Obed—he had brought a quart of Medford rum with him and had been sampling it—stood up and objected. 'Aw, don't call it off altogether, parson,' he said. 'It sounded to me like a first-class funeral, what I heard of it. Don't call it off altogether; let's just postpone it.'

"And that," he continued, after the laughter had subsided, "is what I think those outside prophets I mentioned would have thought if they had heard, as I did, what was going on in this caucus. They would have figured that the funeral they expected must have been postponed."

Franklin was beginning to understand why Gideon Bates was not only a great man but a popular man in Wellmouth. It was not his money alone, nor his success and power—it was his natural shrewd ability as a leader. He had the priceless faculty of making those who disagreed with his policies and resented his domineering manner, respect him and even like him. In those few minutes he had brought good humor and a measure of unity to a gathering which had been on the point of—goodness knew what.

He stood there, his thumbs still in his waistcoat pockets, waiting for the opportunity to continue. He had ceased smiling now, and his next words were serious enough.

"I liked what I heard," he declared, emphatically. "Maybe you think that's a queer thing to say, but it's the truth. I liked it because it proved that the Republican voters of the town I've lived in all my life are not just—er—jumping jacks, puppets that move only when somebody pulls the strings.

A meeting like this proves to me that they are free and independent men, with wills of their own and not scared to speak out and say what they think. That's fine, but—*but,*" with sudden gravity, "that sort of thing can be carried a little bit too far. As loyal Republicans, who mean to see our candidates elected—as they will be elected—we must take care not to disturb the harmony and pull-together of our party. When there's a little—well, say disagreement, as there seems to be here just now, there must be sacrifices made. Yes, and made not by one side alone, but by both sides. That's the way I look at it."

He paused again. Franklin, turning to look about him, saw heads nodding approval. There were murmurs of "Hear, hear!" and "You're right." The speaker heard them. "Why, yes, *I* think I'm right," he agreed, good-naturedly. "If I didn't think so I shouldn't say it. Now, as I understand it, the particular point that is upsetting the pull-together of our meeting isn't a very serious one, after all. We've picked our delegates, and now it's just a question of whether or not they shall be sent to the convention 'instructed' or 'uninstructed.' Now, personally, I'd be satisfied either way, but"— he stilled the applause with a wave of the hand—"but I *shan't* be satisfied to see this rumpus last another hour or so, with this caucus of ours ending in hard feelings. That won't do. And so, I'm offering a suggestion. Not an 'order,' understand," with a smile, "but just a suggestion. Suppose we don't 'instruct' those delegates of ours— Hold on! Wait a minute! Suppose, I say, we send them uninstructed, but with the recommendation—make it as strong as you want to— that they cast their votes for that A 1 sailor and citizen Captain Carmi Blake. If we do that they'll have a fortnight to think things over and some matters that seem to be troubling Mr. Holway and others may be settled in that time. That's my suggestion, and I believe it's a good one. Much obliged to you."

He turned away. Cornelius Haven rushed toward him with a chair and he sat down, took a cigar from his pocket, lighted it and puffed serenely.

The Honorable Joel rapped for order. "You have heard Captain Bates's suggestion," he proclaimed. "I think you will agree with me that it is a fair and wise one. Mr. Briar, your motion to instruct the delegates is before the house. Are you willing to withdraw it and substitute one to the effect that they be sent uninstructed but recommended to vote for Captain Blake? If so—"

But Briar was already on his feet.

"No, *sir!*" he snarled. "I won't do any such thing. It was the understandin' when we came to this caucus that the delegates be instructed for Carmi. All hands know it, the whole South Side expects it. I won't withdraw my motion. I call for a vote."

So the tumult began again. In the midst of it the chair recognized Abiathar Blake. Abiathar's face was purple.

"All this is a put-up job," he shouted. "It was all settled— you know it was, Joe Dean. You and the committee agreed, when we talked with you last, that the delegates should go instructed for my brother. . . . Be still, Carmi! Let me alone! I don't care what you want; it's what the South Side wants and has been promised it should have. . . . Why, consarn it," waving his fist, "if we hadn't been promised it do you suppose there wouldn't have been more South Siders here? . . . Mr. Chairman, if we can't have fair play I want this caucus adjourned till to-morrow. *Then* we'll have our crowd here and you see how the vote'll go! I tell you—"

He went on to tell them, but what he said was inaudible beyond a few feet from where he stood. "Vote! Vote! Vote!" yelled his fellow Republicans, many of whom were tired and aware that supper time was approaching.

Dean pounded and shouted.

"Are you ready for the vote?" he screamed. "Those in

favor of instructing the delegates to vote for Carmi Blake will rise. Those not in favor will remain seated. . . . The no's have it. The motion is defeated. . . . Captain Bates?"

Captain Gideon was again standing His smile was still in evidence, his serenity was undisturbed.

"Mr. Chairman," he said, "I move—and I hope there won't be any negative votes this time—that our delegates be sent to the convention uninstructed but strongly recommended to work and vote for Carmi Blake as our district's choice as candidate for representative to the lower house of the State Legislature."

"Second it! Second the motion! Hooray!"

"All those in favor will rise. . . . No's? There seem to be none. The motion is carried unanimously. The business of the caucus having been transacted, a motion to adjourn is in order."

And so ended the most eventful and, because of its after effects, the most significant caucus in the history of the Republican party of Wellmouth township.

CHAPTER XIX

FRANKLIN came hurrying from the damp grayness of the late afternoon's out-of-doors into the ink-smelling stuffiness and gloom of the "B. Higham" print shop. Cahoon and the bookkeeper had just left for home and Elisha Dodson was in the little back room. He was seated at the editorial desk, his hair, as always, looking as if his head had just been removed from the shaft of a ventilating fan and the shabby green eye-shade cocked jauntily over his left ear. He was writing busily, his nose close to the paper.

He looked up absently. "Oh, Hello, Frank!" he said. "I've been waitin' for you. Longer session than we cal'lated 'twould be, wasn't it?"

Cobb, who had run almost all the way from the hall, was out of breath. Also he was ruffled and disappointed by the outcome of the caucus.

"For heaven's sake, Elisha," he demanded, impatiently, "why don't you light a lamp or two? I think I fell over almost everything there is in that press room; my shins feel that way."

Elisha peered through his spectacles. "Well, now, sho!" he said, repentantly, "that's too bad. I was thinkin' 'twas gettin' kind of hard to see in here. Thought 'twas 'cause my specs needed cleanin'. I'll light a lamp right off this minute."

He rose to do so, but Franklin interfered.

"Never mind that now," he ordered. "We can talk just as well in the dark, and there is plenty to talk about. Have you heard what happened down at the caucus?"

"Why no, I ain't. Tip, he left a minute ago, said he guessed he'd stop on his way along and find out, but he ain't come back. Why, what's the matter, Frank? You act kind of—er—upset, don't you?"

"Upset! The whole frying pan is upset. Listen to this."

He told, as briefly as he could, the story of the afternoon's happenings. When he had finished Dodson was the more upset of the two.

"Gorry!" he exclaimed. "Why, gorry, Frank, that's—that's the funniest thing ever I heard!"

"Funny!"

"Oh, I don't mean funny like—like Tip Cahoon's new hat. I mean queer. And—and what's it all about? A week ago —yes, a couple of days ago—I was as sure, from everything I heard, that those delegates would go instructed for Carmi as I am that I'm here. Seems as if there must be somethin' behind this, Frank; but what? What does this all-of-a-sudden whirlaround *mean*?"

"Huh! That's what I'd like to have you tell me. Where does this harbor improvement thing come in? . . . Oh, of course I know about the schemes for improving the harbor and Blue River. I've heard them more or less talked about ever since I came to Wellmouth. But why did Holway and Bascom get up on their hind legs about them just now? And why do they suspect Blake of being opposed to the Blue River plan? By George, you know, I think he *is* opposed, too. If not, why wouldn't he promise to support it? There's news in this, Elisha; big news, if we can get hold of it."

He was growing excited at the prospect. Dodson shook his head.

"Tell me again what Carmi said when they put it up to him, will you, Frank?" he asked.

"He wouldn't say anything, except that his mind was not made up and that he wouldn't promise that or anything else to anybody. He would do the best he could for the district always—that is, what seemed to him best—and if they couldn't trust him to that extent they shouldn't trust him with the job."

"Yes. . . . Yes, that's sounds like Cap'n Carmi. Ever strike you that he was—well, kind of obstinate? Oh, a fine fellow and an honest one, but sort of, as you might say, sot in his way? That ever strike you, Frank?"

Franklin stared at him; it was hard to believe him serious.

"Strike me!" he repeated. "Elisha, I think I've told you— I certainly told some one—that I considered Carmi Blake about as tactful and diplomatic as a charging rhinoceros. But what has he got in that rhinoceros head of his now? That's what we've got to find out. Everybody is going to ask it, you know."

"Um-hm, and nobody's goin' to be answered until Carmi's ready, I guess. I take it you judged that not even Abiathar knows yet?"

"He didn't act as if he did. Why, that caucus was turning into a free for all. It would have been one still, I imagine, if Bates hadn't told a funny story and got them to laughing. Then he came out with his proposal to recommend instead of instruct and they—the majority of them—fell into line like soldiers."

"Yes. They would, of course. Say, Frank, *there's* what you'd call a diplomat, wouldn't you? Cap'n Gideon, I mean. . . . Um-hm. A smart, able man, a big man. Makes you like him, whether you want to or not."

"Yes, he does. I don't like Dean—don't trust him some-how—and I always want to kick Eldredge; but old Bates is a square fighter as well as a darned smooth one. . . . Well, they sent us 'recommended' for Blake, that's something. . . . Eh? What's the trouble? It *is* something, isn't it?"

"Ye-es, it's somethin' but whether it's much or little depends on what's behind all this. You fellows are sent up to that convention with a—a hint that you'd better nominate Carmi; but if, when you get there, you decide it might be better for the party and for that harmony Gideon was talkin' about to drop Blake and compromise on somebody else—why, that's your privilege. Most folks won't find fault with you; it's been done often enough."

Franklin Cobb struck the desk with his fist.

"*I* won't drop—no, nor even compromise while there's a shot in the locker," he vowed, grimly. "I promised Dean to support Blake and I promised publicly this afternoon to work for him through thick and thin. . . . Well, no use our gassing here all night. What next?"

Elisha rose from the desk. "I was just layin' out a spread for next week hurrahin' because Carmi was as good as nominated. Might as well tear it up now, I guess. . . . Suppose you and I go home to supper, Frank. Nellie'll be anxious to hear all this. . . . Humph! Sho! I wonder how the Orham caucus worked out. Did *they* instruct or didn't they?"

They learned the answer to that question before they descended the steps of the Higham building. Elisha was just locking the door when Tip Cahoon came tearing along the sidewalk. Tip was, as Dodson said afterwards, "all fizzled up" with excitement.

"Cripes!" he panted, breathlessly, as he caught sight of them. "There you be, 'Lish, eh? Who's that with you? Oh, Mr. Cobb! Why, I took it for granted you must have gone right home. Say, wasn't it surprisin' the way that caucus turned out? Why— Oh, and have you heard about Orham? I have. Bi Blake just had a telegram come, and I heard him read it out loud to Cap'n Zenas and Briar and them. Orham sent its delegates uninstructed. What do you think about that now! Ain't that the darndest ever you heard tell of? 'Biathar he's just all knocked of a heap. You see, him and the South Side gang figured 'twas all settled for Carmi and— Where you goin'? There's lots more I ain't told you yet."

"Tell it to-morrow," was Dodson's blunt suggestion. "You'll have more wind by that time, maybe. . . . Come on, Frank."

They walked down the South Side road together. Franklin was deep in thought and Elisha had to limp fast to keep beside him. But one remark was made during the homeward walk and Dodson made it.

"There *is* somethin' behind it all," he soliloquized. "Yes, sir, there certainly is; this Orham business proves it. But what— Say, Frank, would you mind shuttin' off steam a little mite? Whew! Since we turned the corner you've kept me hoppin' like a sand flea in a clambake fire. . . . Whew! thanks, that's consider'ble better."

It was a rather gloomy trio who sat about the Dodson supper table after the meal was over. Franklin had little to say; he was too busy reviewing the events of the afternoon and speculating as to their causes. Helen, too, seemed to be in a reverie. Elisha was the most talkative of the three and, being an optimist by nature, he was beginning to convince himself that the action of the caucus might have been unpremeditated, after all.

"Maybe there wasn't anything underneath it," he observed, though still rather doubtfully. "I don't see how there could have been hardly. It was Joe Dean himself who came and asked you to have the *Eagle* whoop things up for Blake. And he told you that the town committee had picked Carmi for candidate. He said that very thing, didn't he, Frank?"

"He certainly did."

"Um-hm. Then it *couldn't* have been a put-up job. Noah Holway just—"

Helen interrupted. "Nonsense, Father!" she broke in. "Noah Holway has been in town politics for years and years; did you ever hear of his saying anything in a caucus before? Anything but 'yes' or 'no' or 'Second the motion'? I don't believe you ever did. Of course it was a put-up job; every bit of it was planned beforehand."

"Aw, come now, Nellie! If it was a put-up job who put it up? Not Dean and Manasseh and them, because they—"

"Oh, Father, Father!" wearily. "Who else could do it? Who else has managed politics in this town—yes, and this district—since the war?"

"Eh? . . . Why," triumphantly. "I'll tell you who. Gideon Bates, that's who. Joe Dean and Manasseh and Haven and all them, they just take orders from Cap'n Gideon. Yes, and so does Isaac Shotwell and his crowd in Orham. And you can't tell me, Nellie, that Gideon Bates gave Carmi Blake his word to work for him and then played an underhand trick like this one. He don't do things that way, I know it. You know it too, Frank; now don't you?"

Franklin was inclined to agree. "It doesn't seem like him, that's a fact," he admitted. "If this is a deliberate plan to put Blake out of the running, it is a sly one. And I can't see slyness in Gideon Bates. Shrewdness, yes, and bossiness; but slyness and double-crossing—no."

"That's what I say," declared Elisha. "There you are, Nellie! You see? And it's Bates who handles politics in Wellmouth."

"Yes; but isn't it possible that somebody else may handle Captain Bates—sometimes and in certain cases? He is used to being obeyed and flattered and bowed down to. And, you must remember, to him the Republican party is—next to his daughter—the one really perfect thing in the world. If I were trying to manage him in a case like this one—never forgetting that it must go very much against his grain to see a South Sider nominated anyway—I think I should flatter him and ask for his judgment every few minutes and agree with it, and then, when the time came, begin to throw out hints about talk of discord in the party and the bad effect it would have, and the need of harmony above everything else and— Oh, well!" with a nod, "I believe *I* could handle him and perhaps bring him around. And I am not Judge Dean either."

Cobb had not been listening intently to all this. He had been thinking of his own unpleasant situation.

"Well, anyhow," he said, before Elisha could speak, "the convention hasn't been held yet and Carmi Blake may win out, after all. The nominee this year must come from Wellmouth—all precedents would be smashed if he didn't—and every other name was withdrawn long ago. The South Side people will work harder than ever for the next two weeks and," slapping the tablecloth with his hand, "so, you can bet, will the *Eagle*. If Dean—or any one else—is playing any such game as you seem to be hinting at, Helen, I don't know anything about it. What I do know is that I promised the old Sardine himself that my paper should support Blake and this afternoon in that confounded caucus I publicly promised to work and vote for him. I should feel like a coward and look like a fool if I began to hedge now. So fight is the word for you and me for the next fortnight, eh, Elisha? We won't be licked till they sink us."

"You bet you! We'll keep hollerin' 'Victory' long as there's a plank left afloat to hang on to. You just watch us, Nellie!"

Helen was watching them, watching Franklin in particular. As he rose from his chair, she asked a question.

"How are you going to fight?" she asked. "I mean what are you going to do first?"

"What? Oh, I don't know; haven't had much chance to think. I mean to go down to the South Side to-morrow morning and try to get Blake to tell me the inside story of this harbor improvement thing—if there is any."

"And, if there should be any, do you think he'd tell you?"

"Why shouldn't he?"

"Because he is Carmi Blake. You just said that even Abiathar seemed to be puzzled and troubled about it. You thought he didn't know what it was all about. Now if Carmi won't tell his own brother, do you think he will tell you?"

"Why—why—" A sudden thought struck him. "Helen," he asked, looking at her intently, "do *you* know anything about it? Has Carmi told you?"

She met his look frankly and answered without the least hesitation.

"No," she said.

"That seems queer. I should have thought— Humph! Has he seemed to you—well, troubled or worried about anything lately?"

And now there was a momentary hesitation.

"Was he in good spirits? Or did he seem down in the mouth?" Franklin persisted.

"He was not in very good spirits, but—but I didn't think politics had anything to do with that. . . . Well, well," quickly, "we have been sitting here for hours. No, no, I don't need any help with the dishes, Father. Take Frank into the sitting room or, better still, both of you go to bed. It is getting late and I am sure one of you, at least, must be tired."

Elisha did go to his room soon afterward, but Franklin remained in the sitting room. He was not sleepy; the caucus had been exciting and the problem of what, if anything more than the obvious, was beneath the surprises of the afternoon was intriguing. There must be an account of the meeting in the *Eagle*, of course. Just how much of the real proceedings should be told in print? He ought to have some one's advice about that, some one experienced in politics.

He began to remember little things which had been said to him, or which he had overheard said. His interview with Carmi Blake at the latter's office that day when, following the frank talk with Helen, he had called to suggest that he and the big fishing skipper forgive and forget past differences. He had congratulated Blake then upon winning his fight for the nomination and Blake's reply had been a gruff, "Oh, so it's won, is it?" That, as he considered it now, sounded almost as if the speaker had doubts of winning. Had he—even then?

And that scrap of dialogue at the post office between Manas-

seh Eldredge and Judge Dean. "He won't promise . . .
means to look into it first?" . . . Promise what?

Helen entered the sitting room. He heard her come in but,
as he was slouched down in the big rocker, she did not notice
him. He turned his head. Her eyes were moist; if the idea
were not so ridiculous he would have thought she had been
crying.

He sprang to his feet. "Why, hello!" he exclaimed. "I had
almost forgotten that there was another wide awake person in
the house."

She started, glanced in his direction and then turned away.
"I thought you had gone to bed long ago," she said hurriedly, and without looking at him. "Father has, I suppose?"

"Oh, yes. And I must follow suit. I have been sitting here
trying to think this business out, but I haven't got anywhere
in particular. . . . Well, good night."

"Good night, Frank."

Still she was not looking at him, but he was looking at her
and, as he moved toward the door, the lamplight shone for
an instant upon her face. Her cheeks were wet. She *had*
been crying.

And he guessed why. Of course!

He paused. "Helen," he stammered, awkwardly. "I—I
wouldn't feel too badly about it, if I were you. It isn't over
by any means. Carmi is sure to win in the convention."

"Is he?" Her tone was surprisingly listless, he thought.

"Why, honestly, I don't see how he can help it. Every one
of his friends—and he has hundreds of them in the district—
will work harder than ever for him now. The *Eagle*—"

She broke in. "The *Eagle* mustn't take sides," she cried,
impulsively. "Don't you see it mustn't?"

He stared at her. "Take sides! Why, it has taken sides
almost since the beginning. It has been red-hot for Carmi
Blake for the past two months or more. You don't expect
it is going to cool off now, when there is some prospect of a

real fight? That *would* be a yellow trick! What would the South Side think of me? Come now, what would you think of me, yourself?"

She hesitated, but only for a moment.

"It doesn't make any difference what any one else thinks. It doesn't really. You must think of yourself. Oh, don't you *see?*" impatiently. "You must. If this *is* what Father calls a put-up job, the people behind it are the most influential people in the county. They have been good friends of yours; they have helped you in ever so many ways. If you should oppose them too openly you might lose their friendship and then where would you be—you and the paper? They could ruin you. . . . Oh, I know a lot of things, a lot more than you think. Father has told me some and—and I have guessed more. Frank, tell me this: Didn't you borrow money to pay for those new presses and the repairs and everything? . . . Oh, of course, it isn't my business at all and you needn't tell me unless you want to; but you have told me a great deal about your business affairs and I know you were awfully worried for a while. And then, all at once, you bought those presses and— And I couldn't think where all that money came from unless you borrowed it. . . . But you mustn't tell me; of course you mustn't."

He had never told a single soul, but he told her then. Afterward, when he thought of it, he wondered why, but tell he did.

"Yes," he confessed, "I borrowed four thousand dollars at the bank. They have my note. Captain Bates arranged it for me. He told me I could pay it whenever convenient, a little at a time and not to worry."

She gasped. "Four thousand dollars!" she repeated, in a whisper. "Oh, I didn't dream it was as bad as that!"

"Bad? I thought it was pretty fine at the time. It just about saved my life. I shall pay some of it back pretty soon, too.

I have been able to save a little during the last few months. We're doing pretty well," with a satisfied nod.

"But suppose—oh, just suppose they turned against you. They could ask for the whole of it right away, couldn't they?"

"I suppose they could—but they won't. Captain Bates—"

"That is just it! Oh, why can't you see? Who are Captain Bates's closest friends? Judge Dean and Mr. Haven and Manasseh Eldredge. And Dean and Haven are on the bank board. You mustn't lose their friendship. You *must* be careful. Promise me you will be?"

He was amazed; he could not understand.

"Why now, see here, Helen—why—why, what is all this? I shan't do anything—the *Eagle* won't do anything more than it has already done, more than Dean and Bates themselves wanted it to do—that is, support Blake. They were behind him then; I can't believe they are not behind him now. . . . Oh, I know you are disappointed; we all are. We expected both caucuses to instruct their delegates for Carmi. They haven't, but he will be nominated yet. Now is when his real friends must stick by him. We'll pull him through for you yet. As your father said just now—watch us."

Her eyes flashed. "What *do* you suppose I care about all that?" she cried. "I wanted Carmi to be nominated and elected, of course I did. He wanted to be and—yes, I think he should be. But whether he is or not doesn't really matter at all."

"Doesn't *matter?* . . . . Why—why, I thought you—you— When I saw you come in just now I thought you had been crying and I—well, naturally, I supposed—"

"Did you suppose I had been crying because Carmi Blake might lose the nomination? I don't cry so easily. I was troubled about you. Whenever you and Father have preached your—your independence, and whenever you have said that the *Eagle* should stand for what you thought right, no matter who thought it wrong, I have encouraged you. You know I have. And now, when I realize what that sort of encouragement may have led you into, I—oh, I feel so *guilty!*"

She turned away. He was in a curious state of mind. To see her there, in tears—to listen that it was for his sake that she was so troubled—why, it—it— Impulsively he took a step toward her, but she turned again and faced him. She was trying to smile.

"This is all awfully silly, I suppose," she said. "I have been brooding over it out there in the kitchen and I—well, I am rather tired to-night anyway. But, you see, I was sure you must have borrowed money and I felt so responsible. . . . Oh well, that may be all right—the money, I mean."

"Of course it is all right. I told you that Captain Bates arranged the loan for me. I don't believe he would play me a mean trick just because I stood by my guns in a political row. I have seen a good deal of him lately, and I don't believe he is that kind."

"Probably he isn't . . . but," after a moment's pause, "I think you should be careful not to make him your enemy. Now don't *you* think so—everything—and," with a slight emphasis, "everybody considered? . . . Well, good night, Frank. No, no, you mustn't mind all this foolishness of mine. I am just tired, that's all. I shall be all right—and more sensible, I hope—in the morning."

She lighted the hand-lamp on the shelf in the corner and gave it to him. He took it absently. There seemed to be much that he wanted to say, but the saying was hard.

"Helen," he faltered, "I—you mustn't worry about me. If I am in any scrape at all it isn't any one's fault but mine. Certainly it isn't yours. I—I can't bear to think that you have been so troubled on my account. I didn't realize—"

"There, there, of course you didn't. Why should you? Good night."

In his room on the dressing table were a few letters. Neither he nor Elisha had called at the post office that afternoon, but Helen had evidently done so. One of the letters was from Victoria. He *didn't* mind because she had not written for almost a week, *did* he? She had been *so* busy. And she would see him very, very soon. Her friends had persuaded her to stay "just a weeny little bit longer" but she should start for home—"really and truly start"—on September twentieth.

The news should have thrilled him. He tried to believe that it did, but the attempt was not very successful. A few months before and he would have been blissfully happy, would have been able to think of nothing else but that home-coming. Now, when he tried to concentrate on that, he found his thoughts straying to subjects which should have been vastly less important—the caucus—and Carmi Blake—and Helen Dodson.

What the deuce was the matter with him, anyhow?

CHAPTER XX

Next morning Cornelius Haven called at the print shop. He was, as always, the pattern of urbanity.

"You hurried away from the caucus before I could prepare your credentials as a delegate, Franklin. Here it is. Oh, and have you selected your substitute? Of course, we all hope and expect that you will be on hand yourself, but in case you can't—sickness or any other reason—why, you should have an alternate, of course. Who is he to be?"

Franklin had forgotten the matter of a substitute. Nothing short of paralysis or death should keep him away from that convention, but nevertheless— He had an inspiration.

"How about Elisha Dodson?" he suggested. "I haven't spoken to him about it, but he'll do it if I ask him. Yes, make Elisha my substitute, Mr. Haven."

Haven nodded. "A very good choice, I should say," was his comment. "Dodson is an—er—well, an odd stick, but honest and a good citizen."

Franklin resented the touch of condescension.

"He is one of the finest fellows I know," he declared, sharply.

"Yes, yes," hastily, "of course—of course. Well, I will list him as your alternate. Good day, Franklin."

When Elisha was informed of his appointment he was inclined to demur. Why, he had never been a delegate to anything in his life. Suppose he had to make a speech! Gorry! That would be a nice mess.

"You couldn't make a worse one than I made at that caucus. But don't worry, you won't have to be there. Unless I am struck by lightning, I shall attend the convention myself. Now let's get down to cases. How much of the truth about the row in the caucus should the *Eagle* print, do you think?"

Elisha was uncertain. There would have to be some sort of story, of course, but he doubted the wisdom of saying a great deal concerning the harbor improvement.

"We don't want to start any more talk than is necessary, Frank. There's bound to be enough of it anyhow, and we've got to be awful careful, for Carmi's sake. If we only knew what set it goin'—the inside of it all, I mean."

"Well, we don't. And who is going to tell us?"

"Carmi could, I should think likely. He must know. But Nellie seems pretty sure that he won't open his mouth about it, and you said Abiathar acted as if he was as much in the fog as anybody else. Goin' to see Carmi pretty soon, are you, Frank?"

"I'm going to see him now, this very morning. We'll let the caucus story wait till I come back."

"Um-hm. I tore up that front page spread hurrahin' because he was as good as nominated. What about that?"

"We'll have another playing up the 'strong recommendation' stuff. But that can wait, too. I'm off for the South Side."

The Blake wharf was busily crowded when he reached it. Abiathar was superintending the final fitting out of the fishing schooner, the *Spread Wing*—she was to sail for the Banks that afternoon—and Franklin walked over to where he was standing. Abiathar turned impatiently when his name was spoken, but when he recognized his visitor he grunted a greeting.

"Carmi's in the back office," he said. "Yes, yes, you can see him, far's I'm concerned. What do you want of him?"

Franklin smiled. "A good Yankee like you ought to guess that. Captain," he said, "I want—or the *Eagle* wants—to get some inside information about that funny business at the caucus yesterday. What is all this about harbor improvement?"

Abiathar Blake looked at him. Then, taking him by the arm, he led him away from the crowd of workers.

"Look here, Cobb," he said, lowering his voice, "did you mean what you said in the meetin' yesterday about you and your paper workin' hard for Carmi?"

"Of course I meant it. Why not?"

"And nobody's come to you yet and told you you'd better not work for him any longer?"

"No. Who would? And if they did, it wouldn't have made any difference."

"You're goin' to vote for him in the convention?"

"Certainly."

"I told Zenas that, unless I was mistaken in my man, we could count on you. You and he and I; that makes three sure."

"Three! Why not all seven? ... Oh, of course there is Holway. But the vote to recommend for your brother was unanimous."

"Oh, I know," testily. "That was because Bates made the motion. But I wouldn't trust Holway—and I'm a long ways from certain about Haven and Dean and Manasseh. I don't like the looks of Joe Dean's sleeve; it wouldn't be the first time he's had somethin' up it that nobody but his pet dogs knew about."

"But Captain Bates is no one's pet dog. They always take orders from him, don't they? I have never heard anything to the contrary since I've been in Wellmouth."

"Huh! Sometimes a dog is smart enough to fool the one that owns him. I don't know what this harbor game is nor who is really playin' it—nor why."

"But Carmi must know."

"Maybe he does, but if he does he won't tell me. He's my own brother, but he's the stubbornnest mule, when he sets out to be, that ever balked in the traces. He won't say one word. Why wouldn't he promise to back up the Blue River plan? If he had our whole program would have slid through slick as an eel through axle grease. But he wouldn't—you heard him say so—and he won't now. And he won't tell why. Zenas and I set pleadin' and beggin' with him half of last night. We told him that, if he'd found out somethin' was out of kilter with the Blue River scheme, all he had to do was say what it was and show proofs and Holway and the rest of 'em wouldn't have a leg to stand on. The only answer he made was that Noah Holway's legs didn't interest him. Between you and me, Frank, he hasn't been like himself lately —laughin' and good-natured; seems to be blue and glum half the time. I don't know whether it's politics or somethin' else, but it's somethin'. . . . But we can count on the *Eagle,* can't we, Frank?"

"Yes, you can."

"Fine! Now you run along and see what that darned fool brother of mine has to say to you."

Captain Carmi did not seem inclined to say anything at first. He tipped back in his desk chair, his hands thrust into his trousers pockets, and, after acknowledging his caller's "Good morning" with a brief "How are you?" waited for the next remark.

"Well, Captain," began Franklin, "I came down to see if you had anything for the *Eagle* this morning. Anything about the action of the caucus you'd like to have us print?"

"No."

"We've got to print something, you know. A statement from you would interest a great many people."

"I made all my statements in the caucus. You heard 'em, you were there."

"Yes. I heard you say that you would not bind yourself by any pledges or promises."

"That's right. I won't."

271

"I see. You don't care to add anything to that?"

"There is nothin' to add. Plain enough, isn't it?"

"Perfectly. Of course you realize that, after what Holway and Bascom said about the Blue River improvement plan there will be a great many questions asked."

"Let 'em ask 'em of Holway. I presume likely he's got his answers ready—or," with a twitch of the lips, "they've been got ready for him."

Franklin's "nose for news" caught the whiff of a possible hint.

"Got ready for him?" he repeated. "Now that sounds interesting. You mean you believe—"

Blake interrupted. "I ain't sure that I believe anything," he said, with sharp emphasis, "and if I ever should it won't be given out to the paper. Look here, Cobb, I'm willin' the *Eagle* should print what I said about not goin' to the State House pledged to anything or anybody. You can make that just as strong as you want to; but," tipping his chair forward and leaning frowning across the desk, "that's all you must say. Don't you go to speculatin' and guessin' in that paper of yours about me and my actions, because I won't have it. Understand?"

The blood rushed to Franklin's face; he, too, leaned forward. Then, after a moment, he leaned back again.

"Aye, aye, skipper," he agreed, with a shrug and a grin. "I'll obey orders. You can't pick another fuss with me, because this time *I'll* be the one to call the fight off. As the Honorable Dean remarked so gracefully yesterday, there being no further business this meeting is adjourned."

He rose and reached for his hat. Carmi Blake's scowl disappeared, he even smiled slightly.

"No special hurry so far as I'm concerned," he observed. "So long as we've got that point nailed down I'm willin' to talk. Anything else you want to say?"

"Guess not."

"Humph! Bi tells me that you stood up on the floor yesterday and made proclamation that you was goin' to work for my nomination no matter whether they made you a delegate or not. What did you do that for?"

"Oh, I don't know. It was how I felt, I suppose."

"You may feel different—and sorry—later. I may be licked, you know."

"I'm betting you won't. Anyhow, you're not licked yet. Aren't quitting, are you?"

"*What!* No, by the everlastin', I'm not quittin'! And the way I feel now I may not quit even if—"

"Eh? What?"

"Nothin'. . . . But you can bet your life I'm not quittin'."

"Neither is the *Eagle*. Well, good-by. See you later and often, of course."

"So long. . . . Humph! . . . Know what the trouble is with you, Frank Cobb?"

"I imagine there are a good many troubles. Which one do you mean?"

"The trouble is that you're a pretty decent fellow. And," moodily, "I wish you weren't."

"For heaven's sake, why?"

" 'Cause then I could chuck this inkstand at your damned head—and I'd like to. . . . There, there, get out! You're busy and so am I."

A most unsatisfactory interview with a perfectly insane ending. This Blake chap surely was a queer bird.

The *Eagle's* account of the caucus was carefully written. Very little was made of the harbor improvement discussion and a great deal of the fact that Wellmouth's delegates had been sent to the convention "strongly recommended" for Carmi Blake. There was an editorial also and Franklin Cobb wrote that himself. It was a clarion call to the district to rally about the Blake standard.

Captain Blake is the choice of the great majority of our citizens. They have chosen him because of his ability, his integrity and because, knowing him, they know that each action taken by him in the State Legislature will be taken only after careful consideration of what is, or is not, for the welfare of us—his own people. The very fact that he has publicly refused to bind himself by pre-election pledges of any kind should be sufficient proof that he is the sort of representative our district needs and should have. Every Republican voter in Wellmouth and Orham townships should make it his business to impress upon the delegates to the convention this fact: "We want Carmi Blake!"

Elisha Dodson whistled when he was handed the penciled manuscript.

"Gorry!" was his comment. "That's hot enough, Frank. How do you suppose Noah Holway will like that?"

Franklin grinned. "He will realize that I meant what I said in the caucus. Not too hot for you, is it, Elisha?"

"For me? No, sir-ee, not a mite! Nellie, she'll like it, too. She's been pretty sober since the caucus. I'm afraid she had her heart set on Carmi's bein' nominated unanimous. Natural enough she should feel that way. You understand, Frank?"

Franklin nodded. He understood well enough. The interview in the Dodson kitchen had been in his thoughts ever since it took place, and he had reached what he believed to be a fairly convincing explanation of Helen's strange attitude. She *was* worried about his having borrowed the money; she probably did feel a certain measure of responsibility—although she shouldn't, of course; but those feelings were not the real cause of her distress that evening. Her real trouble was precisely that to which her father had just referred. Her heart had been set upon Carmi Blake's unanimous nomination and triumphant election. The shock of the news from the two caucuses had tumbled her from the heights to the depths. She was bitterly disappointed and, temporarily at least, discouraged. She was in the mood to see bugbears in every corner and she saw them in his. That was all. Natural enough, just as Elisha had said.

Yes, of course; but it was up to him to prove that he did understand and was grateful for her interest and thought of him in the midst of her own disappointment and concern for the man she cared for. Whether he actually liked Carmi Blake or not, or whether or not Blake liked him—he was never quite sure in either case—as a matter of common decency he must work harder than ever for the man's success. His own personal feelings—and they were strong ones just now—concerning her and her father must not enter into the matter at all. His own pledge in the convention should be binding enough. It was, certainly; but even that was secondary. Helen's happiness was the only thing that really counted—that and his own self-respect. If Carmi Blake was not nominated and elected it should not be because of any lack of endeavor or fear of consequences on his part. No, it should not!

The story of the caucus and the editorial appeared in the *Eagle* that following week. If they created any sensation at all, it was lost in the whirlpool of political agitation in which Wellmouth was spinning. The South Side was up in arms. Whenever Franklin went down there in search of news items he almost never found any of the leaders at home or at their places of business. Captain Zenas Rogers had gone to Orham; Seth Briar had departed, in his buggy, for a trip around the outlying sections of the township. Carmi was more frequently in his private office, but usually there were a dozen callers in conference with him.

The Corners, however, were placid enough—outwardly at least. Tip Cahoon was wildly excited; he had a new rumor to report every day. The convention was going for Blake on the first ballot; it was not going for him at all; Noah Holway's rheumatiz had got a-holt of him again and like as not he wouldn't be out of doors on convention day; the South Side "wharf gangs" were coming up to stand outside the hall with shotguns, and if Carmi wasn't chosen there would be "reg'lar old Harry" to pay.

When Elisha demanded to know where he had heard this last amazing romance he was a trifle reticent.

"Well," he finally admitted under cross-examination, "you see, I've been cruisin' down to the South Side consider'ble lately—nights, I mean. There's a girl there; her folks live over to Bayport, you know, and she works in Burgess' hardware store. Her and I have been kind of—er—well, goin' 'round together some lately. Say, 'Lish, she's a pippin. Yes, *sir!* don't know when I ever see more of a pippin than she is. Anyhow, she—"

"Back up a minute, Tip! What is a pippin?"

"Eh? Why, it's a—a pippin is—er—er— Don't you know yourself?"

"Yes, I know, but I wondered if you did."

"Course I do. It's a—a—well she's one, anyhow. And she's sort of mashed on me, you understand."

"That's enough. If she is mashed on you I know what she is. Heave ahead!"

"She told me—night afore last 'twas—that that very afternoon she'd sold no less than three dozen loaded shotgun shells —cartridges—to fellers that work on the wharves and around down there. Course they *said* they was layin' 'em in gettin' ready for the duck and goose shootin' soon as the law went off. But *I* said to her, says I, 'I have my doubts. Yes, sir, I have my doubts. Considerin' who them fellers are—all of 'em crazy for Carmi Blake—it looks funny to *me*.' That's what I told her."

"Did she say you looked funny to her? . . . No? Well, she missed a chance. I don't know whether those shells will land any geese or not, but I judge *she* has landed one already— yes, and has been stuffin' it. If I was you I wouldn't tell that yarn down to the South Side. There isn't any game law on idiots, as I know of."

Franklin had been rather expecting a call from some of the Corners "group," Eldredge or Dean, possibly. He wondered if the *Eagle's* editorial, "red-hot" as it was, had found favor or disfavor in high places. But it was not until a few days prior to that set for the convention that an important caller came. And he was the most important of all.

"Hello, young man!" hailed Captain Gideon Bates, walking unannounced into the little back office. "Haven't seen much of you lately. Don't get up to the house nowadays as often as you used to. Well, Vic will be home on the twenty-second. You knew that, I suppose?"

"Why—yes, sir."

"Imagined you would. . . . No, thank you, I won't sit down; got to go across to Joe Dean's in a few minutes. You're pretty busy these days, I guess. I read that editorial of yours last week."

"Did you? I hope you liked it?"

"Liked the spirit of it first-rate. Carmi Blake must have liked it, too. Nailed his flag to the main truck, didn't you?"

"I only drove an extra spike or two. It has been nailed there for a good while."

"Has it?"

"Why, of course it has, sir," with surprise. "You and Judge Dean were the ones who asked me to hoist it there in the beginning."

"To hoist it—yes; but there is a good deal of difference between hoisting and nailing. A flag that is hoisted can be lowered if it's necessary. When it's nailed getting it down isn't such an easy job—no, nor quite such a pretty one, either. I rather wish you had shown me that editorial before you printed it, son."

"Why? I don't understand. Surely, Captain Bates, you don't mean that the *Eagle* should give up—"

"Haven't asked you to give up anything yet, have I? And your editorial has been printed so there's no use talking about it now. You're pretty green in politics, Frank Cobb, and I'm an old hand. I've learned a lot of things that you'll have to learn. One of 'em is just what I said there in the caucus: you heard me say it. In a campaign there is just one thing that really matters—the good of the party. That comes ahead of everything else. Maybe some of us may think that our candidate is a whole lot better than the others or that he is entitled to the nomination and ought to have it. We may be right, too; but, right or wrong, that is secondary to the main idea, which is the success of the party on election day. Nothing—*nothing,* I tell you—must be allowed to interfere with that. You're a good Republican, aren't you?"

"Why—why, yes, sir, I suppose I am. I have never voted any other ticket."

"I should hope you hadn't! Well then, like any Republican worth the name, you are willing to sacrifice something for the party? . . . If it comes to that, I mean?"

"Of course. But, Captain Bates—"

"Hold on! I've said more than I meant to. I've said it because you're a pretty smart young chap and I like you and you and Vic are good friends. You're just getting a good start in this town and county and I don't want you to make mistakes that you may be sorry for later on. You bear in mind what I've just said about sacrificing everything for the party's good, your own ideas of what's what and all that. Sacrifices of that kind have to be made in politics; we all have to make 'em. Confound it, yes!" with an impatient frown. "Some of us may come to feel we must do things that, when you get to be as old and settled as I am, you hate the very thought of doing. . . . Oh, well, that's all perhaps and maybe as yet. But just think over what I've told you and, the next editorial you write, make it plain that the name of any one candidate—I don't care how good a name it is—

doesn't count for a tin nickel beside the success of the Republican party on election day. That's my advice, boy, and I'm giving it just because I know it's safe. Yes, and I shouldn't bother to give it to everybody either. . . . So long. I must hurry over to Dean's."

He was walking out of the office, but Franklin sprang after him.

"Oh, wait just a minute, Captain Bates," he pleaded. "You've said too much or too little, and I don't know which. Can't you—"

"No," gruffly, "I can't. I've said all there is to say just now, and I shouldn't wonder if that was too much."

"But, Blake—"

"Blake may be nominated, for all I know. I hope he will be. Good-by."

Franklin, returning to the desk, thought over this astonishing interview. The more he considered it the less he liked it. He was on the point of calling Dodson in for a consultation but then dismissed the idea. Why worry Elisha, who would of course pass on his worriment to Helen? The convention was but two days off. Everything would be settled then.

The morning of the fourteenth of September dawned fair and beautifully clear. Blue sky, a northwest breeze, not a cloud. But at dinner time, Elisha, glancing at the barometer in the front hall of the Dodson cottage, shook his head dubiously.

"Told you this mornin', Frank, didn't I," he said, "that this kind of a day this time of year was liable to be a weather breeder? Glass is fallin' and it's smurrin' up over to the west'ard. We missed our reg'lar August twister this year, but I vow I'm afraid we may be goin' to get it now. Wind's hauled around to the no'theast, too. Tut, tut! Yes, sir, we're in for a storm, or I'm all wrong. Hope I am."

He was not. By supper time that evening the wind had

increased to a fair-sized gale, and the rain was dashing against the windows. Franklin, waking in the night, heard the gutters roaring and the trees groaning as their branches thrashed against the roof of the little house. A wicked night, with the promise of a still more wicked day to follow.

CHAPTER XXI

THE promise was fulfilled. Franklin during the next morning could feel the little house shake as the gusts tore at its gables and, when he came down to breakfast, Elisha excitedly informed him that one of the ancient silver leaf trees by the road had been blown down.

"How the kitchen chimney has ever stood up long as this I don't know," he declared. "I was up and down a dozen times in the night, makin' blinds fast and watchin' out for trouble. And it's blowin' harder this minute than it has any time yet. This ain't any common fall twister, Frank; this is a reg'lar February snorter landed onto us ahead of time. The papers'll have plenty of wreck news to-morrow; gorry, yes! Say, this is tough weather to hold conventions in. Those Orham delegates'll have a hard time gettin' here this afternoon, won't they?"

"I tell Father that he simply must not try to walk up to the shop this morning," Helen insisted. "It is bad enough for a young man with a pair of sound legs, but for a person his age who is lame it is impossible."

"Never you mind my lame leg nor my age either, Nellie. That leg has hopped me a good many mile. It won't blow off, not with my heft on top of it to hold it down. Suppose I'm goin' to stay away from the *Eagle* office while Frank's off to that convention? Who's goin' to 'tend to things, I ask you? Tip and that kid bookkeeper? Not if I know it!"

Franklin had a happy thought.

"I'll stop in at the livery stable," he said, "and have them send a closed carriage for you, Elisha. Yes, I shall. Who is boss of this business, you or I?"

Elisha's vehement protests that he wasn't going to be loaded into a carryall like an old woman bound for a funeral were ignored. Franklin, garbed in a wrinkled oilskin slicker, an old cap on his head and an umbrella in his hand, started for the livery stable. It took the combined strength of both the Dodsons to pull the kitchen door shut after his exit. The umbrella blew inside out before he reached the gate.

At the stable he left orders for the carriage to be sent at once and splashed on to the Higham shop. Main Street at the Corners was strewn with dead leaves, twigs and broken branches. Cahoon had not arrived yet, but he came in soon afterward, as did the bookkeeper. Both were very wet and Tip was, as usual, voluble.

"Did you ever see it blow so like time?" he panted. "And rain—don't talk! I couldn't more'n half see where I was bound to, and I walked into a puddle front of Joe Dean's place that wa'n't less'n two foot deep. I started to swear, but there wa'n't no comfort in it 'cause every swear I swore never got no further than my front teeth; blowed right back again down my throat. Cripes, what a day!"

The hiring of the livery equipage had given Franklin another idea. When Elisha arrived, moderately dry but still irritable because of the humiliation of being "battened down in a buggy and towed astern of a horse" he mentioned his intention of driving to the South Side.

"I want another talk with Abiathar Blake before that convention this afternoon," he said. "He can tell me just what I ought to do and say to help pull his brother through and his advice should be valuable. I'll be back before dinner time."

He dropped the driver at the stable door and took the reins himself. He had ordered a closed carriage, but the only vehicle the livery had been able to supply was a buggy with a leather "boot." The boot protected the lower two-thirds of his body when in place but its fastenings were old and flimsy and the wind twice tore it loose. Replacing and securing the slippery, flapping thing was a patience-trying and time-wasting operation. It was nearly half-past nine when he fastened the horse to the hitching post before the door of the Blake Brothers' place of business.

He had no sooner entered the outer office than he became aware that something out of the ordinary was going on. One of the two clerks was at his desk, but the other was not in sight. Through the rain-streaked windows he could dimly see the wharf, bare, wet and wind swept, with the tumbling gray and white water beyond. There were no craft of any kind beside the string-pieces and—which was very unusual in his experience—no busy crowd of laborers. From the private office at his left came the rumble of voices, one of them, Abiathar Blake's, loud and sharply authoritative. He could not catch the words, but there was no doubt that Captain Abiathar was much excited about something.

"What's the matter?" asked Franklin of Jerry Nickerson, the clerk, who had hailed him as he entered. Nickerson, too, was excited.

"There's the devil and all to pay," he answered, dropping his pen and coming out from behind the tall desk. "We've got a schooner ashore on the Razor Bank down off the Point of Beach of North Wellmouth. We was lookin' for her in 'most any time, but this mornin', an hour or so ago 'twas, we got a telegram from North Wellmouth sayin' that the life-savin' crew had sighted her, hard and fast on the shoal, and was goin' off to her. Cap'n Carmi was here and he wouldn't wait a minute; jumped into his buggy and started. He took Seth Baker and Abner Taylor with him. I hustled up to Cap'n Bi's house and rousted him out. We've tried to telegraph for more particulars, but the wires are down now somewheres, and we can't get through. Taylor and Baker were the only ones of the wharf gang on hand early this mornin'; all the rest have got the day off 'count of that Odd

Fellows doin's over to Bayport. Cap'n Bi, he's in a regular stew, I tell you. Between worryin' about the men on the *Mary M.* and, it bein' convention day, he's pretty nigh crazy. He's in there now. Jim Hammond and Henry's with him. I guess likely you can go right in, too, Mr. Cobb, if you want to."

Franklin opened the door of the private office. Abiathar Blake was pacing the floor. With him were the firm's head bookkeeper, Henry Wing, and Jim Hammond, foreman of the wharf crew. Blake nodded perfunctory recognition.

"Eh? Oh, hello, Frank!" he grunted. "Can't talk to you now, I'm too busy. We've got a wreck on our hands; Jerry's told you about it, I suppose. . . . There's no other way, Jim," addressing Hammond. "Somebody must go right down, and you'll have to be the one. Get a rig somewheres and start. If you should see a couple of our boys along the way, take 'em with you, but don't waste time huntin' 'em up. Get goin', that's the main thing."

Hammond, oil-skinned and rubber-booted, shook his head dubiously. "It's liable to take time gettin' a horse 'n' team this forenoon," he said. "There's that county Odd Fellows' all day meetin' and dinner over to Bayport and about every rig that could be got ahold of was spoke for long ago. About all our gang are goin' and I'm afraid most of 'em's started by this time."

"I know, I know," nervously. "If only Carmi had sent word to me before he started. And if only I could get away myself! Well, I can't, with that convention on my hands, and a man my age wouldn't be much use anyhow. Oh, good Lord! to think that my own horse has to be dead lame now, of all times. Well, go and ask Zenas Rogers to lend you his. He'll do it, I know. . . . Yes, and say, Jim: If everything is all right down there, if the crew's ashore—and they should be, for the life-savers must have got to 'em long ago—you tell Carmi that he's *got* to come right back. Tell him I say that a whole lot depends on his bein' on hand to see some of those Orham delegates before they go into the convention. Make him understand that. Tell him I say it's almighty important. . . . Well, well," testily, "what is it, Cobb? Don't bother me with politics now. If you'll just wait—"

Franklin had stepped forward. Now he interrupted.

"Captain Blake," he said, eagerly—"Hold on a minute, Jim; you're in this. Captain Blake, I have a horse and buggy outside here. Jim can have them just as well as not."

"Eh? Oh, fine, fine! Much obliged to you, Frank. Go on, Jim. If I can scare up another bunch to help out down there I'll send 'em after you soon's I can. Tell Carmi I'll fix all that and, if the *Mary M.'s* crew are safe ashore, not to mind the schooner, but to come home quick's he can get here."

Franklin was already on his way through the outer office. Even as he started the thought was in his mind and before he, with Hammond at his heels, reached the hitching post his mind was made up. He unbuckled the halter and scrambled to the buggy seat.

"Get in, Jim," he ordered.

Hammond stared at him. "What are you doin' aboard there?" he demanded.

"I'm going with you. Come—move!"

It is a long seven miles from Wellmouth South Shore to North Wellmouth Point of Beach. The road leaves the main highway at the fork just before that highway enters North Wellmouth village and turns right, to wind over low hills and between high dunes, until at last it emerges upon the open beach at the beginning of the mile-wide neck of sand which divides Wellmouth Bay from the Atlantic. The Wellmouth life-saving station then stood—it has been moved since—on the Bay shore just where this neck, the Point of Beach, joins the mainland. Nowadays the first half of the journey may be made over hard, smooth macadam and, in summer, venturesome picnic parties of young people in automobiles make

Point of Beach their objective, although there is always the risk of a heavy car's being caught and held by the soft sand.

But at the time when Cobb and Hammond made their trip there were no really good roads in Ostable County. The highways through the town were sometimes surfaced with clam or oyster shells, but the roads between villages were uneven and deeply rutted, with grass and weed-grown ridges between the ruts. To drive to Point of Beach on a pleasant day was a tiring ordeal for horse and passengers. And this particular day was distinctly unpleasant.

Franklin drove for the first few miles while his companion fought with the flapping boot and yelled encouragement to the plodding horse. The ruts were filled with water which the wheels splashed over the buggy and its occupants and, although the pines and scrub oak by the roadside shut off a little of the wind, there was much more than enough left.

Jim, for the first few minutes, had shouted questions in his companion's ear. What on earth was *he* taking such a devilish cruise as this for? There wasn't any need of it; he—Hammond—could have gone alone. What good did Cobb think he could do down there at the Point? What did he go *for?*

"Oh—because— Oh, I don't know why. Because I wanted to, I guess."

This was no more nor less than the truth. He didn't know exactly why he had suddenly made up his mind to go to the Point. He had never seen a wreck—a wreck in being, so to speak. He had heard many stories about them since coming to Wellmouth, for wrecks along that coast were not rarities, but he had never seen one, nor the life-savers at work; had never even visited an exposed spot like Point of Beach in a storm like this one. And here was his chance. There was the convention, of course, but he could easily get back in time for that. He was young, the adventure and excitement appealed to his imagination and so, just as he had told Hammond, he went—because he wanted to.

Jim's comment was frank. "You must be a darned fool to want to—*this* day. Creepin' Moses, how that rain does slant along!"

"This is about as bad a storm as you ever saw, isn't it?"

"Eh? . . . Lord, no! This ain't a patch on some of 'em I've seen, and been afloat in, too; but I had a good vessel underneath me then and the whole Atlantic ocean for steerage room. You're off the road again. Here, let me take the helm a spell."

They exchanged places on the buggy seat and Hammond drove. After what seemed to Franklin hours and hours—his watch was in his waistcoat pocket and to get at it would have meant a struggle not worth while—they came to a second fork, with a sign bearing a hand pointing to the right and the words "Life-Saving Station."

"We'll go to the station," screamed Jim. "They must have fetched the schooner folks ashore before this, and that's where they'll be, and Carmi, too."

Mrs. Erastus Bean, wife of the station keeper, had seen them coming and met them at the door. Yes, her husband and the crew had started for the wrecked schooner hours before. They knew she must be the *Mary M.* because late in the previous afternoon, before the storm was really bad, the lookout in the towers had seen and recognized her through the glass. She was making heavy weather of it even then, and Captain Bean was anxious. Then, the first thing in the morning the beach patrol sighted her fast on the shoal.

"So 'Rastus sent our spare man over to telegraph you folks," explained Mrs. Bean, "and him and the crew started in the boat. They ought to have been back long ago if everything was all right. I've been up in the tower watchin', but it's only once in a while that it's clear enough to see as far as the Bank, and I haven't seen anything of the boat. Oh, dear! I'm gettin' awful worried, and it takes consider'ble to worry a woman

287

whose husband is a life-saver. Mr. Hammond, do you think—"

Jim did not let her finish. "I think everything's goin' to be all right," he declared, with brusque cheerfulness. "They've probably had to lay by quite a spell waitin' for a chance to get alongside. Don't fret, Mrs. Bean; they'll turn up pretty soon. . . . Oh, say, has Cap'n Carmi been here?"

Yes, he had been there, "quite a while ago 'twas," but he went right on down to the Point.

"Then that's where we'll go. All aboard, Frank."

They drove back to the fork and turned left. "I don't like this over 'n' above fust-rate," Hammond confided. "There's somethin' wrong or they would have been back. Well, now comes the dirty part."

They emerged from between the last of the dunes upon the upper edge of the outer beach. Here the gale had clear, unimpeded sweep. It leaped, shrieking, out of the northeast, plowing the ocean into deep furrows between high, white-crested hills. Lifting those watery hills ever higher and higher, pushing them before it, it flung them at last in crashing, churning, thundering smother upon the shore, shooting their frothing edges up and up to the very brink of the crooked, rutted wagon track.

Jim Hammond shook the raindrops from his brows and mustache and gasped for breath.

"Whew!" he sputtered. "Reminds me of old times off the Georges, this does. Well, we'll get there pretty soon now, if the horse'n' team hold together. See anything of the *Mary M.*, Frank? If she's on the Razor Bank she ought to lay somewheres off about yonder."

Seaward the view ended a few hundred yards beyond the outermost line of breakers. The rest was blank grayness, diagonally streaked with rain. Franklin shouted that he could see nothing of the wreck.

"All right. Never mind her now. Keep a lookout ahead;

this darned road is about half washed away and I don't want
to get off what's left of it. . . . There! See? There's Darius
Bassett's weir shanty. We've made it. Now where's Cap'n
Carmi?"

The little fishing settlement at the tip of the Point, a rather
busy place during the summer months, was now, in mid-September,
almost deserted. The fish traps had been taken up,
and all but three of the fifteen or sixteen rough shanties were
closed, their owners having gone back to Wellmouth or
Trumet to remain during the winter. Cobb, peering from
the buggy, could see no one.

"They'll be down at the cove nigh the lighthouse," explained
Jim. "We'll put the horse under Cahoon's shed here and
hoof it the rest of the way."

It was laborious "hoofing" through the soft sand, but the
distance was not more than a quarter of a mile and when they
came in sight of the lighthouse they saw a clump of people
standing in the lee of the lightkeeper's cottage and peering
out to sea. It was a small group, not more than a dozen altogether. There was at least one woman there—Franklin could
see a skirt flapping.

They hurried on. As they drew nearer it was plain that
Hammond was surprised and puzzled. "Where is everybody?" he soliloquized. "Darius Bassett and his gang haven't
left the Point for good yet; anyhow they hadn't as late as
day afore yesterday. Where are they? There ain't a man
younger'n sixty in that bunch. And where's Carmi? Don't
see Cap'n Carmi anywhere's, do you, Frank? There's somethin' funny about this."

He shouted, but the group by the corner of the house did
not hear him. Their approach was unnoticed until Jim, seiz-
ing the shoulder of a man at the rear of the huddle, spun him
around.

"Where's the cap'n?" he yelled. "Where's Carmi Blake?"

The man, a white-haired, white-whiskered, weatherbeaten

little old chap, Cobb recognized as Ebenezer Bassett, father of the Darius Bassett whose name Hammond had just mentioned. Darius was a trap fisherman, whose weirs were, during the summer months, set along the edge of the channel on the sheltered side of the Point. Ebenezer stared, openmouthed at his questioner.

"Eh? Why, good land!" he quavered. "Why, it's Jim Hammond, ain't it? Where'd you come from?"

"Drove down. Just got here."

.."*Drove* down! From the South Side? In this no'theaster? How you talk! And—why, hello, Mr. Cobb! Did you drive along with him?"

"Course he did! Did you think he flew? . . . Where's Carmi Blake? I want to see him right off."

"Sho! Drove a horse 'n' team all the way down here a day like this! Well, Carmi drove it, of course, and fetched Seth Baker and Abner Taylor along with him, but nothin' on earth's goin' to stop Carmi Blake from doin' what he sets out to. If he ain't—"

Jim Hammond lost patience. Pushing old Mr. Bassett to one side he addressed the man next him, another veteran. The group had, by this time, become aware of the arrivals and were crowding about. There were two women among them, bundled in oilskins, their wet hair plastered about their faces. One of them—Mrs. Darius Bassett—was crying.

"Where's Carmi Blake?" Hammond roared again. "Somebody tell me, will you?"

They all began to tell him then. Every one was excited and Mrs. Bassett was close to hysterics. Carmi Blake had gone; so had Seth Baker and Abner Taylor and Darius Bassett and Alpheus Cahoon. They—every one present—had told them not to, it was crazy; there wasn't any sense in it; if the lifesavers couldn't make it in a reg'lar lifeboat what chance would they have with their rig? It was—

"Oh, shut up!" Jim Hammond was frantic. "Stop screechin'

all to one time, for God sakes, and let's hear somethin' sensible. Here, Olsen, you tell it. And the rest of you keep still."

Olsen was the keeper of the Point light, a sixty-year-old Swede. His habit of speech was provokingly slow, but he was by far the calmest of the crowd.

"Vell, I tell you, Yim," he drawled, "it vas dis vay."

Carmi Blake, with Taylor and Baker crowded on the buggy seat beside him, had arrived at the Point about ten or thereabouts.

"I tell you, Yim," declared Olsen, with a shake of his head, "dey moost have come a-boilin'. Dot horse, he vas all of a lather. He is in my shed now, yust aboot played out. *He* von't go no more dis day, I bate you."

Captain Carmi, so the lightkeeper said and the others agreed with him, was in a savage state of impatience and worry.

"I never seen him like that," put in old Mr. Bassett. "You know how he 'most generally is, Jim—quiet and never sayin' much more than is needful, don't never get upset nor nervous-like. Well, he didn't say much now, but you could tell how nervous he was. Walkin' up and down the edge of the surf over yonder, scowlin' and mutterin' once in a while all to himself. D'rius, he talked with him a little, and, accordin' to him, Carmi was all of a fume, not on account of losin' his schooner —pretty nigh brand-new she is, but he didn't seem to care a cuss about that—what was troublin' him was the fellers aboard her. All Wellmouth men they are, and they'd sailed along with him, or under him or for him, almost ever since he first went to sea. They was his boys, he told D'rius, and he was responsible for 'em. What in time had become of that lifeboat? That's what he wanted to know?"

Olsen and Ebenezer, sometimes one and sometimes the other, went on with the story. Time passed and the storm was just as bad as ever—yes, worse. They could not see the wreck at all, and there was no sign of the returning lifeboat. On her return trip she should, in order to avoid the "wickedest water"—that along the inner edge of the shoals—pass near the Point, within sight of it even on a day like this. But she did not do so. Blake ordered Taylor to take the lightkeeper's horse and ride to the station on the chance that the boat might have returned the long way, back of the shoal, although that was very unlikely because of the additional danger. Taylor was about to start when the lifeboat was sighted.

"Carmi had gone down to tramp up and down the tip end of the Point again," continued Bassett, "when one of us— Alpheus Cahoon, seems to me 'twas—caught sight of the life-boat. She wa'n't where she'd ought to have been, neither; she was around in the easy water on the inside of the Point. And then we noticed that she was 'way low in the water, al-most awash. She was in trouble, bad trouble—even I, with my eyes, could see that. Seth Baker run down to the cove, jumped into D'rius's dory and pulled off to where she was. It was a hard pull for him, but he made it, and when he got back he had news."

According to what Bean, in command of the boat, had told Baker during their brief shouted colloquy, the boat had got within hailing distance of the schooner and found her lying almost on her beam ends at the upper end of the shoal, the seas breaking over her. Her crew, all six of them, were lashed in the rigging. The life-savers made several attempts to get alongside, but were driven off by the wind and waves time and time again. At last, just as their attempt seemed likely to succeed, the boat was thrown from the crest of a sea down upon a heavy piece of floating wreckage—part of the deckhouse it was—and her bow was badly stove. Being a lifeboat she could not sink, but she filled with water and to bring her alongside the wreck, to say nothing of loading six helpless and half drowned men aboard her, was an impossibility. So Bean had decided to return to the station, get the spare boat, and set out again.

"She was in such bad shape," went on Bassett, "pretty nigh

awash, same as I said—that 'Rastus didn't dare risk comin' down along the outside and beachin' her in the breakers, so he give orders to pull around and go up the inside of the Point. It's a long haul and they'll have a good mile tramp acrost the beach when they get there. Besides, it'll take 'em quite a spell to launch the spare boat; but you can't blame Cap'n Bean, 'twas the only thing he could do."

When they told Carmi Blake, however, he was frantic. It would be another two hours before the spare boat could reach the *Mary M.* and, meanwhile, she might go to pieces. And there were those poor fellows aboard her—fellows he had known all his life—what would become of them? No, sir, he would not let them drown. Not if he went after them himself—alone—and in a dory.

Darius Bassett's weir boat, an eighteen-foot whaleboat she was—Darius had bought her in New Bedford, second hand—was anchored in the cove at the rear of the light. Bassett and his crew had been dismantling their fish traps and storing them for the winter and had been staying at the Point while the operation was in progress. Mrs. Bassett and Ebenezer had come down a day or two before, "just for a sort of campin'-out picnic, as you might say." They were all going back to Wellmouth together to-morrow.

"Well sir, Cap'n Carmi, he see that weir boat layin' there and, next thing we knew, he was headin' for that cove beach. 'Come on, boys!' he sings out. 'Here's a good tight seaworthy craft ready and waitin' for us. Who's comin' along?' 'Along where?' somebody wanted to know—and no wonder! 'Why, off to the Razor Bank,' says he. 'We ain't goin' to let those poor devils die—neighbors and chums every one of 'em—just because Rat Bean is a fussy old woman. Come on! What are you waitin' for? It's an easy job. Am I the only one with a man's allowance of guts in this crowd?'

"Sounds crazy, don't it? It *was* crazy, too, but—well, if you'd heard him say it! And seen him! You know how big he is and what a will he's got when he sets out to use it. He stood there, tightenin' the strap to his sou'wester under his chin, and grinnin' at us. Yes, sir, grinnin'!

"'Well?' he says again. '*Am* I the only man in the bunch? Looks so. All right, then I'll go alone. So long, girls.'

"I don't presume likely he would really have gone alone. Anyhow he didn't have to. Seth Baker started swearin'. 'By the great and holy, nobody's goin' to talk like that to me and get away with it!' he growled and headed for the beach. Alpheus Cahoon and my D'rius and Abner Taylor was right astern of him. We tried to stop 'em, but you might as well have tried to stop the tide comin' in. They was aboard that weir boat and pullin' around the tip of the Point afore we knew what had happened, as you might say."

Ebenezer paused, out of breath. Mrs. Darius Bassett sobbed and wrung her hands.

"I'll never see my husband again," she wailed. "Never, never! And it's Carmi Blake's fault. Oh—oh, what shall I do! What *shall* I do!"

Jim Hammond struck one fist into the palm of the other. "Lord! if I'd only been here!" he muttered. "How long since they started, Olsen?"

The lightkeeper slowly shook his head. "Ah don't know," he replied. "Ah guess nobody bane tank aboot clocks or dings like dat, Yim."

"Have they been gone five minutes—or ten—or an hour? Can't anybody tell me that much. How about it, Ebenezer?"

"It seems about a year, but I cal'late it's been much as an hour—wouldn't you say so, 'Bial?"

Abial Smalley, another member of the Bassett "camping-out party," agreed that it was at least that. Franklin caught Hammond by the arm. "What can we do, Jim?" he demanded. "We must do something, mustn't we?"

"Huh!" savagely. "What can we do except wait? Creepin'!

if we could only *see* somethin'. Come on down to the beach, Frank. We'll be that much nigher, anyway."

The wind, so Hammond seemed to think, was subsiding a bit, but the rain and flying spray from the huge breakers still filled the air and at the tip of the Point the outlook seaward was but little more extended than from the lighthouse. They walked up and down the weed-strewn shore, saying little or nothing, but looking, always looking.

Once Jim caught Cobb by the arm and shouted in his ear.

"I'm scared, Frank," he said. "Yes, I am, scared! Carmi's about as good a sailor as there is on earth, but in this gale—and in nothin' better'n a weir boat—! Lord, Lord! If anything happens to him—now!"

Franklin shook his head. He had been thinking of Helen Dodson and what this might mean to her.

And then, at that moment, away out over the farthest notched and wind-torn wall of jumping, heaving water, he caught sight of a dark object. It had been tossed high and now it had sunk again.

"Look, Jim! Look!" he shouted, pointing.

Hammond turned. "What is it?" he cried.

"Out there! I'm sure I saw something. . . . Yes, yes! See! There it is again."

They both saw it now. It rose into sight and fell, then rose again. Jim Hammond waved his fists and yelled.

"It's the boat!" he whooped. "It's them—comin' back. By the creepin' Moses, boy, he's done it!"

The dark object drew nearer, always rising and falling, but always making progress. They could see it plainly now, a boat, with men straining at the oars and one tall bulky figure standing in the stern, a hand upon the tiller. It was almost abreast the tip of the Point where they stood when it changed direction and moved farther to the left.

"That's right! That's the stuff!" roared Hammond. "He's headin' around into the cove. Come on, Frank."

They scrambled over the sand ridges, reached the knoll at the top of the rise and plowed downward toward the cove beach. The group by the lightkeeper's house had seen the boat, for they were hurrying in the same direction.

There were several dories with the oars lying in them, pulled up on the beach. Jim, who was wearing rubber boots, splashed alongside the stern of the nearest and began pulling it into deeper water. Franklin had no rubber boots but he splashed in beside him.

"Where are you going?" he shouted.

"Off to give 'em a hand, of course. They'll need it, with that boat packed full the way she is."

"Then you think they've got the men from the schooner?"

"Eh?" scornfully. "They've come back, ain't they? Do you cal'late Carmi Blake would come back if he *hadn't* got 'em? . . . Here! No use your goin'. You don't know anything about this kind of job."

"I can row a boat. And I *am* going."

He was already settling himself on one of the thwarts. Hammond floundered in after him, gave a final shove with his oar and they started.

They met the weir boat just inside the entrance to the cove. It was low in the water and as they drew near Franklin could see over the side. Beside the men at the oars and Blake at the tiller, there were others—dripping, draggled heaps of humanity lying along the bottom between the legs of the rowers. He glimpsed one or two faces, blue-white, with closed eyes and open mouths. Were they all dead? They looked so.

Captain Carmi, the brim of his sou'wester pushed back, a cut in his forehead and the blood running down his cheek, was shouting encouragement to the rowers.

"That's it, boys," he cried. "That's the way. Lay into it. Fun's all over; we're home now. Keep her goin'. We'll run her in far as she'll float."

Then, apparently noticing the dory and its occupants for

the first time, he lifted a hand from the tiller and waved it peremptorily.

"Get out of the way, Jim," he ordered, "you're blockin' the channel. No, no, you can't help any yet. Get out of the way!"

Hammond and Cobb hurriedly pulled the dory aside. The weir boat passed them and kept on toward the beach and the excited, screaming, waving group at the water's edge. It kept on until its bow struck a sand bar about thirty feet from the shore. Without an instant's hesitation Carmi Blake was overboard, wading to the bow, holding the boat steady.

"Now you fellows get ashore and up to Olsen's," he ordered. "You've done a good job and you're played out. Yes, yes, go! There's enough of us around here to attend to everything. Drop those oars and get ashore! . . . Move! or I'll heave you overboard myself."

There was some hesitancy and objection, but not much. One by one the men who had been doing the rowing rose from their places, lifted themselves heavily over the rail and splashed toward the beach. They moved slowly and stiffly, some of them staggering and reeling as if utterly exhausted. As they reached the shore the little crowd surrounded them, shouting, cheering, laughing hysterically. Franklin heard Mrs. Bassett's sobs and screams of thanksgiving as she threw her arms about her husband's neck.

The dory was now alongside the weir boat again. Hammond, without waiting for orders, had thrown over the larger craft's anchor.

"All right, Cap'n," he said. "She'll lay where she is. What next?"

Blake, who had been stooping over the figures in the bottom of the boat, turned to look at him. With the blood, and the haggard lines about his eyes and mouth, he looked, so Franklin thought, as if he might collapse at any moment; but there was nothing in his voice or action to indicate collapse or even weariness.

"Get these poor devils somewhere where it's warm and dry, that's the first thing," he announced. "They'll have to be carried. No, no," impatiently, "they're all alive. Half frozen and half drowned, that's all; been hangin' in that riggin' most of the night and day. Here, lift this one's feet so I can get hold of him. Then you and—who's that with you? What! Cobb! What on earth are you doin' down here? . . . Never mind. You two can carry a man between you, can't you? No, no, I've got this fellow. You take the next."

He stood erect, one of the helpless castaways in his great arms. Holding him as if he were a baby, he strode toward the beach. Franklin and Jim followed, bearing another between them. As they deposited their burdens on land they were taken over by Ebenezer Bassett, Olsen and the rest who, partly carrying and partly dragging, assisted them up the slope toward the lightkeeper's cottage. As Hammond and Cobb turned to wade back to the boat, they saw Carmi Blake already stooping to lift a third man from the weir boat's bottom.

There were six of them altogether and when, at last, all were in the little house, Franklin, for one, was ready to sit down and rest. The crew and skipper of the *Mary M.* were put to bed or stretched, wrapped in blankets and comforters, upon the kitchen or sitting-room floors. Mrs. Olsen and Mrs. Bassett—the latter now more or less calm—had built fires in the two stoves and were heating water and making coffee. Ebenezer and Smalley had gone over to the Bassett shanty in search of clothes and more quilts and blankets. Darius Bassett and Alpheus Cahoon had gone there, too—to shed their wet garments and "turn in for a spell." Seth Baker and Abner Taylor, however, the pair who had accompanied Carmi Blake from the South Side that morning, were sprawled in the kitchen and it was Baker who answered Cobb's questions.

It had been a devil of a cruise off to the Razor Bank, so Baker declared, but getting there was a "snap" compared to laying their craft alongside the wrecked *Mary M.,* boarding her, cutting the helpless crew loose from the rigging and lowering them safely into the weir boat.

"It was all Cap'n Carmi," vowed Seth. "Every darned bit of it. We'd have give up half a dozen times if it wa'n't for him. He wouldn't let nobody give up. He bullyragged and bedamned us most of the time, and the rest of it he was laughin' and crackin' jokes. Yes, sir, jokes! I remember his hollerin' to Alph'us Cahoon that he understood he'd come down to the Point with Darius on a picnic. Well, he was havin' a picnic, wasn't he? And so on. All nothin', of course. 'Twasn't what he said, 'twas the way he said it and the way he acted. Well, I've sailed under him in storms just as bad as this, and he always acts that way. The worse things get, the more he behaves as if he liked it. Scared? Why, of course I was scared, but he makes a fellow ashamed to show his scare. And, great Jingo, how he did handle that boat; never let her get broadside to a sea once. He's about as big as two men anyway and he's worth six in a time like this."

When at last they did reach the wreck still it was all Carmi Blake. It was he who first climbed aboard. A sea knocked him end over end and it was only the mercy of Providence that he was not killed or washed overboard. But he grabbed something and held on and, although his head was cut and bleeding, he was on his way up the rigging in another jiffy. Oh, yes, some of the others had gone aboard too, but it was Carmi who did everything worth while.

"He's a man, that boy," vowed Seth. "By the great and holy, he's the best man that ever lived! And when you think of Noah Holway and Bascom and them tryin' to sneak him out of the nomination, it makes you think that doin' some kinds of murder ought to fetch a feller into heaven, 'stead of t'other place. Don't it now, Frank? . . . Eh? What's the matter with you?"

Franklin Cobb had sprung to his feet. The convention! He had forgotten it altogether—had not thought of it since

he and Hammond reached Point of Beach. It was to meet at
two that afternoon. He looked at his watch. Twenty minutes
after four. Why, it might be—yes, very likely was—over by
this time.

Mrs. Olsen was crossing the kitchen, a pail of steaming
coffee in each hand. He ran toward her.

"Where is Jim Hammond?" he asked.

She jerked her head in the direction of the door. "Outside,"
she said; "him and Cap'n Carmi. There is some more fellers
from the South Side yust got here."

Around the corner, in the lee of the house, Jim and Blake
were talking with the newcomers. There were three of them,
all members of the Blake wharf crew. The buggy in which
they had come was standing, the horse drooping wearily between the shafts, a short distance away.

"Cap'n Bi never got hold of us till 'most noon," one of
them was explaining as Cobb joined the group, "and we had
a high old cruise down. Wheel fetched loose in that sand
track over acrost from the station and dumped us all out.
Took land knows how long to get it on again. . . . Oh, hello,
Frank Cobb! Here's where you are, eh? Say, Cap'n Bi's
been tearin' his hair about you. Jerry told him he see you
drivin' off in that buggy with Jim here and that he cal'lated
you must have gone to the Point, too. You're supposed to
be a convention delegate, ain't you? Well then, what are you
down here for?"

It was a hard question to answer. Every one in the group
was looking at him. And what reasonable excuse had he to
offer? None—none at all.

"I didn't realize—" he stammered, hopelessly. "I came because— Oh, I don't know why I came. I wanted to see—I
thought of course I could get back before— Oh, I was a fool,
that's all. I'm sorry, Carmi."

Hammond shrugged. "I told him when we first started
that he wouldn't be any use down here, but nothin' short of

a ship's cable could have held him back. He was comin'—
and come he did. The convention must be over and done
with by this time and you was short one delegate, I'm afraid,
Cap'n."

Another of the new arrivals put in a word.

"Not quite as bad as that, Jim," he said. "Soon's 'Biathar
found out he'd gone he sent word to 'Lish Dodson to 'tend
convention in his place. 'Lish was his substitute, you remember. Oh, Cap'n Bi's no fool, even if other folks are."

Carmi Blake broke in gruffly. "Come, come, Ben," he protested, "there's no use callin' names. Cobb's no fool and you
know it. As to his not bein' any use, Jim, it strikes me he's
worked about as hard as anybody since we got back with the
boat."

Franklin shook his head.

"Thanks, Carmi," he said, "but these fellows are dead right.
I *was* a fool, and I feel like a deserter. If you should lose
that nomination—"

"There, there! How do you know I have lost? Anyhow,
if I have, I can always go to sea again. I don't know but
what— Oh, well," with a sudden change of tone. "To the
devil with politics, I'm hungry. Let's go in and see if those
women have got anything to eat and drink. Come on, all
hands."

At nine that evening, Franklin, chilled, drenched and tired
to the last extremity, opened the kitchen door of the Dodson
cottage. His place at the supper table in the dining room
was still set and waiting and Elisha and Helen came hurrying
from the sitting room to greet him.

"Well, by gorry!" cried the former, "if we ain't glad to see
you! Nellie's been up and down to that window about every
other minute since six o'clock. And look at him, Nellie!
Looks's if he'd been through the wars, don't he? Ain't had
any supper, I'll bet you! Set right down to that table and—"

Helen broke in. "Hush, hush, Father," she commanded. "Give him a chance to breathe. And to rest. He looks completely worn out. Frank, don't you want to go right to your room? Father can bring in your supper when you're ready. Now, please—"

But Franklin was thinking of neither bed nor supper. There had been but one thought in his mind during the long, dark ride with Hammond from Point of Beach.

"Elisha," he demanded, "you went to the convention in my place, didn't you?"

"Eh? Why, yes, Frank, I did. Cap'n Abiathar sent me word and so I went. Course I knew beforehand that I wouldn't be much good at the job, but—"

"Wait! This is what I want to know: Did they nominate Carmi Blake?"

The Dodsons looked at each other. "Tell him, Father," ordered Helen. Elisha drew a long breath.

"Well, no, Frank," he admitted, "I'm awful sorry, but— they didn't nominate Carmi. . . . There, there!" hastily. "Don't look like that. You're all shook to pieces. You go and turn in now, and I'll tell you a little later."

"You'll tell me now. They nominated some one, of course?"

"Why—why, yes, they did. You'll never guess who, neither. I never was so surprised—"

"Who was it? Quick!"

"Well, you see . . . well, Frank, I'll tell you. They gave the nomination to Gideon Bates."

"*What!*"

"Um-hm. They voted the nomination to Cap'n Gideon— and he accepted."

CHAPTER XXII

ELISHA, himself very much excited, might have gone on
to tell his story then and there, had not Helen interrupted.

"No, Father," she said, firmly. "Not yet. Don't you see
that he is wet through and tired almost to death? And hungry, too, I am sure. There will be time enough to talk after
he has taken off those soaked clothes and had something to
eat."

Franklin suddenly remembered. "By George!" he exclaimed, conscience stricken. "I haven't told you a word
about the wreck, have I? And of course you have been very
anxious. Well, everything is all right. The crew are safe."

Elisha nodded. "Yes, we've heard that much," he said.
"Jerry Nickerson stopped in a little while ago. He said Carmi
had telegraphed his brother from North Wellmouth that the
Mary M. was a total loss, but that the men were all ashore.
Carmi's stayin' down at the Point over night, but he'll be up
to-morrow mornin'. I meant to ask Jerry if Bi had telegraphed him about the convention, but—"

Again Helen broke in. Both stories must wait, she declared. Franklin must go to his room that minute. Protests
were unavailing. It ended in a compromise; Elisha accompanied their lodger to the bedroom and talked while he
changed.

The Dodson tale was a long one. Elisha, on receiving the
summons from Abiathar Blake, had hurried to the hall. It
was nearly two o'clock when he reached there, and he found
Abiathar with Captain Zenas Rogers and two of the Orham
delegates, in conference in the lobby. The Orham representatives were staunch Blake adherents and the quartet were

very anxious and disturbed. Something was up, they did not know what. There was a mystery afoot, they were sure of it, but they were not in the secret. One of the Orham men —his name was Waters—declared that there had been a marked change in the attitude of the delegates from his town during the last three weeks. One week before the caucus the sentiment favorable to Carmi Blake had been unanimous. Then, little by little, it had changed and, at the caucus, the delegation had been sent uninstructed.

"What's behind it, or who's behind it, I don't know," said Waters. "Ike Shotwell's been busy, I know that much, but he hasn't come near Crowell here or me. He knows, I guess likely, that we're for Carmi, first, last and all the time. I've tried to talk to some of the other fellows who are here with us now but I can't get much out of 'em. They all say they like Carmi first-rate, but that's all they will say. Two of 'em are Shotwell's hired men, out and out. The other two seem to be—well, scared to commit themselves to anything definite. If Carmi himself was only here to talk to 'em it would help a whole lot. They like him—yes, and I think they'd like to vote for him. Maybe they will anyway, only— By the Lord Harry, I wish he was here now, before the convention begins!"

Abiathar shook his head. "So do we all," he growled. "He ought to be, too. There was plenty of others to attend to that wreck, but when any of his own boys are in trouble—well, you know Carmi. But Frank Cobb's runnin' off down there, without any reason at all, like a kid runnin' to a fire! By thunder, I did think we could depend on Cobb!"

Elisha, of course, although knowing nothing whatever of his employer's actions or the reasons prompting them, stoutly defended Franklin.

"There is nobody in this town who has worked harder or done more to make Carmi the nominee than Frank Cobb and the *Eagle*," he vowed indignantly. "Frank's no runaway and you know it mighty well, Cap'n Bi."

"Well, he *has* run away, hasn't he? He isn't here."

"I'm here, and my vote'll count just as much as his. He knows that, too, I guess likely."

Seymour Sears, an Orham man, was made chairman of the convention and Cornelius Haven secretary. The first business of the meeting, ratifying the choices of the two caucuses for nominees for State Senator and member of the Governor's council, was put through perfunctorily and without debate. Then came the nomination for representative to the lower branch of the State Legislature. Zenas Rogers was on his feet instantly and, with earnestness and emphasis, presented the name of Carmi Blake. Blake was deserving of the honor, he was in every way capable, he had been promised the nomination, the district confidently expected it to be given him. "And," concluded Rogers, solemnly, "I warn this convention here and now that the Republican voters, whose delegates we are, will not be satisfied unless we carry out their wishes and nominate him."

There was applause—"real hearty applause, too," so Elisha said. Waters seconded the nomination. And then Captain Isaac Shotwell, of Orham, took the floor. His speech was long, persuasive, placating and eloquent. He, he began by saying, like so many others, honored and respected Captain Blake. He recognized his ability and integrity, believed that, under ordinary circumstances, he would make a first-class representative. He was glad to pay such a tribute to such a man.

"When he got as far as that," said Elisha, "I was hurrahin' with the rest. I'd begun to believe all Bi's notions about put-up jobs and mysteries was moonshine and that Carmi would go in without any hitch at all. But, a minute or so later, the smell of rat got so rank that even a fellow with a cold in the head couldn't help noticin' it."

For Shotwell's next sentence was the declaration that these

were not ordinary circumstances. Unfortunately, very unfortunately, some differences of opinion had arisen as to certain projects of public improvement in which all dwellers in the district, particularly those here in Wellmouth, were deeply interested. Captain Blake, openly, publicly—in the Wellmouth caucus—had refused to pledge himself to work for these projects.

Abiathar Blake was on his feet.

"That isn't so, Shotwell," cried Abiathar. "Carmi never said he wouldn't work for the harbor improvement. He just said that he wouldn't make promises of any kind to anybody. You know that and so does everybody else. Tell us the truth, why don't you?"

Captain Shotwell was not in the least ruffled. His old friend, Captain Blake, in defending his brother, was perfectly right. It was true that Captain Carmi had refused to make any promises for or against the harbor improvement bills. But that very fact would cause, was already causing, discussion and dissension among the voters of the district. In the weeks prior to election that dissension was certain to become hotter and more bitter. This must not be. It was therefore, with this one thought, the good of the party, in their minds, that he and certain others had been in consultation, had held many conferences during the days and nights since the holding of the caucuses.

"Fellow Republicans," went on Shotwell, lifting an impressive forefinger, "at those conferences opinion was unanimous. It was our duty to try and find some one to act as our standard bearer and nominee who was known to be above all questions of this policy and that; who stands, and has always stood, for true Republicanism and unselfish devotion to the public welfare, and whose nomination would unite all factions in the party. The name of one such person occurred to all of us, but we did not believe it would be possible to get him to stand for the nomination. He has already served this district for two terms in the State House and to serve another term we knew would mean a great personal sacrifice for him. But, gentlemen," the forefinger very impressive indeed, "he *has* consented. If he is nominated by this convention—as I am perfectly sure he will be—our troubles are over. I have the honor to present for nomination the Honorable Gideon Bates, of Wellmouth."

According to Elisha the presentation of that name to the convention caused a sensation such as no previous political meeting in his experience had ever known. To at least half of those present it came as a complete surprise; they sat dumb and speechless. The others, however, were evidently expecting it. They cheered and applauded wildly.

"By gorry, I thought Noah Holway was goin' to have a conniption! His specs flew right off his nose and smashed to flinders, but he didn't seem to notice—and when Noah don't notice two dollars goin' to smash then the seven wonders of the world have moved up to eight. *I* didn't holler—no, nor do anything but choke for breath. Thinks I, 'Here it is.' Here's the put-up job! This means the end of poor Carmi."

Judge Joel Dean rose, a paper in his hand. He wished, he said, to second the nomination and in doing so he would read a letter from the distinguished gentleman whose name had just been presented. The letter was short, but to the point. Gideon Bates had written that, although he had long since determined never again to seek or hold political office, he had always preached the doctrine of personal sacrifice for the public good. "It's a poor preacher who doesn't practice," he concluded. "Some of my friends in whose opinion I have confidence seem to feel that I should give up my plans for rest and retirement for the sake of the party and the district. If they are right I must, of course. If my fellow citizens and fellow Republicans nominate and elect me I shall do my best to further their interests in the State Legislature."

That was not the end, of course. Zenas Rogers and Abiathar

fought to the last ditch. They had little help. The mention of the magic name of Bates had taken the fight out of most of the delegates who had been friendly to Captain Carmi.

"But Zenas was fine, Frank," declared Elisha, "I won't forget what he said. 'Are you goin' to sit here,' says he, 'you fellows who were so strong for Carmi a month ago, and see him voted down—now, to-day, while he's down at Point of Beach in a howlin' no'theaster, payin' no attention to himself or the nomination and thinkin' only of those poor sailors wrecked on the Razor Bank? If you are I'm ashamed of you. And I tell you this: there will be a whole lot of people in your own district who will be ashamed of you, too.'"

But when the vote was counted—it was by ballot, Judge Dean saw to that—Gideon Bates had won.

"I cal'lated," concluded Dodson, "that Shotwell or somebody would move to make it unanimous, but they didn't. Knew better than to take the risk, I guess likely. . . . Well, Frank, we're licked. The *Eagle* will have to back water, I suppose. That 'll be a sweet job, won't it?"

Helen had rapped on the bedroom door several times, but now she would not be denied. Franklin's supper was ready, and he must come and eat it while it was hot. Politics and all the rest could wait, the supper could not.

He had eaten almost nothing since breakfast, but he had little appetite even now. Nor did he feel in the least like talking. The sense of disappointment and depression caused by Elisha's amazing news was heavy and, besides, he was very much exhausted, nervously and physically. He gave them a brief résumé of the exciting events at the Point, but his answers to Elisha's questions were far from satisfactory. He realized it himself.

"I can't seem to think clearly," he confessed. "Goodness knows there is enough to tell and more still that I want to hear, but—well, I— Oh, I don't know what *is* the matter with me."

There was no question of that kind in Helen's mind. "I do," she said, with emphasis. "You are tired out. Now you are going straight to bed—and so is Father. Not another word from either of you until morning."

The session at the breakfast table was gloomy. Franklin's mind was clear enough now. He woke early, he had been thinking ever since, and his depression was heavier than ever. Coupled with it was his sense of guilt at having deserted his duty at the convention to, just as Abiathar Blake had expressed it, run away to that wreck "like a kid to a fire."

The Dodsons did their best to reassure him. His absence made not the least difference; the whole business was planned beforehand to the last detail. Gideon Bates was as good as nominated before the convention began; the letter of acceptance in Judge Dean's pocket proved that.

"You couldn't have done a thing to stop it if you'd been there," urged Elisha. "Nobody could. If Carmi himself had buttonholed every delegate afore the doors opened 'twouldn't have helped. The minute I heard Cap'n Shotwell come out with Gideon's name I knew we was done for. 'Twas the one name that could settle everything. Gorry! Joe Dean and Cornelius and Ike and the rest of 'em are slick politicians. When you beat them you've got to get up before the chickens do, now I tell you!"

Franklin sighed. "I can understand now what Bates meant about making personal sacrifices for the party's good. But he said something, too, about having to do things that, as old and settled as he was, he hated the very thought of doing. That doesn't sound as if he wanted the nomination, does it? If he did he is as big a hypocrite as old Dean—and I never thought him that."

"I don't believe he did want it," was Helen's comment, "but Dean and Haven and Shotwell have coaxed and flattered him into running. They have probably told him that it is his duty to be the life-saver of the party."

"Well, he'll have a whoppin' majority," prophesied Elisha. "He's the one man that can make the South Side forget Carmi Blake."

Franklin nodded. "I suppose so. And when I think of Carmi Blake as I saw him yesterday! He was the whole thing down there, I tell you. Why, it was he—practically just he alone—who saved those poor devils on that wreck. He's a great man, I tell you! He ought to get the Humane Society medal. And instead of that they swindle him out of the nomination while his back is turned. It's a confounded shame! . . . Well, come on, Elisha; I suppose we ought to be at the office."

Elisha went to the kitchen for his hat and coat. Franklin rose dejectedly to follow him.

"I am awfully sorry, Helen," he said. "I am all broken up about it. I know how you feel. And I still feel as if it were partly my fault."

"Why, of course it wasn't. Don't be ridiculous, Frank."

"I'd like to print just what I think of the dirty trick. Well, the *Eagle* shall have a story of that wreck that will make people sit up. And if they expect me to be enthusiastic about their precious candidate they'll find themselves mistaken, that's all."

"Frank! Frank, be careful. Captain Bates's friendship means a great deal to you—in many ways."

"If it wasn't for that borrowed money!"

She regarded him gravely. "The money isn't the only reason."

He said no more. He and Elisha started for the office a moment later.

Cahoon and the bookkeeper were there when they arrived. Tip was jubilant over the result of the convention.

"I told you, Mr. Cobb," he cackled. "And I told 'Lish here much as a dozen times. Says I, 'I don't believe Cap'n Bates and Joe Dean and the rest of 'em are goin' to let no South

Sider be our candidate. When 'twas our turn to send a Wellmouth man to the State House it's always been a Four Corners man that went, and I'm bettin' 'twon't be no different this year.' That's what I said. Didn' I, 'Lish?"

"You say so much I can't remember it all. Long as you've won all your bets you ought to have money to lend. Let me have ten dollars for a couple of weeks, will you? Or five—five 'll do."

"Aw, now, quit your foolin'."

"No foolin'. Here, I'll make you a business offer. Let me have the five this minute and I'll pay you ten when the fortni't's up."

"I— Why, consarn it, 'Lish, I ain't got five dollars—not on me, I ain't."

"Have you got fifty cents?"

"Huh? Why, yes, I guess I've got that much. Only—"

"Take it and go buy yourself another necktie."

"What you talkin' about? What's the matter with the necktie I've got on?"

"It's too loud. Mr. Cobb likes quiet neckties—and people—around this shop. You think that over, Tip."

CHAPTER XXIII

THE vote in the convention was already the principal topic
of Wellmouth's conversation. At the post office that noon,
when Franklin called for his mail, they were talking of nothing else. Even the wreck of the *Mary M.* was given but
secondary consideration. On the platform of the Eldredge
store Cobb saw Manasseh, the center of an eagerly listening
group. He was obviously in a happy frame of mind. The
sound of his loud laughter drifted across the road.

A half-dozen callers dropped in at the print shop to talk
the subject over with its proprietor and Dodson. Franklin
shut himself in the back office. He was far from happy and
had no wish to talk. The only one of the visitors who gained
admission was Elkanah Rogers, who had come up to the
Corners on bank business, and even he was encouraged to
remain but a few minutes.

"There's the old Harry to pay down to the South Side,
Frank," he confided. "They're crazy mad down there. The
Blake wharf crew and a lot of the other fellows who are ashore
from fishin' are makin' brags about what they'll do to old
Shotwell the next time he comes over here. Those men who
were aboard the wreck are the worst—them and their relations. They figure the dogfish would be eatin' 'em by now if
it hadn't been for Cap'n Carmi. 'Twas him, so they and
Baker and Hammond vow and declare—just Carmi and nobody else—who saved 'em from drownin'."

"Have you seen Carmi to-day?"

"No, I ain't. I went in to see him, but he was shut up in
the office with Bi and Cap'n Zenas and Briar and that man
Waters from Orham. Henry told me there'd been a reg'lar

312

string of folks from all 'round the district there the whole forenoon. Henry said there was somethin' goin' on, but he didn't know what. Just as I was leavin' Bi came out and him and Waters jumped aboard a horse 'n' team and started off. I wondered if they was goin' to Orham. Think they was, Frank?"

"I don't know. Why should they go to Orham?"

Elkanah hesitated. He glanced toward the door and then leaned forward. "Say, Frank," he whispered, "you don't suppose they're tryin' to coax Carmi to run independent, do you?"

Cobb was for the first time interested. He looked at his caller.

"He *could* do that, couldn't he!" he exclaimed. "By George, so he could!"

"Yes," dubiously, "he could, but I don't believe 'twould get him much of anywhere. This is a solid Republican district. Pretty nigh everybody votes the straight ticket and, besides, look who is runnin' on that ticket this year. How can anybody beat Gideon Bates? Might as well try to beat Saint Peter. No, Carmi won't try it; he's got too much sense."

"Probably you're right, Rogers. But, just for fun, how about yourself? Suppose Carmi Blake did run independently, would you vote for him?"

Elkanah was taken aback by the blunt question. He hesitated, rubbed his chin and looked very uncomfortable. Then, suddenly, to Cobb's great surprise, he struck his knee with his hand, and answered just as bluntly.

"Yes, by the Almighty, I would!" he declared. "Cap'n Bates is a fine man, and I've been proud to vote for him afore—and—and all like that. And I never scratched a ticket in my life. But Carmi Blake is a fine man too. I've been for him since the beginnin' and I'm for him now. You're dead right; he *was* cheated out of that nomination and if he runs

I'll vote for him. . . . Now hold on," hastily, "don't you tell anybody I said that, for the land sakes!"

This brief interview gave Franklin Cobb more food for thought. Elkanah Rogers was, although a patriotic South Sider, a staunch regular in the party. His declaration was astonishing and illuminating. Franklin wondered how many other regulars were feeling as he did. And suppose—it was very unlikely, but suppose—Carmi Blake could be persuaded to run independently, what would be the *Eagle's* attitude toward his campaign? It was a disturbing and staggering thought.

Three o'clock brought another caller. Franklin was writing the story of the wreck and finding huge, almost malicious, satisfaction in emphasizing in detail the bravery, coolness and entire adequacy of Captain Carmi Blake, when Tip knocked at the door and opened it.

"Judge Dean's here," he announced, importantly. "I knew you'd want to see him, Mr. Cobb, so I fetched him right in. Here he is."

The judge accepted Cobb's invitation to be seated, placed his silk hat upon the desk, stroked his beard and beamed upon the world in general. That he was very well satisfied with that world just at present was evident. Franklin, himself decidedly unsatisfied, resented the attitude. He was more than ever sure that he did not like the Honorable Joel Dean.

The judge mentioned the weather, of course; it seemed to be his customary manner of beginning any conversation. He referred to the wreck and expressed gratification at the rescue of the crew.

"You were there, I understand, Franklin," he said.

"I was at the Point—yes. I had nothing to do with saving the crew. Captain Blake did that, the whole of it."

"Oh, scarcely the whole. I understand that Hammond and Bassett and—er—several others went with him to the wreck."

"They went because he made them go. He made them

ashamed to stay behind. I've never taken much stock in this
hero stuff in books, but I saw some of it yesterday. If Carmi
Blake isn't a hero then there never was one."

"Yes—oh, yes, no doubt. . . . We missed you at the convention, Franklin."

"I should have been there," bitterly. "That was where I
belonged."

"Oh, well, your substitute was on hand, so it was all right.
. . . I imagine you were surprised at the nomination of Captain Bates."

"Yes, very much surprised."

"But pleased, I hope?"

Franklin did not answer. Judge Dean regarded him
benignantly.

"Every good citizen of this district should be pleased—yes,
and proud," he said, with solemn emphasis. "We should all
be very grateful to Captain Bates. He did not wish the
nomination. He felt that he had earned a rest from public
service and its cares. He accepted with great—ahem—reluctance and solely for the party's welfare."

"So Elisha told me. He says you read a letter from Captain
Bates stating that some of his friends in whom he had confidence were certain it was his duty to run."

"Yes. I—er—have a copy of the letter with me. It is a
very fine letter indeed. I hope the *Eagle* will print that letter
in its next issue. As a campaign document I can think of
nothing better."

He laid the letter on the desk. Franklin glanced at it, but
he did not touch nor read it.

"Who were the 'friends' whose influence was so strong with
Bates?" he asked.

"Captain Isaac Shotwell of Orham was one. There is no
person in the county who knows the ins and outs of the
political situation better than Captain Shotwell. He and Captain Bates have been intimate friends for years. Mr. Haven

was another, so was Mr. Eldredge—yes, and Mr. Holway. Noah Holway is—shall we say, something of a rough diamond?—but a shrewd, able man."

"You were another advisor, of course, Judge?"

"Why—er—yes, certainly. Gideon would have consulted with me in any event. I am—er—perhaps his closest friend as well as his lawyer."

Franklin picked up the Bates letter, but dropped it again.

"You yourself were the first person to suggest the *Eagle's* playing up Carmi Blake's name as a possible candidate, Judge Dean," he said. "And, later, I remember your coming here to urge the paper's coming out openly in his support. At that time you told me the Republican town committee had decided that he should be nominated."

"Yes—er—yes, that is true, but—"

"Shotwell and the Orham committee were for him then, weren't they?"

"Why, yes—in a measure. Of course—"

"I don't remember your mentioning any qualifying measures. I think you said the feeling was unanimous throughout the district. Just when—and why—did you and the others change your minds?"

Joel Dean was too old and war-wise a political veteran to show discomfort, even if he felt it. He stroked his beard and smiled tolerantly upon his young cross-examiner.

"It wasn't a sudden change, Franklin. It was—er—gradual. Little by little we learned—heard in various ways—that there was objection, decided objection in some quarters, to Captain Blake as the party nominee. He is undoubtedly honest."

"You never heard that he wasn't; I'll bet on that!"

"Oh, no, no. He is honest and smart and—er—capable. Quite so, quite so. But you will agree with me that he is—ahem—obstinate and—er—very plain-spoken and, as we say, 'set' in his ways. Now a man like that makes enemies, more enemies than he is aware of, of course. This year it is *very*

316

important that the party majority everywhere in the State should be large. The party's welfare—"

Cobb broke in. He had heard all this before.

"All right, I understand that, Judge. But I'd like to have you tell me this: Was it Carmi's attitude on the harbor improvement plans that made you and the rest decide against him?"

Judge Dean's answer was very prompt indeed. It lacked, or so Franklin thought, a little of his usual deliberation.

"Only partially—only partially. Of course his stubborn attitude in the caucus was the final convincing proof to most of us that he was not the right man for this particular year, but that was only—"

"Just a minute. Do you know any reason why Blake should refuse to pledge himself to the Blue River plan?"

"Why—why, certainly not. . . . Really, Franklin, I don't understand— Why do you ask *me* such a question? How should I know?"

"I wanted to ask somebody. Abiathar Blake, Carmi's own brother, declares that *he* doesn't know. And Carmi himself won't say a word. . . . Well then, one other thing. Why didn't you, or Captain Bates or somebody, drop me or the *Eagle* a hint? Why did you let me go on shouting for Blake, announcing his nomination as a sure thing, up to the very holding of the caucuses? In that caucus I pledged my paper and myself to keep on working for him. I gather, from what you say now, that you had grown doubtful of the wisdom of nominating him some time before that."

The judge smiled. He bent forward to lay a hand upon the Cobb shoulder.

"My boy," he said, "in politics it isn't always wise to speak your thoughts to too many people. It wasn't sure, by any means, that Blake might not be nominated, after all. Besides," with a still broader smile, "we did not wish the Blake crowd to be able to say that we were not playing fair. They had

been promised the *Eagle's* support and that they have had.
. . . But now—now," patting the shoulder upon which his
hand still rested, "we are counting on you and your paper
to work just as hard for Gideon Bates. Of course as a loyal
Republican you will do that anyway; and as a friend of—
shall I say a friend of the entire Bates family—you will be
glad to do it. I expect to see Gideon this evening and I know
it will please him to hear that the *Eagle* is enthusiastically
pledged to his cause."

Franklin shrugged. "Pledges don't seem to mean much
in this campaign," he observed, tartly. ". . . Oh, well," after
a moment, "what is it you want the *Eagle* to do now? The
last time you begged its help you—"

"Now—now"—Judge Dean raised a protesting hand—"I
didn't beg, young man; I suggested, that was all. And, if I
suggest now, it is quite as much for your sake," with significant emphasis, "as for Captain Bates's. He will be elected
without your paper's—ahem—valued support; there is no
question of his election."

"All right, probably there isn't, but you seem to want its
support, just the same."

"Yes; yes, we do. There are only a few weeks before
election, and the *Eagle* is read by practically everybody in the
district. There is some hard feeling still, some rough spots
to be smoothed down, and your paper can smooth them
easier and quicker than anything else. Carmi Blake is out
of the race, and Gideon Bates is very much in it. Make that
perfectly plain, but do it diplomatically. The *Eagle* must
continue to speak highly of Blake as a man and a citizen.
It might well—er—glorify the rescue at the Point, praise his
bravery—and so on. You understand?"

Franklin glanced at the sheets of manuscript on his desk.
"Don't worry," he said, grimly. "It will do that."

"Yes. Yes, that is quite as it should be. But editorially it
must state that the convention did itself proud in its selection

of a candidate. Stress the point that all differences of opinion must be forgotten. With Gideon Bates as our standard bearer the Republican voters of Wellmouth and Orham will march unitedly to certain victory at the polls in November. . . . That sort of thing. Do you see?"

Cobb did not answer. The judge continued.

"Do it gracefully, of course. Don't jump—don't be too abrupt. Ease yourself and your paper out of Blake into Bates. That is what the committees of the two towns will do when they meet the voters. 'We,'" with a smile which, for him, was surprisingly close to a chuckle, "'love and admire Carmi Blake, but for the welfare of the party and the greater good of the communities in which we live, we stand triumphantly together behind Gideon Bates.' That is all. It is simple enough. Our motto from now on is 'The sword of the Lord and of Gideon.' Hum! No, I wouldn't print that. Some of our good friends might think it irreverent. . . . Well, I must run on now, Franklin. We shall look for your editorials in the *Eagle*."

He rose. Franklin Cobb rose also.

"Judge Dean," he said, after a moment of frowning reflection, "I may follow your suggestion. As things are now I don't see anything else to do. . . . But," sharply, "I want you and Captain Bates to understand that I am not at all happy about this business. Personally I am just as strong—no, stronger for Carmi Blake than I ever was. I think he is one of the finest, squarest men I ever knew, and I think this thimblerigging him out of the nomination is a dirty trick. That is exactly how I feel; but what the *Eagle* will do is a different matter. Good afternoon."

Judge Dean did not seem to resent this plain speaking. Franklin rather hoped he might, but he did not appear to. His smile was still gracious.

"When you are older, my boy," he said, "you will realize that what you call 'thimblerigging' is often necessary—especially in politics. Good day. . . . Oh, by the way, Captain Bates wished me to tell you that he had just received a telegram from Victoria. She is leaving the West earlier than they expected. She will arrive here on the afternoon train to-morrow."

He bowed himself out of the office. If ever a person was tempted to assist an exit with a well-placed kick, Franklin Cobb was that person at that moment. The suave, sanctimonious, patronizing old trickster. A kick might do him good—it would at least upset that precious dignity of his. But kicks were expensive luxuries. Signers of four-thousand-dollar notes could not afford them. He turned back to the desk. Why had he borrowed that money? He needed it and, at the time, Bates's kind offer had seemed like a gift from the gods: but now—at this humiliating moment—it seemed like the price of slavery. He had traded his independence for two new printing presses and a water-tight roof. The alternative might have been smash, but it would have been a self-respecting smash.

So Victoria was coming home, would actually be in Wellmouth to-morrow. She had telegraphed her father of her change of plans but she had not telegraphed him; apparently she had not thought it worth while. He should have been resentful, as he had been when she had neglected him before, but, oddly enough, now he was not. He did not seem to care. Victoria was not in this. He was—and so was Carmi—and Helen—but Victoria was not. She did not belong. . . . And yet she did, for she was Gideon Bates's daughter and he and she were engaged—or something like it. Heavens, what a mess!

He busied himself with the story of the wreck, but now the words did not slide as rapidly from his pen. What he had written already was, when he read it over, pretty poor stuff. He began again, but the new beginning was poor stuff, too. He gave it up, temporarily, and sat there thinking.

Victoria was coming home—he and she would be together
again. . . . And Helen—what effect would the upset of Carmi
Blake's plans have upon her?

They *were* in love with each other. Carmi had as much
as admitted it, and Elisha had intimated that she "thought a
sight of him." Probably they would be married soon. Helen
had never hinted at their marriage, nor their engagement,
but he had accepted the latter as a settled fact. . . . And yet
Carmi had not been visiting the cottage quite as frequently
of late. . . . Oh, well! Carmi was a great fellow, a wonderful
fellow; but Helen—she was—

This would not do; this would not do at all. He dipped
his pen in the ink and once more tackled the story of the
rescue. He wrote doggedly on, rising after a time to light
the bracket lamp. Elisha rapped and put in his head at the
door.

"Pretty nigh supper time, Frank," he announced. "Tip
and the other fellow have gone long ago. Almost ready to
start, are you?"

Franklin looked up. "I guess I won't go yet awhile, Elisha,"
he said. "I want to finish this thing and I'm not half through.
Tell Helen not to keep supper for me. She may leave out
the milk pitcher and some crackers or something, if she cares
to. I'm not hungry to-night. . . . Yes, yes, go on. I don't
want you to wait."

Mr. Dodson went finally, but under protest. Franklin continued to write. An hour or so later he heard the street door
open and voices and footsteps in the outer office. He could
not imagine who was calling, at that time in the evening, but
he shouted a hail.

"Here I am," he cried, peering out into the darkness of the
print shop. "Who is it? What do you want?"

The footsteps drew nearer. Three men came groping between the presses toward the little back room. When they

reached it he recognized them as Abiathar Blake, Captain Zenas Rogers, and Briar, all South Siders.

"Hope we ain't botherin' you too much, Frank," said Captain Abiathar. "We stopped in at 'Lisha's, but Nellie said you were up here. Can you spare us a few minutes? We've got somethin' pretty important to talk about."

He invited them in, of course, and as there were not chairs enough to provide for all, Rogers took the editorial seat, Abiathar the visitor's armchair, and Cobb and Briar perched on the edge of the desk.

"Well?" inquired Franklin, after a moment during which the delegation said nothing. "What is it, gentlemen?"

"You see, Frank—" began Blake. "You see— Oh, you tell him, Zenas!"

Captain Rogers pulled at his mustache.

"Mr. Cobb," he began, rather formally, "we three have made ourselves a sort of committee, as you might say, to come here and talk to you. We've been doing a good deal of hustling around since that packed convention put over its little game. We've seen a good many people, here and over at Orham, and we find that many of 'em—a whole lot of 'em—don't like that game any better than we do. They don't want to stand for it—and we *won't* stand for it. We've talked to Carmi for two hours or more steady and at last we've got him to say 'yes.' We're going to run him as the independent candidate for representative to the State House from this district. . . . Yes, we are. It's settled."

Franklin Cobb stared at them. They were deadly serious. He whistled. "Great Scott!" he exclaimed. . . . "Against Bates? Do you think Carmi would have a chance?"

"We think he's got a fighting chance. And it will *be* a fight, don't make any mistake about that. He's going to need all the help he can get—and so—"

He paused. Briar finished the sentence for him.

"And so we've come here—knowin' how strong the *Eagle*

322

has stood for Carmi and after hearin' your promise in the caucus to stick by him through thick and thin—we've come here to ask you if you mean it, that's all. Will you and your paper stick by him now? That's what we want to know."

CHAPTER XXIV

FRANKLIN ignored Briar's question. "Tell me some more about all this," he ordered. "This is—well, this *is* news!"

Captain Zenas, who seemed to be spokesman of the self-appointed committee, gave the reasons prompting their decision to break with political precedent in Wellmouth and Orham townships.

"Running an independent in this district is risky, we know that," he declared; "but there are some risks that decent, self-respecting folks ought to take if they want to stay self-respecting. Carmi Blake was promised that nomination. Joe Dean himself promised Bi and me that he should have it. He *did* have it; a month ago it was as good as in his pocket. Then that pocket was picked. Just why the job was done we don't know, but we do know that we won't sit down and say 'Thank ye, kindly' to the pickpockets. We're going to fight for what belongs to us even if somebody gets hurt. That's right, isn't it, Seth?"

Seth Briar nodded. "It's right enough," he agreed, grimly. "Of course, Frank, you mustn't get the notion that we don't know what we're up against. We've got the quarter-deck of both towns against us. Bates and Dean and Shotwell have been givin' orders for a long spell, and they're smart navigators, too. And the very smartest thing they could have done was nominate Gideon. If this was an everyday election I'd say nobody would have a two-cent chance against him. But this election ain't an everyday one, and Carmi Blake ain't an everyday man. I wouldn't bet on his winnin'—fact, I'd count the odds consider'ble on the other side—but I'll fight for him and keep on fightin' long's there's a kick left in me.

. . . And now, as I said before, are you with us or against us, Frank Cobb?"

Still Franklin ignored the question. He asked one of his own.

"Has an independent candidate ever won in this district?"

"No. Not for any office that amounted to anything," admitted Rogers.

"How do you go about putting him on the ticket?"

"Could do it two ways. Print stickers and have 'em handed out at the polls; or print our own tickets, all straight except for representative, where we'd put Carmi's name instead of Gideon's. The last way's best. Before that, of course, we must get up a petition announcing his running and get it signed. That part's easy; I can get thirty signers without going off the main road at the South Side."

"How does Carmi feel about it? Captain Rogers, you said, didn't you, that you three had talked to him for hours and 'at last' he had consented to run. That doesn't sound as if he were very enthusiastic."

Abiathar Blake sniffed. "Carmi ain't enthusiastic about much of anything these days," he grumbled. "Seems to have lost interest in everything, politics and business and everything else. Been actin' queer for weeks. Only time I've seen him really like himself lately was when the *Mary M.* came ashore. *Then* he was Carmi Blake. . . . But he's agreed to let us put his name on the ticket and to make the fight. And he'll make it, too. Carmi's not a quitter."

Rogers nodded agreement. "He'll fight," he said. "Only he made us understand that he won't shift one inch from the position he took in the caucus—no promises or pledges of any kind to anybody. . . . There's something behind it, something to do with the harbor improvement, I'll bet—but, if so, he won't tell us."

He paused. Then after a glance at his companions, he went on.

"Frank," he said, "we're going to need all the help we can get between now and election day. The *Eagle* could help us more than anything else, if it would. You and it have done a lot for Carmi so far. Do you feel as if you could keep on doing it? Seth's put it to you straight enough. Are you with us or against us?"

Franklin thrust his hands into his pockets and stared, frowningly, at the wall above the speaker's head. "Well, Captain Rogers," he said, after a moment, "I can't answer that question to-night. What you have told me is a surprise and—well, I must think it over carefully—very carefully. You see—"

Abiathar Blake leaned forward. "Boy," he cut in earnestly, "you mustn't get the idea that we don't realize this is a pretty ticklish place for you. We understand that all right. You've got yourself and your private feelin's and the way your bread's buttered to consider. We know, everybody knows, that you are pretty thick with—well, with all the Bateses. We shan't hold it against you if you tell us you and the *Eagle* have got to stand for Gideon. But you said some fine things about Carmi in the caucus and so—well, there it is."

"Yes, I know. I meant what I said. . . . But I can't answer you to-night."

"That's all right. Of course we've got to know who we can count on and where we stand, but if we know within the next day or so it will do. . . . I guess that's all, ain't it, Zenas?"

He rose and the others rose also. Each said good night and turned to the door. Franklin spoke again.

"Gentlemen," he said, impulsively, "I can't let you go without saying this much. No matter how I may decide—how I may feel that I must decide about my paper's position— I want you to know that my sympathies are with you. I think Carmi Blake deserved the nomination and should have had it. Speaking for myself personally I'm for him first, last and all the time. But my paper— Well, that is all I can say now. Good night."

He told the Dodsons not a word, either that evening or the following day, of the call of the South Side delegation. This does not mean that he did not think of it, for he thought of little else. All his natural inclinations were pulling him one way and his prudence, and such practical common sense as he had acquired during his brief business career, the other. If he were a free man, if there was no note in the bank, if some one other than Gideon Bates had been nominated, even if that some one were the powerful Joel Dean himself, he would not have hesitated. He was young and therefore something of a hero worshiper and Blake's bravery and coolness the day of the wreck appealed to his imagination. A good fighter for a cause worth fighting for always allured him. Carmi Blake had been tricked and cheated. Carmi Blake was a fine chap. Helen apparently cared for him—there was a pang in that thought too—but if for no other reason than that she did care for him he, Franklin Cobb, as a decent fellow ought to help her and her man.

But how could he? Gideon Bates had been very kind to him. Leaving out all questions of business success or failure there was such a thing as gratitude. Yes, and loyalty—for there was Victoria.

He finished the story of the wreck and rescue and turned it over to Elisha and Cahoon at the type cases. At one o'clock, as he and Dodson were walking back after dinner, to the Higham shop, he heard the train whistle. Victoria was on that train. He had debated whether or not to meet her at the station, but, as she had neither written nor wired him, he had decided not to do so. Only a few months ago and he would have been at that station a half-hour before train time regardless of letter or telegram, a significant fact of itself if he had realized its significance.

But before he left the back office that afternoon a note was handed in by Tip Cahoon. A boy had brought it with the message that Mr. Cobb was to have it "right away"; if he had gone home the boy and the note were to follow him.

Tip, returning to the type cases, winked at Elisha.

"Girl's writin'," he whispered, confidently. "Oh, I've had notes like that, plenty of 'em in my time, and I can always tell. All smelled up 'twas, too—some kind of cologne or Florida water on it. Bet you 'twas from Vic Bates, 'Lish. She was due home to-day. Cripes! Frank Cobb's a lucky fellow to have her and her old man's money on the string."

Tip would have won his bet. The note was from Victoria, evidently written in a great hurry and scrawled over four sheets of violet-tinted paper. Why in the world hadn't he met her at the depot? She was *so* disappointed. He must come to the house *right* after dinner that very evening. She should expect him. "P.S. Isn't it wonderful about Papa's going to the Legislature again!"

At eight he rang the Bates doorbell. It had been a long while since he last did that, and many things had happened in the interval. The trim maid admitted him and smiled as she did so. Yes, Miss Victoria was in the front parlor. He was to go right in.

Victoria was there and her parents were with her. Mrs. Bates was, as always, graciously condescending and coolly cordial. Captain Gideon was bluff, good-natured and cordial without the coolness. Victoria sprang from the piano stool, both hands extended.

"Why, Frank!" she cried. "I'm *so* glad you came. It has been ages and ages since I saw you, hasn't it? You look —why, goodness gracious, you look *older!* He does, doesn't he, Papa? Why, you haven't been sick or anything, have you?"

Her father chuckled. "Shouldn't wonder if he was tired, Vic," he observed. "Guess we all are, a little. . . . Well," turning to the caller, "we're through the worst of it, I guess. All but me, my trouble is just beginning. I swore, a good while ago, that I'd never hold public office again, but they made me take my swear back. Have to do some things in this world whether you want to or not. Seems to me I hinted something of that kind to you last time I was in that back room of yours, eh?" with another chuckle.

Franklin smiled. "I believe you did, sir," he admitted. "I understand now better than I did then. I suppose I should congratulate you on your nomination, Captain Bates."

"And on his election, too," put in Victoria. "It's the same thing."

"Not quite, not quite, young lady. Have to count the votes first. They may put in a Democrat, you can't tell."

Mrs. Bates sniffed. "Don't be silly, Gideon," she said, loftily. "When a Democrat is elected in this district *I* shall move out of it."

The older people remained but a short while.

"Mother," suggested Captain Gideon, "you remember I promised Cornelius Haven that you and I would run in a few minutes this evenin'. Better get under way, hadn't we?"

It did seem to Franklin that Mrs. Bates was not at all eager to get "under way." The look she gave her husband was not over affectionate. However, after informing her daughter that they would be back *very* soon, she and the captain left the room. Victoria and Franklin were alone together for the first time in months.

She came over to where he was standing and looked up into his face. He looked down into hers. She was as pretty as ever.

"Well?" she asked, after a moment. "Aren't you glad to see me?"

"Why—why, of course I am."

"You don't say it very enthusiastically," with a pout. "And you don't act very glad. You haven't even kissed me. . . .

Oh, no, no!" drawing away. "I don't have to beg people to kiss me; I have known them to actually *want* to do it."

He kissed her then. It was not a very satisfactory kiss, at least she did not seem to find it so. She drew away.

"Frank Cobb," she demanded, pettishly, "what *is* the matter with you? . . . You aren't really glad to see me at all."

"Why, yes, I—"

"No, you're not. Why didn't you meet me at the station?"

"I wasn't sure that I should be welcome. If it hadn't been for Judge Dean I shouldn't have known you were coming home to-day. The last word I had from you was that you were not leaving your friends until the twentieth."

For some, to him quite unexplained, reason, this statement seemed to amuse her. She clapped her hands. "You were mad at me!" she exclaimed, with a little giggle. "You· *were!* Oh, that's lovely!"

"Lovely! Why?"

"Oh, because it is! I began to think you were too—oh, noble or something—ever to get really cross at anybody."

"Well, as a matter of fact, I wasn't exactly cross with you, Vic."

"Why not? You ought to have been. *I* should have been furious. . . . Or was it because you didn't care whether I ever came or not?"

"Now, Vic, don't be silly! I think you should have written or wired me, just as I think you should have let me know about your plans for going away for the summer."

"Why, what do you mean? I did write you."

"Not until everything was settled. You didn't as much as hint to me that you were considering such a thing. . . . Oh, well, it doesn't make any difference now."

"Yes, it does, too. It makes a difference to me. I've just got home and—and, instead of being glad to see me, you scold me for something that happened away back in June.

I suppose you have been brooding over it ever since. I wouldn't have believed you could be so disagreeable."

"I don't mean to be disagreeable."

"You are. You're just horrid. I almost wish I had stayed another week with Belle. She coaxed me and coaxed me to do it, but I wouldn't. I was having a good time there. The people I met didn't find fault with me. *Some* of them," with a toss of the head, "seemed to find me *perfectly* satisfactory."

If there was a hint in this last sentence Franklin refused to accept it. Possibly, he reflected, he had been a trifle disagreeable, he was not in the happiest of moods. However, he had no wish to quarrel.

"I'm sorry, Vic," he said. "Let's forget it. I know you have had a wonderful time. Now tell me all about everything."

"Of course! That's what I want to do. If you'll only be nice. . . . Oh, come along! Papa and Mother will be back before long and we have *so* much to talk about, haven't we?"

She took his hand and led him to the sofa. They sat there together, just as they used to sit during those evenings when she was at home on her vacations from the Academy. They had been wonderful—those evenings. This one should be just as blissful—even more so, if possible, for they had not seen each other for so long. And yet it was not. There was something lacking. She was just as charming; her eyes, when they looked up into his, had the same demure twinkle which used, when he first knew her, to tempt him almost beyond resistance. He used to think the allure in those eyes was innocent, uncalculated, unrehearsed. Now he found himself wondering into how many other masculine eyes she had looked in just that way. . . . Yet, as the thought occurred to him, he was ashamed of it. What *was* the matter with him?

And the difference was not entirely on his side. She was eager to talk of her glorious holiday in the Michigan camp.

She had had a perfectly gorgeous time. He had already gathered from her letters that the "camp" was a summer home considerably larger than the Wellmouth town hall, but with furniture and fittings vastly different; that it was the social center of a fashionable summer colony and that life in that colony was never dull either during the day or night. And now, as she chattered and rhapsodized, he could readily understand why she had been too "busy" to write frequently. She had met such a nice crowd of young people. Sailing excursions, picnics, parties, dances—oh, something going on every single minute. Occasionally, carried away by her enthusiasm, she said things which were illuminating, things she had never mentioned in the letters.

"No one shall ever talk to me again," she declared, "about the East being more—oh, you know—used to things—culture —and all that. Why, almost every boy I met was at college somewhere, or just had been, and most of them belonged to families with loads and loads of money. There was one in particular. He and I—"

She stopped suddenly, glanced quickly at Franklin and added: "Oh, he wasn't as nice as you are, of course. Nobody is—when you *are* nice. But," with a sigh, "how in the world I shall ever be able to content myself in dull old Wellmouth again I *don't* know. . . . There! Now tell me a little about yourself. What have you been doing? Oh, I know you wrote lots of letters, but we don't put everything in letters, now do we?"

He was by this time certain that she had not put everything in hers. A year before and he would have asked questions, many searching questions, concerning that "boy"—the "one in particular" whom she had mentioned and then so suddenly ceased to mention. Now he asked not one. Curiously enough —he vaguely realized how curious it was—he was not in the least interested in the young gentleman.

And he soon began to suspect that, although she had asked

to be told about him—Franklin—and what he had been doing during her absence, her interest was more pretended than real. As he described the progress of the *Eagle* and the slow but sure improvement in his business and prospects he grew excited and eloquent.

"I really believe that I may have a pretty good thing here," he asserted. "Oh, I'll never get rich out of it, of course— nothing like that—but I like the work, like it a lot. And I like the town and the people—most of them. You see—"

He paused. Carried away by his enthusiasm he had been speaking rapidly and had not been looking at her. Now, turning, he caught her lifting a hand to hide a yawn.

"Don't you think so?" he asked, with calculated irrelevance.

She started and, meeting his look, smiled.

"Yes, of course," she agreed, beaming. "Of course I do."

His suspicion was confirmed. She had not been listening. The certainty acted upon his enthusiasm like a bucket of water on a fire. He gazed moodily at the carpet.

"Well, go on," she urged, after a moment. "Tell me more."

"There isn't any more to tell."

"Oh, but there must be."

"There isn't."

"Now, Frank, how can you! You haven't said a word about politics or about Papa's nomination or anything. Don't you think it is splendid?"

"Is it?"

"*Is* it? Why, the idea! Oh, I know what you mean; you think he didn't really want the nomination. Well, he didn't, but Mother and I are delighted. Now we can spend the winter—or a good part of it—in Boston, just as we used to when he was in the Legislature before. That will be *fun!* And, besides, I am so glad that Carmi Blake didn't win. If he were our representative, I should be more ashamed than ever to tell people I lived in Wellmouth. A common South Side fisherman! *He* getting up and making speeches! What *sort* of barbarians would people think we were down here!"

There are certain times when the saying of certain things leads to certain—and quite unforeseen—consequences. This was one of the times. Franklin was disappointed, unhappy, and therefore more than usually reckless.

"I think Blake should have been nominated," he declared, with emphasis.

Victoria gasped. She moved away from him on the sofa.

"Why! . . . Why, Franklin Cobb!" she cried, aghast. "How can you— Are you crazy?"

"Perhaps so, but if I am, there are a great many other people in this district who are crazy in the same way. Carmi Blake and the South Side had been promised that nomination. At the last minute the promise was broken, and I think it was a mean trick. That's the truth, Vic. It is the way I feel and I can't help it."

She was staring at him, wide-eyed and incredulous.

"Why, I never heard such a thing in my life!" she vowed. "You think—you say you think that that Blake man should have been nominated instead of my *father!* Oh, you're making fun of me!"

"I'm not. I should tell your father the same thing if he asked me. Perhaps I shall tell him anyway. A promise is a promise, no matter who makes it."

"I don't believe there was any such promise," hotly. "Why should those South Side people be promised anything? What do they amount to, anyway?"

"They were in a position this year to demand what they wanted and get it. Judge Dean himself admitted that to me. He told me that the promise had been made."

"Well, what of it? He changed his mind, I suppose, after he realized how ridiculous it was. And, besides, how could Judge Dean promise anything unless my father told him he might? Do you imagine that he, of all people would do such a thing without consulting Papa? Indeed he would not! He wouldn't *dare!*"

"But your father told me the same thing—that Carmi had been promised the nomination this year."

She sprang to her feet.

"So you think my father is a liar! That is what you are telling me?"

"Why—why, no, not— Well, he wouldn't consider it a lie, of course. It was a political promise and, from what little I've learned about politics, I judge that promises of that kind count only as long as it seems advisable to count them. Your father believes—"

She stamped her foot. "I won't hear a word!" she cried, furiously. "Not another word! You ought to be ashamed of yourself. After all Father has done for you!"

Her cheeks were crimson. She looked as if she might fly at him like an angry cat. He had never seen her in a temper before. This was not the purring, cuddling, temptingly feminine creature he had known. This was a different Victoria altogether.

He rose from the sofa. "Why, Vic," he protested, "you mustn't misunderstand me. I am not saying a word against your father. I am sure he thinks he is doing exactly the right thing. I only—"

He stepped toward her, but she pushed him away.

"Don't you touch me," she ordered.

"But—oh, well, all right. I only want you to understand how I feel about this Blake business."

"Carmi Blake! *That* man! You are actually sorry that Carmi Blake was beaten! A common, South Side toughy! A great, hulking, awkward fish peddler who talks of nothing but codfish—yes, and smells like one most of the time! You dare to stand there and tell me that Papa—my own father— the finest man in the county—yes, and the richest, too—a man that everybody looks up to and respects—you tell me to my face that he should have stood aside and let a—a *thing* like that Carmi Blake make us all a laughing-stock before the whole State! And you have the impudence. . . . Oh, I hate you! I *hate* you!"

She sobbed hysterically. He was bewildered; he scarcely knew what to say in face of this tirade.

"Now, Vic," he begged. "You've got this all wrong. I'm awfully sorry I offended you. . . . Please don't cry."

Her sobbing had already ceased. She avoided his approach and when she next spoke her tone was cuttingly sarcastic.

"Oh, don't let it trouble you," she said, airily. "It doesn't trouble me. Perhaps it is just as well. I have been thinking a good deal while I have been away, and I guess it is better just as it is. . . . Well, we were never engaged, that's one comfort."

"Why, Vic—"

"We *weren't*," fiercely. "You said we were, but *I* never said so. I liked you. I used to think you were almost as nice a boy as I ever knew—in Wellmouth, at any rate. You were—oh, queer, and dreadfully serious about your silly little paper and things like that. But I did think you were a gentleman."

"Come, come, Victoria!"

"Yes, I thought you were. Perhaps I didn't know as much about real gentlemen as I do now. I have learned a good deal this summer. . . . Well, I had a good time at any rate," triumphantly. "Now I'm glad of it."

"Oh! . . . Oh, I see. . . . Well, then, perhaps—"

"There isn't any perhaps. And when I think of how I tried to help you! How I coaxed my father into lending you that money. Why, where would you and that—that miserable *Eagle* of yours be this minute if it wasn't for us? Oh, well, you can ask Carmi Blake and the rest of his South Side fish hawkers to help you now. Maybe they will," with a laugh; "they seem to be your own kind. You love them so much."

His conscience was troubling him no longer. He squared his shoulders.

"I respect and admire Captain Blake," he said. "I have reason to. And I do believe that he has been tricked and cheated. . . . However, there is no use talking about that now. You would like to have me go, I suppose?"

"Oh, I don't care what you do. I'm not the least bit interested. We should have had to have an understanding some time, and now we have had it."

He nodded. "And Carmi Blake was as good an excuse as any to bring it about. Yes, I understand. Good night, Victoria."

"Good-by, Mr. Cobb," with significant emphasis. Then, with a laugh, "I suppose you will go home now and tell the Dodson girl how I have abused you. She will sympathize, I'm sure. The whole town knows that she is another admirer— a *great* admirer—of your precious fisherman."

At the outer door he met Captain Bates and his wife returning from their call on the Havens.

"Going so soon, Frank!" inquired Captain Gideon. "Why, I thought you and Vic would have enough to talk about to keep you going till twelve anyhow."

"We have had our talk. Good night, Mrs. Bates. Good night, Captain."

CHAPTER XXV

HE WALKED home in a daze. Two or three late—late for Wellmouth—pedestrians met him but he neither noticed them nor answered their hails. As he approached the Dodson side door that door opened and a man came out. The man was Carmi Blake.

Franklin awoke from his reverie sufficiently to recognize and greet him.

"Good evening, Captain," he said. Blake started and looked up. "Eh? . . . Oh, hello!" he grunted, and walked on. Franklin did not detain him. If Blake was not inclined to conversation he was even less so.

He opened the door quietly and entered. The little hall was dark, but the lamp was burning in the dining room and by its light he saw Helen. She was seated in a chair by the table. A handkerchief was in her hand and, as he looked, he saw her lift it to her eyes. He closed the door behind him. She heard him and rose to her feet, hastily hiding the handkerchief as she did so.

"Oh, it is you!" she exclaimed. "I—I wasn't expecting you so early."

"What is the matter, Helen?"

"Matter? . . . Why—why, nothing."

"Yes, there is. I am sure there is."

"No—there isn't really. I was sitting here thinking—and—oh, *don't* look at me like that, please!"

"But, Helen—"

"Don't! . . . Frank," impulsively, "does it ever seem to you that this world is all wrong? Wrong from top to bottom?"

"Yes," promptly.

"Sometimes I think it is. Do you ever wish you weren't a human being, but something else, a—oh, a cow, for instance?"

"A *cow?*"

His expression caused her to burst out laughing, but the laugh lasted but a moment.

"Yes, a cow," she repeated. "A cow hasn't any conscience—at least I imagine she hasn't. *She* wouldn't care if she made her friends miserable; she wouldn't feel the least bit wicked or even be sorry for them. . . . There, that is foolishness enough for one evening. I'm going to lock up now. No, I don't need any help, and I don't feel like talking. I'm going straight to bed. Good night."

He went to his room. Her peculiar manner and behavior puzzled him. Had she and Blake quarreled? If so, the quarrel must have been all on Carmi's side. He could not imagine her losing her temper. He had known her a good while, had watched when her father's absent-mindedness and well-intentioned blunders were enough to try the sweetest temper, and she was always forbearing, good-humored and quietly sensible. He could not picture *her* as flying into a rage, stamping her foot, saying things that cut, mean things—

So it was all over, his and Victoria's romance. It was—over and ended. He realized now—and his hurt pride writhed under the realization—that she had intended it should end, if not that very evening, then soon afterward. She was tired of him, probably there was another love affair already under way—one of those fellows whom she had met at the camp—and she had returned home determined to find some excuse to send him packing. His defense of Carmi Blake had furnished the excuse, that was all.

Well? . . . And what now? . . . He was free. There was no longer the heavy responsibility of an engagement upon his shoulders. Of course there were other responsibilities, his business, the note in the bank—that sort of thing; but these were his own, no one shared them. His future was his own. He could take chances and if the chances ended in ruin— why, he was young, and Wellmouth was not the only place in the world. So far as the four thousand dollars was concerned there was money enough already to take care of part of the sum and the building and its contents, to say nothing of the *Eagle* and the business, would be worth much more than the remainder. Yes, he could do what he liked. And, so long as it was his, his paper could speak out for what its owner honestly believed to be right.

There was much more of this, hours more. And, considering how suddenly all his plans and dreams had come to nothing, Victoria Bates had surprisingly little share in his thoughts. His pride was wounded, he was humiliated and chagrined because she had made a fool of him, and he had been such an innocent, trusting idiot, but he was not in the least heartbroken. No, there was no dodging it, his principal feeling was one of relief.

As soon as he and Elisha reached the print shop next morning he went into the little office, closed the door, and, seating himself at the desk, wrote busily until eleven. Then he put on his hat and overcoat and came out into the shop.

Elisha, his eyeshade cocked jauntily, was setting the Bayport locals. Franklin stopped beside him.

"Elisha," he said, "I have written the leading editorial for this week and left it on my desk. Set it as soon as you can and have a proof ready for me. I am going out and probably won't be back before noon. I'll see you at dinner down at the house. I don't think I shall be late."

With a word to Bearse, the bookkeeper, concerning his proposed absence, he left the building and walked toward the corner. As he came opposite the Dean law office, however, he was hailed by Seth Briar. Seth had driven up from the South Side and, leaning forward in his buggy seat, beckoned to him. Franklin stepped out into the road beside the buggy.

Briar was chuckling. "Well, Frank," he whispered, "the news is gettin' round. There's a confab under way over yonder this minute, and I'll bet I know what it's about. Cornelius Haven and Manasseh went into Joe Dean's five minutes ago, and just now I saw Gideon himself goin' in there. They've probably heard about Carmi's runnin' and I shouldn't wonder if they were a little mite nervous. Well, maybe we'll make 'em more so before election's over. The South Side's beginnin' to boil up already. We may not elect our man—I can't believe there's any real chance of that—but we'll make the Corners gang work to win, and that's somethin'. It won't be quite the walk-away they counted on. Say, Frank," eagerly, "you haven't made up your mind yet about—about what we asked you the other night, have you? Won't keep us waitin' too long? We ought to know one way or the other."

Franklin stepped back to the sidewalk.

"I can't talk now, Seth," he said. "I'm in a hurry. See you again soon. Good-by."

Franklin waited until the buggy turned the corner. Then he crossed the road and stood before the door of the Dean office. There he hesitated. The hesitation, however, was but momentary. He opened the door and entered.

The outer room was empty, but the door of the private office beyond was closed and from behind it he heard the murmur of conversation. He rapped upon the panel. The conversation ceased. A chair was drawn back. A moment later he and Judge Dean faced each other across the threshold.

That the judge was surprised to see him there was evident. Nevertheless his "Good morning" was prompt and his presence of mind in evidence. He closed the door behind him and led his visitor a few feet away from it.

"Well, Franklin," he said, "this is an unexpected pleasure. What can I do for you?"

"Captain Bates is here, isn't he, Judge?"

"Why—why yes, he is here. He is busy just at the moment. In an hour, perhaps—"

"I should like to see him now, if it is possible. I won't keep him but a minute or two."

"We are in the midst of a rather important—er—conference. I wonder if you have heard that our—ahem—South Side friends are turning out to be poor losers?"

"I know that Carmi Blake is to run independently, if that is what you mean."

The Dean beard was stroked. The judge regarded his caller with speculative scrutiny.

"Is that what you wished to speak with Captain Bates about?" he inquired.

"Yes, sir. In a way."

"Hum! Mr. Haven and Eldredge are in there with him now. We are all interested, of course. Perhaps you might tell us all what you have in mind?"

"If the captain chooses to tell you afterward I have no objection, but I must speak with him first."

Judge Dean said "Hum" again. Then he turned, and, opening the door behind him, entered the private office. He did not close the door and Franklin could see the gathering in the lawyer's sanctum. It reminded him of that day when, in that same room, he had refused the offer of the "group" to buy the Higham property. Now, as then, the portly figure of Gideon Bates filled the chair behind the flat-topped desk. Manasseh Eldredge, coat thrown open and left thumb in the armhole of his vest, slouched by the window. Little Mr. Haven was the only one who had not been present on that former occasion. Haven and Eldredge waved a greeting. Bates, too, must have seen and recognized him, but he made no sign.

Dean bent to whisper in the captain's ear. Bates listened and then, rising from the chair, walked into the room where Franklin stood awaiting him.

"Well, young fellow?" he asked. "What is it?"

Three pairs of eyes in the inner office were turned in their direction and Franklin was acutely conscious that the corresponding pairs of ears were straining to listen. Before replying he closed the door tightly. Then—

"Captain Bates," he stammered— It was hard to begin— "Captain Bates, I don't know whether or not Victoria has told you of our—of our disagreement last night. If she has, she probably told you why we disagreed and of some things I said about the way I thought Blake had been treated in this campaign."

He paused. Gideon Bates made no reply. His expression was grave, almost grim, and it changed not in the least when Cobb referred to his daughter. So Victoria *had* told him. She would, of course. Well, so much the better; that part of the matter need not be mentioned again. Still what must follow would be hard enough. He went on.

"Captain Bates," he said, "it was at your suggestion—yours and Judge Dean's—that the *Eagle* supported Carmi Blake for the nomination. I didn't know him very well then at the beginning, but as I came to know him better I respected and admired him more and more. I was glad to have my paper push his campaign and glad to do so personally whenever I could. I meant what I said in the caucus, that I should stick by him and fight with him to the finish."

The great man's lip twitched. "Making quite a speech, aren't you?" he observed, dryly.

Franklin caught his breath. "Why—why, I guess I am," he admitted, with a one-sided grin. "I beg your pardon. I just wanted you to know that I really do think Carmi Blake is a splendid fellow. If you had seen him, as I did, down at that wreck, you— But that hasn't anything to do with what I came here to say to you. If Victoria has told you about— about last evening she probably told you that I believe Blake was—yes, was tricked in the convention."

"Um-hm. Well?"

"Well, he was. Now wasn't he, Captain Bates?"

"He was licked. There were reasons why he had to be licked."

"Do you know what the reasons were? . . . Oh, I don't mean harmony in the party and all that stuff. Those were the reasons given, but I don't believe they were the true ones."

For the first time Gideon Bates showed real interest.

"Do *you* know any other reasons?" he demanded, sharply. "If you do *I* don't know anything about 'em and I want to know. . . . Come, come! What are they?"

"I don't know. I only feel that—that there must have been some."

"Bosh! . . . Well, well? What else?"

"Why, just this. I have been thinking this thing over ever since the convention. The *Eagle* was pledged to Carmi Blake. It was; there weren't any 'ifs' and 'ands' about it. When Judge Dean came to the office the other day I told him, just as I have told you and Victoria, that I thought Blake had been swindled. I thought, of course, that it was all over and so I was prepared to make the best of it and support you."

"Humph! Much obliged."

"Oh, don't think for a minute that I don't believe you are the best man who could have been nominated. You are, of course. I respect you and you've been a good friend to me. I'm very grateful to you, sir; you *must* understand that. It's just the way the thing was done that—"

"All right, all right," impatiently. "I'm pretty busy just now and those fellows in yonder are waiting for me. Let's get it over. You've come here to tell me that you and the *Eagle,* being too righteous to stand for swindling and political tricks, are going to support Carmi Blake as an independent. That's about it, isn't it?"

"Why—why, yes, sir, it is. I'm sorry, Captain Bates. There isn't anything personal in this at all. And it does seem so—

so darned ungrateful. But, honestly, sir, I—I can't do anything else without feeling like a hypocrite and—liar—yes, and
a yellow dog. That's the truth."

"Um-hm. Well, then us other yellow dogs will have to get
along without your valuable help, I suppose. Maybe we can;
miracles *have* happened, you know. . . . Think Blake'll be
elected, do you?"

"I haven't the least idea he will be."

"I rather doubt it myself. . . . Good-by."

"Just one more word, Captain Bates. You must believe—
you've *got* to believe—that the trouble between Victoria and
me had no influence at all on my deciding to do this thing.
My mind was practically made up before I came to your house
last evening. Perhaps I wasn't quite aware then that it was,
but now I realize it."

"Well. . . . Anything more?"

"No, sir, I guess not. Except that I'm sorry."

"So am I, so far as that goes. Good-by."

So that, too, was over. There remained but one more unpleasant session and for that Franklin was prepared. He
looked at his watch. It was after twelve, dinner time, and
Elisha would be at the cottage. He walked briskly down the
South Side road.

The Dodsons were in the kitchen when he entered. Elisha,
his hat and coat on the floor where he had thrown them when
he came in, was limping up and down the room, gesticulating
wildly. Helen, white-faced and very solemn, was standing by
the stove. Franklin hailed them cheerfully.

"Hope I'm not late," he said. "I was detained longer than
I expected." Then with a smile, "Elisha, you look excited.
What's the trouble?"

Elisha choked. "What's the trouble!" he spluttered. "You
ask *me* that, Frank Cobb? . . . Oh, my gorry! I ain't been
in anything *but* trouble since I read that editorial of yours.
Of all the crazy craziness— Aw, Frank, you can't mean it!"

"I mean every word of it. Has Helen read it, too?"

"Course she has. I fetched it home for her to read. And she's just as upset about it as I am. That's so, ain't it, Nellie?"

Helen sighed. "Yes," she agreed. "Franklin, you mustn't do this thing. . . . Oh, I know how you feel about Carmi and the way he has been treated. Father and I feel the same way, of course. It is fine—it's splendid; but for your own sake you mustn't do it. It is just what Father called it—craziness. It will mean ruin for you; you can't afford it. Please—please don't."

Elisha was on the point of breaking out again, but Franklin motioned him to silence.

"Listen, both of you," he ordered. "There is no use arguing, it is all settled. I realize what it may mean—probably will mean—but I'm going through with it just the same. When I first came here to Wellmouth I talked pretty loudly about independence. Either that talk was all bluff or there was something behind it. Now, it seems to me, I am at the point where the independence must be made good or the bluff shown up. You know, both of you, how I feel about Carmi. I was for him when I thought he was sure to be nominated and elected. What sort of a thing would I be if I deserted him now, just because he hasn't an outside chance of election? Come now, be honest. What would you two think of me if I did that? I'll tell you. You would think I was what I just told Captain Bates I would be if I did it—a yellow pup."

Helen did not speak. Her father, however, had caught a name in the concluding sentence and he repeated it.

"Cap'n Bates!" he gasped. "Do you mean you've told Cap'n Gideon to his face that the *Eagle* is against him?"

"Yes. I'll tell you all about that pretty soon. Just now though I want to say something else. So far as I am concerned, and the *Eagle* is concerned, it is settled—done with—my mind is made up and it won't be changed. I'm going to face the music and if it is my last dance here in Wellmouth

I shall try and make it a lively one. But for you, Elisha, the situation is quite different. I want you to resign as editor of the *Eagle,* give up your job to-morrow. That will let you out and put you right with Bates and Dean and the others. Then, by and by, when I am frozen out—when they take over the shop and the paper for debt, which of course they are likely to do at any time—they will have to have an editor and they will hire you, just as they were going to do before I came here at all. Of course I'll pay your salary just the same until—"

But here Helen interrupted. *"Frank!"* she cried, indignantly. "How can you!"

"But it is plain common sense, that's all. I have thought it all out."

"You have, have you?" This from Elisha. "You've thought it all out and your notion is that you're too good to be a yellow pup, but that I *am* one—comes natural to me, I presume likely. Frank Cobb, if you say another word like that, I'll haul off and hit you over the head with this cane."

"But, look here, Elisha—"

"Shut up! Now talk sense or don't talk at all. Have you actually made up your mind—honestly made it up for good?"

"I've been trying to tell you so."

A long breath. Then— "Well, that's that. Nellie, how about dinner?"

"But, Elisha—"

"Don't bother me. If I've got to answer all the questions Tip Cahoon'll fire at me when he reads that editorial I'm goin' to need steam in the boiler."

"But, Elisha, I'm serious about this."

"By gorry, so am I! Didn't fetch home a dog biscuit to put on my plate, did you? Yeller pup! Well, some pups bite; don't forget that."

As they were going into the dining room Helen touched their lodger's sleeve.

"Franklin," she whispered, anxiously. "I—I *must* say this

to you. It isn't really my concern at all, but I *must* say it. Have you thought about—about Victoria?"

Franklin Cobb laughed aloud.

"Victoria," he repeated. "Why, Victoria is the least of my worries."

And he meant it.

CHAPTER XXVI

During the meal Franklin said no more about Elisha's resigning from his employ, but, later on, while on his way to the South Side for an interview with the Blakes and Captain Rogers, he stopped at the cottage and did his best to convince Helen that such a procedure was the plainest of common sense.

"Tip and Bearse and I can get along until after election," he declared. "I didn't say anything to your father, but I imagine I shan't be permitted to own the *Eagle* and the printing business much longer than that. The bank can demand payment at any time."

"I know. I have been thinking of nothing else since Father came home with that editorial. But, Frank, do you think Captain Bates will do that just because you are against him politically? It would be such a *mean* trick."

"He may not consider it so. He has been mighty decent to me, and he may think the mean trick is on my side. Besides, there are others who won't have any scruples. Dean and Eldredge and the rest of them know about it, and they won't be sympathetic. And—well, there will be other influences. No, I mustn't expect mercy and perhaps, from their viewpoint, I don't deserve any."

"Then, Frank, what makes you do this thing? Carmi won't expect you to do it. There is no reason at all why you should sacrifice anything for his sake."

"It isn't for his sake, really. I think he is a splendid fellow; and he is your friend—"

"Please leave me out of it."

He hesitated. Leaving her out of it was the one thing

which could not be done; he realized that well enough.

"Oh, well!" he said, with a shrug, "there is no use going through all that again. I have told you how I feel. I'm not posing as the high-minded hero. I'm a born gambler, I guess. I took over this business here in Wellmouth just as a gamble, and I've enjoyed playing the game my way. Now I'll be hanged if I'm going to let Dean and his gang stack the cards for me."

"Frank, suppose it all happens just as you say it may; suppose you do lose your property, all of it, what will you do?"

"Oh, I shan't lose everything. There will be something left. I have about fifteen hundred dollars put aside and the shop and business ought to be worth at least the face of the note even under a forced sale. I suppose I might get a fair price from those Wapatomac people who were after it when my uncle died, if I chose to approach them."

"Frank, has it occurred to you that you might be able to borrow enough—you have a little already—to pay that note?"

"Borrow? Again? From whom?"

"Why—I don't know, of course."

"I'm afraid you don't. . . . But now about your father. There is no sense at all in his being dragged into it. Let him drop out now. By and by, if they take over the *Eagle*—as they will, for they don't want the Wapatomac people here— they will have to have an editor. Elisha, if he isn't tied up with my Judas Iscariotism, will naturally be the one they will choose."

"Oh, *don't!*" with fiery indignation. "If you, with all it means to you, can stand for what you believe is honest and right, do you think he will sneak out and hide? If he wanted to do such a thing I wouldn't let him. And you heard him this noon. You can judge whether he wants to or not."

"Well, I wish he would. If it wasn't for you two I should be a whole lot easier in my mind. I mean to make this final scrap of mine a lively one, and there would be fun in it if I didn't feel so responsible for you and Elisha. You are, both of you, as stubborn as—well, as Carmi Blake himself, and that's saying a lot."

She smiled, wearily. "I know another stubborn one. . . . Oh, Frank, it isn't too late even yet! Won't you—? No, you won't, of course."

The outer office of the Blake brothers was, when he entered it, deserted except for the two clerks. Abiathar was away on a political errand, so Nickerson informed Franklin.

"Lively doin's these days, Mr. Cobb. Cap'n Bi and Cap'n Zenas are over to Orham this afternoon. Cap'n Carmi's inside though. He don't seem to take half the interest that the rest of 'em do. Funny, ain't it?"

Carmi Blake was at his desk. They had not met—except that evening when they passed each other at the Dodson door —since convention day, the day of the wreck of the *Mary M*.

"Hello, Cobb," he grunted. "What are you doin' here? This is the den of the Forty Thieves; hasn't Joe Dean told you that yet? Takin' some chances, aren't you?"

Franklin grinned. "I belong here," he said. "I came to tell you fellows that I've decided to be the forty-first thief."

Blake looked at him.

"Now what in blazes does that mean?" he demanded.

"Means that I've joined the outlaws. Your brother and Rogers and Blair called the other evening to ask me if I was herding with the sheep or the goats in this election. I told them I would think it over. I have thought and here I am. I'm a brother goat, Captain. The *Eagle* is bleating for you in this campaign. Got another statement ready? We are waiting to print it."

"*What!* Beriah Higham's paper backin' an independent? . . . What's the joke? Oh, come; tell me, so *I* can laugh."

"Laugh now. It may be easier for us both to laugh now than later on. And Uncle Beriah hasn't owned the *Eagle* for some time; I thought you knew that."

"But—but— Oh, quit your foolin'; let me get this straight, if I can. You and your paper are comin' out for *me* against *Gideon Bates?*"

"Yes."

"For the Lord's sake, why?"

"Oh, just because. Give me a good hot blast to start us off with. Whatever you say goes on the front page."

The big man could not seem to believe it, even yet.

"Well, I swear!" he muttered. "I told Bi and Zenas that they were darned fools even to hint at your comin' in with us. I never supposed you'd be the biggest fool of the lot. You realize you are that, don't you?"

"Not altogether. Why did *you* decide to fight?"

"Why?" The Blake fist clenched. "Why, because I've been kicked when my back was turned. That never happened yet without a fight afterwards.".

"All right. That is my reason for fighting, too. You weren't the only one kicked in the same place."

"Humph! . . . Well, I'll— Say," suspiciously, "who's been talkin' to you? Who put you up to this?"

"Nobody. I don't know what you're hinting at."

"Don't you? . . . Well, never mind. Suppose I should tell you I didn't want your paper's support?"

"You told me that once or twice before, but you had it just the same. It is still my paper, you know."

Carmi Blake's big fingers toyed with the pen in the rack before him. He looked at his visitor and then at the pen.

"Say, Frank Cobb," he blurted, after a minute, "probably you won't like this—I shouldn't if I were you—but here it is. Does Vic Bates know that you are goin' to work for my election instead of her father's?"

Franklin stiffened. "I don't see exactly what— Oh, well then—yes."

"She does!"

"She knows how I feel. And her father knows that the *Eagle* is behind you in the campaign. I told him so a few hours ago."

"You *didn't!* Told the old man himself? To his face? . . . Well, I swear! Cobb, you may not have good judgment, but you've certainly got more sand in your craw than there is on Point of Beach. . . . So Vic knows, eh?"

It was a subject Franklin did not care to discuss further.

"Carmi," he said, impatiently, "I'll tell you what I told Helen. Victoria Bates is the least of my worries."

The pen dropped from the Blake fingers.

"Oh," he observed, slowly, "you told Nellie that, did you?"

"I did. And now we'll let that end it, if you don't mind."

Captain Carmi said very little more during the remainder of the interview. He promised to prepare a statement immediately, and the *Eagle* should have it that afternoon. Abiathar and Zenas would be up to see Cobb as soon as they returned from Orham; they knew a good deal more about whatever plans had been made than he did. His final remark as his visitor rose to go was characteristic. In it and in his tone and manner was that same reluctant, almost grudging, quality which Franklin had learned to expect of him.

"I suppose I ought to thank you, Cobb. Bi and Zenas and Seth will be mighty glad to hear what you've told me. They'll figure that havin' the *Eagle* with us will mean a whole lot. Why you do it I'll be hanged if I quite see, and I think, for your own sake, you're a fool *to* do it. But I'm much obliged to you—for that."

Franklin left him at the desk, still toying with the penholder.

The following morning things began to happen and they continued to happen for three long, hard weeks. The South Side committee, Rogers and Abiathar Blake and Briar, came and discussed plans. Of course they were exuberant over the addition of the *Eagle* and its owner to their ranks and said many flattering things concerning the Cobb courage and honesty. Franklin brushed the praise aside.

"Thanks," he said, "but just forget all that stuff, please. I know what two-thirds of the district will be saying about me in a day or two and what you say now isn't likely to swell my head. Tell me what you want me to do, and I'll do it. I want to be kept busy, that's the main thing."

They had no doubt of their ability to keep him busy. The *Eagle* must print every line favorable to the independent candidate for which it could find space. The ballots with Carmi Blake's name on them must be prepared; the Higham shop would print them, of course. There were to be many meetings in the two townships and speakers would be needed. Franklin had demonstrated, at the caucus, that he could "think on his feet," and if he could spare time to do some of the platform work it would help a lot.

"And," urged Captain Abiathar, the most excited of the three, "more than anything else we've got to talk Carmi up to everybody we meet. Catch 'em down to the post office; lay for 'em Sunday mornin's after meetin'; grab 'em at the lodge—and, whenever you do, just put Carmi to 'em strong. I tell you," brandishing a fist, "we ain't dead yet, not by a long sight! The way some of the boys talked to Zenas and me over to Orham yesterday makes me feel that we'll poll more votes than the Bates crowd are reckonin' on. They figure Gideon is in already. Maybe—well, yes, probably he is —but they better not risk sleepin' on watch, just the same."

The *Eagle*, when it appeared, caused the greatest sensation of that sensational first week. The news of Carmi Blake's independent candidacy was already spread abroad, so the formal announcement, with his own statement, was more or less of an anticlimax. But Franklin's ringing editorial and the front page story of Blake's heroism at the wreck were read aloud at every supper table. Captain Rogers drove up from the South Side and strode into the back room, a copy of the paper in his hand.

"That's the stuff to give him, young fellow!" he crowed. "That yarn about what happened down at Point of Beach! More than half the folks who read that yesterday, didn't realize what Carmi did and when you say that, while the convention was bunkoing him out of the nomination, he was saving the lives of our fellow townsmen, you've said something that makes them all sit up. That story of yours will do more good than anything else ever could. Keep it up. You were there, right on hand. You saw it. Give it to 'em hot and heavy."

Franklin could not help smiling. "How does Carmi himself like the hero rôle?" he inquired.

Captain Rogers sniffed. "He's sorer than a peppered blister, of course; you know him. If he had his way he would burn every *Eagle* in the county. But don't let that hinder you. Give us more fireworks of the same kind next week. They are what will make votes."

This was one side of the picture. The other side began to show itself. Tip Cahoon handed in his resignation; verbally, of course—as a writer Benjamin Harrison Cahoon was not a fluent success.

He marched into the shop the morning after the sensational broadcast was distributed and, cornering Elisha by a printing press, made his announcement.

"I'm through," he declared, red-faced and sputtering. "I see it comin' when I read that stuff Frank Cobb wrote and that you set up, 'Lish Dodson. I says to myself then, says I, 'This is the finishin' tail end of it. The Wellmouth *Eagle* will be through inside of six months and *I* might as well get through afore the whole town is ashamed of me. . . .' Eh? What's that?"

"Oh, nothin'. Only, if all you was waitin' for was for the

town to feel ashamed of you, you've wasted a lot of time already, seems to me, Tip."

"Aw, dry up! I ain't funny this mornin', if you are."

"Not the same way, anyhow. Well, go ahead. What's the rest?"

"There ain't no rest. I'm through. I'm heavin' up my job, that's what I'm doin'. I met Manasseh Eldredge just now, and I says 'Hello, Manasseh,' and what do you think he said to me?"

"'Hello,' I presume likely. A good many folks do say it."

"He never said *nothin'*. And then Judge Dean came in and never said nothin' neither. They just looked at me as if— as if I smelt bad or somethin'. I tell you, 'Lish Dodson, when a man like the Honorable Joel R. Dean won't speak to you, it makes you feel pretty sick. I can't afford to have folks like that down on me."

"Um-hm."

"'*Um-hm!*' Is that all you've got to say? You've heard about rats leavin' a sinkin' ship, ain't you? Well, if this ship ain't sinkin' then there never was one. *I* won't sink with it and you can tell Frank Cobb I said so."

"I'll tell him—if I think of it. . . . Well, what are you hangin' around here for? Clear out—*rat!*"

Tip's desertion made double work for Elisha, of course, but he stoutly declared himself equal to it until some other compositor and printer could be located and hired. Enoch Bearse, the young bookkeeper, volunteered to do the morning and evening sweeping and cleaning in addition to his other duties—for extra pay, of course. Franklin believed that he, himself, could fill in, as a green hand assistant, while printing was done. They would get along somehow, they must. The opposition should not have the satisfaction of seeing the Wellmouth *Eagle* falter in its flight. That flight might, and probably would, be short in its duration, but the bird should soar high and proudly while life was in him.

Each morning that dawned brought with it the expectation that before night a notice would be delivered by the bank messenger demanding immediate payment of the note. But day after day passed, and no notice came. He could not understand the delay.

That it was merely delay and not forgiveness nor forgetfulness he had more than one reminder. Manasseh Eldredge met him on the post office steps. As usual, Manasseh was the center of a listening group and it was this group he addressed as the *Eagle's* owner passed.

"Yes, sir," proclaimed Eldredge, loudly, "as I was sayin', runnin' into debt is a darned sight easier than runnin' out of it. Some folks in this world borrow money off their friends and then forget all about the money and the friends, too. Debts are debts, though; they have to be paid. My old grand-dad used to say that independence was a fine thing, but it took cash to buy rum. Haw haw! I guess I'll have that sayin' printed on a card and hang it up in my store. I'll have it printed over to the Higham shop. They'd do a good job on that kind of thing, don't you think? . . . Eh? Oh, never you fellers mind what I'm drivin' at. *I* know—and so does somebody else, I shouldn't wonder."

Judge Dean and Cornelius Haven were standing by the cashier's rail in the bank when Franklin cashed a check at the teller's window. They looked at him and whispered together. Dean nodded and Haven nodded in apparent agreement. Franklin knew what they were whispering about; his ears tingled.

As he came out of the bank the Bates's dogcart was drawing up at the edge of the sidewalk. Victoria was driving and her mother was on the seat beside her. He raised his hat. Mrs. Bates turned her head. Victoria looked at him, but he might have been the hitching post, so far as any sign of recognition on her part was concerned.

And yet, a little farther along the road, Captain Gideon

Bates met him. "Morning, Cobb," said the captain, briefly. "Nice weather."

To offset all this there were other, and more pleasant, happenings. At the South Side, and during his speech-making trips to Orham and North and East Wellmouth, he met a good many people who shook his hand and said unexpectedly gratifying things concerning him, the *Eagle,* and the Blake cause. Blair had declared that Carmi would have the "quarter-deck" of both towns against him. In the main that appeared to be true; the enthusiasm at the meetings was, for the most part, furnished by the rougher element, the fishermen and workers on the wharves and alongshore, but there were some exceptions. Several times men of prominence, men whom he would not in the least have suspected of approving the election of Captain Blake, came to him when his short speech was ended and expressed themselves as gratified and in agreement.

"I know," said one of these; "Captain Gideon is a fine man and an honest one, but he told me, only a couple of months ago, that he was through with office-holding for good and all. Yes, and he told me, too, that he was convinced Carmi Blake ought to be nominated and elected, even if he was a South Sider. Now did he change his mind, or did Dean and Ike Shotwell change it for him? And what is behind this harbor improvement thing that upset the frying pan in your caucus? Nothing, Ike Shotwell says. And Blake won't talk about it, you say? Well, as a general thing, I'm for a man who talks too little rather than one who talks too much. My vote goes to Carmi Blake this year, and I hope the Lord will forgive me for doing what I never forgave anybody else for doing—that's scratching my party ticket."

One of the most amazing converts to the Blake cause was Miss Alma Perry. This prim little person, who prided herself upon being a member of "one of the very oldest families in the Old Colony, Mr. Cobb," who was a Four Cornerite *of* the Four Cornerites; who shuddered at the vulgarity of the South Side and had been shocked beyond description when the name of a resident of that section was first mentioned for the high honor of representing her beloved township in the State Legislature—that she should enlist in the ragged army of rebellion was beyond understanding and almost beyond belief. One of Elisha's first observations the day after Franklin announced his decision, was to the effect that the Poet's Corner was liable to be pretty empty from then on.

"We'll have to depend on scissors and paste, Frank," prophesied Elisha. "And I wouldn't wonder if we had to scare up somebody else to do the 'Gleanin's' for us. Alma's read that editorial by this time, and she's probably burnin' sugar in a saucepan to get the smell of it out of her house. It was bad enough when the Four Corners stood by and let a South Sider run for representative. She told me more than once that she couldn't understand how gentlemen of breeding like you and Gideon and Judge Dean could countenance such a thing, let alone aidin' and abettin' it. What her dear mother would have said if she was alive she didn't like to imagine. She bore up under it though, but mainly, I guess, because you and the captain and Joel seemed to be in favor of it. Now though, when the *Eagle* not only keeps on cheerin' for Carmi, but dares to say the great and sacred Cap'n Bates shouldn't be elected, she—well, she must feel the way Deacon Eleazir Foster felt when the Come-Outer chapel was sold at auction, and Mike Gonzales' Portygee widow bought it and turned it into a billiard saloon. Eleazir said the proverb told him that you couldn't make a silk purse out of a sow's ear, but he noticed it didn't say nothin' about what a sow's purse could make of a church. Alma won't say it that way, of course—she wouldn't speak of a sow if she could help it, and if she did she'd call it a lady pig—but old Eleazir couldn't be more horrified than she'll be at what her beloved *Eagle* has been turned into. . . . No, I'm afraid Alma won't darken our doors again. Not that she ever darkened 'em much; there ain't enough of her for that."

Franklin laughed and admitted that he was probably right. And yet, the very day following that upon which the editorial appeared Miss Perry minced into the outer office and genteelly requested Enoch Bearse to inform Mr. Cobb that she was there and would very much like to speak with him.

Franklin, being summoned, hastened to greet her. He and Elisha exchanged significant glances as they passed each other in the print shop.

"Good afternoon, Mr. Cobb," said the little spinster. "I trust I have not interrupted you in your work. I realize quite well from—ahem—my own experience that the breaking of a train of thought is no light matter, although so many—may I say untrained—minds seem to consider it so."

Franklin assured her that his particular train of thought had not been permanently derailed. She smiled, murmured that it was so nice of him to say so, and produced from her reticule one of the familiar rolls of pink paper.

"Mr. Cobb," she said, and Franklin noticed that she appeared greatly agitated, "first of all let me thank you for one of the most perfect experiences of my life. Your account of the dreadful disaster at Point of Beach and of the heroic conduct of Captain Blake was—well, I'm sure you won't mind my saying that it thrilled me to the very core of my spirit. It did— Oh, I can't tell you *how* it did!"

"Why, thank you, Miss Perry. I was thrilled myself that day at the Point. Blake was pretty fine. I didn't exaggerate."

"I am sure of it. You are a true artist. . . . Oh, Mr. Cobb," tremulously. "I—I must confess that I read your editorial first and when I learned that the *Eagle*—the paper which I have read so many years and to which I have, in a humble way, so often contributed my own little—ahem—thoughts— was not only advocating the election of a South Side fisherman to the halls of our State congress, but was actually demanding the defeat of our great and good citizen, Captain Gideon Bates, I—I was paralyzed with astonishment. I was shocked, horrified—yes, I must admit it—I was actually ashamed of having read it."

"I am not surprised at that, Miss Perry. I imagine many others felt the same way."

"Oh, but wait! *Then* I read that wonderful story of the wreck. And as I read and thrilled and thrilled at Captain Blake's valor and self-sacrifice and—and all like that—I began to see, I began to comprehend. I said to myself: I understand now why Mr. Cobb felt that he must support Captain Blake. He couldn't do anything else. As a true gentleman and an admirer of the grand and noble, no matter in what walk of life it is found, he could do nothing but his duty. And that duty was to help the hero to his just reward. After all, what difference does it make where a hero was born and where he lives? 'Kind hearts are more than coronets and simple faith than Norman blood.' *We* realize that, don't we, Mr. Cobb?"

"Well—we should, I suppose."

"Yes. And so—so I have come here to-day to tell you that in spite of my admiration for Captain Bates, and my pride in being one of the residents of the—you *will* let me speak of it as the better section of our town, won't you? In spite of everything I have come here to tell you that the *Eagle* may depend upon me. Yes, and Captain Blake may depend upon me. No matter," with a slight shudder, "what friends may say of my conduct, I—I shall continue to contribute to our dear paper. Here," extending the pink scroll, "is a little proof of my feeling. A little tribute, written under—under stress, I assure you. I hope you may find it worthy, Mr. Cobb. . . . You will excuse me if I don't remain longer. Good day."

She hurried out. At the threshold she paused to dab at her eyes with a lace-edged handkerchief. Franklin turned to Bearse who had been an eager listener.

"Well, by George!" he exclaimed. Then, hurrying into the

shop, he displayed the roll. "Elisha," he cried, "miracles do happen. Come in here with me."

They read the "tribute" together. It was entitled "To Well-mouth's Hero."

> The great waves burst upon the shoal
>   And leaped above the sands.
> There was panic in the hardy skipper's soul
>   And in those of all hands.
> "Oh, must we die in sight of home!
>   Oh, wives and children dear!"
> So rang the shrieks from out the foam
>   If there had been any one to hear.

> But see! upon the Point of Beach
>   There beats a gallant heart.
> Though all cheeks except his may bleach,
>   His courage doth impart.
> "They shall not drown, our kin our kith!"
>   He cries. "Yon whaleboat take
> And to the rescue hasten with
>   Your comrade, Carmi Blake."

Eight more verses describing the row to the *Mary M.*, the rescue of the crew and the return to the cove. Then the grand finale:

> And shall we falter in the race
>   And e'en forget him now
> When South Side and Corners both do place
>   The laurels on his brow?
> No! Duty calls us to remember
>   Reward for valor's sake.
> So each and all vote this November
>   For heroic Carmi G. Blake.

Elisha whistled. "Say!" he exclaimed. "Well, by gorry! I'd as soon have expected the Old Scratch to get religion. Goin' to put it all in, Frank? It's pretty long for the Poet's Corner."

"Then we'll make the Corner longer. Put in every word, Elisha. It is pretty terrible poetry, but it means a lot to her. I doubt if you or I can realize the struggle that poor soul went through before she could bring herself to this. There's your New England conscience, Elisha."

But Elisha had his own ideas. He mentioned them to Bearse later in the day.

"Enoch," he said, "I hate to give in that Tip Cahoon was ever right about anything, but I shouldn't wonder if he was right once. He always vowed that Alma was 'mashed,' as he called it, on Frank Cobb. It seems ridiculous to think of, but I do begin to believe it's so. You can't tell where lightnin' will strike, that's a fact."

The political fight grew hotter and hotter with the approach of election day. That the Blake campaign was something more than a merely perfunctory protest was increasingly evident. Captain Abiathar, always the most optimistic of the leaders, grew more and more hopeful.

"I tell you, Frank," he declared, "I'm beginnin' to think we've got more than a bare chance. Oh, the odds are against us yet and always will be, but the signs show better every day. The South Side will be for Carmi almost solid. Even some of those who have stood by Cap'n Gideon and his crowd through every other election are beginnin' to shake. The Corners, of course, will be Bates, same as usual; they hate us South Siders, and they're scared of the way we're goin' ahead. But, all around on the edges, North and East Wellmouth and the like of that, Carmi is strong and gettin' stronger. Waters tells us that the shore end of Orham is for him, too. And the best symptom of all is that the opposition is beginnin' to fight. They started by goin' around with their noses in the air; we wasn't worth noticin'. Now, though, they're holdin' Bates rallies on their own account."

"Does Captain Bates himself speak at any of those meetings?"

"No; no, he don't. Too dignified, I guess likely. But Joe Dean and Haven are speech-makin' over in South Orham this very evenin'. Keep up your Blake stuff in the *Eagle*, Frank. That's helpin' us more than anything else."

Election day was the first Tuesday in November. On Sunday Elisha announced, between sneezes, that he cal'lated he'd been fool enough to catch cold. " 'Twon't amount to nothin' though, Frank. Can't afford to be laid up now. Hot brick to my feet to-night and a kettle or so of boilin' strong ginger tea and I'll be fit as a fiddle to-morrow."

But he was not fit. Neither his employer's orders nor his daughter's coaxing prevented his going to the shop, however. He worked as usual all that day and on Tuesday morning he hobbled to the town hall where he cast his ballot. He was so exhausted when this duty was fulfilled that he reluctantly consented to return home and "turn in." "Won't be much to do this afternoon, that's a fact. Say, Frank, the minute you hear anything about how the vote's goin' you'll get word to me, won't you? By gorry, I wish the fellow who invented colds had this one!"

Franklin's late dinner that noon was a sketchy affair. There was, as always, an abundance on the table, but his appetite was missing. He, too, was feeling the reaction from the days and nights of work and worry and the excitement of speechmaking and political argument. It was over now. There remained nothing but the counting of the votes and, as the polls would not close until six, the result would not be known before seven at the earliest. He had no inclination to hang about the hall, where Captain Abiathar and Rogers and Briar were distributing ballots and laboring with the few, if any, still undecided minds among Wellmouth's male citizens. He was worn out, physically and mentally, and a little after four he left the excited crowd and went to the Higham shop, where at his desk in the back room he could be alone. He had told Helen not to keep supper waiting. He would not return home until he could bring the news of victory or defeat.

That it would be defeat he had little or no doubt. It had been a forlorn hope in the beginning and, in spite of Abiathar's growing optimism and Captain Rogers' more guarded admissions of encouragement, he could but consider it hopeless still. The odds were too great. Carmi Blake might make a good showing, his vote might even be astonishingly large, but it would not be large enough to win against Gideon Bates. Too bad for Carmi; he deserved to win, but he was sure to lose.

As far as he—Franklin Cobb—was concerned it would make little difference. His goose was cooked. He had dared to oppose the rich and great and respectable in Wellmouth, and he must pay the price of his impudent temerity. So far—and he could not understand why—the powers that were had not demanded payment of the four-thousand-dollar note. The "group" held him in the hollow of its fist and the fist had not yet closed to crush him. Why had he been kept waiting? He did not know, nor could he imagine. Perhaps—it was but one of the perhaps—Captain Bates was responsible for the delay. The proud old magnate might not care to fight in that way. After the victory—well, that would be different. The fist could close then, purely as a matter of business.

It was inevitable. It had been from the moment when he made his decision. He knew it then, he knew it now. He had been too busy to make definite plans for his future, but it was high time he did. As he had told Helen—

Helen! . . . Yes, although he had never permitted himself to admit it before, there was the real trouble, the great trouble, all that really mattered. He must go away and leave Helen

365

Dodson and, in all probability never see her again. Of course he must not see her again; he must forget her, for she belonged to another man.

For a time—it seemed a long while ago—he had fancied himself in love with Victoria Bates. Now he could laugh at the idea. All that foolishness had really amounted to nothing, either to Victoria or to him. But Helen—

This was not getting him anywhere. There was nothing new in it. He had known, ever since he came to Wellmouth, that she and Carmi were in love with each other. It was because of that fact, more than anything else, that he had made his decision to fight for Blake's election. Blake was a great chap, but it was Helen's happiness that really counted. Yes; yes, that was what he had told himself; but to-day—now—how about his own?

Well, the sooner he got out of Wellmouth the better. If the bank messenger came into that office at that moment he would be welcome.

Some one was coming in. It could not be Enoch Bearse, the bookkeeper, because Enoch had gone home at half-past five and it was much later than that now. He had been sitting in the dark and now he hastily rose and lit the bracket lamp. He glanced at his watch. It was after seven.

The visitor, whoever he was, was pounding on the counter of the outer office and shouting his name. Franklin shouted in return.

"Yes," he called. "What do you want?"

"Want to see you. Enoch said you was here when he left. Shall I come in?"

"Of course. Come ahead. . . . Why—why, hello, Carmi! What's up?"

Blake did not answer immediately. He bent forward, seized the visitor's chair, which was standing in the far corner, swung it over the desk and sat down.

"Ain't too busy to talk, are you?" he observed.

"Not busy at all. But, see here, Carmi, what's the matter? You haven't heard—"

"How bad I'm licked? No, haven't heard anything definite. Too early yet. Bi and Zenas will let me know soon as they know themselves."

"Did you tell them you were coming here?"

"No, but Bearse will tell 'em, I guess likely. They are hangin' around the town hall with their ears to the ground. For two men their age they're the most excited lunatics you ever saw. . . . Haven't got a cigar, have you, Cobb? No, never mind; got a couple in my pocket, after all. Have one?"

"No, thanks." Franklin watched while his caller bit the end from the cigar and lighted it. Then he spoke what was in his mind.

"Well, *you* don't seem very excited yourself, I'll say that," he observed, with emphasis.

"I'm not. What's the use? Don't make much difference anyhow."

"What! Doesn't make much difference whether you are elected or not? What are you talking about!"

"Talkin' the way I feel. It's a comfort to be able to talk that way; I haven't done it for quite a spell. That's why I came in here."

"But—but, hang it all, Carmi, don't you *want* to be elected? Why, you've been putting up a grand fight. You've got the other side scared; I've heard that from a dozen different sources this past week. What did you make the fight for if you didn't care whether you won or not? Oh, you're joking, of course."

Carmi grunted. "I haven't felt much like jokin' for a good while," he said, grimly. "When I do go into a fight I generally aim to scare the other fellow before I finish. I told Bi and Zenas that I'd make the run, but I did it to please them, not because I really cared a whole lot about goin' to the State House."

"Well, by George! . . . Why, I understood you gave up going to sea in order to take up politics."

"So I did. I thought—well, I've changed my mind since then, or had it changed for me. Now, provided I get the lickin' I guess is comin' to me, I can go to sea again. Think probably I shall. I've had the best times of my life on salt water."

Franklin shook his head. He could not understand this at all. Blake blew a puff of smoke toward the ceiling and changed the subject.

"So you and Victoria Bates are off each other for good, eh?" he observed.

"Yes. . . . Now, Captain, if you don't mind—"

"All right, all right. . . . I was thinkin' out loud, that's all. That wasn't what I came to talk about, anyway. Zenas Rogers came to me last night with a yarn that he'd just heard. Where he got it I don't know. It's about you and your affairs and is supposed to be a dead secret. It worried him, and when he told me I was worried too. If you hadn't been mighty decent to me all through this runnin' for office game I shouldn't mention it now, but you have been more than decent and— well, neither he nor I are goin' to let you get into trouble, or stay in trouble, on our account. Look here, Frank; is it so that you've borrowed money, a good deal of money, from the Wellmouth bank and Gideon Bates and Joe Dean are holdin' a note over your head?"

Franklin leaned back in his chair. "So it is town talk already, is it?"

"No, no," hastily. "No town talk about it. Whoever told Zenas said that only a very few knew about it. But is it so? I'd like to have you tell me, if you will."

"Yes, it is so. I borrowed four thousand dollars when I repaired and refitted this place. Captain Bates himself suggested my doing it and I gave the bank my demand note for the amount."

"You did, eh? That was what Zenas said. And in spite of that, you and your paper stood up for me with Gideon himself runnin' on the other side! What in the devil did you do that for? Can you pay that note if they come down on you for it?"

"No. I have been expecting them to demand payment at any minute. Why they haven't done it yet I don't understand."

"Nor I, neither. What will you do when they do?"

"Pay what I can and let them take over the business and property for the rest, I guess. Either that or try and sell to outsiders."

"Hum! And what will you do—yourself, I mean?"

"Go to Boston, or New York, or somewhere and hunt for a job."

"Leave Wellmouth and—and everybody in it?"

"I shall have to."

Carmi Blake slapped the desk. "I'll be darned if you do!" he vowed. "That would be a healthy thing for us South Siders to let you do after the way you've stood for us with a smash hangin' over you. Look here, boy, you owe how much—four thousand, is it?"

"Yes. But I have about fifteen hundred put aside, so the debt is but twenty-five hundred altogether. Oh, don't worry about me, I—"

"Shut up! Zenas Rogers is well fixed; Abiathar has got considerable laid by; and I'm not broke exactly. We'll take over that four thousand amongst us, and you can pay off the bank note and give us another one. We won't nag you for our pay, I promise you that. . . . Come, it's settled, ain't it?"

He put his big hand on Franklin's knee. Franklin shook his head.

"No," he said, firmly, "I'm afraid it isn't, Carmi—not that way. It was suggested to me, some time ago, that I try to borrow the money elsewhere, but I decided not to do it. It might be years before I could pay it off; perhaps, now that I have offended and antagonized so many people in the district, I might never be able to pay it. I won't run the risk of sticking my friends."

"Stick be hanged! You listen—"

"No. I'm more obliged than I can tell you, and I will promise you to think it over, but I tell you now what I'm sure I shall tell you in the end—that I won't borrow of you or any one again. I have had enough of that."

There was more pleading and argument on Blake's part, but it accomplished nothing. Franklin's determination did not move; he would think it over, but the thinking would not change his mind, he was certain.

"That's enough of that, Carmi," he declared. "Don't you think we may as well walk down to the hall and see if the returns are all in, from Orham and the other places?"

"No. I tell you I don't care whether they're in or not. Say, look here, Frank Cobb; if you clear out of Wellmouth what about Elisha Dodson?"

"Oh, Elisha will be all right. Whoever takes over the *Eagle* will need him. They will have to have him, he will be indispensable."

"Hum! . . . And Nellie?"

"Why on earth do *you* ask *me* that? Helen is provided for, I should say."

"She is, eh? Who is providin' for her?"

"Well, I supposed you and she would— Well, you'll take her to Boston with you if you should be elected, won't you? And if you're not—"

"What the blue blazes are you talkin' about *now?*"

Again Franklin shook his head, this time in impatient bewilderment.

"Since you force me to say it," he said, "I will. You and she are going to marry some day, I presume, and I thought—"

"Hold on there!" Carmi Blake rose to his feet. He was frowning and his hands were clenched.

"Young fellow," he growled, "I wonder if— Say, are you playin' innocent with me? Don't you know that Nellie gave me my walkin' papers over a month ago? Of course you do!"

Franklin stared at him. "Gave you—your—your—"

"I swear I believe you *didn't* know it! Have you seen me up at her house very often lately?"

"Why—why no, but I—I supposed you were so busy with politics that—"

"Don't talk like a jackass! Did you think politics would keep me away from *her?* . . ." He turned away, walked to the window, looked out into the blackness, and then turned back again. "She told me I better stay away; that it was no use my hangin' around any longer, or what amounted to that. That night when you met me comin' out of her door was the last time we spoke of it and the last we ever will. I'd been there to find out if she really meant it, if she couldn't change her mind. She couldn't—so there it is."

Franklin was dumfounded. His feelings were strangely mingled. There was pity for the man before him, but with it was—something else.

"Carmi," he stammered. "I—I'm sorry— I—I didn't know."

"Hum!" with a shrug, "I begin to believe you didn't. Well, that's enough of that. You can understand now why goin' to sea again looks good to me. I wanted to be something bigger than a fishin' skipper on her account. Now I don't care. . . . But *you* ought to care."

Franklin was still suffering from shock. The last sentence he scarcely heard.

"But why?" he queried. "I supposed you and she— Well, by George! Why did she do it?"

Captain Carmi sniffed impatiently.

"She did it because she liked somebody else better than she did me. Anyhow I judged that was it. She's too straight a girl to marry one fellow when she cared for another one. She didn't say that, but it was plain enough. I'd guessed as much for some time."

Franklin sank into his chair once more. He said not a word. Blake looked down at him.

"There was a spell when I thought you was playin' a two-handed game," he growled. "I know you better now and I guess you wasn't, on purpose anyhow. You're a good deal of a kid, but you're square. . . . Oh, confound you, Frank Cobb!" with a sudden snarl. "I wonder how I kept from knockin' your head off long ago. I'd do it this minute if—if I wasn't ashamed to."

There was a thunder of footsteps on the front platform. The front door flew open with a crash. A half dozen men ran through the print shop. Seth Briar was in the lead, with Zenas Rogers and Captain Abiathar and Elkanah Rogers at his heels.

"Frank! Frank!" shouted Seth. "Are you there? Do you know where Carmi is? Have you seen him?"

Carmi himself answered. "I'm right here," he announced calmly. "You need specs, Seth, if you can't see anything my size."

They leaped upon him, they thumped his shoulders, they yelled.

"You cussed old lobscouser!" whooped Elkanah. "You're in, did you know it! You're elected! You're elected! Whe-e-e!"

He was dancing. Seth Briar tossed his hat to the ceiling.

"What's the matter with the South Side?" he demanded of the world in general. *"It's* all right!"

Captain Carmi seized Zenas Rogers by the shoulders.

"Shut up, all hands of you!" he roared. "What's all this, anyhow? Zenas—"

Captain Zenas was as excited as the rest, but not so noisy. His florid face glowed.

"It's so, Carmi," he crowed. "Close enough vote, the land knows; probably not more than twenty-five over in the whole district, but it's enough. You've won! You've licked Gideon! You're our next representative."

CHAPTER XXVII

IT was true. Carmi Blake's name was on but twenty-two more ballots than that of his opponent, but, as Captain Rogers had said, that twenty-two was enough. The Four Corners was no longer, and was destined never again to be, the seat of Wellmouth's political mighty. The South Side was in the saddle.

All that night the celebration kept up. Franklin, in his bed in the Dodson cottage, could hear the bell of the Second Meeting House at the South Side ringing. At four the next morning two tremendous "booms" shook his windows. The hilarious fishing crews and wharf gangs had marched silently to the Corners and there, arrogantly triumphant, had loaded and fired the two old cannon, under the very noses of their deposed rulers. Gates were lifted and carried away, black crape was hung on the aristocratic doorknob of Judge Joel Dean's law office, and the platform of Manasseh Eldredge's store displayed a large, black-bordered sheet of pasteboard, cut in the shape of a tombstone and lettered "Sacred to the Memory of a Dead Political Job." It was the night before the Fourth all over again, with additional trimmings.

Franklin, as soon as he could get rid of the hysterical enthusiasts in his office, had hurried home to tell the Dodsons the marvelous news. They had heard it already, he found. Helen was quietly happy. Elisha, who had insisted upon getting up, was in the sitting room, wrapped in a blanket. His exclamations of astonishment and his jubilations were hoarse but hilarious. He refused obstinately to return to bed and yielded only when his daughter declared that she should send for Dr. Williams. "You know his treatment for one of your colds, Father," she warned him. *"He* won't let you up for a week."

Even after he was again tucked in he insisted that the sitting room door be left open. Franklin had no opportunity for a word with Helen alone and he did not mention Carmi Blake's visit.

In the morning Elisha, his cold still with him, but much less severe, announced that he was going to accompany his employer to the print shop.

"Think likely I'd stay at home to-day!" he snorted. "You couldn't keep me here with a chain cable and a kedge anchor."

All that forenoon callers came to the office of the Wellmouth *Eagle.* Franklin at his desk in the little back room and Dodson and Bearse in the shop and front office listened to the chorus of congratulations and the "I wouldn't have believed it's" and the "It beats anything I heard of's." Miss Perry came with a brand-new poem.

"It wrote itself, if I may say so," she declared. "If ever I was inspired it was when the milkman told me this morning of Captain Blake's election. I sat right down, and the thoughts simply flowed from my pen. I haven't eaten a mouthful of breakfast yet."

Captain Zenas Rogers drove up from the South Side about eleven and, in the back office with the door shut, he told Franklin some things which were decidedly interesting.

"Bi and I had a long talk with Carmi last night before we went to bed," he said. "We know now the inside of that harbor improvement fuss."

Franklin turned quickly. "Do you, really!" he exclaimed. "So Carmi told you, at last?"

"Yes, he told us. And he said we might tell you, provided you promised to keep it to yourself. We three are supposed to keep it a secret. Not that it ought to be kept," disgustedly, "but just because he wants it to be."

"All right, Captain Rogers, he can depend on me. I won't tell."

"Certain; he said you wouldn't. It don't amount to much, after all, in one way; anybody but Carmi would have out with it right there in the caucus. If he had— Whew!"

He chuckled and shook his head.

"Well?" eagerly. "What was it?"

"Just this. Remember Noah Holway's saying that it was the Blue River plan that ought to go through? How much improving the river mouth up there meant to East Wellmouth, and all like that? It was Carmi's not promising to use his influence for that particular plan that Noah objected to."

"Yes. Of course I remember that."

"Well, you know, don't you, that there is a lot of land along both sides of Blue River where it empties into the harbor? . . . Um-hm. Well, that land hasn't ever been good for anything; nothing but a few scallop shanties and lobster shacks on it. It might come to be worth considerable, though, if the river abreast it was dredged and deepened so vessels could go up in there."

"Why, yes. But—"

"Wait a minute. Who do you suppose owns that land now?"

"The people that own the scallop and lobster shanties, I suppose."

"Oh, no, they don't. One after the other, beginning two years ago, when the harbor improvement was first talked about —and before deepening the Blue River was even mentioned as a part of it—that river front land was bought up, piece by piece and for a few dollars a lot, by a man who said he represented a Boston company. This company, so the fellow said, might, maybe, some day put up a summer hotel there. There was nothing sure about it yet so the folks who sold must give their solemn words not to tell a soul. They all did; they'd have promised anything to get a few cents a foot for sand land that wasn't good for anything except to clean knives with."

Franklin whistled. "I—see," he said slowly.

"I doubt if you see the whole yet. Carmi looked into the affair pretty thoroughly and, as near as he could make out, there never was any Boston company at all. That fellow who did the buying was a stranger of course, he had to be, but the land is really owned by Joe Dean, and Manasseh, and Haven, and Ike Shotwell and his brother, and Noah Holway, and three or four more in different parts of Wellmouth and Orham. *Now* you can see why they didn't intend to put a man into the State House who wasn't pledged to improving Blue River."

"Pshaw! . . . Yes, yes. That's plain enough. But—but does that mean that Bates was in it, too? It doesn't just seem like him, does it?"

"Why no, it don't. And Carmi says he hasn't heard Gideon's name mentioned by whoever it was—Carmi won't tell—that whispered it to him. Carmi guesses that Bates doesn't know anything about it. Joe Dean has probably given him all kinds of smooth reasons why the Blue River plan is the best, and it was he and Shotwell who filled him full of 'harmony in the party' and all that."

Franklin thought it over. "That was a shrewd trick," he observed. "There wasn't anything really crooked in it, though. You can't put people in jail for speculating in land."

"No, but if Carmi Blake had stood up there in that caucus and told the story I don't believe he would have lost the nomination. There is just enough slick monkey business in it to make folks mad."

"Why didn't he tell?"

"Because he is Carmi. For one thing he had given Dean his word that he wouldn't tell a soul until after election. When he first got wind of it—and before he really found out what he found out afterwards—he went to the judge and asked for the true story. Dean hemmed and hawed and owned up that he and a few others did own a little land up there, but they had owned it for a long time. They just bought it because it was cheap and might be worth holding. Carmi was a good Republican, wasn't he? He wouldn't start a lot of gossip and talk which might raise hob with the party's chances in the election and perhaps delay the whole improvement idea for years and years? It was all perfectly square and honest, just a business deal. Anyway he surely would be fair enough to promise not to mention it to any one till he was elected. So Carmi promised not to tell till after election, but he wouldn't promise to back the plan till he'd gone into it from main truck to keelson. That wouldn't do for Dean and the rest, of course, so they set out to lick him.

"Carmi is fair enough about it, even now," Rogers went on. "If the State engineers say the Blue River scheme is the best, he'll endorse it and work for it. If they say 'no' he won't. And you and Bi and I must keep our mouths shut. He says he won't be responsible for starting a row that might upset the whole district, when there is nothing to be gained by it. He told the voters where he stood and that they could take him that way or leave him. . . . Well, they took him. Ho, ho, they did so! That's one in the eye for the Four Corners! Some of us South Siders have waited years for this."

He lingered a few minutes longer. Just before he left he referred to the matter of the note.

"Carmi told Bi and me that he tried to get you to let three or four of us take that note over from the bank," he said, "but that you wouldn't have it. I hope that isn't so."

"I said I would think it over, but I don't think I shall change my mind, Captain Rogers."

"We wish you would. We owe you and your paper a whole lot more than four thousand dollars, Frank Cobb. Yes, and we want you to keep on running the *Eagle* right here in Wellmouth. If only— Oh, well; you keep on thinking."

Another caller of importance came to that office before the day was over. About three in the afternoon, as Elisha and Franklin were discussing matters pertaining to the next issue, this visitor made his appearance. Elisha had just imparted a bit of news.

"The wind must be cantin' our way a little mite, Frank," he observed, with a broad grin. "Who do you suppose was in the front room just now askin' to see you?"

"Don't know. I can't waste the whole day talking about the election. Whoever it was, I hope you told him I was busy."

"Oh, I did, don't worry. But his comin' was just a sign that the wind was changin', that's all. 'Twas Tip Cahoon and, although he didn't say so in so many words, I rather cal'late that he'd like his job back."

"No?"

"Yes. Tip acted to me pretty well shook up. I haven't seen him so mealy-mouthed and polite since that girl from East Wellmouth came in here with her father to ask if he was goin' to give back the five dollars he borrowed of her. Seems she'd found out that he borrowed it to buy a Christmas present for another girl with, and she and her dad were a little mite peeved. Tip was humble and soft-soapy enough then, but no more so than he was just now. . . . Eh? Yes, Enoch, what is it?"

The bookkeeper stood in the doorway, a peculiar expression on his face.

"Cap'n Gideon Bates is out front," he confided in an agitated whisper, "and he says he wants to see you, Mr. Cobb."

Elisha and Franklin looked at each other. "Gorry!" gasped the former.

"Ask him to come in, of course," ordered Franklin. "All right, Elisha; I've been expecting him, or some one representing him, for some time. Run along. If he gets too violent for one man to handle, I'll call you."

Elisha limped out, looking anxious. Franklin squared his

shoulders. Here it was at last. The dance was over, and the fiddler had come for his pay.

Captain Bates's greeting was pleasant enough—surprisingly so, recent events considered. He accepted Franklin's invitation to be seated.

"Shan't keep you long," he said. "Just stopped in as I was going by. Are you too busy to waste a minute or two on a man whose neighbors and—h'm—friends have decided isn't fit to represent 'em up at the State House?"

"Oh, now here, Captain Bates—"

"All right, all right. Never mind the flowers. Maybe I'm not quite ready for the 'Rest in Peace' wreaths yet. . . . Well, you licked me, didn't you? And proud of it, I suppose?"

"Captain Bates, I tried to make it plain when I came to you at Judge Dean's office that day, that there wasn't anything personal in my opposition. I should have been proud to work for your election at any other time, under other circumstances. It was just that—well, I felt that Blake had had a raw deal. You know— But there is no use going over all that again."

"Not a bit. No matter what kind of a deal he had he's won the game. Maybe he deserved to, I won't say he didn't. What are they going to give you for your help in winning it? Make you postmaster or county sheriff, or something?"

"They haven't mentioned anything of the kind."

"They ought to do something for you. It was this blasted paper of yours that did more than anything else to put Carmi in. You're a good hard fighter, young fellow; I've said that before, and I'll say it again. Well, I don't hold any grudge against you for that."

"I was sure you wouldn't."

"I don't. . . . The only grudge I've got against you is that you're so confounded young. Wait till you get to be as old as I am and you'll understand what I mean. I don't like being licked any better than I ever did, but, so far as holding office is concerned, I'm glad I haven't got to go through it again. A dog may hate to realize that he's had his day, but when that realization is jammed down his throat, the best thing he can do is swallow and go back to his kennel. We folks up here at the Corners must understand that we've had our days, I'm afraid. The South Side will run this town from now on, or I miss my guess. . . . Lord A'mighty," with a sudden growl, "how I do hate to say that! But it's the truth; I've seen it coming for a good while."

He frowned and did not speak again for a long interval. Franklin, too, was silent. He was wondering when the real subject which was the excuse for this call would be reached.

Captain Bates looked up.

"Well," he said, slowly, "that's about all, I shouldn't wonder. You get back to your job and I'll crawl back to my kennel the way an old dog ought to. I just wanted you to understand that there were no hard feelings on my part, that's all. . . . So long, son."

"But—but Captain Bates—surely this isn't all you came here to say?"

"Eh? Yes, it is. . . . There are one or two other things I might say, but they're not the kind of things one man talks about with another. . . . You and—er—Vic aren't as—er—friendly as you used to be. I'm sorry for that."

Franklin did not know how to reply. He was embarrassed and troubled. His caller nodded.

"Yes, I'm sorry," he mused, "but that's your affair, of course—yours and hers. Vic's the only child I've got and, naturally, she and what she does with her life means a whole lot to me. Her mother and I have different ideas about what's best for her, but I suppose that is so in a whole lot of families. And she has her own ideas, too—and her own way, generally speaking. It is hard to know when you're spoiling a child. You want her to be happy and have anything you can give her and so . . . H'm. . . . You don't want to hear all this stuff. Good-by, young fellow. You won't be coming up to see me, I suppose, but I shall probably drop in and see you once in a while. If there's anything I can do for you, let me know. . . . Oh, by the way, how are you getting on with your business here? Everything going as smooth as it was when we talked about it last?"

"No, sir, not quite, but as well as I have any right to expect. I have made some enemies—naturally I would—by the *Eagle's* attitude in backing an independent candidate."

Gideon Bates rubbed his chin. "What do you mean—enemies?" he demanded. "Have they been trying to hurt you in a business way?"

"Well, the *Eagle* has lost some advertising but perhaps—"

"Whose?"

"Oh, Manasseh Eldredge has withdrawn his store advertisements, and there are some Orham storekeepers who have done the same thing."

"Humph! . . . So Manasseh has stopped his ads, has he? He always was a sorehead. I'll see to him. I may be an old dog, but I haven't lost all my teeth. Don't worry about Manasseh."

"But, Captain Bates, there is one thing you haven't mentioned at all. I thought when you came in here you had come to tell me that that note of mine your bank holds must be paid. Why you haven't called for payment before this I don't see. You were very kind when you let me have that money without security and, whatever you say, you must feel that I have treated you perfectly rotten in this election business."

"Here, here! What's all this? I haven't said anything about any note, have I?"

"No, you haven't yet—"

"Anybody else said anything about it?"

"Not directly. I heard Eldredge—"

"Eldredge be damned! Can't pay it yet, can you?"

"No, sir. I might pay a little of it, but not the whole. I don't know when I can pay the whole."

"When that money was lent you it was understood that, as long as you paid your interest, the note would stand just as was?"

"Yes, sir. But then—"

"Be still! Pay that money when you are able to pay it. That was the bargain between us and I'll see that the bank's end of it is lived up to."

"But—but Captain Bates, I—I— Why, you make me ashamed of myself. I didn't expect—I—I can't thank—"

"Didn't ask you for thanks, as I know of. For God's sake," sharply, "what sort of a skunk do you think I am? I don't mix my banking with my politics. Gave you my word, didn't I? . . . Well, good-by."

He walked out. Franklin did not accompany him to the street door. It was not until he heard that door close that he thoroughly realized his visitor had departed. Then he sprang to his feet and would have hastened after him, but it was too late. He sank down into the chair again. This was— why, it was unbelievable. It changed everything.

He tried to think—to realize the change. The debt was still a debt of course, but without the prospect of demand for immediate payment, he could face the future with courage and confidence. He need not give up the printing business and the *Eagle*. He need not leave Wellmouth. He was back again exactly where he was before he made his momentous decision to fight the "group" and the power it represented. He was, if no better off, certainly very little worse than he had been two months ago. Why, he was free. He could keep on—

Elisha tiptoed to the door.

"What did he say, Frank?" he whispered, fearfully. "Was he awful mad? What's he goin' to do to you?"

Franklin looked up. "Elisha," he said, "I—I've had a shock.

383

... So far as that goes," with a long breath, "I've had two; one last night—and now this. If you don't mind I'd rather not talk just now."

"Sure! Sartin! That's all right. Only if he said anything —er—er—shockin' to you I'll tell him what I think of him. I don't care if he *is* the biggest old rooster in the hen yard. I'll—"

"Hush!" Franklin lifted his hand. "Elisha," he declared, with emphasis, "there are two of the finest men on earth right here in this little town of Wellmouth. One of them is Carmi Blake, and the other is Gideon Bates. And blessed if I know which is the finer. I do know that I'm not fit to hold a candle to either. . . . There, there! Don't ask me what I mean. I'll tell you some time. Just now I—I want to be alone."

A half-hour later he left the shop. "I'm going out—for a walk, I guess," he told Bearse. "I may be back before closing time, or I may not. If I'm not tell Elisha to lock up."

Helen was sewing in the sitting room when he came up the Dodson walk. She saw him and hurried to the side door.

"Why, Frank," she asked anxiously, "what are you doing here at this time in the afternoon? . . . Father isn't—sick?"

"No, no. Your father is all right. I came here to see you. I wanted to tell you something."

He told her of the Bates call and what Captain Gideon had said about the note. She was delighted.

"Why, that is wonderful!" she cried. "Why, Franklin, that means—"

"It means a lot of things. Just how much it may mean depends on—well, on you, Helen."

"On me? What have I to do with it?"

"Everything. Helen, I haven't told you before, but I am going to tell you now. Carmi Blake and I had a long talk last evening. He came to the office when I was there alone.

384

He said. . . . Helen, is it true that you and he are—are friends —and that's all?"

She looked at him. The color rushed to her cheeks.

"Why—why, of course we are friends," she faltered. "I don't know what you mean. Carmi and I have always been friends."

"Yes, but he told me he had hoped you might be more than that. He cares a great deal for you, Helen. I know he does."

Her sewing fell from her lap as she rose from the rocking chair.

"Really, Frank," she protested, "I—I—"

"Don't be angry. That isn't my affair of course. . . . Oh, yes it is, but I shouldn't dream of speaking of it if he hadn't spoken first. He told me that he—well, he as much as told me that he loved you and wanted to marry you, but that you, as he said, sent him about his business because you didn't— couldn't love him. Carmi is a splendid fellow. Helen, I—"

Her eyes flashed. "Stop!" she cried. "What *do* you mean? Did *he* send you here to—to—"

"No, no. Of course he didn't. But, Helen, don't you see how this changes everything for me? Ever since I came to Wellmouth I have been given to understand that you and Carmi were—well, in love with each other. Even your own father hinted that. . . . Don't blame him; he didn't really say it, but—"

"Oh!" indignantly, "I won't hear any more. It isn't true. And Father should be— Oh, I won't listen to you. I'm going away."

But he stepped in front of her.

"No, Helen," he said, firmly, "you're not going—yet. Whether I go or not depends on you. Whether I stay on here in Wellmouth depends on you, too. Yes, it does. Helen, I—I— No, you must listen. You've got to."

"I won't. . . . I am going out of this room this minute. . . . Let me be!"

But he had caught her in his arms and was holding her fast. This was not at all the way in which he had meant to say it, but—what did that matter now?

"Helen," he pleaded, "please—please listen. I love you. I suppose I have really loved you from the beginning, although I didn't realize it. I doubt if I should have made a fool of myself with—with Victoria if I hadn't supposed you and Carmi belonged to each other. When I did realize how much I cared for you I—I tried to put it out of my mind because it seemed so useless. But I couldn't—I just couldn't, although I swore you should never know. And when he told me that you didn't care for him—last night, I mean—I—I. . . . Oh, well, there," releasing her, "you see how it is. Don't cry, I won't say any more."

She was crying, fumbling for her handkerchief. He waited a moment and then turned wearily away.

"I've made you miserable," he sighed. "I'm sorry."

Another long moment. Then he heard her speak his name. He turned back. She was not crying now. Her eyes were wet, but they were very bright.

"Frank," she said, "you—you are sure you do care for me? Really and truly care?"

"Sure? . . . Did I sound as if I were making believe? Helen—dearest—"

"Wait! And if—if I don't say that I care for you, you will go away from Wellmouth?"

"Yes. I made up my mind to that while I was walking down to this house just now."

"In spite of what Captain Bates said about the money you borrowed? That trouble is over. You won't have to lose your business."

"Yes, in spite of everything. I have made up my mind. It isn't worth while. Nothing is worth while but you."

"Then—then I think you will have to stay, because—"

"Because what? . . . Oh, my darling, you don't mean—"

386

"Of course I do. . . . Even when you were chasing after Victoria Bates, you could have seen—if you had had eyes for any one but her. . . . I—oh, my dear, be careful! The window shade is up."

They sat there in the gathering dusk talking, talking, with intervals of silence during which talk would have been a superfluous nuisance. He told her again all that Captain Bates had said that afternoon and all that Carmi Blake said the previous evening. He spoke of his business prospects, his hopes, his plans for their future. Marriage must be postponed for a while. Let him pay off at least half of the bank debt and then—

"But I'll make good," he declared. "I've got something to work for now, something real."

At last she rose from the chair. It was not a large one but it was quite big enough for two just then.

"I must light the lamps and get supper," she said. "Father may be home almost any minute, and what *will* he think?"

Franklin, alone in the sitting room, happening to put his hand in his coat pocket, found there a pink scroll. It was the poem Alma Perry had handed him that morning. He had not read it.

Alma had declared herself "inspired" when she wrote that particular poem and the facility with which she found rhymes when an uninspired person would have found only discouragement went far toward proving her statement. Her "tribute" was not lengthy this time, only five verses.

VICTORIOUS PEACE
by
ALMA DIADAMA PERRY

The battle's roar had died away
Upon the air of even.

> *"Who won?" "Who lost?" did Wellmouth say.*
> *For the polls closed at six and it was then seven.*
> *But when Aurora lit the dawn*
> *All knew the laurel's bough*
> *Had bent to shed its leaves upon*
> *A hero's noble brow.*

Franklin read thus far. Then, chuckling, he went into the kitchen where Helen was very busy indeed.

"Listen to this," he said, and read the five stanzas aloud. The final one was as follows:

> *"Oh, men of Wellmouth, hear my voice,*
> *And fear not for the future.*
> *Forget your quarrels and rejoice,*
> *Though now things may not suit you.*
> *The trouble's o'er, the strife has fled,*
> *Let all united stand.*
> *Forget the past and look ahead.*
> *God bless our native land!"*

"And that's that," he said, in conclusion. "If there are any leaves left on that laurel bough I vote them to Miss Perry. Any one who can rhyme 'future' with 'suit you' deserves to be crowned. I only hope the 'men of Wellmouth' take her advice and forget their quarrels, but I'm afraid that is too much to expect—immediately at any rate. For instance I doubt if Eldredge and Dean will love me for some time."

Helen laughed happily. "Never mind that, dear," she said. "There is another line in that wonderful poem for you and me. 'Forget the past and look ahead.' That is what we are going to do, aren't we?"

(1)

THE END